More critica

"Correa's *Spy's Fate* is a must fo. an important political statement, and being written in a Cuban voice, it is an amazing one. It will interest anyone concerned with Cuban-American relations, with the intelligence community here, there, or anywhere, or with international diplomatic relations, real or fictional. Its release, when Americans have just been informed that Cuba is, yes indeed, part of the 'axis of evil,' could hardly be more timely."

—*Pop Matters*

"Arnaldo Correa is Cuba's answer to le Carré . . . This is an extremely well written, humorous, and suspenseful novel, made all the more believable by the fallibility of the characters and the absurdity of bureaucratic communications. A truly great ending! I found *Spy's Fate* refreshing and look forward to more English-language thrillers from this Cuban Noir writer."

—*Kate's Mystery Books Newsletter*

"*Spy's Fate* is a refreshing change from ideologically molded tales of the U.S.-Cuban spy wars . . . *Spy's Fate* is an illuminating read and a fine introduction to this Cuban author."

—*Drood Review of Mystery*

"[A] detailed excursion into the Byzantine world of Cuban secret service and rivalries among the island's ruling elite. This is a layered, complex, and engaging novel that warrants comparison with Graham Greene's 'entertainments' and John le Carré's recent fiction."

—*In These Times*

"An engrossing portrait, highly recommended."

—*Library Journal*

"If spy thrillers are your thing and Cuba is on your list of places to visit, this first novel, written in English by Cuban author Arnaldo Correa, may be your cup of tea . . . Correa is particularly adept at describing the economic realities that have affected younger Cubans and spawned intergenerational conflicts . . . If you have any doubt about the collusion between the U.S. government and the Cuban exile community, either review President Bush's speech in Miami on Cuban Independence Day or sample Arnaldo Correa's perspective in *Spy's Fate*."

—*Worldview*

"Arnaldo Correa has crafted a fast-paced, sociological, and political spy novel comparable to any in its genre. Insightful, the book takes most 'American' readers into Cuba and allows for us to see a side of the country from an insider's point of view . . . An engrossing novel that you can't easily put down. It demands your attention. I hope other works by this talented author will be translated into English as well. I would hate to be deprived of any of his future works."

—BookBrowser.com

Critical praise for Arnaldo Correa's *Cold Havana Ground*:

"Correa offers a tantalizing glimpse into the world of Afro-Cuban religion and folklore . . . With its detailed ethnographic background . . . this is apt to appeal to fans of such authors as Janwillem Van de Wetering and Eliot Pattison, whose mysteries contain strong spiritual elements."

—*Publishers Weekly*

"Crafting parallel stories that follow a police search for a missing Chinese cadaver and a *Santera* who discovers that a malignant spirit has taken hold of her brother, Correa offers a uniquely riveting mystery that offers a window into little-known Afro-Cuban traditions."

—Nicholas Shumaker, *The Brooklyn Rail*

"In Florida, it's almost impossible to cast a stone without hitting a mystery novelist. In Cuba, ninety miles away, the odds of hitting a Cuban-born mystery author are almost nil, unless you aim for Correa . . . Recommended for fans of literary mysteries set in exotic locations and readers interested in Cuban culture."

—*Library Journal*

"This mystery, based on an actual case from the Havana Police Department's files, is a heat-infused look at the steamier side of contemporary Cuba. It is a story in which nothing is as it seems and everyone has a secret. This suspenseful mix of magic, mystery, and lust is expertly woven by the author, who pulls you along as it slowly becomes clear how each of the stories are related and what crimes have been committed."

—*Puerto Rico Sun*

"An unusual mystery . . . Basing his tale on actual events, Correa takes us inside the Afro-Cuban religions of Santería, Palo Monte, and the Abakuá Secret Society. Though we're most drawn to the sly, likable oddball Alvaro, the mystery unfolds through many points of view . . . Correa's poker-faced humor and colorful storytelling—plus the chance to look at unfamiliar groups in an off-limits country—make this a worthwhile read."

—*Booklist*

SPY'S FATE

ARNALDO CORREA

AKASHIC BOOKS
NEW YORK

Published by Akashic Books
Original Akashic Books hardcover edition published in 2002
©2002, 2005 Arnaldo Correa

ISBN-13: 978-1-888451-65-8
ISBN-10: 1-888451-65-3
Library of Congress Control Number: 2004115737
All rights reserved
First paperback printing

Printed in Canada

Akashic Books
PO Box 1456
New York, NY 10009
Akashic7@aol.com
www.akashicbooks.com

To Bill, Stacie, and the boys: Taylor, Max, and Mr. Parker

A Note from the Author

This novel would not have been written without Bill Heffernan's encouragement, blasting criticisms, and much other help. Marjorie Moore took care of correcting my English and assuring me of how good it could be if I ever managed to decipher the correct order of the words, the proper tense of the verbs, and the right prepositions to use. Her comments on the novel were also a great help.

The characters and the plot, I must swear, are fictitious. But many of the situations depicted here are only too real; they are part of the fate of a whole country, caught in the middle of a never-ending clash between unyielding forces.

TIMOTHY SIDNEY KING, head of the CIA's Cuba section, opened the envelope stamped "URGENT" that had just been handed to him by one of the director's aides. King read the note inside: *"An important officer of the Cuban Intelligence Service has reportedly defected. It's believed he hijacked a yacht late last night and left Cuban waters heading north. Source: P.G."*

For many years, King had read messages coming from the same agent, highly placed within the Cuban government. The recipients of the original messages were the CIA director and the Deputy Director of Operations. King signed the receipt for the message and immediately contacted his liaisons at the FBI and the Immigration and Naturalization Service, each of whom was involved in screening the thousands of Cubans arriving in Florida in August 1994. Replies came back soon after: There was no ranking Cuban officer of any kind among the current batch of Cuban immigrants.

Initially, King was annoyed. But perhaps there hadn't been enough time for the officer to reach the Florida coast. It was possible he had not been spotted and picked up by any of the vessels patrolling the Straits. Or maybe the guy had shown up in the Bahamas, or decided to go to Mexico. Most likely, the defector would reveal his identity as soon as he was rescued or made it to land. Then he'd certainly ask to talk to the CIA. There was nowhere else to go. At the moment, he and his section were overwhelmed with work as a result of the immigration mess. But this high-ranking Cuban Intelligence officer was too important to miss—a diamond in a big wave of shit, King thought. No, he would not miss him. He picked up his phone and called Florida again to make sure that as soon as the intelligence officer was detected, he would be sent directly to King's section in the CIA for questioning.

King got up from his seat and moved around his office to stretch his muscles. He looked at his belly and renewed his vows to get rid of the twenty pounds of excess weight he had accumulated over the last ten years. It was stupid to carry all that dead weight, especially at fifty-five. But the mere thought of doing physical exercise bored him, and eating was the only real pleasure he had left. He forced his mind back to the Cuban Intelligence officer.

"The rats are leaving the doomed ship," King said in a loud voice.

Nada es un hombre en sí, y lo que es,
lo pone en él su pueblo.
(A man alone is nothing; his people make him what he is.)
—José Martí

THE FAN STOPPED with the screech of a dying animal. The heat, pushed aside all this time, invaded the room again. He remained motionless, staring into the darkness. Another power failure, he told himself, feeling immediate guilt for not jumping out of bed to unplug the refrigerator. The coils might burn if the power went on too soon or if there was a surge of high voltage on the lines, but still he refused to move. He was tired, very tired. Tired of the heat in that miserable 1994 Havana summer. Tired of the sleepless nights thinking about the problems that harassed him. Tired of waking up every time the power went off and on. Tired of everything he had done during the last twenty years.

A month earlier, in July, he had come back from Africa after a three-year assignment, pursuing one of the most complex missions of his life. Returning, he had been full of joy. Finally he was going to live a normal life, spending most of his time with his children—who were not children anymore—enjoying the grandchildren to come as he had never enjoyed his own kids. But his homecoming at the airport had been cool and polite. His two sons, who were twenty and twenty-two now, seemed uneasy and inhibited, and they made him feel the same way. His daughter, now seventeen, had not come to the airport at all. She had gone to the beach instead. Two days later, when she came back, she had excused her-self, saying, "Imagine, Dad, two days in Varadero, what an oppor-tunity! You know, Varadero Beach is only for the tourists and for the big shots' families now. I hadn't been there since you took us when I was twelve."

When they arrived at his apartment from the airport, he had found all three bedrooms taken. His sons were living with girlfriends in two of them. The master bedroom, now belonging to his daughter, was locked. It was clear he did not fit into his children's plans. Worst of all, though, was Cecilia's absence. Sitting in the living room, trying to make conversation and being attended to like an unwelcome visitor, he realized that his whole past life had vanished with her death. The place was no longer the sweet home that had filled his dreams for so many years of patient waiting in distant lands. It was a territory invaded by three hostile strangers. The small boys he remembered taking turns to wear his boots and the tiny girl who liked so much to fall asleep on his lap had vanished forever. Just like their mother.

During the conversation, he decided to make a tactical retreat to study his new situation. He told his children he had to attend a work meeting for a few days just outside of Havana but would keep in touch by phone and drop by to see them as often as the meeting allowed.

The first couple of days, he stayed at a friend's house, telling his friend that his whole family had been at the beach when he arrived and he had no keys to get in. He thought of discussing the situation with his superiors at the Service and asking for a place to stay for a few weeks, but rejected the idea for the moment, deciding to look for a room instead.

The next day, he stopped by for a short visit at an hour that seemed convenient to his children. They kept themselves distant and silent, asking no questions and showing no interest in where or how he was going to live. The presents he had brought were lying in the same place, as if they didn't want to touch them. Sometime during the visit he stopped making conversation to gaze at the three sad faces staring through him and wondered what had become of his children now that they were grown-ups. It was clear they had a lot to say but did not want to say anything. For his part, he thought it wiser not to rush into the unavoidable bitter discussion. It would be better to first find out exactly what had happened, and why they had changed so much.

Later that afternoon, he left "his" apartment on Twentieth Street close to Third Avenue in Miramar feeling empty and defeated, as never before. He started to walk south along Twentieth toward Fifth Avenue when he suddenly heard the high-pitched squeal of a heavy vehicle braking behind him. He jumped toward the sidewalk. Glancing back, he saw a 1952 green Chevy pickup that had stopped barely six feet from where he had been walking. He started to move on, then felt someone at his back. Two arms held him from behind in a grip too powerful to shake off. He was bracing to try some defensive movements when he heard a voice thundering:

"This is how I wanted to catch you, sonofabitch!"

"Floro!" He recognized the voice of a buddy who had taken parachuting lessons with him fifteen years back. Later they'd worked together in Africa for several months. Floro was one of the most remarkable guys he'd ever met. Fearless, with the energy of a battalion, he could find solutions—sometimes crazy—for everything. Floro had reached the rank of lieutenant colonel twice and been demoted both times for some foolish mistake. He was finally dismissed from his short and brilliant career in the Intelligence Service five years ago for seeming to have lost the capacity to observe any sort of discipline or to obey any authority. Nevertheless, they had all liked him and were sorry to see him go.

Floro sat down on the curb, invited him to do the same, and began to relate the course of his life since they'd last met. A few minutes later, he finished, saying, "I work now as a construction foreman. Never had it easier in my whole life. I'm in charge of rebuilding houses. Once a house is rebuilt, it's rented for dollars to foreigners living in Havana or to one of the new enterprises that work only with dollars. Dollars, dollars, that's all that counts these days. What about you?"

"Floro, I'm in a hell of a mess. I just got back from too long a stint away from home. During that time, my wife died and my kids have changed completely—they're downright hostile. They don't even want me in the house anymore."

Floro's face looked grim. "They don't have a right to do that to you!" His voice was angry.

"But it would be worse still if I tried to force them to share the house with me."

"Yeah, I guess you're right." Floro remained silent for a while, then spoke emphatically. "Your situation is extreme, but don't think you're the only one in that boat. It's a general problem with this generation. A lot of them have careers, and they know enough of the world to compare their income with what they could have if they were in another country. They have wings and they want to fly. They don't ask themselves for one minute how and why they got their wings. They want to eat well, have their own place to live, own a car, and be able to travel with their own money. Basically, they want to do the things they see in American films and on TV. When they look at what they have now, they become convinced they'll never have anything near what they desire. Then they begin to resent the government as the cause of all their miseries. So they turn against people like you and me, as if we were part of the forces that keep them grounded while life passes them by."

"You've become quite a philosopher, Floro. But the thing that worries me most now is that I don't have a place to stay and I can't afford to rent a room. This morning, a lady wanted one hundred dollars a month for a room. That's two thousand pesos—four months of my salary!"

Floro slapped his friend on the shoulder, leapt up as if he'd been bitten on the ass, and pulled him from the sidewalk. "Let's go. I have the perfect solution for you. The saints want to help you. They made me turn at Twentieth and not at Tenth, as I always do. Do you believe in our African voodoo saints? *Shangó, Oshún, Yemayá* . . . You better. Miracles are the only thing keeping the Cuban people alive nowadays." Floro pushed him into his beat-up Chevy pickup and started driving.

"This vehicle is better now than when it came out of the Detroit factory. It had a gasoline motor, but I put in a new 100-hp Volvo diesel engine. A little heavy, though."

After a short hop to Twenty-sixth Street, Floro stopped in front of a three-story apartment house being rebuilt into an office building a block away from the seafront. He led the way into the place, walking with his usual big strides. His old Russian boots with no shoelaces sounded like the hooves of a horse. He greeted the workers he met along the way, slapping his big hand hard on the shoulders of the ones he caught off guard.

"We'll work on the top floor until it's finished," Floro said. "Then we'll come down floor by floor. Most of the workers I have come from the eastern provinces. I give them some rooms on the second floor to live in. We keep the tools and the construction materials locked up in rooms on the first floor."

Floro opened doors as he walked, showing him everything as he kept talking, jumping from one subject to another. When they reached a door at the end of a dark hall on the first floor, Floro pulled a big bundle of keys from his pocket and started testing each key in the lock. The last one opened the door to a room even darker than the hall. A stale odor welcomed them.

"I can let you use this room and the kitchen in the back. Take the key; it's yours. But whenever you want to screw a woman, don't bring her in here. Can you imagine what would happen if I let the men living upstairs do their fucking here? As my buddy, I'll lend you the key to an empty house I keep furnished as a dormitory. You'll have to make sure nobody's using it before you go in with a lady. When you use it, you have to put up a signal in the window—your shirt, a shoe, the woman's panties—anything."

His friend disappeared into the darkness, stumbled twice, and cursed. Finally, he heard the sound of Venetian blinds being opened. Sunshine poured in and changed the place like magic. A rush of fresh air swept the dead odor out. Floro kept opening more windows and doors. "As long as I'm the one who pisses the farthest in this business, you don't have to worry about a place to stay. After we finish here, there'll be another house to rebuild somewhere else, then another and another. There are hundreds of empty houses to be rebuilt in Miramar alone." Floro grabbed his friend's shoulder in a steel grip. "Listen, man, I can even put you on the payroll as a night watchman. I'm talking seriously. An extra couple of hundred pesos a month come in handy, even if they aren't worth shit these days. You'll have to sign up with another name, but you're used to that, aren't you?" He paused a moment, then shook his head. "Well, maybe that's not such a hot idea; for only two hundred pesos a month, we could both end up in jail."

He pushed the thoughts—the unwanted memories—away, got up from the bed naked, and walked into the shadows of the kitchen, stumbling here and there against walls and furniture, searching for the electrical cord that had to be disconnected. Afterwards, he wrapped a wet towel around his waist and walked to the end of the kitchen to open the back door. A gust of sea breeze cooled by a full bright moon freshened the place.

"It would be heaven if this door could be kept open all night." He muttered the words aloud and immediately realized that the invitation would be accepted by all the burglars on the coast, with the sure loss of the few irreplaceable items he still owned. The priceless electric fan first of all.

He closed his eyes and told himself again that his children and his present living conditions were only a partial cause of the bitterness he felt. There were other woes, as well. He had come back to a country very different from the one he'd left. The economy seemed to have collapsed rapidly once trade and other economic relations with the Soviet Union and the socialist bloc had stopped—almost overnight—in 1991. In that same year, the United States had intensified its thirty-five-year economic war against Cuba. Now everything was in short supply: food, fuel, electricity, medicine, and transportation. Everybody he met had lost more than ten pounds on average in the last three years. Prostitution had flourished overnight. Young, beautiful, educated girls were selling themselves for almost nothing. Political unrest was growing because most people could see no way out of the current situation. Many desperate emigrants were trying to reach Florida at any cost to enjoy the privileged asylum granted to Cubans under a U.S. law dating back to the sixties. That was a card the American government had been playing against the Cuban Revolution for many years, to encourage demoralizing defections and the use of force to procure vessels. In the last few months, numerous armed assaults had been made to seize small crafts from fishing enterprises, dockyards, and Coast Guard stations. Even a passenger ferry servicing Havana Bay had been hijacked, ending up at the bottom of the sea, its passengers drowned.

Finally, the situation out of hand, the Cuban government had issued a decree permitting free migration in any sort of vessel. The clear objective was to create a huge wave of emigrants in search of the land of milk and honey in Florida. The human tidal wave, the government had believed, would act as a boomerang forcing the United States—already overwhelmed by immigration from everywhere—to stop rewarding all Cubans arriving on U.S. coasts with privileges not granted to any other nationality.

As soon as the new decree was known, thousands of desperate people began to gather whatever floatable material they could put their hands on to assemble all kinds of rafts. Working in their neighborhoods until they were ready, they would then carry everything to some place on the coast where the rafts could be assembled and launched out to the sea. Usually, they would take off late in the

afternoon or at night to avoid the blazing tropical sun. Seamen recommended just past midnight as the best launching time, the period when the *terral* sets in, the friendly wind that blows from the
land toward the sea until mid-morning the next day, taking sailing
vessels easily into the open sea. Then, in the late morning, the trade
winds set in, blowing steadily westward.

In good weather, crossing the ninety miles from Havana's coast
to Key West takes a day with a decent sailboat—a couple of days or
more for a strong raft with oars and a sail. But still there are dangers. Weather in the summer changes quickly. Frequent thunder-
storms with strong winds, heavy rains, and lightning are a deadly
threat for any small vessel. Toward the end of summer, low-pressure centers can develop into hurricanes. On a poorly built raft, the
odds against voyagers crossing the Florida Straits are great. In
those cases, with luck, they might be spotted by a small U.S. reconnaissance plane and picked up long before they reach the Florida
coast by one of the many U.S. Navy ships patrolling the area.

Someone he didn't know came to take him to the safe house for a
luncheon meeting with the chief of the Intelligence Service. What
was happening? No outsider had ever been used before for these
types of chores. He had never seen the guy and was about to refuse
the ride, but dismissed the idea, deciding that the explanation must
be quite simple, most probably it was the only available car. He got
into the automobile, but discouraged the driver's efforts to start a
conversation and let his eyes wander along Miramar's Fifth
Avenue, always a pleasant view. The beautiful, often opulent houses
on either side of the wide avenue vanished ten minutes later as they
entered the small town of Jaimanitas and then Santa Fe. Some of
the old wooden houses his father had shown him when he first
came to Havana at the age of twelve were still there. He could
remember his father's voice and the poetry in all he said, as in all he
did. "Those homes were built at the beginning of the century when
these two fishing villages, always crossed by fresh winds coming

from or going to the sea, became a fashionable summer resort for the rich people of Havana. Only the best wood was used to withstand the relentless attack of all the decaying agents that thrive in this high temperature and humidity year-round." The old wooden houses stood as ghosts amid an assorted collection of new and refurbished dwellings, from the humble and plain apartment houses of the government housing program—for many years, all of them as alike as beehives—to the modern chalets of those who had somehow prospered.

The driver turned left into an area where numerous shacks sprouted like mushrooms trying to hide in a forest of low, thorny shrubs. These were the quarters of *orientales*, newcomers from the eastern provinces where the economic situation was always much worse than in the rest of the country. "In a few years, no one will be living like that in Cuba," his father used to tell him. "The only thing we need is an honest government. This country can be very rich if we just let the people work." His father's prophecy never came true, though by the 1980s the economic situation had improved notably. Now it was worse than ever.

Past the shacks, the car took a right turn onto a well-maintained dirt road and climbed uphill until it halted before a gate half-hidden by a hedge of thick bushes. Beyond and above the hedge he could see a weathered, red-tiled roof under a glaring August sun poised in the exact middle of a naked sky. The heat became oppressive as soon as the car stopped, and they waited for the guarded gate to be opened.

"This is it," the driver said to his lone and silent passenger, as he parked under the shadow of an avocado tree in the front drive. Three other cars were tucked under the heavier shadow of a stand of very old mango trees at the top of the hill, just beyond the house. He stepped onto the veranda surrounding the house and followed the driver into the living room of the high-ceilinged, wooden, colonial-style dwelling. The driver motioned for him to wait and kept walking toward the back of the house.

All doors and windows were open, and from the living room he could hear the voice of a woman complaining about something. Another woman laughed. The breeze coming unchallenged from the northeast cooled the place and made the mahogany rocking chairs seem exceedingly inviting. The view facing the sea extended to the north, east, and west as far as the curvature of the earth allowed the gaze to reach. Just below the house, a patchy landscape of roofs and patios stretched amid streets that ran to the seafront to meet the blue water. His eyes scrutinized the shoreline to the west where the Marina Hemingway—a conglomerate of modern buildings, bungalows, channels, and yachts—seemed to belong to another world.

He heard the steps of two people on the mosaic floor and got up as the chief of the Intelligence Service came into the living room from the back of the house. The man looked much older and thinner than the last time he had seen him. The framework of the massive, strong, bull-necked man he remembered was still there, but the flesh had withered away and weakened. His once long, thick beard with a reddish glow was now white and thin, and his face was sweeter, like the face of any grandfather.

A few steps behind him stood Marcelo, his second-in-command, always silent and almost invisible before the top chiefs, one of the keys to his success in the trade. Marcelo nodded and smiled warmly, something he rarely did.

"You look now very much like your father did, with those streaks of gray in your sideburns," the old man said, embracing him softly with what used to be a bear hug. "Time flies. Life is gone before we realize it. I was with your father in New York the day you were born, back in 1950. I asked him what he was going to name his first male child and he answered quickly, 'Carlos Manuel, just like Céspedes.' After a few drinks, celebrating your birth, I remarked, joking, 'That's quite a responsibility for such a small boy, bearing the name of the father of our country—a man who shot himself rather than be taken alive by the enemy.' Your father stared at me. 'That's exactly the way I want him to be,' he answered, his face very grave."

The old man stopped for a moment, then added, "You have honored your name. Your father would have been proud of you, if he were with us today."

"You look in pretty good shape," Carlos Manuel said, trying to change the subject of the embarrassing conversation.

"Don't lie, telling me I also look good. I've lost thirty pounds, and I know I look like hell. When you grow old, you learn suddenly one day that your cholesterol and triglycerides are about to clog you up from head to toe. You find out that pissing so often is a sure sign of diabetes. In the morning, when you wake up with a bladder about to explode and you almost can't piss, it's because your prostate is all swollen up and one of these days you're not going to be able to piss at all. All sorts of pitiable woes fall upon you with age. It's the payment for all you ate in excess during your whole life. 'You are what you eat.' Who said that? A Greek philosopher, I'm sure. Greek philosophers said just about everything worth saying. I used to know who said that, too. And that's the worst; you begin to forget everything."

The old man seated himself at the head of a dining table covered with a white tablecloth, Marcelo at his right. As they sat down, two women hurried in to serve the meal, a large bowl of steaming black beans, a platter of white rice, another platter of *tostones*—double-fried smashed slices of banana plantain—and individual plates of sliced tomatoes and roasted chicken. The salt was in a small saucer beside bottles of vinegar and cooking oil for dressing the salad. One of the women brought a big pitcher with cold water and three glasses, all of them different. She raised her eyes to meet his after he cast a fast glance at her round and solid breasts, the nipples trying to pierce the cloth of the blouse.

"Can you imagine that I am only allowed to eat three spoonfuls of rice and three of beans?" the old man said sadly. Then he went on to explain how many calories he was supposed to eat during the whole day. "The secret of the diet is not to fight hunger. If you're hungry, you're lost. A hungry man can't think straight. To beat hunger and still eat only a little, you have to spread out the food you're allowed during the day, every three hours. Never eat much. Just little by little."

The old man, still in the same sorrowful tone, changed the subject.

"Carlos Manuel, you have been away for a long time, and you're beginning now to really know what happened when the Soviet Union and all the other socialist countries collapsed. Our imports dropped from eight billion dollars a year to less than three. Can you imagine that? Suddenly, having to carry on this country's entire economy with a third of what it used to have? I never imagined that the Soviet Union was going to melt like that. Nobody did. Not even the Americans guessed that."

"Carlos Manuel" sounded awkward. The name triggered something in his mind that made it wander away from the old man's conversation. For most of his life he had been using names other than his own. Single, short war names very few people knew about: Aurelio, Mauricio, Marco, Roberto, Rudolph . . . all in keeping with the best tradition of the Russian secret service that had trained them all. False public-identity names, each one with a complete life of its own. Each with a different look, different mother and father, a whole set of friends, a special way of talking, dressing, and eating to go with the country, the education, and the roots of this new identity. With each change of public name, a long painful private metamorphosis, until one day it was complete, and he had fully become this other being. He had left behind many names and many other lives, like some species of animals leave behind outgrown skins. Now his real name, Carlos Manuel, sounded remote, strangely alien, with a life that hardly seemed to belong to him.

Normally, in this sort of gathering, after a long time away, he would have done most of the talking, briefing his two bosses on the highlights of his work abroad. On this occasion, however, the old man seemed uninterested, speaking only about his illness and the difficult economic situation the country was facing. Carlos Manuel kept silent, feeling that something important was about to happen. He sensed the moment had arrived when the old man turned his head and glanced at him with the same vivid expression in his eyes that he remembered so well, although he kept talking in the same low key.

"Listen, son, the days of Cuba taking so active a part helping liberation movements all over the world, even waging full-scale wars in Africa, are over. Many people have had to go into civilian life, or to other posts within the armed forces, now that we have to produce everything we consume. I'll show you what we are doing here. In a couple of years, we'll be producing more than thirty tons of chicken, pork, and rabbit meat on this small farm alone." The old man stopped talking, as if giving him time to absorb that information.

"Don't you worry. In your case, you'll be transferred to the police for one year, until you reach the retirement age of forty-five. In that way, you won't lose the very favorable pension plan from the Ministry of the Interior after almost twenty-five years in the service. Once retired, we will find a good position for you in one of the many new enterprises that are being created with foreign firms. In fact, you can pick whatever job you like."

He could not believe what he was hearing. Marcelo only nodded his head now and then, approving everything. Why were they putting him away? What had he done wrong? Since the moment he was ordered to return home, he had been under the impression that he was going to be promoted.

"We need to place our men in key places in the joint ventures with foreign capital. Besides, in addition to your pension, you will have full salary and some of the other economic advantages these new enterprises offer."

The old man seemed uneasy in his new role as salesman. In the past, he had always emphasized the *needs of the Revolution* when he presented a subordinate with a new task. Now he was talking about material advantages. "Nothing to worry about." The old man repeated the words over and over.

He had been stunned, had wanted to bluntly ask why they were dumping him. But if he had learned one thing over the last twenty years, it was never to ask why. He had to figure it out for himself. It was true that the glorious days of Cuba as a mini–world power had been over for quite some time, and that fact had compelled many people in the armed forces to change jobs. Yet, in spite of that, he knew this did not apply to men of his expertise, at a time when the confrontation with the United States was increasing day by day. The reasons for his dismissal had to be found elsewhere.

Marcelo came to see him two days after his release from the Service. He came alone, at dusk, wearing a pair of jeans with no belt and a black, worn-out polo shirt faded to a dirty gray around the neck and sleeves. There was no place to sit in his dwelling. They went to the kitchen and he invited Marcelo to sit on the floor close to the back door, a spot always blessed by the sea breeze.

Marcelo had brought a bottle of Havana Club rum, just like the good old days. Carlos Manuel looked inside the fifty-year-old General Electric refrigerator and, after some hammering, was able to rescue some ice. He gave Marcelo the only glass available and took an empty condensed-milk can for himself. The visitor didn't wait until the rum was served to start talking.

"Sorry, brother, we failed you. I, especially, failed you completely." Marcelo let out a deep breath, as if a weight had been lifted off his chest, then continued in a low voice as he sipped his rum, staring into his friend's eyes. "For many years, Cecilia kept everything so much under control that we trusted her blindfolded, thinking that if she was around, everything was okay. We weren't able to see how many things had changed within your family when your children stopped being children and Cecilia lost control. The economic situation turned bad from one day to the next; there were so many needs for all the people that we just attended to the ones who cried the loudest. It's the truth. There was no possible way to make ends meet. On the other hand, amazingly, a lot of people managed to get by one way or another. Our families are so closely knit that any cash always gets spread among everyone. In some cases, someone in the family would get a job in tourism and earn a few dollars a month. Others had relatives with farms who provided food. Many of the people who went away to the United States or elsewhere send money to their families here. That money is one of the main sources of support for the country nowadays. And then there is the hidden economy that feeds and is fed by a strange black market. A lot of the workers and administrative personnel derive most of their income from stolen goods from their workplaces. It's been going on for some time, and has become a lifesaver for a lot of families and a curse for the whole country. I myself close my eyes to what my wife does. In the last few years she's been selling the cigarettes and cigars that we get on our ration card at higher prices. Now she and the woman who lives in front are making soft drinks and candies for the kids in the high school nearby. I just don't want to know how and from whom she's buying the sugar, the wheat, and the oil to make those things. Nevertheless, my children have stopped complaining about food. It's amazing how things have turned out."

Marcelo kept silent for a while. The rum at his side remained almost untouched. Then he continued, looking out at the sea as if talking to himself.

"We just kept making the routine calls once in a long while to chat a bit with Cecilia. Asking her if she needed anything. Her standard reply was, 'Everything is okay, don't worry about us.' If she asked for something, it was always simple. Once she needed a mechanic to fix your car brakes. We sent somebody who worked for over a week fixing everything wrong with your Lada. Another time, I remember, she asked us to send someone to fix the water pump in the building. She never mentioned that she barely ate so the kids would have enough food. She never said the money wasn't enough, she never complained about anything. Finally, she got ill, but never mentioned it. Little by little, your kids became hostile to everything. They blamed you, they blamed us, and they blamed the government. Above all, they felt you didn't care about them. They could never understand why you weren't able to be at their mother's funeral.

"The main thing we became aware of, finally, was the drastic change in your children's attitude. We came to the conclusion that they had the final say in this situation. The only thing to do was to get you out of the big game. Bring you home to see if you could gain control. It was too late to try anything else. As you know, we could not pull you out in a hurry, and there was no use telling you anything while you were there. You might have lost your concentration, and that could have had fatal consequences for you and many other people as well.

"We also found out quite late that your sister had contacted your kids, and that she was calling your daughter frequently on a neighbor's phone. After your wife's death, she started sending money to Claudia through a third party. There was nothing left to do. With a link between your sister in the U.S. and your kids in Cuba, it was only a matter of time before your real identity would become known. When you all came to Cuba, your father managed to swap your identities with another family to protect your sister and to dodge the CIA's surveillance. Once the CIA knows who you are, many things will come into place for them."

There was a long silence. Marcelo drank his shot of rum in a hurry. Carlos Manuel realized that Marcelo's face had aged in the last few years, especially around the eyes, although he still kept a boyish look and the thin, wiry body that made him look much younger than he really was. They had been together in school and on many risky missions, and they had come to feel like blood brothers.

"Do you have any idea why she killed herself?"

Marcelo shrugged and asked in return, "Did she leave you a letter?"

"Sort of. Almost since the beginning of our marriage, she wrote everything she wanted to tell me in school notebooks. I discovered them by chance, although I never told her, because I wasn't supposed to prowl in her things. Somehow, she came to know that I was aware of her writings, and that became her way of telling me the things that she didn't dare speak. After I got back this time, I read all those notebooks, starting with the first. About six months before she killed herself, there's a subtle change in her writings; I can't pinpoint what it is, but it's there—maybe a more open way of saying things. A month before she poisoned herself, there's another change; she started writing as if she was going somewhere and she might not be here when I came back. I've read those parts many times, but I can't find a single clue as to why she ended her life." Carlos Manuel closed his eyes as if bringing Cecilia back to his memory. "It's like just one last long talk with me, like she used to enjoy when we were lying in bed, very late at night, after we'd made love." Carlos Manuel put a hand on Marcelo's shoulder, pressed it hard, and asked, "How ill was she, really?"

Marcelo shook his head. "Not that ill."

"I wish I'd known all of this before."

"Don't torture yourself. There's nothing you can do now. You have to take all of this as a spy's fate—a price we all have to pay for what we do." Then Marcelo added in a lower tone of voice, as if talking to himself, "She was so closed in on herself, so self-restrained. Why didn't she tell me she couldn't hold on anymore? I guess she wasn't that sort of person; I guess it was the only way out she could see. *The only way she could make us think about our families.*"

Marcelo got up slowly and walked out through the back door. He jumped over a small fence at the rear of the patio, disappearing into the shadows of the building and the growing darkness of the evening. He never looked back or said goodbye, as if he was running away.

* * *

The visit had been so brief and so decisive that for a moment Carlos Manuel doubted it had even happened. He remained in the kitchen doorway, feeling the cool draft of air coming from the sea and watching the moon gain strength. He thought about how little he knew the people he had thought he knew best. He had never imagined that Cecilia would kill herself; he'd never dreamed Marcelo cared anything for any person in particular. To him, Marcelo represented the paradigm of the people in his trade—a man detached from feelings, just a brain applying what Baruch Spinoza, the great Jewish-Dutch philosopher, often said: "Never cry or laugh on account of men's deeds, only understand them."

The moon took hold of the night. From where he stood he could see many people crossing the big empty lot at the back of the building where he now lived, going to and from one of the raft-launching sites on Havana's coast, at Twenty-eighth Street in Miramar. They all moved in the same way, passing through the lot with their heads down, walking in zigzag patterns to avoid the holes in the coral reef and the debris left behind by others, their faces and hands reflecting the moonlight as if they were covered in a coat of aluminum paint.

When he had moved to this makeshift apartment, he had become curious about the exodus. Several times he had started to cross the empty lot, but each time he had stopped before reaching the launching site, as if he were about to look into a pestilent wound inside his own gut. Something had grown inside him during these last days, during these last hours. That night he had an urgent need to see it.

H E PUT ON an old pair of jeans, a bright yellow cap that glowed in the dark, an orange T-shirt, and a pair of tennis shoes without socks. He joined the stream of people crossing the back lot, watching his step as he walked on the sharp coral reef that continued up to the shore. Soon he reached the shadows of an old building and started to stumble against obstacles. Somebody at his back—a fat man was all he could tell—turned on a flashlight, and he suddenly remembered that he needed batteries for an old flashlight he had found among his belongings when he moved to his new room. It was a useless thought, but it was there, filling his mind as he waited for the man with the torch to take the lead.

Then the fat man turned abruptly to warn him. "Watch it! There are stairs just ahead." He thanked the man and started to walk beside him on the sidewalk that ran along the back of a building, parallel to the coast. The sidewalk was slippery from the sea hammering the shore, but the sharp sea odor was inviting, and the sound of the waves hitting the reef was pleasant and relaxing. Soon he reached the ruins of a small pier. The moon had painted the sea with a much lighter coat of aluminum paint, until it resembled a big pool of mercury.

Below, on the pier almost at water level, a crowd of curious bystanders had gathered around the relatives of two crews getting ready to leave, seeming to join them in their sad farewell. One of the rafts was about to be launched and both crews were cooperating to make final adjustments. He surveyed the raft with an expert eye. It was well made out of six empty oil drums welded firmly together in two, three-drum clusters. The framework was built with four-inch steel U-beams fastened with bolts so it could be carried to the seashore in sections for assembly.

Once the raft was completed with a wooden board on top of the floating drums, it was lowered into the water with two strong ropes. Immediately, six men, five youngsters, and one old man boarded the raft and began loading the supplies handed down by people on the dock. Everything was tightly fastened to the steel frame of the raft under the close supervision of the old man. Four long oars were pulled out of the baggage and the vessel began moving slowly northward away from shore. The sea surface began to ripple, pushed gently by a breeze, and the people left behind cheered and shouted to the rafters, wishing them a safe journey. When the raft was about a hundred yards from the coast, a white sail was hoisted, the wind filled it, and the vessel gained speed. The people on the pier yelled again. Some wept.

The next raft was poorly made. A weak frame of nailed wooden pieces embraced a big pine box with a double bottom, that was filled with polyurethane to make it float better. Carlos Manuel recognized one of the members of the crew, a young man who had frequented his house in the past, a friend of his older son. He stepped down to the pier to get a closer look. The boy he remembered was now an athletic young man as tall as he was, but his features were unmistakable.

"Andrés."

"Hello," the youngster answered without looking up, showing he had noticed him already.

"Are you travelling on *this*?"

Andrés remained mute and gave only a short nod.

"Why, Andrés? You know a black man doesn't have much future in the United States."

"What future does anybody have here?" The voice was high-pitched in anger.

He stood silent. After a while, Andrés faced him.

"Sorry, man. This is not easy, you know. But I have to do it. I have to do it for my family's sake." Andrés spoke as if he were trying to convince himself.

"Why don't we talk? Let's see what sort of problems you have."

Andrés did not answer. He just bent back down to the raft.

"Maybe I can help you. Besides, look at this raft. It will explode into pieces against the first wave."

"Why don't you leave me alone?" Andrés snapped, facing him again.

"I'm sure I can help you."

"If you want to help somebody, why don't you help your own kids? They're leaving from Cojímar right now."

DRIVING AS FAST as he could to Cojímar, Carlos Manuel reviewed his past family life, trying to understand why his children were running away from him and from the country he had wanted them to love above all things.

Now he realized he had been like Santa Claus, arriving home with presents for everyone, staying for a few weeks, giving them everything they wanted, trying to please them to make up for so much time away. When he was at home, everything was put aside, every day was a holiday: dinners in restaurants, vacations at the beach, trips to the Escambray Mountains to see uncles, aunts, and grandparents, days of kisses and hugs with all three children fighting for his attention. Cecilia smiling all the time, trying to appear cool and collected, as if she were saying, "What's the fuss? Daddy has just come home from work like everybody else."

Then he would disappear again, leaving one unexpected night for another long stretch of time. Gone somewhere. Usually to a place that could not be known and, if known, could not be mentioned. All that emptiness filled only by letters brought by someone every once in a long while, letters always saying the same thing: He loved her and the kids very much. He missed them very much. He was well and counting the days before he came back, but never knowing when.

Suddenly, his mind jumped to something that had occurred to him the first time he had played chess with a computer. He had made a mistake and was about to take it back when he thought that, in life, you can't really take back what you've done wrong. The only thing you can do is to improve your way of playing from there on to make up for your mistake. He had decided then that he would never take back a move when playing chess with a computer. Sometimes with a winning game, he made a bad move and lost. He then went back step by step to find the move that had lost the game. That self-imposed discipline not only improved his game, it made him more thoughtful in life.

When and how did I lose my life's game? he asked himself now.

The last time he was in Cuba, he had spent several months with his family. Then he had had a winning game in his hand; in fact, a terrific game. Antonio, his oldest son, then eighteen, had just entered the Medical University of Havana. He had finished high school in the Camilo Cienfuegos military school. There he had been an honor student, finishing among the best in his class. He seemed to do everything well. He was bright, modest, responsible, excellent in both sports and studies, a good worker in the month he spent each year harvesting citrus on a state-owned farm. Then, instead of following the military career for which he had seemed so fit, he had decided to study medicine. Antonio had always been too old for his age, he thought. Antonio had crossed the line from childhood to manhood with no transition.

Felipe, his second son, then sixteen, was not at all a good student. He spent too much time with girls, going to parties and raising all sorts of hell. Cecilia, as all mothers do, blamed it on "these modern girls with no moral principles and no respect for their own sex, always chasing him like bitches in heat." Good-looking, an excellent dancer, a loyal friend to everyone, excessively generous even with things that did not belong to him, Felipe, since birth, seemed to be blessed by a good star. Felipe never lost his temper. He was always in a good mood, a permanent rush of fresh air in the house.

"I think I'm going to be an artist, Dad," Felipe had announced one day when they were travelling by car to a mountain resort, and he had asked his son what he planned to do with his life.

"What sort of artist do you want to be?"

Felipe remained silent for a moment.

"I don't know yet. Can you give me a good idea? What about a painter like you?"

He had smiled, not knowing how to answer. "I'm not a painter, son. I just like to draw a little."

Now, five years later, their entire apartment was decorated with Felipe's paintings. He had liked them very much. Felipe was a gifted student in the National School of Art.

His mind came back again to his life chess game. In this past month, he had tried very hard to understand what had happened during his last assignment in Africa. Little by little, he realized that his work had imposed tremendous hardships on his family, until it had reached the point of disaster. During his last three-year tour of duty, the purchasing power of his salary, the only regular income in the house, had devaluated to almost nothing. When he went away, most of the necessary goods could still be bought at very low prices through the rationing system. Additional food or goods had to be bought in a parallel market at much higher prices, but had still been accessible with his salary. Now, very little could be acquired with the rations system, and the parallel market had disappeared. Most food had to be purchased at very high prices on the black market. The value of the peso against the dollar, once about par, had gone down to a hundred pesos to the dollar for some time, then settled around twenty pesos to the dollar. His monthly salary, 450 pesos, could now buy very little outside the rationing system. In addition to the economic problems, Cecilia's illness—and finally her suicide—was the final blow for all of them.

A good chess player never gives up. He has to find a way to save the game by stalemate if it's impossible to win it. Now he had to study the board to decide on his next move. First, he had to know what he had in his hand. He viewed the members of his family in his mind as chess pieces. Antonio always seemed to him like a tower, the rook, capable of defending the entire family if necessary. Felipe was like a bishop, able to get deep into enemy territory almost unnoticed. His daughter, Claudia, was more like a horse, the knight. Yes, she was a very young mare, unpredictable in her moves, with a powerful kick. She was the most independent of his three children, very hard-headed, with a strong sense of leadership. And Cecilia? She had been the queen of the family, the most powerful piece, already lost. *And he had been the king, protected by his family, all the time at all costs.* Now the game was almost over. Time was overdue for the king to go out and fight.

H E DROVE THROUGH the half-mile-long tunnel under the mouth of Havana's bay, coming out the other end on the six-lane Carretera Monumental, an expressway running eastward, built in the fifties to astonish Havana's dwellers with its width and its name. He slowed down and paid attention to the surroundings, careful not to miss the turn for the old road to Cojímar. In 1990, many sports arenas, roads, and buildings had been constructed here for the first celebration of the Pan-American games in Cuba, and he wasn't familiar with the new look of the area. Nevertheless, the old landmarks were easy to follow, and soon he was on the right track to Cojímar, reaching the top of the hill at the entrance to the town in a few minutes. For an instant he saw all the lights of the town below, ending with the silhouette of the fortress built centuries earlier by the Spaniards at the mouth of the small bay it guarded. He slowed down as he entered the village, swarming with people coming and going, walking in the streets instead of on the sidewalks, even though it was close to midnight.

As he travelled through the familiar places depicted in *The Old Man and the Sea*, pleasant memories of the times he had brought his family there flashed through his mind. On those lazy afternoons they invariably ate in the restaurant La Terraza, always sitting at one of the tables overlooking the bay so the kids could watch the slow passing of the fishermen in their sailboats, coming into town after a day's work out in the Gulf Stream. Once, the restaurant's cook had come to sit at their table to tell the kids anecdotes of when he used to work for Cojímar's most famous fisherman, Ernest Hemingway, on his yacht *Pilar*.

He came out of his reverie abruptly as he approached the pier and the people in the streets became a compact crowd of more than a thousand, watching rafts being assembled and launched out to sea. He parked the car on a side street and worked his way into the multitude to access the pier.

"Manicero, mani." The voice of a vendor suddenly made him hungry for the home-cooked roasted peanuts being sold.

"Manicero, mani." The voice was right at his back now. Someone called the vendor and bought all the packs of peanuts left. He kept pushing ahead until he reached a narrow pier where several crews were busy assembling their rafts. He spotted his younger son Felipe, already on a raft at the end of the pier, receiving gear from his brother and sister. Their supplies were well-packed inside heavy nylon sacks, each one marked with a number in red ink, as if they had been ready for a long time. Was that the reason they had not wanted him at the apartment, the reason his bedroom, taken over by his daughter, had been locked against him?

He stood there watching them, not knowing what to do. He felt empty and weak as he looked at the most important part of his world preparing to run away from him. The three of them saw him suddenly, surprise and dismay showing on their faces. The two boys looked down, as they always did when caught doing something wrong. He knew he had lost that battle. He had no right to interfere with their lives now, but he would try one last time anyway. Putting his arm around the shoulders of his elder son, he drew him ten feet away. He couldn't find in his mind what to say. Before he realized it, he was speaking the way he used to when Antonio was a boy.

"I thought there was an understanding between us that in my absence you had to look after them." As he spoke, his own words sounded silly, out of place, absurd.

"That's exactly what I'm doing now, Dad," Antonio answered shortly, and turned away to continue his preparations.

He then tried to convince Antonio to let him go along on the raft. Antonio hesitated, then joined Felipe and Claudia to discuss the matter with them.

Carlos Manuel jumped onto the raft and started to check the way it was built, the amount of water and food they carried, the way they had designed the sail and fastened it to the raft.

Antonio came back from the meeting to give him the final word.

"How are you planning to keep on course?" he asked his son, before he could say anything.

Antonio showed him a small compass fastened inside a water-proof kangaroo belt.

"We'll try to always go due north. The wind is coming now from the south. If it holds until morning, according to the fishermen, we could average about three knots, not counting the help of the pad-dles. At sunrise, we should be way out into international water, more than twenty miles off the coast. With luck, U.S. ships will pick us up in the morning—at the latest, in the afternoon." His son saw the doubt in his eyes and tried to answer it. "The fishermen say the American vessels are right out there." Antonio evaded his eyes, still full of doubt. "Dad, you can't come with us. We all think it's not good."

He gave Antonio his cap and T-shirt to be fastened to the top of the sail mast.

"The yellow and orange color should contrast sharply against the blue of the sea and the white of the clouds, so the raft can be spot-ted more easily. It will bring you luck. You already have it with the wind. There's a strong and steady *terral* tonight; it will hold until morning," he said, trying to be convincing. "Do you know the strength of the Gulf Stream near the coast?"

Antonio's blank face gave him the answer.

"The Gulf Stream will make the raft drift to the east, maybe as much as it advances to the north," he added.

"I brought your metal case, the one you use for tools," Antonio said.

"What for?" he asked.

"It should reflect radar waves better. I filled it with polyurethane so it will also float, in case . . ." Antonio did not complete his sentence.

"Good thinking" was the last thing he said to his son. He looked around and found that everything was ready. He tried to say something aloud to all of them, but the words stuck in his throat, and he only whispered, "Isn't there anything I can do to help?"

"Daddy, you're too late for that."

It was his daughter Claudia who came forward. She spoke the words looking directly into his eyes, then turned her back on him and jumped onto the raft.

He bid a brief farewell with his hand, then walked as fast as he could away from the pier. He found he was weeping, the first time he could remember doing so since childhood.

05

HE WAS DEVASTATED. The whole outfit his children had gathered together was worthless. It had no chance of withstanding any mildly rough sea. He looked around and realized it was no better and no worse than the rest of the rafts being assembled at the pier. *But they were his kids!*

On his way back to Havana, he considered his chances of getting any sort of motor vessel to follow his children's raft and find it in the middle of the Florida Straits before anything happened to them. He reached his old apartment half an hour later, still with no plan in mind. He found three farewell letters addressed to him lying on the dining room table. He didn't have time to read them now and only noticed that Felipe's letter was thicker and heavier than the others. As he looked around for whatever would be useful for the voyage he intended to make, he turned on the radio already tuned to Radio Reloj, a station that broadcast only news and the exact time. The announcer said it was midnight and forecasted heavy rains and winds for the central part of the island due to a low-pressure wave, a usual event at this time of the year. The bad weather was travelling westward and was expected to hit the western provinces during the morning that same day: Monday, August 15. He shook his head. That was bad news, and there was no telling when the change of weather would really reach the Havana coast. Weather reports were not that trustworthy.

He decided to call Marcelo at his house. By now, he might be asleep. He dialed the first two digits and stopped, anticipating what was going to happen: Marcelo's aide, sleeping by the phone, would wake up to answer this late call. Nervous at being awakened at that hour, he'd relax when he heard who was calling. Then he'd try to find out what was wanted of his boss before he decided whether to rouse him. Lies wouldn't work. The man was no fool. He would tell him that it was a personal matter and that he needed to talk with Marcelo very urgently. Maybe he would add it was a matter of life or death. The aide would hesitate, but finally he would awaken Marcelo. A few minutes later, Marcelo, bad-humored and bewildered by the call, would pick up the phone. What was he going to say to him? That he needed a fast and sure vessel to search for his loving children and then take them safely into enemy territory? All the youngsters on all the rafts—and the overwhelming majority of the rafters were young—were somebody's beloved children. He had seen the faces of the parents trying to look as if they were happy to see their sons and daughters leave in those frail and stupid vessels. They loved them as much as he loved his. What made his children special? He put the telephone down.

On the other hand, he told himself, the situation he was in now was due mainly to the nature of his work. Marcelo himself had taken the blame for it. He dialed Marcelo's number at his office. Maybe he was still working. An unknown voice answered. He identified himself and asked to talk to Colonel Marcelo.

"One moment, please." There was a long silence. Was Marcelo hesitating before answering his call?

"Marcelo is not in the office," said another voice.

He decided to dial the private phone number only a few people knew. The familiar voice of Marcelo's aide answered immediately. Without his asking, the aide put Marcelo on the phone.

"What's the matter, old boy?" Marcelo was trying to be casual.

"My kids left on a raft from Cojímar about an hour ago. I've just heard on the radio there's going to be bad weather in the next few hours. The shit they're on will not stand any rough sea. I need some kind of motorboat to find them and see they reach wherever they're going safely."

There was a long and heavy silence.

"Get ahold of Floro. Have him call me back."

He put down the phone, contemplating the meaning of the answer he'd received. Yes, it was positive, something was going to be done. At the same time, he smiled, remembering his "casual" encounter with Floro. So, Floro was his guardian angel! He should have known.

IT WAS ALREADY seven o'clock, and the sun still wasn't able to break through the thick mass of clouds coming from the east. Lightning and thunder on the horizon announced a thunderstorm knocking at the door. He remembered the weather forecast he'd heard on the radio and damned its accuracy. According to what he saw on the radar screen and his own calculations, he was already twenty-two miles due north of Cojímar, and he still hadn't found a trace of any raft on the radar. He wondered how much drift the Gulf Stream could cause, this current flowing eastward in the Florida Straits like an immense blue river. He had no idea how strong the Stream was that close to Cuba this time of year. He guessed it would be at least two to three knots, maybe even five. That meant he had to look for his children's raft twelve to eighteen miles to the east of Cojímar, possibly up to thirty. He sped up the yacht, looking at the fuel gauge and wondering how many more miles he could travel with the little diesel fuel left in the tank. The further east he travelled, the foggier it became, the darker the horizon, the more restless the sea. On the radar he could see heavy rain ahead.

Off and on his radar screen started to pick up what could be three rafts or small vessels close to each other about twenty miles to the northeast in an area of heavy rain. He changed course by almost ninety degrees. Instead of due east, the compass now pointed almost due north. He was going to intercept whatever objects gave those radar readings.

He headed for the closest one, the weakest signal. Twenty minutes later, he hit the bad weather. Suddenly, the remains of a raft floated in front of the yacht. There was nobody among the wooden flotsam and bundles wrapped in nylon bags that went by. "No survivors," he said aloud to himself. His heart sank.

It became harder to keep heading north with the strong wind and waves coming from the east. The yacht was taking a lot of water with every wave, and he feared the motor would stop at any moment. He turned on the electric pump to get as much water out as possible, but it was not enough. With visibility reduced to less than a mile, he kept constant watch, trying to decipher the signals on the radar screen. The two small floating objects drifting westward stayed for only a few seconds then went off, the radar only detecting them when they were on top of the waves. The yacht, forcing its way northward, was getting closer to them.

Half an hour later, the rain thinned and the sun began to pierce the clouds. The wind had calmed down a little, but there were still strong gusts. The waves continued to beat fiercely against the yacht. He was sure now he'd passed the front of the low-pressure tropical wave where major weather disturbances are always found. The yacht had taken too much water, though, in spite of the pump working steadily all this time. It began to lift its bow more slowly after each wave, and it was becoming harder to steer. The fuel gauge was already in the red zone. He had no other choice but to change course into the waves, slow down the engine, save whatever fuel was left to keep the batteries that operated the pump fully charged, and wait for the current and the wind to bring toward him whatever was being reflected on the radar.

The wind started to bring the echo of voices from a long distance. Was he going mad? Trying to pierce the fog with his eyes, he sought to distinguish that maddening sound. He knew that he should only go after one of the objects signaling on the radar, it was impossible to reach both. He decided to head toward the strongest flash on the screen, praying it was Antonio's steel case.

The wind and the waves he was facing pushed the object westward. He had to try to stay put and let the wind do the rest. With the improvement in visibility, he hoped to see any small floating object in his course for at least a mile or two. Suddenly, he saw a yellow and orange blot moving in the fog like a tiny hand waving hello.

"Claudia! Antonio! Felipe!" he yelled at the top of his voice, knowing that the wind made it impossible for them to hear him. Like sounds from another world, he started to hear human voices more clearly. The passengers on the raft must have spotted the yacht and were calling for help. He tried to distinguish the voices of his children. Was that Claudia? It had to be them! Was that yellow and orange rag on top of the mast real? He began to struggle against the waves. He had to maneuver to be able to catch the raft as it passed by, because there was no way for him to turn the wounded yacht around without capsizing in such a heavy sea. He had anticipated this moment and had a long rope ready, tied to a big life preserver. He threw it starboard.

Everything happened very fast. He glimpsed all three of them rising up from under the water. Their sail had been torn to pieces and had blown away. It was easy to see that the raft was badly damaged and they were hanging on to what was left. His children spotted the preserver and were desperately trying to catch it, but the raft, the yacht, and the rope were in a hell's dance. It seemed they were going to pass right by and that it would be impossible for them to catch the rope. But at the last instant, he gunned the throttle of the engine. The yacht, in a final effort, jumped forward. Antonio and Felipe caught the rope, and his three children, clinging to what was left of their raft, banged against the yacht. Pale and sick, they seemed so little and helpless! The engine of the yacht stopped with the same dying-animal screech as his electric fan.

He shouted at his children that he had to abandon the yacht and that they would all have to use the lifeboat fastened to the top of the deck. He managed to lower the boat with its four oars inside. Antonio jumped into the lifeboat, and Claudia and Felipe started to hand him the few bundles that hadn't been swept away from the raft, probably water and food. He went inside the yacht's cabin and emerged with three life preservers like the one he was wearing. He handed them down to Antonio. Then he went inside the yacht again to pick up whatever else he could find of use. He salvaged the signal pistol and some shells, a case of plastic bottles with water, and a few cans of food. He put everything into a big plastic bag and started to come back out.

Something caught his eye as he glanced through a porthole at the lifeboat. Several men had appeared out of nowhere and were throwing his kids into the water. Immediately, he felt a shift in the yacht, and sensed that someone had jumped aboard and halted somewhere aft. Whoever it was must now be positioned to ambush him as he came out.

He crept out through the bow hatch. From there, he could see four men in the lifeboat and a big husky mulatto with a knife standing before him, blocking his way. He glanced at his kids. They had managed to reach what was left of their raft and were screaming, trying to warn him. He waved a hand to them and made a gesture to take it easy. He was relieved they were safe for the moment. He put on a smile to ease the tension when he faced the pirates.

"Okay, big boys. You have to get out of the boat. I can help you save yourselves, but first you have to give back the boat." He tried to speak in a gentle tone, as if everything happening was just a kid's prank.

One of the men in the boat shouted up at the mulatto with the knife. "Loco, come on! There's enough water and food in the boat. Leave the man alone."

The mulatto ignored him and simply stared at the man who had been advancing little by little with a silly smile on his face and was now two steps away. Loco made a gesture as if to say he had decided to spare the life of such an insignificant and foolish foe. He jumped back into the lifeboat and started to use his knife to cut the thick rope that tied the boat to the yacht.

"Stop that or I'll kill you!"

The sudden change of tone in the man's voice made Loco halt what he was doing to measure the yachtsman again.

"Ay, que miedo!" Loco put on a feminine gesture and voice, imitating fear. A couple of the men beside him laughed.

The man on the yacht also laughed. He seemed powerless to stop the theft of his only means of survival. It was clear the yacht was doomed. Every wave poured more water into it and its bow had already begun to sink. The mulatto went back to cutting the rope. Then the man on the yacht withdrew a small pistol from his rear pocket and knelt down on the deck to get closer to the raft. Four of the men stared back, surprised by the sudden change in this seemingly harmless man.

"Look at me, Loco!"

The mulatto raised his head and received the shot in his left eye. He fell back on the boat, and a jet of blood streamed out of the hole in his face. The other men sat back, dumb with disbelief, staring at the corpse that rocked as the craft was hit by the waves.

"Out of the boat." The man on the yacht spoke again without raising his voice, aiming his small pistol at the eye of the one who seemed to be the leader of the group.

The four men dropped into the water, leaving the dead man rolling in his own pool of blood.

"Now, listen to me! Those kids are going to board the boat. Then I'm going to get some things out of the yacht. From now on, I'll kill anyone who gets closer than fifteen feet to any of them. I can guarantee each one of you a painless death. At this range, I never miss the brain through the eye." He pointed his gun again at the leader of the group, who seemed stunned. The four men swam quickly away from the boat.

The youngsters again took possession of the lifeboat as their father got ready to abandon the condemned yacht. Quickly, he threw a sack full of the yacht's salvage into the boat. He then jumped in, took the knife from Loco's hand, and pushed the body into the water. Finally, he spoke once again to the men hanging onto what remained of the raft.

"Listen to me. In a minute, this water will be full of sharks after the blood. You can save yourselves if you follow my instructions *exactly*. Board the yacht. It will take at least three hours to sink. The sea has calmed down quite a bit and it isn't taking much water now."

He threw Loco's knife onto the deck of the sinking craft. Then he told the frightened men to chop down both of its outriggers with an ax they'd find at stern; then to tie any buoyant material they could salvage between the two outriggers, using the mooring ropes. If they managed that, they could ride safely, sitting on the joined outriggers. He also told them to make short paddles with plywood scavenged from the boat. He said he would give them some water and food to last a couple of days. Also, he said, he was willing to wait until they were ready and he would guide them. He had a compass, so he knew which way to go.

He kept his word. He waited until they had their new, makeshift raft built, threw them a rope, and began towing them with the lifeboat. The men rode sitting on the outriggers, paddling like madmen with the oars they had managed to make to keep pace with the lifeboat.

That afternoon they saw a ship on the horizon travelling westward. Carlos Manuel fired two shells with the signal gun. When the ship spotted them and changed course to pick them up, he cut the rope and abandoned the lifeboat to join the four men. The youngsters rowed ahead to meet the rescuers. The yachtsman told the scared men what he wanted them to tell the Americans about the mulatto. They must all say the man had disappeared the night the raft was torn to pieces. Nothing should be said about the yacht, or that the youngsters had ever been with them. He told them his name was Ramiro Ramos. They should say he was the carpenter who had built the raft in exchange for coming with them. If anybody asked about the gear they had taken from the yacht, they would say they had found it floating in the debris after the storm. If necessary, they could say the mulatto had brought him into the group and they didn't really know anything about him.

The men had simply stared back at him, too frightened by what they had seen him do to argue. He felt sure they would do as they had been told. At least, for a while.

WHEN KING ENTERED his office in the morning, he glanced at the items written on his memo pad. Atop the list of most pressing issues were two big capital letters—P.G.—put there so he would not forget about the lost intelligence officer. It became his first order of business. Going over reconnaissance reports on Cuba, he finally found one that could explain why the defecting officer had not arrived at any "friendly" port. The day before, late in the morning, a reconnaissance plane had reported the sinking of a small yacht about fifty miles southeast of Key West. King had set up an immediate watch for all information that might throw some light on the event.

Later that day, a report was received from the Netherlands that seemed to piece together what they already knew. Two days earlier, a radio call had been received at the headquarters of a Dutch shipping company from the captain of the reefer *Silver Star IV*. The captain, en route to Rotterdam with frozen concentrate and single-strength orange juice from Belize, described a small vessel being chased by what appeared to be a gunboat, perhaps belonging to the Cuban Coast Guard. The incident occurred at 04:15, August 15, eleven miles northeast of Havana, very close to Cuba's territorial limit. The chase took place several hours before dawn, after moonset, and was followed mainly on radar. Calm seas and winds, however, allowed the crew to hear heavy machine-gun fire, followed by what seemed to be an explosion. On the radar they watched the gunboat turn south and the other vessel continue northward at about the same speed. The captain said he received no call for help. The incident, King decided, could explain the sinking yacht later reported by the reconnaissance aircraft.

King requested full information on the sunken yacht from the National Reconnaissance Office. The U.S. government had been maintaining heavy surveillance on the Florida Straits since the raft exodus started. A special group within the National Intelligence Agency was already under presidential order to monitor events. Its task was to keep the White House updated on estimates of the number of people emigrating on rafts and other vessels, to forecast possible casualties due to weather changes, and to oversee all Cuban naval operations. The National Reconnaissance Office and the National Imagery and Mapping Agency reinforced their normal operations in the area. They followed all activities with a network of satellites that provided most of the visual information, and with special stations to monitor radio and television broadcasts in Cuba and international communication to and from the island.

On the same day, King received additional information about the sunken yacht. Several of his men were able to go through the mass of raw data and draw a clear picture of what had happened. The yacht had left Cuba two days before at 03:05 hours, shortly after it was stolen from the Almendares River dockyard. When the yacht left the mouth of the river to enter the sea, the local post of the Cuban Coast Guard reported to its headquarters that the motorboat *Elvirita* had departed without having been properly dispatched. The Cuban Coast Guard headquarters ordered a gunboat stationed at Mariel, a port town twenty-five miles west of Havana, to intercept the yacht before it reached Cuba's territorial limit. It also warned the crew of the gunboat to be on the lookout for rafts, and to be especially careful to avoid running over any of them. The gunboat left Mariel at 03:20. The maximum speed for that type of boat is forty knots. On this mission, the craft averaged only about twenty due to many rafts encountered on its course. The yacht being chased pushed a steady fifteen knots, which seemed to be its maximum speed. As soon as the *Elvirita* left the coast, it headed toward two cargo ships travelling close to the Cuban international water limit, twelve miles from the coast. The nearest one was a Cuban ship loaded with 1500 tons of cement from the Mariel cement plant. It was doing ten knots about eleven miles north of Havana, heading for Nassau in the Bahamas. Four miles from the Cuban ship, the Dutch reefer travelled northeast, doing twelve knots.

The gunboat made several attempts to talk with the person or persons on the yacht. All the attempts were recorded, but there were no responses. Finally, the gunboat shot a warning round of tracer shells ahead of the yacht. The fugitive craft maneuvered to hide itself behind the ship loaded with cement. For a few minutes, the gunboat could not fire on the yacht without hitting the cargo ship. After the gunboat passed the Cuban cargo ship, the stolen yacht tailed the reefer to repeat the defensive maneuver. When the gunboat reached the international water limit, it asked for instructions from its headquarters. It was ordered to return to Mariel.

King asked the CIA station in Havana to open an investigation on the incident involving a yacht in the Almendares River dockyard. Two days later, he received two versions of the hijacking of the yacht *Elvirita*. The first one indicated that Major Alfredo Cazalis, with the help of two workers at the dockyard, José Rodriguez and another man named Chicho, had taken the yacht. The workers boarded the vessel at the yard to test some repairs they'd done, since the yacht had to be ready in the morning. They made a short stop at the gardens of the restaurant 1830, located at the river mouth, to pick up Cazalis, who was waiting there. The yacht took off at maximum speed to open sea without stopping at the Coast Guard post to get its permit. Another source indicated that only one man was on the yacht, and no one knew his name. This unknown man had come to the yard late at night in a car with the yard's manager, who gave him the best boat he had under repair, "because he had an order from a big shot in the Ministry of the Interior."

Even though the incident had been witnessed by many people and included the involvement of a Cuban cargo ship and a Dutch reefer, nothing was published by Cuban sources, which was another strong indication that the person involved was someone important. In the past, the hijacking of vessels to flee the island had always been made public, and was even cited as a primary reason the Cuban government had allowed the ongoing raft exodus. In the inquiry carried out by the Havana CIA station, the real Major Alfredo Cazalis was reported working normally in his army unit deployed near the U.S. Guantanamo naval base. Cazalis was a known wrestler who had won a silver medal in the 1992 Barcelona Olympic Games. José Rodriguez and Chicho were in fact workers at the yard and neither had shown up for work since. Further inquiries with Chicho's wife indicated that both friends were in jail in Villa Marista, the dreaded headquarters of the State Security Police in Havana.

King went to see CIA Director of Operations Austin Cabot, explaining briefly what had happened so far.

"We're facing a fog curtain thrown up by the Cubans. They'll cover up what really happened in many ways. It will take a long time and much effort to find out the truth. We need to know who this man is and what really happened to him. Do you have any way to ask P.G. if he can give some more details?"

Cabot considered King's request longer than he usually did.

"You well know, Sidney, we seldom ask this person anything. He normally sends us a lot of first-rate info. It's simply not wise to get in contact with him unless there's a very pressing reason. It so happens, however, that I have to send him a present and congratulations from the president himself. His information and advice on this raft crisis have been most valuable." He paused, closed his eyes, and then said, "Okay, this is what we'll do. Just to tease P.G., I'll tell him his yacht and his intelligence officer vanished into thin air. Then I'll ask him if he dreamed that up."

A day later, Austin Cabot personally brought King the reply from P.G. It read:

> *Austin, you're losing your old touch. I suggest you change your glasses to improve your vision. Surely there was a boat taken from the Almendares dockyard with only one man on it. Judging from the fuss I hear, this guy must be the cream of intelligence officers. That's all. Remember, I never ask questions, I only hear things.*

Going over the case carefully before closing it, King decided that the only relevant new fact was the curious wandering of the yacht before it sank. After the gunboat chase ended, the yacht travelled due east at low speed for about twenty miles, always staying parallel to the Cuban coast but in international waters. Then it turned north and hit a storm. From that point the yacht roamed around the area for almost an hour, as if it had trouble with its rudder or nobody was in command. From 08:35 on, the vessel seemed totally at the mercy of the waves and the wind, sinking before noon.

After the last message from P.G., there was nothing but silence from the Cuban side. King considered this another strong indication of the veracity of the initial report and the importance of the officer. No further information came in about the case, and it was subsequently filed with the following conclusion: "The unidentified intelligence officer was apparently lost at sea when his yacht sank after being hit by gunfire from the Cuban Coast Guard. He is believed to have been wounded or killed during the attack, which explains why there was no call for help."

O N SEPTEMBER 2, a newly arrived Cuban exile was arrested for an incident with a girl at Jacksonville Beach. The girl started to yell when the man grabbed her hand and wouldn't let her go. Police from a patrol car intervened and the man was put in jail, charged with intent of assault and battery. The girl was taken to the hospital and the physical examination showed no signs of violence on her body. Since the girl pressed no charges, the prisoner was to be released once the investigation was duly completed. Unaware of this, the man, after a full day in jail, suddenly claimed he had information to sell in exchange for his liberty. The statement actually prompted a postponement of his release when the county sheriff decided to forward the information to the FBI. According to the prisoner, he had witnessed the murder of one of his raft partners while escaping to the United States. Since the alleged murder had taken place at sea, the sheriff filed a report with the FBI. Two days later, an agent was sent to question the prisoner, who told his story with an assortment of gestures and noises to make up for his limited English. Out of all these communications, the FBI agent gathered that a month earlier the man had been fleeing Cuba by raft with several other refugees, when a small yacht intercepted his makeshift vessel. Without warning, the lone occupant of the yacht shot one of the refugees in the eye.

The FBI agent recommended that, before pursuing any further investigation, psychological tests be administered to the prisoner, who he felt had "all the earmarks of a pathological liar." Since the report dealt with a foreign exile, it eventually ended up in the hands of the CIA liaison, who promptly forwarded it to the Cuban section at CIA headquarters. The information set off immediate alarms when it reached T.S. King's desk.

Although P.G.'s initial report from Havana had been closed, sporadic information had continued to trickle in from Cuba, adding further details about the intelligence officer believed killed during an attempt to defect. One in particular had mentioned some gossip about a river dockyard manager who had been charged with negligence and possible collaboration with a high-ranking officer of the Ministry of the Interior who had escaped in one of the boats anchored at the yard. Now the testimony of the Jacksonville Beach prisoner added yet another twist. King decided to send somebody who spoke fluent Spanish to the Jacksonville Beach County Jail without delay.

William T. Barter, forty-one, new at CIA headquarters but already a seasoned field officer in Latin America, was the man selected for the inquiry. He read the FBI transcript on the Jacksonville Beach prisoner and decided he needed more information about the mission. In his short time at headquarters he had become more than a little friendly with Martha Jackson, T.S. King's secretary. Now he invited her to lunch to see what he could find out.

"What do you know about this, Martha?" Barter put a plane ticket and the FBI transcript on the table.

"You've told everybody you wanted some action. There, you have some action," Martha said, smiling.

"You call action going all the way to Florida to talk to a loony?" Barter was a tall, bony man with a big jaw, but his eyes had long lashes that gave his face an air of sensuality. He took one shoe off and began rubbing his left foot along Martha's left leg.

"You have me to thank for this mission."

"How was I selected?"

"The old man asked me to find out which of the new guys had the best command of Spanish."

"How did you find that out?"

"Over the past few months, I've discovered you're quite good at everything you do." Martha smiled and lowered her eyes shyly. "What time do you have to catch your flight tonight, Bill?"

"Have to be at the airport at ten-thirty. What do you have in mind, Martha?"

"I wondered if you had time to stop by my apartment for a cup of coffee before you go . . . I won't be seeing you for a while."

"Yes, there's plenty of time."

Barter smiled, amused by the expression of unconcealed delight on Martha's face. He was amazed at the transformation that had taken place in the woman in the few months since their intimate relationship had begun. The plump, serious woman in her forties, who had used the last twenty years of her life to become one of the best executive secretaries in the CIA—as if that were her only purpose in life—had transformed herself into a totally new female. She had lost ten pounds, dyed her hair red, and changed her way of dressing, her way of talking, and, above all, her way of making love. It was as though she had just discovered a new joy, and was amazed, surprised, and scared by her increasing response in every sexual situation.

"What's behind all of this?" Barter came back to the papers on the table.

"I don't really know. But it relates to a Cuban deserter who never reached the States. King is taking a special interest in this matter. He even asked me to announce your visit to the Jacksonville Beach sheriff and see that you get red-carpet treatment. I called the guy on the phone and he'll meet you at the airport."

"How am I supposed to know him?"

"You're not. He'll know you. I sent him your photo by fax."

"When do you think I can take a look at the T.S. file?"

"You know I have to wait for the right moment."

"You understand why I need the lowdown on the chief? To make any progress in this dead hole, I have to know this guy inside out."

"You already sold me on that devilish idea. You just have to be patient."

William Barter looked at the prisoner in front of him. A handsome head, with black wavy hair, a big mustache very well trimmed, and a sad look in his dreamy eyes—all of that on top of a frail and skinny body. Barter glanced over the first page of a file with a photo of the prisoner and his general data. As he went through it, he read aloud: "Alberto García Machado, born in Havana, Jan. 1, 1959." Barter laughed.

"Born with the revolution! How do you like that? Amazing your parents didn't name you Fidel. How does it sound, 'Fidel García Machado'? To honor that name, you might have been a good bare-ass communist all your life, stayed at home working hard all the time, and then you wouldn't be in this shit hole." Barter spoke in Spanish.

The man stood silent and desolate. It was clear he didn't appreciate the joke. The sheriff had warned Barter that the prisoner was no longer cooperative. In the close to a week that he'd been in jail, other inmates had coached him on the American judiciary system and state laws. He was now following the advice of his "lawyers," who wanted an official written document withdrawing charges before he confessed anything.

"Look, man. I came all the way from the CIA just to hear your story and you don't want to tell me anything. I can't promise you immunity unless I know what you have to sell us. You have to show the merchandise first."

"If I tell you what I know, there would be no merchandise to sell." The man had a faint smile on his face.

"If things worked like that, there would be no prisoners in any jail in this country. All they'd have to do is to say they had a secret to exchange for their freedom and off they'd go, free as birds. You seem an intelligent enough man to see the point." Barter imitated the voice and the gestures of the prisoner.

"Look, I understand what you say, and I wish you could understand my point, too. I have never been in jail before in my life. I haven't killed anybody or robbed a bank, sold drugs, or anything like that. Eleven days ago, I was a little rough with a woman who wanted to play with me as if I were a schoolboy. I just held her hand and she started crying in the middle of the street as if I were killing her . . ." The eyes of the man grew moist and he could not continue speaking for a while. Finally he added, almost whispering, "Everybody here has told me not to say anything until I have a signed paper in my hand, withdrawing charges and letting me off. I don't trust that man behind you. Nobody trusts him here. He's full of tricks. He's a mean guy. He likes to destroy every Latino who gets in here."

"Jailers are mean guys. They have to be to deal with liars like you. According to this record"—Barter waved the file—"you were let out of Krome Detention Center fifteen days ago to come to Jacksonville Beach to work, earning twenty-five bucks a day plus room and board. Two days after you got here, the police arrested you red-handed when you attacked a woman who didn't comply with your love requests. I believe you're a jailbird. You can't live anymore outside a pretty cage."

"You're wrong. I've never been in jail before in my life."

Barter turned his back to the prisoner and faced the sheriff, who had been watching.

"I think this guy's got something, but he won't let it out unless he's released."

"Do you want me to release him? There are no charges against him."

Barter hesitated, thinking that once free the prisoner could change his mind. He decided to look deeper into the case. A couple of extra days in Florida wouldn't hurt anybody.

"Not for the moment. Maybe I can get around him after talking with the guys who came on the same raft with him. The navy plucked him off the water along with four other partners. I'm going to take a look at the immigration and naturalization records. I'll call you when I decide what to do. Thanks a lot for the lift from the airport and all the help."

That afternoon, William Barter flew to Miami after talking by phone with three of the prisoner's raft partners. He told them that he was working for a charity organization, helping refugees all over the world. He wanted to meet them to see what financial aid they needed and to explain the different training programs his organization had to offer them so they could get better jobs. All three men were very interested. He asked them to meet him at ten o'clock sharp the next day at the Miami Beach Holiday Inn.

He could not locate the fourth rafter, named Ramiro Ramos. At Krome Detention Center, where the refugee had stayed for almost a month, Barter obtained the address and phone number of a large bakery where he was supposed to be working. He called him there, but nobody in the bakery had ever heard of him.

He arrived in Miami around four o'clock that afternoon, September 8, a Thursday. He rented a car at the airport and went directly to the Pinos Nuevos Bakery to talk to the management. According to the information he had, Ramiro Ramos had been let out of Krome Center on September 5 to fill a vacancy at the bakery. Ramiro never got there. The personnel manager agreed to show him the only five Cuban refugees he had received from Krome. In less than fifteen minutes, the riddle was unraveled. The last refugee sent had swapped jobs with Ramiro. The man now working at the bakery had wanted to remain in Miami. Ramiro, on the contrary, wanted to get as close as possible to Tampa. It was past six o'clock, too late now to find out his new address.

* * *

Barter slept until nine in the morning. After a shower and shave, he went down for breakfast, seating himself so he could watch the arrival of his guests as he ate. From the photos on his copy of their records, he picked each of them out as they entered the lobby. All three were impressed when they were called by their names and invited to sit down at Barter's table and order whatever they wanted. After he finished his breakfast, he called Krome Detention Center on his cellular phone to find out the work address assigned to the man who had swapped jobs with Ramiro. It turned out to be a small construction contractor in Sarasota. Ramiro Ramos had just started to work up there four days earlier as a pipe fitter's helper in a crew that moved from one place to another. The general manager of the outfit gave him the cellular phone number of the pipe fitters' foreman. After a short while, he had Ramiro on the phone. He talked to him in Spanish, loud enough for his breakfast guests to hear.

"Hello, Ramiro! This is Joseph de la Torre speaking, from IORA, *International Organization for Refugee Aid*. This is a nonprofit religious organization that helps refugees all over the world. We provide financial aid when it's needed and we have a lot of training centers where refugees can learn all sorts of trades to enable them to get better jobs. In fact, the IORA has an employment agency of its own," Barter said, smiling at the men before him.

The man, Ramiro, seemed interested, and immediately asked if the IORA had any training program for work as a miner. "A friend here says that in Nevada they pay twenty-five dollars an hour to work in underground copper mines." He added, "I don't care how dangerous the work might be. I can take care of myself."

To Barter, Ramiro seemed ignorant and naïve. He couldn't resist bullshitting the man, describing the wonderful school for miner-trainees his organization ran right in the middle of the Rocky Mountains, next to the Colorado School of Mines. The other three Cubans listened open-mouthed and delighted with the wonders of this charity organization that could only exist in America.

"When can I see you? Do you want me to come to Miami right now?" Ramiro asked eagerly.

"No, I'll call you again tomorrow and we can decide when and where to meet." Barter kept smiling the whole time at the men sitting at his table. He ordered the check and, after signing the bill, led them to his room. The CIA officer closed the door behind him after all three guests were inside. He pulled up a chair and sat down, blocking the door. He showed his CIA credentials and spoke in a threatening tone, very different from the one he had used until then.

"Okay. Now we can stop the bullshit. I brought you here because you're involved in a problem that could be very damaging for all of you."

The men were astonished to find they'd been fooled and were now being accused of some unknown crime. To further pressure them, Barter took off his coat, showing his .357 Magnum in a shoulder holster.

"According to Alberto García, all of you lied when you entered this country. He is in the Jacksonville Beach jail now and he said that you all witnessed a murder you didn't report." Barter spoke in Spanish with a heavy Mexican accent that sounded almost comical to the Cubans.

The three men stood silent, staring at Barter. One of them took the lead, speaking in perfect English. "We don't know what Alberto has invented to get himself out of jail. We answered all the questions the immigration officers asked us to the best of our knowledge. We don't know anything about this murderer Alberto mentioned. Anyway, in the end, it's the word of the three of us against Alberto's word."

Barter measured the odds. He was completely out of line in detaining the men, and was even crossing the holy barrier that divided CIA and FBI authority. The CIA had no authority in domestic affairs, and he had no real evidence this was anything more. Still, it seemed impossible to break the silence of the man in jail without giving him what he wanted. He stood a better chance with these three guys, one of whom at least spoke fluent English. The man was blond and blue-eyed. Most likely he had a university degree. One of the others was a black man, so he had to be careful. He didn't want the sonofabitch claiming later he had been discriminated against and harassed because of his race.

Barter decided on a softer approach. He smiled at the blond man. "I'm glad you speak perfect English. Now we can understand each other much better." Barter continued in English, "Don't get me wrong. I don't really care if you exterminated each other for whatever reason. The problem is that Alberto García spoke about a murder committed while you were on the same raft. If I decide to believe him and write down in my report that you're trying to cover up a crime, that you lied your way into this country, I'm sure you'll be put in jail and sent back to Cuba."

"That has to be proven," said the blond man. Barter detected a hint of doubt in his voice.

"Nothing has to be proven because there would be no trial to settle the matter. The U.S. government decides who is and who isn't accepted in this country. And let me tell you that my word is going to outweigh the word of all of you."

The other men asked the blond to explain what was going on. When he had translated, the black man stood in front of Barter and shouted in anger: "*Eso no es justo!*"

"*No, no es justo. Pocas cosas son justas en este mundo*. You should know that by now, there's not much justice in this world," Barter answered.

The Cubans began arguing amongst themselves. The blond took the others to a corner of the room to continue talking in a whisper. While this went on, Barter grabbed a beer out of the fridge and started drinking it. The Cubans came back to him to bargain, this time in Spanish. He made them wait until he finished the beer.

"Okay. If we agree to change our declaration, what will happen to us?"

Barter smiled at the men. "Look, I just want to find out the truth. If this crime was committed in international waters, I guess U.S. law has no jurisdiction. I don't think anything will happen to you for not telling the whole truth when you arrived." He shrugged. "You'll have to think up some good reason why you didn't. For instance, maybe you were afraid you'd be killed if you told." He gave them another shrug.

"What do we have to do now?"

"We'll fly to Jacksonville this afternoon. You will make a joint statement with this Alberto García to a lawyer, with the sheriff and me as witnesses. That will do. After that, all of you can leave. The CIA will pay all expenses."

Barter made reservations on a plane leaving in four hours. He placed another call to the sheriff in Jacksonville Beach to arrange everything there. Then he drank another beer and treated the Cubans to the last beers in the room's mini-fridge. He paid the hotel bill and drove to the airport, where he turned in the rental car. On the plane, he sat next to the blond Cuban.

"Why don't you tell me the story while we travel?" Barter asked, once they were airborne.

"Then I'd have to tell it twice." The blond man leaned back in his seat and closed his eyes.

The sheriff was waiting at the Jacksonville airport with two other policemen in two cars. The three refugees were handcuffed and pushed into one of the cars under protest. When they reached the small county jail, an attorney was waiting for them, and without delay, they all entered a large cell, where preparations had been made to take their statement. Alberto García, also handcuffed, was brought in.

"Okay, birds. Time to sing your song. Who is going to do it?"

The blond man asked that the handcuffs be removed. Barter made a gesture of assent to the sheriff, who gave the order to the deputy. They went on with the formalities explained by the attorney. The refugees designated the man with the blond hair and blue eyes to speak for them, with Barter translating into English simultaneously. The story began with their departure from Cuba and went into full detail, step by step. When it was clear that Ramiro had killed the mulatto, Barter jumped from his seat. He pointed a menacing finger at the blond man.

"Son of a bitch! Why didn't you tell me before that Ramiro was the killer?"

"Who the hell fooled us in the first place? What do you think we are? Little lambs?"

Barter rushed out of the cell, reached for his mobile phone, and started to call the FBI to provide him with a helicopter and backup to detain Ramiro Ramos. The sheriff and the attorney followed him out, not knowing what was happening. Barter gave them instructions as he continued trying to contact somebody with authority at the FBI in Florida.

"Get that paper signed by these bastards. I need the original to take with me."

At that moment, they heard the noise of chairs banging and someone screaming in the cell. They raced back to see what was going on. Alberto García was crawling on the floor, bleeding from a cut on his mouth. The other three were kicking and punching him.

"He deserves it," murmured Barter.

"What do I do with these people? Charge them with attempting to murder this other guy?" the sheriff asked, bewildered by everything happening, and by the conduct of the CIA officer.

"This Alberto García just fell off his chair. Keep them locked up until tomorrow. Then let all of them go. No charges. See that these three get back to Miami. I'm going to drive to Sarasota right now to catch that motherfucker Ramiro in the middle of his sweet dreams."

H E FELT SURE he was about to be discovered. Somebody had gone to all the trouble to track him down in Sarasota. There was no charity organization so aggressively helping people. The call was probably made to locate where he was and the CIA or the FBI was on their way to catch him. He had no time to lose.

"*Muchas gracias*," he said to the pipe-fitter foreman when he handed back the cellular phone. His boss was a very short man with a lot of Mayan blood in his veins who had arrived in the U.S. from Nicaragua a decade earlier.

"You look upset. Did you receive bad news?" the foreman asked.

"Not at all, Don Manuel. On the contrary, I got good news. The problem is that I don't know what to do now. I need some good advice."

"Can I help?" the Nicaraguan asked.

"I've been offered a very good job as a miner. The pay is wonderful, but the mine is very far away in a place called Nevada. It must be freezing all the time there. I've never seen snow before. I want to know more about this offer before I accept it."

"Nevada is far away, but it's not so bad."

"There is another big problem for me. I have to meet this guy in

Miami right away, but I have no money. Could I get paid for the time I've worked?"

"Hop in the pickup. I'll drive you to the office and see you get paid."

He was sure the Nicaraguan didn't believe him. It must have been clear to his boss that he had been taken aback by the call and was trying to get away as soon as possible. He tried to mend it. "I would like to keep this job open if you allow me. In the end, I don't think I'll go to Nevada."

The Nicaraguan didn't reply and there was no way of reading his thoughts from his facial expression, which might have been carved in wood.

They rode to the office of the small construction company where a woman with a round face and thick glasses took care of all the paperwork. The Nicaraguan told him before they went in: "They have a rule to pay salaries only on Saturdays. Let me do all the talking."

The foreman explained to the woman that the new man in his outfit had to go back to Miami because his wife was having a baby a month ahead of time. The woman smiled and said sweetly, "How are the baby and the mother?"

"They are fine," said the foreman, smiling with a smirk that was intended to be sweet, too.

The woman prepared the pay. One hundred and fifty-two dollars for three and a half days of work, after income tax, social security, safety shoes, room, and board were deducted. They walked out of the office to the company pickup.

"Let's go to your room to pick up your things before I take you to the bus depot."

"There is no need to go by the room. I have all I need in this toolbox." He felt he had no way of concealing from the Nicaraguan that he was on the run. "Besides," he added, "there is not much in the room. You can keep it or give it to someone else if I don't come back."

The Nicaraguan started the motor, but didn't move for a moment, staring at the road.

"I have to purchase some fittings in Tampa. I think it's much better that you take a bus in Tampa."

"I'll be very grateful to you. Tampa would be much better."

The Nicaraguan took the old Route 41, which ran near the coast, instead of the newer U.S. 75. As they drove, Carlos Manuel glanced at the many vessels anchored along the waterfront from Sarasota to Tampa. His plan for getting back to Cuba involved finding a job on a fishing boat or a yacht that travelled to the Caribbean. Once off the coasts of the U.S., any place was safe for him.

Very soon, they were driving along Tampa Bay, full of big cargo ships coming from and going to all parts of the world. After some time driving in Tampa, the Nicaraguan stopped the vehicle in front of the bus depot and reached for his wallet.

"Are you sure you can reach where you're going with the money you got?"

"Thanks, Don Manuel. I have enough." He grabbed the hand of the Nicaraguan and held it while he said, "I'll never forget this."

"Hoy por ti, mañana por mi."

When he was in Cuba he had given up all his secret accounts that held money for coping with emergencies like the one he was in now. He counted his money and it amounted to a little less than two hundred dollars. He'd also had to hand over his emergency caches where he kept new identities and other tools of the trade. All he had now was a steel toolbox with a clean set of clothes, a pair of shoes, his shaving gear, toothbrush, toothpaste, a small pair of scissors, Band-Aids, pain relievers, and such. Still, he thought, he had been in situations far worse than this.

The first thing to do was change his looks. In the restroom of the bus depot he washed up, shaved his mustache, trimmed his sideburns, and changed clothes. He looked at himself in the mirror and was shocked by his face after so many years with a mustache and thick sideburns. Below his nose there was now an ugly white patch that would need a lot of sunlight to match the color of the rest of his face. His lips looked thinner than he remembered, and he felt dismayed by all the space between his nose and upper lip. He smiled at this other guy in the mirror, who seemed younger and much less serious than he'd been for many years. The peasant from the eastern provinces of Cuba had disappeared. He was now compelled to grow another personality in a hurry to match the new look.

For the first time he had no rules to follow, no special aim but to be a totally different person than he had been in the last month. No other task but to hide himself for some days until he could find his way back to Cuba. There was no burden of a mission to carry out and no other lives at stake besides his own, if he failed. He had a sense of freedom he had not experienced for many years. He went across the street to buy a shirt and a pair of sneakers to match this new personality. When he slipped on the pullover and tennis shoes and looked in the mirror, he was struck by the resemblance to his son Felipe.

The only thing he could do now, he thought, was use his sister's help. On the other hand, maybe it was just an excuse his mind was inventing to meet with her after so many years. From a public phone, he called his sister in New York for the first time in thirty-two years. He recognized her voice immediately when she answered—it hadn't changed in all that time. "Margarita . . ." He was the only one who called her by that name after their father died. She was Marjorie to everybody else. "Listen to me, I don't have much time. I need you to fly to Orlando to meet me tomorrow afternoon at the Great Western Hotel. I'll wait for you there. Do you understand?"

For a few seconds there was an awkward silence. Finally, a calm voice said, "It's going to be fun. See you tomorrow."

Upon arrival in Orlando, he chose to stay at one of the La Quinta Inns, close to the international airport. He called the Great Western

Hotel and made a reservation for his sister. Early the next day, from a convenient place in front of the hotel, he began a careful surveillance for anything suspicious. As time passed, his mind went back to his children. They had stayed in Krome Detention Center for only a short time. While in the lifeboat, he had told them the real nature of his work and instructed them on what to do once they were in Miami. They must call their aunt and ask her to deposit money in a Miami bank. Then, they must ask her to file an affidavit of support on their behalf through a lawyer, so her name wouldn't be involved. He also told them not to mention him to anyone, even his sister. They should say they'd found the lifeboat floating among the debris after a storm. They should deny having seen the yacht, if asked, and, of course, they should forget forever the attempt to steal the lifeboat and the mulatto's death. Once they were safely out of the camp, they should not contact him there or try to help him in any way. Whenever he managed to get out, he would call his sister and find out their address and make an attempt to meet them before he went back to Cuba.

He decided to tell his sister all about his life as soon as they met. Even so, he thought, it was impossible for any of them to grasp the far-reaching implications of the fact that he had been an intelligence officer in Cuba for more than twenty years.

It was close to sunset when he saw his sister getting out of a limousine in front of the Great Western. To his amazement, his kids also popped out of the back of the car. There they were, all three of them clad in bright new clothes. They had all put on some weight and looked so at ease in their new situation that he was, for a moment, astonished. He stepped behind a public phone booth as they walked into the hotel lobby. Felipe looked toward the place where he stood, as if searching for something his instinct told him was there. His sister, he thought, had changed her naïve and irresponsible way of doing things very little in all these years.

He stepped into the phone booth once his children were out of sight and called the reception desk where Marjorie was getting ready to check in. He told her there had been a change of plan and gave her the address of the La Quinta Inn at the Orlando airport. As they left the hotel, he followed in another cab, making sure that no one was tailing them. He understood the fragility of the security measures he was taking, but it was the best he could do.

KING APPEARED TO BE measuring the man in front of him. In fact, he'd been measuring him ever since William Barter, Jr. had joined his section five months ago. Perhaps Barter would be a good replacement for him when he decided to retire. About a year earlier, after a meeting, he had had a brief social chat with the CIA director over a cup of coffee. Casually, as if the thought had just entered his mind, the director had asked him: "Sidney, have you thought of a successor?" He had been taken aback by the mere thought of retirement. To soften the effect that the remark had obviously had on his subordinate, the director had added, "It takes quite some time to find and train the right man, you know. Think about it."

Certainly nobody else in the Cuba section was capable enough to step into his shoes. Most of the veterans were about his age or older, already disenchanted with the game, each one counting the days until retirement. Up to that point, the few young men who had come into the section with some field experience weren't worth shit. Most of them lacked guts, something you either have or don't have, something that, unlike a beard, doesn't grow with time. He had made some room for new blood and three younger men had entered the section in the last year. Barter was the last one.

In the beginning, King didn't like this large man with the loud voice. He seemed too eager to get his nose into everything and, above all, he lacked the finesse King thought a man working in this special trade ought to have. On the other hand, the new man had a good university background in economics and philosophy, an excellent record in the CIA, and a knack for being liked by everybody, which was an asset. Now, judging by the report of the field trip that King had read carefully, it was clear that Barter also had initiative, could make decisions on his own, and was willing to take chances. He had come from Florida that same Friday at noon with his report ready in his laptop and had been able to get it to King's desk by three o'clock. He wondered how Barter had managed to get through his boss, Leonard Crawford, a master of delay, a genius at drafting meaningless reports that everybody praised. Perhaps, King thought, it was time to put this guy Barter to a real test.

While waiting for King to finish reading and signing some papers, William Barter glanced at the walls of the office where three big pictures of University of Alabama football games from the sixties were hanging. Barter got up and took a closer look at each of the pictures to see Timothy Sidney King in his days of glory as captain of the 'Bama team during the tenure of legendary coach Bear Bryant. It was hard to believe that King could ever have been the slender, fast, and daring leader of one of the best college football teams in the nation. On the desk, a photo showed him posing for the media with a serious expression on his face and the hard look in his eyes of the gods in their moments of glory. Barter thought the broad shoulders and the steel-gray look were the only thing time had respected.

"Mr. Barter, I just did a first reading of your report. As you know, the whole section is very much tied up with this rafter immigration mess. Nevertheless, this matter you took care of in Florida seems to be urgent; I would like to discuss the follow-up on this issue and leave it entirely up to you."

Barter sat on the edge of his seat. He sensed that something important for his career was about to happen. His main worry was not to reveal in the conversation any of the additional information he had managed to get through Martha.

"Sir, I thought I was spinning my wheels when I got the order to go all the way to Jacksonville Beach to question a madman. When I read the FBI transcript, it seemed like a waste of time, and I was prepared to go there, question the guy for five minutes, and come back the same day."

"Well, Mr. Barter, let me tell you. You have just uncovered a high officer of Cuban Intelligence at large in this country," King said.

"Is that so?" Barter opened his eyes wide and pretended to be startled. "As soon as I found out he killed this man in the boat, I tried to get some backup from the FBI to hunt him down in Sarasota, but I couldn't get ahold of anybody with enough clout at that time of night. So I drove all the way to Sarasota to catch him in his sleep. When I got there, I found out the man had left at noon the day before. I knew this guy was acting like a pro, somebody highly trained. All I could do was talk to the local police and give them copies of the photos of this guy I got from Krome by fax, in case he showed up again. Let me ask you a question, sir. Why didn't he identify himself when he got to the detention center? Why is he hiding away after he defected from Cuba? It doesn't make sense."

"Those are the right questions to ask, Mr. Barter. Why didn't this guy come to us? Usually the ones who defect from Cuba quickly seek shelter under our wings, looking for money, protection, or whatever."

"Maybe he's afraid of being prosecuted for killing the mulatto," Barter said.

"I don't believe that would have mattered to a seasoned intelligence officer. Maybe he didn't really defect. Cuban Intelligence could be using this raft situation to get him and some others into the country, and we just happened to stumble across this one."

"What sort of plan could this guy have, Mr. King?"

"There's no use guessing about his mission." King stopped talking, reached for a mint in a drawer, and put it in his mouth. Then, pointing to Barter, he said, "So as it turns out, you went to Florida to answer one question and came back with three: *Who is this man? Where is he now? And what has he come here to do?*"

"That was the best I could do, sir," Barter said, feeling that King was accusing him in an oblique way.

"Congratulations, Mr. Barter. You did a mighty good job in just four days. Look at everything you brought back: photos of this man, his full description, legal paperwork to charge him all the way from illegal entry to murder. Very well done, indeed." King spoke as if he were reading Barter's mind. He continued: "Let's divide this work to answer those three questions. We'll ask the FBI to find this guy for us. Just to give them some incentive, we'll charge Ramiro Ramos with first-degree murder. Then, we might pass on to some receptive ear within the FBI that we have information, not yet confirmed, that this very dangerous man came here to assassinate a high-ranking U.S. official." King smiled and his face lost twenty years. "Let their imagination take it from there. In that way, we ensure a first-class manhunt from Key West to Nome. How do you like that, Mr. Barter?"

"Sounds good to me, sir."

"The second task is all yours, Mr. Barter. Don't think your job is finished yet. It's just begun. You have to identify this man—find out who the hell this Ramiro Ramos really is. You must go back to Miami to meet the people on a list I'll make for you in a few minutes. Speak with those chaps. They know a lot about the Cuban Intelligence Service. They may give you a hint or two. Once you talk to those men, you're on your own, Mr. Barter. You've been around long enough to know the system. Use it! I suggest in the first place, reproduce by the thousand the photo of this guy. Spread it among the Cuban community to see if anybody recognizes him . . . And about the last task—to find what this man really came here to do—I'm afraid we may have to wait until we catch him." King looked at Barter, who stood, open-eyed, listening to him, knowing he wasn't through.

"Mr. Barter, you should fly right back to Miami. Martha, my secretary, may have to bump some civilian to get you to Florida on a weekend this time of year. I hope you don't mind the rush." King gazed into Barter's blue eyes. He wanted to judge the man's reaction, see how eager he actually was. King punched a key on his telephone and spoke: "Martha, get Mr. Barter on any flight to Miami after . . . let's say, ten o'clock tonight. Is that satisfactory, Mr. Barter?"

"Fine, Mr. King. I don't mind going right back at all. Just give me the list of the people I have to see and I'll be on my way." Barter spoke with a smile on his face that looked almost genuine.

King smiled, too. "You don't have to overdo the eagerness, Mr. Barter. Go home, bathe, and have some supper before you leave. Just spare me five minutes while I fetch the information from my computer for you. Wonderful machines, computers. Who would have guessed twenty years ago that our agency would grind to a halt without them? Go on and check on how Martha is doing with the reservation, while I print the list of those Cubans you're to see in Miami. Oh, Miami, how Cubans love to nest in Miami!"

As soon as he was alone, King picked up his phone and called each of the five men Barter was going to meet. King had always liked operative work, although his days in the field were long past. The recognition his peers afforded him, in fact, had come more from his skill as an administrator. "This guy can produce a vital conclusion just by knowing how much toilet paper is used in a given country," the CIA director had once remarked while King was giving a lecture on Cuba's economic history and deriving from it the reasons for some of the most blatant flaws in U.S. policy toward the island.

In the present case, King sensed that the man they were after was very important, and, at the same time, saw it as an excellent opportunity to test the capabilities of young William Barter, who had performed well so far. Now, he wanted to test his persistence, see how committed he was to his work. Maybe this somewhat raw country boy could be shaped with time into a good successor for his rather complex section.

The subject of training his successor was becoming an obsession. He'd reached the age of fifty-five, and he had to plan for the termination of his working career in the near future. Early retirement was the word of the nineties and, much more, of the century to come. He dreaded that idea. What was going to become of all the work he had done in the section? He needed a good man in whom he could deposit all his knowledge about Cuba, one he could convince of his ideas and the plans he'd laid out so carefully, to make sure they were put into action when the change in Cuba's government occurred in the not-too-distant future.

Aside from that, King wondered, what was he going to do with all his time off? He hated fishing, golfing, and other hobbies. The only things he cared to watch on television were the news reports and good movies of the sixties. Reading fiction was a stupid waste of time for him. He had no children or grandchildren, only nephews from a sister he despised. All the family he cared for was on the verge of extinction. He didn't have friends with whom to play cards. Watching sports bored him to death, except for a good prizefight. The work on Cuba had taken up practically all his thoughts and time since he had become head of the Cuba section. What would happen when it came to an end?

"Bastard, swine, *hijo de la gran puta*. I've been working my ass off for the last four days and he's sending me back tonight! The only sleep I've had in the last thirty-six hours was on the plane coming back. I should have stayed in Florida over the weekend, sleeping like a hog, swimming at the beach . . ." He saw Martha's expression change with his last remark, so he swerved in another direction. "But I had to rush back to see you, Martha. How could I sleep without having you at my side?"

Martha threw back her head and laughed. "You're as good a liar as they come," she said, taking one of Barter's big hands and leading him to her kitchen. "That's the price of success. You made quite an impression on T.S. with your initiative and resourcefulness, finding the enemy agent right under the FBI's nose. Let's celebrate that. I made your flight reservation for a twelve o'clock plane, so we have enough time for a grand meal I'll cook specially for you."

One of the things Barter liked most about Martha was her cooking. She never seemed to repeat herself with a dish, and she always surprised him with something tasty. He put an apron on, getting ready to help her. The apron looked funny on him—too small against his broad body.

"Today I feel like cooking Chinese food," Martha said, handing Barter a package of frozen fish from the fridge. Barter put the fish in a proper container and placed it in the microwave oven, selecting "defrost."

Martha took Barter's hands, turning his attention back to her. "I spent ten years organizing personnel records. I already sold T.S. on the idea of reviewing his records well ahead of retirement to make sure they're in order. I scared him with worst-case scenarios. So he commissioned me to review them for him this coming week. I'll have full access to his personnel record and I'll make you a résumé."

Barter lifted Martha by her buttocks, placing her with ease on the kitchen table. He kissed her on her mouth and worked from there to her left ear and the back of her neck, then managed to free one of her breasts, sucking on it furiously.

"You're going to miss your plane," Martha whispered.

THE THREE DAYS in Florida with her brother, nephews, and niece were among the happiest she'd had in her whole life, Marjorie thought, as she packed to go back to New York. She'd enjoyed every minute of their time together, discovering the fun of one of the best playgrounds in the world. Now she dreaded the moment it all had to end and she feared as never before the emptiness of her apartment in a city which, with time, had become alien to her. This meeting had been a complete turnaround in her life, a rebirth. Now her whole world revolved around these four troubled people, tied to her by blood but in many ways strangers, with another culture, and other beliefs and attitudes toward life. Their problems had become the center of her thoughts and feelings, displacing others that now seemed petty and insignificant.

Carlos Manuel had decided that the kids should go back to Miami by plane while he and Marjorie travelled north by car to some place near New York, where they would separate—this time, perhaps, forever. A ten-minute shuttle-bus ride from the hotel took them to the new Orlando International Airport, a huge compound designed to handle heavy streams of visitors. Even so, they had managed to arrive late—everybody had been reluctant to rush their departure, hoping for something to happen at the last minute that might somehow make it possible to remain together. Once at the airport, the kids had to dash for their plane, which made the farewell much easier.

After the youngsters left, Marjorie rented a car and, navigating through a maze of roads under construction around the airport, managed to get onto U.S. highway 4, heading for Jacksonville. Her plan was to reach I-95 and travel northward along the Atlantic coast. She hadn't driven on a highway in years, but she tried to act in front of her brother as if she did it all time, a deception with which, she suspected, she wasn't entirely successful. *I'm too tense*, she told herself. After they reached Daytona Beach, she decided to take the right lane, slow down, and relax.

She was determined to use the many hours they would be travelling together to convince her brother to stay in the U.S. and take proper care of his own kids. She prayed to God to make him aware of the foolishness of going back to Cuba—maybe to spend the rest of his life in a dungeon. Cuba was a country where nobody who cared for him was left, an island that, for all she knew, was the closest place to hell on earth, a gigantic prison from which no one was allowed to leave.

Suddenly, there was a squeal of tires, followed by the heavy pounding of cars colliding in front of them. One of the vehicles, a new red van, was thrown off the road like a toy. Marjorie braked immediately and pulled deftly onto the shoulder, just in time to avoid being hit from behind. Her brother jumped out of the car and ran to aid the driver trapped inside the van, who was screaming for help. Marjorie could see Carlos Manuel struggling to get a heavy man with thick gray, wavy hair out of the vehicle. Two other men arrived to help lift the man out and carry him to a place beside the road. She felt a bit dizzy and weak, with a sudden desire to urinate.

"Watch it! The gas tank is leaking fuel," somebody yelled, as her brother ran back to the van and salvaged the driver's kangaroo belt and a portfolio. The wounded man tried to get up, maybe to thank her brother, but someone shouted at him to remain lying down.

The gray-haired man shook her brother's hand, then Carlos Manuel headed back to Marjorie, who was standing next to the car, trying to regain control of her bladder, looking around at the mess of wrecked cars and distressed people.

Carlos Manual reached her, smiling. "Sister, I didn't know you were such a hell of a good driver."

"As good as they come," she said, laughing a bit shakily, knowing that her brother was perfectly aware of how rusty at the steering wheel she really was. "To be honest, if you only had a driver's license, I'd gladly turn all the driving over to you."

He smiled and threw his arm around her shoulders, hugging her. "Let's walk up to that café. I'll treat you to a cup of coffee."

"Great! I need a bathroom."

The paramedics and the police reached the accident site a few minutes after they returned to their car. The injured driver of the van was taken away in an ambulance along with a woman suffering severe shock. Marjorie eased back into the driver's seat, fastened her seat belt, and carefully entered the stream of cars flowing northward. She remained silent for quite a while, proud of her brother's prompt and effective intervention and of her own performance as a driver. Then she started to talk excitedly in a euphoria she couldn't control. Until they reached Jacksonville, she spoke continuously about all the petty incidents during the multiple collision. She was elated and surprised by her quick reaction and timely maneuvering to avoid being hit, amazed at how her brother was able to pull such a heavy person out of a car on the brink of catching fire and maybe exploding, at the risk of his own life. She laughed every time she remembered the wild stare of the woman in shock and her funny dress and messed-up hairdo.

"She looked like a sister of the Marx brothers," she repeated many times, laughing.

They spent the night at a motel just off the highway. The next day,

Marjorie observed her brother's changing mood. Right after leaving Orlando, he had seemed worried and sad, surely thinking about his kids. He often fell into spells of deep silence while staring at the boring landscape along the highway. After they left the state of Florida, heading toward Savannah, his humor began to change and he started asking questions. It surprised her how much he already knew about everyday life in the U.S. He was even aware of minute details that seemed irrelevant to her: the cost of all sorts of food and beverages, the names of all brands of cigarettes, the baseball and football teams and how they were doing in their leagues, something she had never managed to learn herself.

At Carlos Manuel's request, she told him about the trips she had made to Mexico and Europe. He spent a long time studying the *Rand McNally Travel Atlas* she had bought at the Orlando airport to select the best roads for her trip back. While reviewing the map, he asked questions about the cities along the U.S.-Mexico border, and about the control the Mexicans had over American visitors.

"Have you ever been on a fishing boat off the West Coast?" he asked.

She was startled by the question, then nodded, remembering. "Some months before Arthur died, we went on a tourist trip from San Diego to Puerto Vallarta in Mexico. The men on board did some fishing along the way."

"Did you have to show your passport to any American authority before you left?"

"I don't remember. I don't think I did." She felt foolish for not recalling the details, but it was such a long time ago. Judging by his questions, she gathered that he was investigating his return to Cuba. That, and the fact that he seemed more cheerful, prompted her to make a first attack on his most vulnerable point. "*Hermano*, I'm worried about the kids. This country is not easy for youngsters, even if they know their way around and have someone watching over them all the time."

Her brother remained silent, looking at the road. She kept on hammering.

"Claudia is very young, she's so pretty . . . so sexy. I think she needs her father to stay near her."

He cut in. "*Hermana*, they had already decided to try their wings and fly on their own. They grew from childhood to adulthood on a raft trip across the ocean from their homeland to the country where they've chosen to live. I don't think they'll really need me around."

Marjorie did not agree. She had never had a child of her own, but she was sure this was not a proper attitude for a parent. She felt a rush of anger.

"Maybe I should rent out my apartment in New York and go live in Miami so they can reach me easily whenever they need me."

Again her brother remained silent for a few minutes, as if digesting her idea, then spoke slowly. "I believe the best you can do is what you have done so far. You don't have to move to Miami."

Marjorie looked at her brother, amazed that he could be so detached about his kids. Aware that she was outraged, he pressed his hand on her shoulder, warning her to pay special attention to what he was about to say.

"Margarita, there is a very important thing you must know." He stopped, as if unsure whether he should continue. He began again, speaking slowly, as if weighing every word. "When I arrived in Orlando, I went into a library and was able to check the FBI web page on the Internet. I found my picture there among the ten most-wanted criminals in this country." He paused. She had slowed the car down almost to a stop, paying full attention.

"At sea, I had to kill one of the five men who tried to steal our lifeboat. They assaulted the kids and threw them into the water while I was inside the sinking yacht. I managed to get close enough to kill the most dangerous of them in such a way that his body and all the blood remained inside the lifeboat. If he had fallen into the water, sharks would have come after the blood, attacking the kids, who at that moment were hanging onto the wreckage of their raft. There was no other way to stop those men."

Marjorie's face registered sorrow and pity, then she reacted. "But that's a clear case of self-defense! You're not a criminal. Why is the FBI harassing you? What about all of Batista's criminals who killed thousands of people in Cuba and were then sheltered and protected once they got to this country? The FBI can't do a thing like that to you. Carlos, you're playing this game in the wrong way. You're in America now. You have to do things the way they're done here. You have to fight those accusations! I can help you—I'll talk to my lawyer. I'll go to see a senator who went to school with Arthur and was his close friend."

Her brother tried to calm her down. "Don't worry. So far, nobody has made a connection between you and me or the kids and me."

Marjorie nodded, but her normally happy, full-moon face showed her distress. Her brother drew a breath, then spoke softly, like a grown-up to a small child. "If we take simple measures, the risks can be minimized. Actually, while we were on the lifeboat, I asked the kids to call you only from public phones and to tell you not to call them. As I feared, those rules were not followed."

"Well." Marjorie felt unjustly blamed. "How was I to know about all this you're telling me now? I just couldn't pay attention to every-thing Claudia told me to do. When I received her first call, I wanted to go to Florida immediately and bring them back to my huge empty apartment in Manhattan, but Claudia practically forbade me to come to Miami. Then she gave me the name and address of a lawyer and told me exactly how to proceed with the affidavits of support. From there on, I was afraid of doing anything on my own. From the begin-ning, Claudia talked in such a mysterious way and gave me such pre-cise and strange instructions that I ended up feeling I was part of a big conspiracy. After a while, I became convinced she was unduly afraid of everything, reacting as she would in her own country, where everyone is being watched all the time."

Carlos Manuel shook his head, ignoring his sister's last comment. "This morning, just before they went back to Miami, I told them to move to another place and have their phone number changed as soon as they got there. Claudia is going to call you every day from a public phone."

Startled, Marjorie looked at her brother. "Aren't you exaggerating the precautions? Anyone listening to my calls will only hear a doting aunt talking nonsense with her niece. I rarely catch either of the boys at home. If they are in, they just say hello and something sweet to me and go on with whatever they're doing."

"All I want is to avoid dragging the kids and you into this and getting you earmarked as close relatives of a dangerous criminal and enemy spy."

Marjorie kept silent for a while. She suddenly realized that her brother was in many ways a total stranger to her. In spite of how much she loved him, she knew nothing about his life for the last thirty-two years. Maybe he had committed other dreadful crimes for which he was now being hunted. A horrendous thought came into her mind: There was no telling what would happen to him if he were caught. He could be sent to the electric chair, poisoned to death, or—at best—thrown in prison for life. She then felt deeply sorry for trying to convey to him the idea that he wasn't being a good father by leaving his kids alone. Now she wanted him to get out of the country as soon as possible. At that very moment, she felt illuminated by an idea that would solve all his problems.

"Listen, Carlos, God has just made clear to me how you can stay safely in this country as long as you want, or get out from any place you wish."

Carlos Manuel smiled with sweet memories of Marjorie's God-inspired ideas. She struggled to explain her vision. "Just be yourself. Nobody knows who you really are. Not even your own children know your real name. You can get an American passport and all sorts of IDs right away. Why not hide behind your own true identity? Why don't you take advantage of all this mess?" Marjorie was thrilled with her discovery.

The scheme was appealing. "How would I go about it?"

"I'll handle it through my lawyer. I'll give him your birth certificate and some recent photos. That's it."

"Sounds too easy."

"That's all I did the first time I went out of the country. If necessary, I'll dig up some other information to prove you were born in Brooklyn and lived in New York until you were twelve."

He smiled, mentally playing with the idea. "Go ahead. I'll keep in contact with you somehow. With the money you gave me, I don't have to risk crossing the border like a wetback, handled like cattle. I'm going to take it easy in California until I find a sure escape gate to Mexico."

"Why don't you come and live with me until you have proper IDs and a passport?" Marjorie watched her brother hesitate. "It seems *Papá* wasn't so crazy to change your names when you all went to Cuba."

"The FBI and the CIA have the means to discover who I am. It's just a matter of time. Since you're my sister, your house is the first place they'll look for me. Better if I stay on the run and try to keep in touch with you."

She didn't listen to her brother's reply. In her mind what she had said seconds before lingered: *"It seems Papá wasn't so crazy to change your names when you all went to Cuba."* This triggered something inside Marjorie. She remained silent for a few moments. When she spoke again, her voice was bitter and her face had turned sullen. "For all those years, I only had a mailbox address to send my letters to Cuba. Letters that were rarely answered, and a telephone number for leaving messages in case of emergency with someone called Plácido. The only one in the family I ever talked to was *Mami*, while she was alive. She had to hide from father in a neighbor's house to receive my calls every month. *All of it was so cruel.*" Marjorie's face expressed deep sorrow, her hands clenched on the steering wheel, her eyes fixed on the road.

He tried to make her see the other side of the story. "Don't forget that the U.S. has been at war with Cuba for all this time, as long as I can remember. Also, it hasn't ever been a clean war. Everything under the sun has been used to try to subdue the rebellious island. *Papá* did what he felt was his duty."

"What did 'war' have to do with calling his only daughter once a year? Just a short call, saying 'Happy birthday, Margarita' was all I ever wanted, all I ever expected."

"Maybe you're right. Severing family relations the way it was done turned out to be a gigantic mistake. Family is and ought to be sacred. Creating such an abyss between Cubans on one side and the other, making foes for life of those who migrated for whatever reason, has hurt the Revolution in the long run more than helped it. But what you're saying about *Papá* is not true. He made us keep an empty seat at the table to remind us that you were missing. Whenever *Mamá* talked with you, she had to give him a full account of what you said; he celebrated all your successes. One of the main reasons he changed our names was because if the CIA or the FBI found out his real identity, it would have messed up your whole life, and your husband's work for the navy and the army would have been jeopardized. Don't ever think he didn't love you. He suffered because you stayed behind."

"What else could I do?" Marjorie reacted indignantly. "I was about to get married to the only man I ever loved. I was finishing school. I was born in this country; I'm American. *I had absolutely nothing to go there for.*" Then, as the meaning of her last statement hit her, Marjorie broke into tears. She pulled off the road, stopped the car, and wept for a long while.

He had been trying to avoid any clash with his sister regarding politics or family affairs. His professional training told him not to antagonize her in any way—on the contrary, he needed to make her feel that she was the one who had made the right decisions all along. But he rebelled against the idea of playing by the book with his own sister, someone for whom he cared so much. He had realized soon after their meeting that they had little in common, only old memories buried in a past that seemed as remote to him as if it came from another life. In contrast, she held onto those memories to the last detail and enjoyed recalling them, as if they had happened the day before.

Adding to the tension was the fact that he felt very awkward trying to be himself. All the characters he had impersonated until then were single men with no families, with lives that weighed on him only in the infinite details that he had to memorize, and in the ways he had to act and react to any situation in order to be consistent with that image. From the time he arrived in Cuba with his parents, still a child, he had spent most of his life away at schools, coming home only for weekends and vacations. Later, he had stayed for long stretches in the Soviet Union and other countries in Eastern Europe, where he had acquired most of his training. During that time, his family interaction had consisted only of the frequent letters he received from his mother, with inserts of short paragraphs in another handwriting from his father. And the month his father had stayed with him in Bulgaria following his mother's death.

After he started to work and got married, living with Cecilia and the kids during his short leaves in Cuba was like visiting a remote, enchanted place, far away from all worries and troubles, where everything was perfect. When he returned for good, he had realized that dealing with the problems of everyday family relations was far more difficult than he had ever anticipated.

On Thursday, September 15, the third day of travelling, they reached Washington, D.C. Marjorie drove around the Potomac River, the Lincoln Memorial, the White House, and other landmarks of the capital he wanted to see. Finally, she parked in front of the National Air and Space Museum of the Smithsonian Institute, which they visited. Later, they strolled from the Library of Congress to the Capitol, where they watched congressmen coming and going and the media always on guard for news.

As they came back to the car, Carlos Manuel asked his sister, "Did you know that Havana has a replica of the Capitol?"

"I remember something vague about that. Yes, *Papá* used to say that all the country folk visiting the city had their photo taken in front of the Capitol as hard proof that they'd been in Havana."

"Havana's capitol is smaller. It has a more human size. It's prettier because its dimensions are more balanced. This whole set of government buildings here strikes me the way the Egyptian pyramids must have impressed common people in ancient times—a big show of the Pharaoh's force."

"Oh, Carlos, like all the partisan leftists, you criticize this country for everything. I used to do it, too. You should have seen me during the demonstrations against the Vietnam War. I used to wear a T-shirt with Che Guevara's image. Arthur would come to the rallies and stay on the sidelines, watching me. I think I did it mostly to embarrass him. I don't know why, but when we're young, we do things to hurt the ones we love most. As I grew older, I became more conservative. I view life now in a totally different way. I've gone back to religion, something I'd put aside for quite some time. Changes frighten me now. Now, I pray to God for everything to remain the same forever."

They finally reached Philadelphia—the place, Carlos Manuel said, where they would separate. Instead of stopping at a motel, this time they went to the Wyndham Plaza right in the center of town. Marjorie wanted to stay in a good place for the two days they had left.

After sleeping late the next morning, they headed out for lunch. She used this last opportunity to buy him, in spite of his protests, more clothes and a new pair of shoes, a fancy shaving kit, and a set of suitcases. These expenses hurt him almost physically. He did not have to see her bank statement to know that the money her husband had left her had mostly dwindled away, surely spent on all the senseless endeavors his sister was capable of dreaming up. His training enabled him to read the real story in the minute details of her behavior. But there was nothing he could do to stop her from spending money on him. It made her happy to have the opportunity to be generous with him and his kids.

When they got back to the hotel, he explained his plans for getting out of the country. Using the travel atlas, he showed her three possible ways he was considering crossing the border to Mexico. His first choice was a fishing trip from the San Diego area to Puerto Vallarta or Manzanillo. The next best possibility was to enroll in a sightseeing and bicycle tour to the Monterrey area. The third way was simply by passing through the border at a busy crossing using the common identification the normal U.S. citizen uses every day: a driver's license and credit cards. In each case, someone would be waiting on Mexican soil with a passport for him.

"I'll keep in touch with you to see if you've been able to get me a passport. If you do, it would be much safer. And here, this is a code book to let you know easily where I am."

He handed her a booklet he'd picked up at the motel where they'd stayed in Orlando. It had maps showing the location of every La Quinta motel in the country. He held another copy of the booklet in his hand.

"When you receive a message saying, for instance, 12-280, it means that I am at the twelfth motel listed from the beginning of this booklet, in room 280. Of course, I'll register using any name, even a woman's name. Don't call me, just send the passport to the hotel administration in my real name."

The next day he went along to the train station to see her off. Just before leaving, he told her, "I want you to promise you won't ever say anything about this trip to anybody—ever, under any circumstance."

She nodded.

"If you have to admit it, don't give any name, or any detail."

"Don't you worry, *hermanito*. Last night a very sweet voice whispered in my ear to fear nothing because an angel is guarding you at all times. I felt so reassured that I slept soundly the rest of the night."

He went back to the hotel to prepare for his departure. He dyed his hair gray and curled it as best he could. He wrapped a couple of hotel towels around his waist and put on an oversized pair of trousers and a set of black-rimmed glasses he had purchased. Then, he compared his likeness in the mirror to the photo on the driver's license of the man he had helped during the accident on I-95, John Wilkinson. He checked out of the hotel, where he was also registered in the same name. He left his set of suitcases in the doorman's care and took a cab to a house on Glenwood Avenue and Broad Street, where the owner of a 1990 Ford Cortina was waiting for him. After driving the car around and engaging in a bit of bargaining, he bought the car for 2900 dollars instead of the 3200 dollars advertised in that morning's newspaper. The car was in fairly good shape and, best of all, had belonged to its original owner. He couldn't take the risk of buying a car that might turn out to have been stolen. Driving his newly acquired car, he picked up his luggage at the hotel, then set off to carry out his carefully laid plan—in the first place, to complete the information he needed to borrow John Wilkinson's identity for a few days.

AFTER THREE HOURS of sleep, Barter got up in a hurry. He was already late for the first meeting King had arranged for him. As he brushed his teeth, he glanced at the short biography of the first man he was scheduled to meet, finishing the reading over a cup of coffee and a couple of doughnuts. He covered the distance between the Miami Beach Holiday Inn and the northwest side of Hialeah in forty minutes and managed to be only an hour late for his appointment. The person he was there to see was Juan Pascual Hernandez ("the Owl"), a man in his seventies. Pascual received him clad in a blue suit and a grayish tie. He looked totally out of place in a Miami of Bermuda shorts and tennis shoes—like Barter himself was wearing—on a glorious Saturday morning replete with blue, open skies and a temperature hovering around seventy-five degrees.

Pascual was a tall, slender, erect man, with the swift and graceful movements of a retired dancer. Only his face, plowed in all directions with deep wrinkles, looked old—very old. Two sunken, colorless eyes flashed from time to time below bushy eyebrows that were surprisingly black, just below a cap of gray hair. The man had been one of the founders of the Cuban Armed Forces' Intelligence Service after Castro's Revolution. He had been trained at West

Point when he was a young and promising officer back in the late forties. Batista's takeover in 1952 had not suited his aspirations, nor the aspirations of a group of young officers like him, all hungry for a social system shaped like the one in the U.S., where they had all been educated. The group began conspiring against the brutal dictator. In 1958, Pascual Hernandez was imprisoned, accused of helping an uprising at the Cayo Loco Naval Base in Cienfuegos Bay. When the Revolution took over in 1959, he was released from prison and became a teacher to a new generation of intelligence officers. As early as 1961, however, he had decided that Fidel Castro was leading the Revolution in the wrong direction, and he offered his services to the CIA, which gladly put him on its secret payroll. He then continued to serve in the Cuban army until 1975, when he defected to the U.S., taking his wife and daughter with him. A son chose to remain behind in Cuba.

Pascual escorted Barter rather ceremoniously to a studio where he had a pile of materials he wanted to show him. Twenty minutes later, Barter realized that King had arranged a whole course on Cuban Intelligence history and organization for him. Pascual, he found, was a natural teacher and a very educated man. But somehow he felt that the man had probably never really understood anything that went on around him during his whole life. He seemed to have been born clad in a mental suit and tie.

The last of the five men Barter met was Alejandro Alcazar, a man five years his junior, who had defected to the CIA on a trip to London in 1986. None of the five men recognized the photos of Ramiro Ramos. The information they offered about Cuba's intelligence service was detailed and interesting, but it did not add much to the knowledge he already had, Barter concluded. Only Alcazar, who belonged to a much younger generation than the others, seemed to Barter to have ideas, points of view, and information worthy of a second encounter in a different scenario. The son of a Cuban ambassador to England when he was a boy, Alcazar had learned the Queen's English as his mother tongue, and he still kept a moderate British drawl as a touch of distinction. He had also lived in several European countries, learning other languages and rounding off a broad and worldly education. Nothing, not even his looks, remotely revealed that he was Cuban. When he defected, he was working for an American company in South Africa and holding a British passport. At that time, Cuba was actively helping the Namibian liberation guerrilla and South African anti-Apartheid movements, while deploying a six-thousand-man army in the south of Angola in preparation for engagement in a full-scale war against South Africa.

Alejandro had been prepared for his intelligence work in a very secret training program that had gone on for many years parallel to the regular courses for intelligence personnel. This program was aimed to train small groups—five persons or fewer per team—of very select agents. These teams were designed to work deeply undercover as totally autonomous units in countries of interest. All of the trainees adopted new nationalities when they had attained full command of the languages and lived for some time in the countries where they would be citizens. They assumed the names of persons who had died leaving no relatives or any easy trail to identify them, since in most countries it's difficult to match death and birth certificates when the two events occur in different locations. Often a death entry can be erased for a price.

For their second encounter, Barter invited Alcazar to dine at Monty's Restaurant in Coconut Grove, a place Alcazar had suggested.

"Do you trust me with the order?"

"Of course. Go ahead and order for both of us. I'll eat any creature that can walk, crawl, swim, or fly." Barter was glad to be relieved of the job, using the time his guest was busy ordering the meal to stroll around the place and take a look at the yachts anchored just a few feet away. A man born and raised deep inland, the open seas and vessels of all sorts fascinated him.

Alcazar put the menu aside and ordered a full-course dinner for two, with plenty of grilled lobster as the main dish and, as appetizers, stone crabs, the specialty of the house, with French white wine while they waited for the meal. Barter was astonished when all the dishes crowded a table for four people. He began to mentally calculate the cost of the dinner and wondered how he was going to justify such a whopping meal. Alcazar started eating the stone crabs and drinking the wine as soon as they were served; at the same time, he began answering the questions Barter posed.

"Each batch of trainees specialized in certain areas of expertise. Some of the recruits had very good scientific or technical backgrounds, permitting them to seek work in international companies in places of special interest to Cuba in Africa, the United States, South America, even in Asia. Their fundamental objective at that time was to procure information and to gain influence in whatever field they were in. A sizeable part of their salaries was devoted to sustaining their own organization, which necessarily included some backup. Once, I heard a big chief, half-drunk, bragging about a group he had overseen that had become very powerful and wealthy. When it was convenient, two or three teams exchanged information or coordinated their actions, becoming a network. There was a center-man for each team who was the only one who knew and was allowed to contact the rest of the members."

Alcazar managed to devour most of the food while at the same time going into more details about the training program, fully aware that the information he provided was his share of the bill. "In the seventies and eighties, some of the trainees were chosen for more active roles. They underwent very thorough military training and were used for tasks related to Cuba's involvement in various wars. Those men were placed in positions that enabled them to procure sensitive political and military information, but also to offer overt military assistance when necessary."

Alcazar continued answering Barter's questions as long as there was food on the table. After the last of it was finished, he invited Barter for a nightcap and to try out his sports car.

"What make?" Barter had always dreamed of owning a sports car.

"Porsche, 911-Turbo. I went to Germany last year to buy it directly from the factory."

"How could you afford something like that? What bank did you rob?"

"To buy a toy like this, you just have to forget about everything else. All my life I longed for one but never could afford it. I still can't, but there it is."

Barter whistled when they got near the car, and he told himself that the price of this baby was well over 100,000 dollars.

"What's its maximum speed?" Barter dove into the seat beside the driver, struggling to fit his extra-long legs under the dash.

"It depends on the driver's sphincter," Alejandro said, taking off as if he were piloting a bullet that had just been fired. "At about 150 miles per hour, mine doesn't hold anymore, and I start shitting my pants."

They tested the car around the neighborhood and finally stopped at Dinner Key, also in Coconut Grove. They were ushered to a table where two gorgeous girls were waiting for them.

"Ladies, it is my pleasure to introduce Mr. Douglas Gates, Bill Gates's brother. Doug, this is Laura, your nightcap, and this is Leticia, my nightcap."

"Who is Bill Gates?" Laura asked.

When Alcazar brought Barter back to his hotel in broad daylight, he reached into the glove compartment of his Porsche and pulled out the photo of Ramiro Ramos taken at the Krome Detention Center in Miami, sent to him a few days earlier by Barter.

"I almost forgot. Look for the real identity of this man in Nicaragua."

"Why Nicaragua?"

Alejandro smiled cynically. "My sources told me that."

"Come on, tell me what you know."

"Look, Bill, I'll be quite frank because I really want to help you be the next general director of the CIA. Nevertheless, I had to quit Fidel's cause because it condemned me to watching pennies my whole life. Do you have any idea of the upkeep on this Porsche and all that goes with it? And the kind of rent I have to pay for a house in Coral Gables? Besides, I have to keep all my contacts greased. The CIA's regular money doesn't go that far."

Barter decided he liked this strange Cuban. Whoever had recruited him for the intelligence service had done both a good and a lousy job. He was perfect for the role, but too fond of the kind of life only a lot of money can buy. No regular state service in the world could afford such an agent. He had the feeling Alcazar had a lot to offer, but it was evident that to keep on living the way he did, he had to be a very good salesman, no matter how much he knew. *Maybe the trick was to sell the same merchandise to many buyers.* It was also clear that Alcazar knew something about the man he was looking for and wanted to get paid for it. Barter decided to start paying. There was a strong CIA paper trail through Nicaragua and an angled confrontation with the Cuban Intelligence Service back in the eighties. That seemed a good road to take.

Barter sent an official request to the CIA for money to extend his search to Central America, to follow some very good leads he had in that direction. "Chances of success are eighty percent with money to pay for the information." He didn't mention Alcazar. He was surprised when he received a call from King the same day he sent the request.

"How well do you know Central America?" Before he had time to answer, King gave him an order phrased as a question: "Why don't you take one or two of those chaps you've met along with you?"

Barter, taken aback, hesitated for a second. "Yes, sir, that's a mighty good idea. I'll take Alcazar."

King delayed his approval for a moment, then said, "Alex is a very bright young man. You'll feel at ease with him. But maybe some of the older guys are more knowledgeable than he is about that neck of the woods."

"Alcazar will be fine, sir," Barter said in a cheerful tone, trying to soften his refusal.

Barter met with Alcazar at midnight to discuss the job he had to offer. By now Barter was aware that Alex was a nocturnal creature and there was no use trying to make any appointment with him during daylight hours.

"You'll get five thousand dollars for 'expenses' when you leave here for Managua. There will be another five if the trip is success-ful. If it's not, I'll see you're hung up by the balls."

Alcazar smiled, as if he were thinking it was a pleasure to work with a guy who could read his mind so well.

"Of course, the dice won't roll unless I know first what you know about this Ramiro Ramos. I don't want to go on a wild-goose chase to any mosquito-ridden country. I have to meet your contacts here and evaluate what they said to you before we go."

Alcazar's smile faded, as if he had been caught off balance. He hesitated a minute. Barter stared at him with a savage look, think-ing the worst.

"I'm afraid . . . this, this"—Alcazar stuttered as if he had been caught in a lie—"this is going to cost you another meal at Monty's, this time for four people." Then Alcazar laughed. "Come on, don't shit your pants; I'll pay for this meal with the money you're going to advance me."

The next night, Alcazar took Barter to meet a Cuban and a Nicaraguan, and to dine in a place that offered "All you can eat for $5.95."

Barter waited for Martha's call. She rang every night around ten o'clock, after she had finished her house chores and was ready to go to bed. He used these long phone conversations to do other things. With a wire hanger he made a telephone holder that liberated both his hands to shine shoes, sort dirty clothes, glance over the newspaper, or list the work he had to do the next day. This time, however, Barter didn't let her start with her stories.

"I'm leaving for Nicaragua in a couple of days, so we won't have a chance to talk to each other for a while."

"You can't call me from Nicaragua? Why not?"

"You know why. Everybody, including our common boss, would be listening to our calls, taped by half a dozen secret service men. Besides, I'm going as a newspaperman to interview a lot of people who were involved in guerrilla warfare there in the eighties. I'll be moving around a lot."

"Are you going to dig into the Iran-Contra affair? Are you out of your mind?"

"No, you know what I'm doing. Listen, this is very important, Martha. I need detailed information on your boss's accident—the one that cost him a leg when he was stationed in Nicaragua. Anything you can dig up on how it happened. Got it?"

"All that data is classified."

"That's why I'm asking you for it. Look, Martha, there's nothing shady about this. But it's very important that I know all the details of that 'accident.' I need it for this job, but for obvious reasons I don't want to ask him for it."

"Jesus, Bill. That's going to be difficult, even for me. I'll do my best, that's all I can promise you."

"That's my girl. You know where and how to send it whenever you get it."

"Take care of yourself. You've really got me worried this time. I love you, you fool."

I DON'T BELIEVE THE CIA is going to all this trouble and expense just to find the identity of an unknown Cuban Intelligence officer who entered this country illegally unless there is something very special about this man or a good reason why they want him so badly. Hunting down spies is an FBI problem; that's the agency in charge of counterintelligence in the U.S., not the CIA." A middle-aged man clad in a two-thousand-dollar dark gray suit sat behind a huge mahogany desk. He spoke the words emphatically, with a warm and well-modulated voice.

It was two o'clock in the morning. The room was barely illuminated. On a silvery tray on the desk rested a bottle of *Añejo Ocho Años, Havana Club* rum, along with two Bohemia glasses that glittered in the twilight with the vestiges of ice cubes and rum.

Alejandro Alcazar, sitting in a chair in front of the desk, shrugged.

"I don't know what's behind all of this yet, but you're right. For the first time, King went to the trouble of calling me and giving me his instructions himself."

"You already told me that, Alex," the middle-aged man said dryly, then stood up abruptly, ending the meeting.

Alcazar rose rapidly and joined the man already on his way out of the room. They walked into a hall that was shrouded almost completely in darkness and headed for the faintly lit living room. As they walked, the middle-aged man kept talking.

"Alex, you have to find out what this fucking cripple is up to. He dreams of going back to the good old sixties, when we all had to dance to the CIA's stupid music. He doesn't accept the fact that we have earned the right to decide all this country's policies on Cuba. We've earned that right with the blood shed by our people who've died trying to overthrow Castro." The man stopped at the front door to the house and opened it.

"Not only that. Miami was a poor, shabby, one-story-high country town when the Cubans arrived in the sixties, and we made it a rich and powerful city. We've linked the U.S. with all the countries south of its borders, making Miami the trade capital with all the Spanish-speaking countries. Our highly qualified labor force has attracted all sorts of industries to this area. Our representatives in Congress have made alliances with other right-wing groups and are invincible. Furthermore, there is very little chance to be president of the United States without Florida's votes, and the Cubans decide where the majority of the votes swing in this state. The Cuban vote is decisive. Once someone is president, he wants to be reelected four years later, and in the meantime he doesn't want to pay the political price of opening relations with Cuba. This goes on and on . . ."

Alejandro Alcazar nodded in response to the often-heard speech.

"Remember. You're responsible for this case and for keeping an eye on this Barter boy to find out what he really wants. I want to know which side he is on."

"Pereda, I am on top of it. Don't you worry," Alcazar said, changing his tone of voice.

The middle-aged man placed his hand on Alcazar's right shoulder in farewell, gently pushed him out of the house, and closed the door. Alcazar stepped onto the veranda and wondered how long he was going to have to wait. Once, he had stood there for more than an hour. This time, the security guards came up immediately, holding a couple of big Dobermans on leashes, to escort him to his Porsche parked at the entrance to this huge mansion in Coconut Plum, the realm of one of the most powerful men in the Cuban community in the United States.

Alcazar liked to drive at that time of the night, when he could push his Porsche almost as fast as he liked for long stretches along I-95, virtually deserted. Close to Boca Raton, he punched a number on his cellphone. After many rings, a sleepy feminine voice finally answered.

"Wake up, baby. We have work to do."

I N REAL LIFE, nothing is completely white or purely black; the most devout nun may dream of penetrating phalluses, the wickedest man may weep during a movie. Everything has to be measured in context; nothing is very meaningful outside of its setting. Cuba today is not the Cuba of the eighties, when there was enough for everybody and the country progressed steadily. Nor is it the Cuba of the sixties, when—like today—there was very little food, clothing, and medicine, but everyone was willing to make all sorts of sacrifices to ensure a better future. Law cannot be enforced today the way it was before, even if it's the same law."

Colonel Francisco had stopped eating, as a clear sign of respect, to listen to General García. While seemingly very attentive to the general's lecture, Francisco fought against a yawn behind a hand discretely held over his mouth. He hated all that crap about how dialectics governed every process in life that the general kept throwing at him—as if he had not read all the same manuals from the pack of cheap Russian philosophers that had converted the bright, but often hard to grasp, works of Marx, Engels, and Lenin into dead recipes to suit all of their obsolete and rigid ideas.

Colonel Francisco, second in command of the High Military Court, was having a lunch meeting with General García, head of the Internal Security Department of the Ministry of the Interior, in a house in Reparto Flores where the general held most of his meetings. Francisco and García had many of these work sessions. In them, Francisco received from García, aside from specific information about the military personnel on trial, the general policies that had to be applied, policies that changed with time and issue. García often even prescribed specific treatments for individuals.

Francisco loved this house surrounded by a lavish garden. He never tired of looking at the lively colors in the stained glass that crowned the doors and windows, or at the swimming pool, shaped like a painter's palette and always full of water, that resembled a shallow sea. Above all, he delighted in the food served at the house, plain but always tasty and well-cooked, with a lot of spices, full of irresistible odors that made his mouth water for a whole hour before lunchtime.

"General, you're absolutely right. I believe that in a moment like this, when the country is having such a rough time and the people are suffering so many hardships, we have to clamp down on criminality as hard as we possibly can. Take a case like the one we have been reviewing today. If we let those corrupt officers go without heavy punishment, it would be demoralizing for the entire armed forces. Nowadays we can't allow any weakness. If it was left to me, I'd shoot all of them."

General García wrinkled his face almost in pain. That was not what he had meant, but all the same, Colonel Francisco would do as he was told. A strange guy, this Francisco, very sharp on many things and so dumb on others, García thought.

Colonel Francisco despised change. He firmly believed that the very essence of law was its permanency in time and circumstance. For each crime or misconduct, there had to be a set of invariable punishments. It was the only way people could eventually learn how to behave in any society. It was the simple physics principle of action and reaction applied to human conduct. The same basic truth ruled the education of a child. Unless it learned to behave according to a given set of unchanging rules, it would never be able to distinguish right from wrong. It was a horrible mistake to punish a child for something one day and let it go the next. The same thing applied to every citizen and society as a whole, regardless of its economic system or set of religious or non-religious beliefs.

Francisco considered General García a man totally ignorant of laws and their purpose. In fact, the general had often shown disrespect for the law and felt and acted as if he were above it, reciting excerpts from Marx and Lenin to suit every occasion, as if they provided the ultimate truth on everything. On the other hand, Francisco recognized that García had a long history as a warrior and a man of action, with a solid and broad education, very rare among soldiers. General García, in spite of his apparent good character and flexibility, was a true hard-liner. A man fully convinced of what he was doing, with a strong internal motivation, capable of carrying out anything for the cause. He was rigorously self-disciplined, frugal, as austere as a Spartan soldier of ancient times. His body was as dried-up and weathered as an old desert rock, especially his head, totally bald. Nevertheless, the general didn't understand law and there was no use arguing with him on that issue.

Before the meal, they had exchanged information and views on several cases, one of them involving twelve civilians and three officers of the Ministry of the Interior. The officers had taken bribes in connection with a gang that stole cars, then dismantled, reassembled, painted, and registered them with different license plates. The officers were accused of completing all the paperwork to legalize the operations. According to Cuban law, any crime involving a member of the armed forces, regardless of the number of civilians involved, had to be resolved by the harsh laws that ruled military courts.

All the people involved in the affair were in jail, some of them for several months already, pending completion of the investigation. Now was the moment for a public trial, and García wanted to make sure the case was presented properly, because at any given moment it could be of political interest to allow press and television coverage. García made it clear that the whole process had to be handled in such a way that demonstrated that the Ministry of the Interior would not accept any sort of corruption. This was necessary from time to time to fight the ever-present shadow of the trial of General Arnaldo Ochoa, a former national hero sentenced to death in 1989 for high treason and drug trafficking with two other members of the security forces; and the later imprisonment of the Minister of the Interior at that time, General José Abrahantes, also implicated in the affair. After these events, the Ministry of the Interior had been completely revamped with officers from the army. These new chiefs didn't know much about the complex work of the beheaded organization, and the whole ministry limped badly, lacking the efficiency of its older days. So, it was good for its morale and for its public image to show how a well-organized criminal band had been captured and severely punished.

The officers implicated in the bribes all came from the army, which could have some political implications, General García thought. Besides, even though all three officers had committed the same criminal offense, they were very different people, with diverse motives and attitudes. One of them was a lieutenant colonel with an outstanding record in Angola, driven into corruption because of intense family problems that required a lot of money to resolve. When he was caught, he declared: "I'd do it again a thousand times if faced with the same circumstances."

Since all three officers had accepted the charges, García was making sure the prosecutors would go easy on them in the trial, avoiding the possibility of negative reactions. García was aware that the real cause of the enormous increase in criminality in the country was the fact that no family could live off the purchasing power of a salary, or even two salaries if both husband and wife worked, and that this fact was demoralizing the core of the people who sustained the whole system. Furthermore, he was convinced that the leaders of the Revolution still hadn't realized this.

* * *

At the end of the meal, after coffee had been served, Francisco opened his arms as if in despair and asked García, "What are we going to do about the guy who snatched the *Elvirita?* I'm getting nowhere with Marcelo." Francisco leaned his head back with a solemn expression on his face and said in a low tone, "Is somebody trying to protect this man?"

As often occurred with García when he was asked a direct question, he stalled. His face was expressionless, as it always was when he had information he could not share. "What is the problem?" García asked blandly, as if it was the first time he had heard about the incident.

Actually, on account of his job, Marcelo had given him a full briefing the morning after the hijacking, and he had followed the case until the investigators concluded that the officer had probably died when the yacht sank. Then, a few days back, Marcelo had told him that the *Elvirita* hijacker was at large in the United States, wanted by the FBI and charged with murder. But, as he recalled now, Marcelo had avoided going deeply into the matter and, so far, had failed to send him a written report with the new information.

Colonel Francisco knew that General García was one of the few people in the Ministry of the Interior who had complete knowledge of the identity of the escapee and had to be fully informed about what had happened. Nevertheless, he gave García a brief account of the yacht's hijacking from the Almendares dockyard. Then, playing with his empty coffee cup, he added, "Now I'll explain where we stand. The State Security investigators received a photo of a man wanted by the FBI and the CIA from their sources in Miami. Two of the dockyard workers and the manager identified the man in the photo as the one who stole the yacht."

Colonel Francisco indicated his empty cup to the man serving lunch. The man went to the kitchen and brought back two clean cups and fresh coffee. After a sip, Francisco charged again, "I ask myself, who is this guy? If he is an intelligence officer, what kind of information does he have? What will happen if the FBI catches him? Possibly, I keep thinking, he has a lot of information that, if known by the enemy, could endanger the country's security, or at least the life of other agents and collaborators. Then, I ask myself again, has the Intelligence Service taken the necessary measures to prevent that? Who is responsible for this mess? I can't get any answers to my questions unless the Intelligence Service cooperates, as I already said. All facts indicate that this man is a very important officer who worked close to Marcelo, maybe an old buddy, and possibly because of that very human reason, Marcelo is not handling this case properly."

"What facts are those?" asked General García, very interested this time.

"In the first place, it's well-known that Floro works only on Marcelo's special assignments. Floro went to the house of the manager of the dockyard that night and yanked the man out of bed, telling him he had an order to give this man a yacht. Whose order? It's very clear it could only be Marcelo's. The manager, a former intelligence officer himself, delayed as much as he could, seeking a proper written authorization, until the yacht was snatched. Floro and two of the workers were jailed for questioning. Floro did not stay locked up for long. Somebody brought a copy of his medical discharge from the service, stating that he isn't responsible for his actions when he is under the influence of alcohol, and that he can't stay secluded in close quarters because he goes nuts. After a couple of days in jail, he was released. Who can get a man arrested on serious charges out of jail in a couple of days? Again the answer is obvious.

"As soon as I learned about all of this, I took charge of the case myself. Still, I repeat, the State Security investigators and I were kept in the dark by lack of cooperation from the Intelligence Service. From Marcelo, to be exact."

"Doesn't it occur to you that this could be an operation to put that man where he is now?"

"General, with all due respect, imagining things is not my job. I have to go by facts. Someone belonging to the armed forces of this country stole and lost a yacht valued at several thousand dollars, then ran away to the United States, all of this aided by very powerful people within the Ministry of the Interior. My duty is to prosecute him and clarify the reason why someone helped him do it. We have to have full, complete, absolute information about what is going on. This is not an internal problem of the Intelligence Service that they can handle any way they choose. This could even be a case of high treason."

A long silence followed, filled with the noises of General García's labored breathing. As a youth he had tried boxing and had his nose broken in his first fight. Since then he had breathed mostly through his mouth. Thirty years of heavy smoking had clogged other parts of his respiratory system, so that García emitted all sorts of strange sounds when the air went in and out of him.

"If you have to get to the bottom of this, do whatever you have to do. That is your duty, isn't it?" García replied.

"That is the order I need, General García."

The colonel smiled, deciding that he would reopen the case immediately and slap Floro and the manager of the dockyard back in jail, charged with being accessories to the theft. *Let's see if Marcelo is willing to surrender his information when Floro goes nuts inside the tank,* Francisco thought. The image of Floro going mad amused him deeply.

ENDING HIS INTERVIEW with the famous Dr. Nicolas Aranguren-Beitía, a Nicaraguan lawyer and poet who had fought alongside Sandino, Barter plugged his modem into an outlet in his host's library. From his laptop he dialed a phone number to his family home in Utah, connecting to his main computer to collect his email. Among many brief letters in plain language there was a coded message from a server in Holland. The connection with his computer lasted less than two minutes. Barter couldn't wait to read what he had received from Martha. Perhaps her message contained information concerning King's accident.

"Don Nicolas, *me permite leer un mensaje de mi madre?*"

The eighty-two-year-old man nodded. "*No hay ningún apuro,*" he said, and continued to sway back and forth in a rocking chair, thinking that the generous five-hundred-dollar fee could cover the call and the reading of many letters.

Barter decoded the message in his laptop and began to read.

> *Querido Mio (is my Spanish right?): I found just what you are looking for. It is a letter Austin sent to headquarters when King had the "accident" that crippled him. I hope it gives you all the clues you need.*

Love, love, love,
M.

La Finca, Honduras, September 8, 1985
To: R.R. Lindsay, D.D.O. CIA, Langley, VA
From: Austin C. Cabot

Dear Bob:

I have a few hours free to give you a preliminary account of the unfortunate events that have taken place in the past two days on this side of hell. I arrived in Tegucigalpa the day before yesterday at noon. (It seems ages ago now.) Pereda and Steve, the field officer in Honduras, were waiting for me.

The weather was too lousy to take a chopper to La Finca, so we spent the night in Tegucigalpa. At 10:30, after a downpour that lasted all morning, we took a jeep. The Honduran army provided another jeep and a truck with soldiers to guard us on the long ten-hour trip to La Finca—a courtesy for which they are being very well paid, I assure you.

I really wanted to get the feeling of the field conditions, because this is the first time I've been over here in the middle of the rainy season everybody talks about. It reminded me of the days on the Mekong Delta. We arrived at La Finca at 20:15. Colonel Dominguez, the head of the Nicaraguan Contras' camp, and a group of his officers were waiting for us with a big meal: roast pork, wine, the works. King wasn't there. I asked Dominguez why. He didn't answer my question but started attacking T.S. and acting as if he were outraged by the accusations T.S. has made against him and his men. The other guys started meddling in Spanish. I told Dominguez to cut the crap—the only thing I'd come to do was to see about King's accusations against them. I hadn't travelled that far to hear complaints about our man that hadn't even been funneled through proper channels. Furthermore, I didn't want to hear

King's name in their mouths, period, and I wasn't in the mood for a big reception meal. All I wanted was a hot shower.

We went to the quarters prepared for us in the main house of La Finca, where the owner of the estate used to live. It's a huge, two-story house. On the first floor there's a big dining room, a kitchen to match, and some of the household servants' quarters. The upper floor was where the owner and his family had lived. We took the three bedrooms in a wing facing north. King's room was in the southern wing. His two bodyguards and a Nicaraguan, who is half–personal aide, half–special cook (King doesn't eat the food cooked downstairs) use the rooms next to his.

The house is at the top of a small hill five hundred feet away from the barracks and about half a mile from the river dividing Honduras and Nicaragua. A double fence encloses the whole compound, protecting the camp and the house. A security force of fifty men with dogs, electronic gadgets, and full communication with all the other camps surrounding the area are supposed to offer full protection to the place. Since La Finca is located in Honduran territory, the camp is thought to be a very safe place (as you know, the Sandinista army has never set foot on Honduran soil to avoid an international incident).

Steve and Pereda went after King, who was supposed to be in a village by the road we had come along, at the river crossing to Nicaragua. Steve came back an hour later and gave me a detailed account of everything King said and did when they had found him in one of the town's whorehouses, already with a few drinks too many. King was surprised to see Steve and Pereda and wasn't pleased by the fact that they wanted to fetch him to come to see me. King said nobody had mentioned the visit before; he was having some of the fun he deserved after six months in that rat hole, working his ass off for nothing. "If this is the same Austin Cabot I worked with in Saigon, I'm going to save a seat and the best whore in town for him," he said, holding onto a brunette with his left arm and lifting a chair with his right. "If it's not the same Austin Cabot, tell that man, with due respect, that I'll see him in the morning. I am now enjoying my time off."

Steve drove me to town to see King. Two years ago, when I came to check over La Finca and close the deal with the owner, there had only been a country store and about ten huts on the road near the river crossing. Now the whole riverbank and both sides of the road for over a mile is a town full of huts thrown up by Nicaraguans fleeing from the war zone. There are dozens of whorehouses and bars swarming with all sorts of people, lured by the dollars we're pouring in here. It's a scene that reminded me again of my Saigon days.

"About time one of the big boys showed up," T.S. said as he greeted me.

Pereda pulled the girls to another table, spooked off some of Dominguez's men who were sitting around, and soon T.S. and I were able to occupy a table in a corner with nobody eavesdropping. (This Cuban, Pereda, can make himself useful wherever he is. He knows exactly when and where to take over. He knows when and where to keep away from the places he shouldn't be and the conversations he shouldn't hear. While he was with the girls, he gathered a lot of the information we needed later to put things in place.)

T.S. went on for a good half hour, listing his complaints about Dominguez and his staff. The thing that really rankled him was Dominguez's use of the land mines he had given them. T.S. said his instructions had been quite specific. The mines were to be used only in conjunction with war operations against the Sandinista army. They were never to be planted in roads used mainly by civilians. But it had all worked out just the other way around. He said Dominguez and his whole lot don't have the guts to put up a regular fight against the Sandinistas, because they don't want to risk their hides. The only thing *they've done so far, he said, is to mine the roads, so every now and then a bus or a truck blows up, causing heavy civilian casualties.*

At first, I tried to lessen the importance of those events, but T.S. tried even harder to convince me of how serious it was. Finally, he pulled out a copy of a newspaper with the photo of a bus hit by a mine that caused twenty-six casualties, including six deaths. In the center of the article was a photo of two small kids, a boy and a girl, all torn apart. King started to weep as soon as he saw the picture. It was a painful sight. Of course, he had been drinking heavily and he was under stress from the whole situation he was in.

I told King he was wrong to take personal blame. Dominguez was the one who should look at that picture. He, King, had nothing to do with it. With that sort of reasoning, I was able to calm him down a little. I decided to bring the girls to the table, freshen up the drinks, and invite some Spanish guitar players and a very fat woman dancer to join us, the most bizarre scene I ever saw. By the time we got out of the place, at one o'clock in the morning, T.S. was in the same high spirits we've always known. We both decided to take a rain check with the girls for the following night, since we had a lot of work to do the next day and I was very tired. Steve and Pereda thought otherwise and took a couple of girls back to La Finca with them.

A loud explosion woke me up just after seven the next morning. I thought immediately that the place was under a mortar attack coming from the woods on the other side of the river. I took cover as best I could in the room and waited, but there were no more explosions. I went out to see what had happened and saw King being carried downstairs, bleeding like a slaughtered bull, his left leg all torn up. I took charge and managed to stop him from bleeding to death. I sent for the doctor at the camp's hospital and ordered a chopper to be readied. After

*the doctor did a fair mending job, I sent King with Steve and
the doctor to our best hospital in Panama, the closest place he
could get decent medical attention.*

*Then, I set myself to find out what had happened. It didn't
take an expert in explosives to see that someone had placed a
mine under King's bed, with a timer or some other device to
detonate it. I ordered them to seal all the rooms in that southern
wing and asked for some specialists to be brought from Langley
to find out what had really happened. While I was thus occupied, Pereda started questioning everybody in the house and
ordered the arrest and isolation of King's bodyguards and all the
men guarding the compound that night. He also questioned
everyone working in the household, one by one.*

*Dominguez seemed to be at a loss about what had hap-
pened, and it was clear he was very much concerned and scared,
because I was there when it happened. He had the good sense
to let Pereda handle the whole inquiry.*

*By noon that day, we had some leads—one of the guards
and the house cook were missing. The cook had come into the
house past midnight with a tall whore, and stayed for about two
hours, supposedly in his room. The pair left together about two
o'clock in the morning. Both of the outer gates of the compound
should have remained locked after ten at night, except to admit
the top officers, but for quite some time that order hadn't been
applied on Saturday nights. The cook and the whore had
entered the compound and left again by a small gate near the
house, used only by house personnel and by some of the higher
officers who don't want to be seen at the main entrance near the
barracks. So, the coming and going through that gate, we
found, was almost unhindered for the people who work at the
house and for higher officers.*

*The missing guard, we learned, had been on duty with
another guard, a very young boy, when the cook and the tall
whore entered the gate. This young boy gave that information*

and described the woman. He was taken to see all the whores in town, close to a hundred, only five of whom could be called tall, but none fit the description he had given and he didn't recognize any of them as the one who had come into the house the night before. From the very beginning, Pereda thought the "whore" was really a man, the one who put the mine under King's bed. Pereda also said the intention was probably only to scare King, not to kill him. Maybe to warn us to keep the war fair, because they could also get nasty. Pereda personally showed me a mark on my door that had not been there the day before. Maybe just a way to warn that they could also have reached me.

A search party with dogs was sent out after the cook's scent. At mid-afternoon, the dogs became very excited and picked up and followed a trail that went along the river for about five miles up to another river crossing. When the party went down the riverbank, they fell into a mined area. Two dogs were maimed and had to be killed. One of the guards was wounded. Late in the afternoon, another party started the search again on the Nicaraguan side, but they advanced very slowly, fearing they would also fall into mined terrain.

That night some "specialists" that Pereda had recommended arrived at La Finca. King's aide and one of the bodyguards were very badly tortured. They confessed they had surrendered a lot of information about King's activities to Dominguez's men and to the cook. Pereda had learned from the girls, the night we came in, that Dominguez, half-drunk, had said on several occasions, "If King keeps on trying to fuck with me, I'll show that stupid American who's boss here."

Nevertheless, Dominguez's men did not stay idle. They went after the missing guard in his hometown, in northern Nicaragua, and brought the man back. He was turned over to Pereda's men to show they didn't have anything to do with the bomb planted under King's bed. As a final outcome of the

*inquiries, Pereda told me that there was no doubt the "whore"
who had made the hit was a very well-trained man that came
from Nicaragua. Pereda followed the dogs' tracks for about ten
miles. He came back and told me the hit against King had been
prepared and carried out by a Cuban intelligence officer. A
reception party had been waiting on the Nicaraguan side. The
whole operation had been extremely well-covered. Later, we
had news that Roberto, a special Cuban intelligence advisor to
the Sandinistas, had dropped out of sight for over two weeks
and got back to the place where he usually works the day after
King was injured.*

*Anyway, I think Dominguez is responsible in many ways
for what happened. We have to reassert the company's authority
here. If you have nothing against it, I will order Pereda to proceed in a couple of weeks when things have calmed down.*

See you this coming week,
A.C. Cabot

MARCELO CALLED a server in Denmark through his laptop. The computer-to-computer connection went on immediately. Once in the server, he called another server in Mexico and opened an email box, sending a coded message and receiving several. He had been expecting a message from Carlos Manuel since his release from Krome Detention Center several days before.

Two weeks after Carlos Manuel had entered Krome, a Cuban intelligence agent who worked undercover in the center had spotted him. Through a religious organization, it had been possible to get a job for him in a bakery and thus arrange his release from the camp. With no knowledge of this, Carlos Manuel had swapped jobs with another Krome inmate and ended up in northern Florida.

An agent from Tampa was sent with his family for an unexpected vacation at a motel in Sarasota to check if Carlos Manuel was under surveillance. This change of location seemed suspicious, and it was important to clear that up before attempting any contact with him. At the same time, everything had been arranged to get him out of the U.S. on a ship flying the Liberian flag but with a Cuban captain and crew, when the ship unloaded fish from Thailand in San Francisco. But Carlos Manuel had disappeared suddenly. A week had passed since then and there was not a clue about what was happening.

In the last few days, two messages from Miami and one from Tampa had given details of a CIA inquiry among Cuban ex-military personnel showing photos of Carlos Manuel and searching for any information about his identity and whereabouts. The CIA station in Havana had also received the same query. Marcelo was concerned about Carlos Manuel's silence. It could be a sign that he had been caught already and that the CIA's search for him was a trick to deceive Cuban intelligence. That would point to a leak in the Cuban intelligence organization in Florida that the CIA was trying to cover up. Marcelo cursed himself for not following his first impulse to leave Carlos Manuel alone. But it could also be that he was on the run and had had no chance to send any messages yet without taking undue risks.

With a gloomy face and dark thoughts, Marcelo finished his call, closed his laptop, and placed it carefully in its case. He turned over a pile of documents awaiting review and started scribbling short notes on a memo pad. An hour later, when Marcelo was almost finished with the paperwork, he spotted Luis, one of the main officers of his staff, standing in the open door of his office. Marcelo signaled him to come inside, knowing that Luis would interrupt him only for an urgent reason. A tall, dark, and strong mulatto in his forties, with an ugly scar on his face that gave him a fierce, difficult-to-forget tribal look, Luis spoke as he walked in.

"Bad news, chief. Floro was jailed this morning."

"What did he do this time?"

"He's been charged as accessory on the *Elvirita* hijacking, obstructing justice . . . the works. I guess Colonel Francisco was pissed off because we've denied him all sorts of information. I believe that he's already got news that our man is alive in the U.S. He wants us to come tamely to our knees and give him everything he wants."

Marcelo stayed silent for a moment. He scribbled something on the pad and, without looking up, said: "He wouldn't go fishing that deep unless he had his ass very well covered. He ought to know that Floro was doing something I told him to do. Francisco is after my head. Now he has the opportunity to put on a big show. He's the executioner of a death sentence someone has dictated."

"That's possible," Luis admitted.

"The only people who might profit from this case and have enough clout for that are General Pablo or General García. I don't believe García has anything against us, but the head of State Security would surely like to get rid of me and a few of you."

Marcelo's secretary came in with two cups. Luis's eyes smiled at the coffee. After finishing his cup, Luis lit a cigarette.

"Did you know I've cut down to five cigarettes a day and I'm only smoking them halfway?"

Marcelo lifted his eyebrows, as if to say he had heard that story before.

"I want you to make sure Floro has everything he needs. Tell him to stay calm. I'll give him the order when to go nuts."

Luis nodded and went away.

Marcelo canceled his appointments for the rest of the morning and personally called Octavio, one of the senior officers of the staff, for an urgent meeting to go over Carlos Manuel's case. While Marcelo waited for Octavio, he began walking around the room, reasoning out the news he'd just received.

As he had so often before, he spared a moment to contemplate how much he hated being locked up in an office with no windows inside of what used to be an apartment building. It had improved a lot after he changed some lights and, following his secretary's advice, placed four nice pictures of open landscapes on the walls. Still, being shut inside four walls for many hours every day was unpleasant. This last thought made him think of Floro, just as Octavio entered the room.

Octavio was a man in his sixties whose very white complexion, black-rimmed glasses, and white beard always reminded Marcelo of the Russian scholars who had occasionally given him lectures when he was a student. Octavio opened a thick file and explained briefly what had been decided and accomplished thus far, then made a final appraisal of the situation.

"All possible immediate damage to the mission Carlos Manual was handling in Africa and the Middle East was identified and the necessary measures implemented within a week after he left Cuba on this dreadful trip. Actually, since my section had been working for a long time on the assumption that he was going to be pulled out and given an open job sooner or later, the new measures needed were few and minor."

Octavio took a sip of the cup of hot tea Marcelo's secretary had specially prepared for him. Very emphatically, as if he had gained vigor with the beverage, he added, "That is not the case with the damage that his possible defection to the enemy may cause the Service as a whole. That would be close to a catastrophe in some of the areas of major concern. He has maximum detailed information on many of our past major operations in Africa and Central America. He knows most of our agents in those areas much better than we do. Worst of all, a lot of the local people who worked with him are still on their jobs. Some big decisions have to be taken on this matter . . . *soon*."

Marcelo stood silent for a moment. Then he spoke softly, as he usually did when he wanted to emphasize an order. "Let's prepare a memo to the minister immediately, not more than two pages. I'll see the old man at home tonight and ask him to sign it so it will be on the minister's desk tomorrow morning. Be prepared for a meeting on this."

Marcelo knew he should have taken this first defensive move long ago. He'd been delaying it for several evolving reasons. In the beginning, the first conclusion was that Carlos Manuel had died when the yacht sank. Later, when he was spotted in Krome, Marcelo didn't want to do anything that might warn the CIA, because there was always the chance of information leakage. Once Carlos Manuel was out of Krome, he had delayed any action because he had arranged his quick and safe return home again and thought it best to keep quiet.

"Carlos Manuel's trip was a hell of a big mistake," Octavio grunted.

"Yes, it was my big mistake. But sometimes big or little mistakes are the only possible solutions to certain problems."

"Making decisions is what bosses are for," Octavio said with soft sarcasm, unconvinced.

Octavio, a living institution in the Service, allowed himself to criticize Marcelo, and even higher officers as well. Marcelo and most of the top chiefs in the Service thought Octavio was a real pain in the ass. He was almost infallible in his judgement, which was founded not only on solid grounds but on a lot of experience acquired while working himself to the top echelon from the very bottom of the ladder. Octavio also spent a lot of his time updating his overall information and learning as much as he could about technical developments in the field. Octavio was implacable in pointing out mistakes, no matter who'd made them.

Now, since Cuba could no longer count on the help of the socialist bloc's intelligence, the few people like Octavio who combined vast experience, sound judgment, and current knowledge had become very important assets. Marcelo often disagreed with the points of view of these old-timers. Maybe it was a matter of age. Probably within twenty years he would be in Octavio's situation.

"What would you do in this case?"

Octavio started to speak, then stopped and shrugged, as if to say there was no use relating what he had in mind.

"Go ahead, tell me what you really think," Marcelo challenged.

"The most important task the Service has today is to make sure *by any means* that Carlos Manuel doesn't fall into the hands of the enemy," Octavio said, and then repeated his words emphatically.

* * *

Marcelo started to pace his office again after Octavio left. A question continued to plague him: *How had the CIA and the FBI known the importance of Carlos Manuel from the beginning?* Almost immediately after he left Cuba, they had started trying to track down his identity. Now an unprecedented search for him was underway in the U.S., with a fat reward attached. Carlos Manuel's identity was one of the best-kept secrets in the Service. Each of the men in the central office who had handled his work from one mission to another thought he was a different person. Even Octavio had been astonished when Marcelo handed him a big pile of files to make an appraisal of the situation that would be confronted in the event Carlos Manuel's identity was uncovered by the CIA.

THE TIRELESS RINGING of his phone interrupted King while he was shaving. The irritation clear in his tone when he answered the call was quickly dispelled by the eagerness in Barter's voice. He was calling from Dulles International Airport, having just arrived from Managua. He explained that he had confirmed the identity of the man he had been chasing, but preferred to give King a short briefing on his findings before he wrote a final report on the case. There were, however, some sensitive issues that had come up, and, for reasons he'd explain personally, he wanted to talk with him outside CIA headquarters. Somewhat intrigued, King made a seldom-heard offer to a subordinate. He invited Barter to come to his home directly from the airport and join him for breakfast.

"I brought back the most astonishing news," Barter said, as he and King were still shaking hands.

King simply nodded and led the way into the dining room. He walked slowly, the best way to hide his lameness, which he despised. He found himself displeased with Barter. He didn't like the smell of the man. Something stale emanated from his body and especially from his hair. It was as if he hadn't bathed since he last saw him.

"Young man, at my age, and with all I've been through, nothing astonishes me anymore," he began.

Barter smiled at King's retreating back. As they walked, he uttered a few compliments about the garden and the large oak tree in the backyard, a splendid landmark to locate the house in a neighborhood of houses and streets very much alike. Breakfast was already served on a sideboard in the dining room. A heavy, middle-aged woman could be glimpsed now and then working in the kitchen.

"Make yourself at home. Help yourself to breakfast while you tell me this extraordinary news." King spoke the words with a slight sarcastic intonation as he used both hands to lower himself slowly into a chair. Every so often, King replaced his mechanical leg with a better and smarter one, so his lameness was hardly noticeable when he moved slowly. To match his personality to his handicap, he had become an outwardly calmer man after he lost his leg. Only on rare occasions did he revert to his old self, letting out the reins, allowing his passionately held ideas to be spiced with the bitterness and loneliness that had filled most of his life. He lived by himself in a house full of iron bars, bulletproof doors, and electronic security gadgets, all the result of his "accident."

Getting ready to eat now seemed to require all of Barter's attention. The younger officer, who had been so anxious to communicate his news, appeared completely distracted by the food before him. He prepared his coffee carefully with cream and sugar. He buttered his toast as if he were plastering a wall. He was about to start eating his ham and eggs when he seemed to remember something and stopped. He took a sip of his coffee, then whispered, "The man is Roberto."

King froze. He remained motionless except for his left hand, which held a spoon halfway toward fetching some sugar. The spoon started to shake.

"Are you sure?"

"Dead positive. I had that hunch for quite some time, after talking with a few Cubans in Miami, but I confirmed it last night in Managua."

A silence followed. Barter studied King's reaction. He saw how King went back into his shell, put sugar in his coffee, and, in the patronizing way he always used with subordinates, said with a sardonic smile, "Mr. Barter, the U.S. is the last place on earth where Roberto would come, at least as long as I'm alive, and he knows that very well. For years I have been chasing him all over the world. I've managed to uncover him twice, but the devil escaped both times, only to pop up somewhere else under another mask. I am on his track in Africa now. It has to be him. And you come to tell me he is, at the same time, in the United States?"

"I'm convinced the man we're after is Roberto. I have no doubt."

"Mr. Barter, that doesn't make any sense. Why would he come here in the first place, and especially on a yacht that capsized in the middle of a storm? You don't know this man, and how resourceful he is. You must be confused, Mr. Barter. As you know, Roberto is a very common name in Cuba and all over Latin America, just like Robert is in English-speaking countries. There are many Robertos in the Latin world, but only one *Roberto*. Do you get the difference?"

"Well, sir, I am sure this is *Roberto*."

King took a long look at the man in front of him. He was beginning to grudgingly admire him again. In spite of his nauseating odor, he was persistent. He would not let go. That was the quality that separated men into two completely different groups—the winners and the losers. Besides that, Barter had been playing a bit with him. He had a feeling in his gut that Barter was pursuing something he had not yet disclosed. What was he after, anyway? Maybe it was wise to keep him at arm's length until he could learn more about this as yet unpolished jewel.

Barter started to talk in a hurry, knowing his time was running out. "As you know, sir, I based myself in Miami to carry out your order to identify this man. All I had on him were the photos and fingerprints taken at Krome Detention Center. I sent them to every place I could think of, always through the proper channels. There wasn't a trace of old information on him in the FBI, our files, or anywhere else. This man seemed to have come from nowhere. I decided to show his photos to Cuban exiles in Miami who had been in the Cuban army or the Ministry of the Interior. I looked up more than fifty of those guys; I thought that if he really was an intelligence officer, someone must have seen him at one time or another. Two of the men I interviewed looked at the photos and thought they'd seen him in Africa in the eighties. But nobody was sure.

"I also sent photos and fingerprints to the CIA station in Havana's U.S. Interest Section and received an encouraging response. The man could be an officer named Colina who did intelligence work in Africa in the eighties. He also might have been in Nicaragua. There was an advisor to the Sandinista army when they were fighting the Contras with the war-name Roberto who fit his description. Havana sent another report, stating that there was a strong possibility this man might be a top Cuban specialist on CIA undercover actions and irregular warfare, who always worked under deep cover, and there was no solid info on him. Then I met one guy who knew key people who would know for sure if this man had been involved in the Nicaraguan war. He was willing to make all the contacts, so I decided to go there to show them photos and question them. It cost some money to get cooperation, but it was worth every penny. Both of the men I spoke to there have no doubts. Our defector is Roberto."

Barter stopped talking and started eating his cold ham and eggs. King had eaten little. At some point in the story he had lit a Cuban cigar, showing he was through with breakfast. He expelled the aromatic smoke away from the table and talked as if he had regained his tranquillity.

"Let me give you some information about the *Roberto* I am talking about. This guy once impersonated a rich Brazilian driver of formula-one race cars and enchanted the daughter of the general-in-chief of the South African army while she was at school in England.

He spent a month with the girl at her parents' home in Cape Town and was able to make a copy of Operation Gazelle that enabled the Cubans to inflict an overwhelming defeat on the South African army at Quito Cuanavale in South Angola. He did that while racing like a madman all over that country in a half-million-dollar Ferrari with the beautiful lady at his side opening all doors for him. The whole thing was so audacious that even the usually efficient South African Secret Service was completely fooled. This blunder cost General Westbrook-Malan his career and his life. He blew his brains out a month after he was demoted. The South Africans finally stumbled onto what had happened when the Ferrari was sold and the romantic racecar driver that Westbrook-Malan had taken into his home disappeared, leaving all his valuables behind in his apartment. He simply went out for his usual morning run and never came back, as though he had vanished into thin air. And he did it right under the nose of the South African Intelligence Service."

King rose from his seat with evident effort and started to walk slowly around the table to where Barter sat, still eating. "Mr. Barter, you have the makings of a good intelligence officer. Beware when some of the pieces of a puzzle seem to fall into place too easily. Making your story believable will require proof, hard undeniable proof, not just the blah-blah-blah of people you have paid generously."

"There is proof, sir." Barter reached into a pocket and withdrew an envelope.

King placed his cigar in an ashtray to have both hands free. He took off his glasses to see the photos, and Barter realized King was nearsighted. The first photo showed a group of military men in camouflage uniforms, gathered on the patio of a country house. Nearby were two jeeps, also camouflaged. It was a typical scene in the endless Nicaraguan war of Sandinistas against Contras. King knew the scenery all too well. The photo had been taken from a high place, perhaps from the window of an adjacent house. The next photo was an enlargement of the head of a man very well-known to King—Tomas Borges, head of the Nicaraguan Ministry of the Interior, a legendary communist leader. The following enlargement showed the man talking to Borges. King knew this guy also, Colonel Marcelo, maybe a general by now, a rising star in the Cuban Intelligence Service. The last photo was an enlargement of the figure standing next to one of the jeeps. It was the same man who called himself Ramiro Ramos.

This was the first time King had seen that revealing picture, undoubtedly coming from a top-level source. While he was stationed in Nicaragua, he had never been able to unveil either of the two Cubans. He knew, felt, and often dreaded their existence, but they were never more than shadows in the dark.

"Sir, these are two very special Cuban intelligence agents. This man," Barter pointed to Ramiro Ramos, "was the guy who put a personal mine under your bed. When he did that, his war-name was Roberto. Isn't this the *Roberto* you're talking about?"

"How do you know about all of that?"

"You ordered me to find out the identity of this man, sir. All those things came up in the inquiry. That is why I came to see you before I made my report. How do you want to handle this piece of information, sir?"

King took a long breath and seemed to collapse into a chair.

The younger officer hid a smile as he took a big bite of ham dipped in egg yolk, swallowed it in a gulp, and chased it with coffee.

King stayed silent for some time as if he was thinking very carefully about what he was going to say. His face looked withered, and at the same time, his expression had become harsh and absent.

"I'm going to put in a request for your promotion this week. You've got yourself another job, Mr. Barter. The FBI has not been able to get one clue on the whereabouts of this man, let alone identify him. Go and find this man. This time we'll have a direct line between us—you'll work under my direct orders. I'll back you up with everything I've got. Now, listen carefully. I'll say it just once: *If you get Roberto alive and deliver him to me, I personally guarantee your career in the company.*"

MICHAEL, SITTING ON the edge of a chair and sobbing deeply with his head buried in his hands, suddenly muttered, as if talking to himself, "I have to kill that son of a bitch."

"Don't say that again, Michael. Promise me!" Janice, covered only with a sheet stained with spots of her fresh blood, began to move slowly toward her son. "Promise me, Michael!" she pleaded again, as she continued moving painfully, trying to reach him. Michael stood up when she got near him and walked out of the room, slamming the door behind him.

Janice dropped back onto the bed in a state of confusion such as she had never known. One idea pushed itself to the forefront of her mind. For the first time, she admitted to herself that she was in a situation she couldn't handle anymore. It was as if she had fallen into a deep pit, and the more she struggled to get out, the deeper she sank. Worst of all, she was dragging Michael down with her.

Janice heard the front door slam downstairs as Michael went out. She managed to get up and walk naked to the bathroom, avoiding the patches of her own vomit. After standing under a hot shower for a long while, trying to wash all the mess from her body, she felt extremely tired. The bathroom was hot and full of steam. As she moved step by step to fetch her robe from the bathroom door, she saw her image reflected in the mist-covered mirror. She stopped and faced it.

She was horrified by her reflection. The droplets had turned into layered drops that, running down the surface of the glass, distorted the expression on her face, with its swollen red-bluish eye. It looked to her like the image of death. She felt weaker and weaker. As she fainted, her reflection transformed through her eyes into the pale and tortured face of Michael. A terrible premonition flashed through her mind before she lost consciousness.

When she came out of her faint, her mind was clear: *She had to kill the son of a bitch, before her son did.*

He abandoned U.S. highway 89 at the intersection with Williston Road, took a left turn toward Burlington, drove for a mile until he reached the University of Vermont, made a right turn at South Williams Street, and rode around campus for a while. "This is it," he said to himself. He checked his wristwatch. It was ten-thirty in the morning, September 20, a Tuesday.

He stopped at a newsstand close to the university health center and bought a map of Burlington. After studying the map, he left campus and turned west onto a street named Buell, surveying the houses as he passed by, searching for a room-for-rent sign. At the intersection with North Union Street, he spotted the sign he was looking for. He slowed down, taking a close look at the house and its backyard. Then he drove around the neighborhood for almost half an hour, spotting several other houses that rented rooms. He decided to go back to the first place.

He rang twice before a boy of about thirteen came to open the door. The kid had blond hair and vivid, inquiring brown eyes set in a round face with cheeks full of pimples. He smiled at the boy. "Son, my name is John Wilkinson and I'm looking for a room to rent. I'll be doing some research at the university library for a few weeks and this place looks convenient for me."

"Four hundred dollars a month," the boy said.

The man nodded. "May I see it?"

The boy assented, leading the way to a room upstairs.

"Is breakfast included?" the man asked, after a thorough inspection of the room and a bathroom across the hall.

"No, but you're allowed to use the kitchen. You can fix your own breakfast and keep anything you need in the fridge. You have to eat the rest of your meals out. No cooking allowed in the room." The boy gave this information in a brisk, businesslike manner.

"May I leave my car parked in the backyard? I had an accident recently and the doctor told me I have to walk as much as possible to regain the full use of my right leg. If I have the car handy, I'll never walk a block."

"Yeah, I guess so," the boy said, smiling slightly.

The man took a last glance at the room and decided to take it.

"A month in advance," the boy said dryly.

The man reached for his wallet, but seemed hesitant to turn over the money.

"I'll give you a receipt signed by my mother. She's sick in bed. That's why I'm handling this," the boy said, reading his mind.

The man gave the boy four one-hundred-dollar bills. The boy went back down the corridor they had passed through and entered the room nearest the stairs, staying inside for quite a long while. When he came back, he handed the man a receipt written in a woman's neat handwriting that ended with a fancy signature: Janice J. Howard.

"What's your name, son?"

"Michael."

The man extended his hand to shake Michael's, sealing the deal.

"Could you help me bring my luggage upstairs, Michael? I can't put much weight on this leg." The man rubbed a hand on his right knee.

"Sure," the boy answered eagerly.

After they carried the bags to the newly rented room, the tenant let Michael park his car in the backyard beside a sailboat about twenty feet long, resting on a trailer. Then he helped take a piece of tarpaulin out of the trunk of the car and cover the automobile with it.

"Nice boat. Is it yours?"

Michael groaned. "It was given to me, but I don't want it."

The tenant was going to ask why but changed his mind. Instead, he decided to make friends with the boy. "Michael, after all this work, we've earned a good lunch. Let's take a walk downtown to eat anywhere you choose. Maybe you can show me your town."

After lunch, they strolled around downtown Burlington, finally settling down on one of the benches in Battery Park overlooking Lake Champlain, where they continued to talk until sunset. It was close to seven when they got back to the house. Michael insisted on making sandwiches and milkshakes. Seated at the table, side by side, they felt like old pals.

"How sick is your mother, Michael?"

"Nothing serious; I guess she'll be around in a week or so . . . I don't know."

By a subtle change in the boy's demeanor when he mentioned his mother, the man sensed that something was wrong.

"It's been a long day for me, Michael. I guess I'm going to hit the hay." The tenant climbed the stairs and glanced casually at the door of Michael's mother's room as he passed.

Carlos Manuel felt that he had found the ideal place to hide for the time being. A couple of weeks would hopefully be enough time to obtain the new identity he needed. When he was ready, he would ask Marcelo to send one of his old passports to a convenient place in Montreal, Canada, which was just a couple of hours drive from Burlington. In the meantime, he was going to fulfill an old dream: He would try to paint the ravishing landscapes around Lake Champlain.

WILLIAM BARTER WORKED for a couple of days with the FBI officer in charge of the search for the man who called himself Ramiro Ramos, becoming convinced that the enormous resources of that institution were being used to their fullest extent in the case. The only thing he had been able to contribute was getting Ramiro moved onto the list of the top ten most-wanted criminals—with a $100,000 reward for any information leading to his capture instead of the usual $25,000. Barter did not reveal the CIA findings about the fugitive and his exploits as an intelligence officer in Nicaragua, confirming to the FBI only that their quarry was a very dangerous man.

Barter sensed that Miami, with a Cuban community of close to a million people, was the key location for his search. He based his operation in a rented house in Miami Beach and began to use the collaboration of Alejandro Alcazar and two other Cuban ex-intelligence officers he had met at the beginning of his inquiries. Soon, photos of Ramiro Ramos and word of the fat reward for any information that might help to reveal the true identity and whereabouts of the fugitive were spread over the city. Barter was sure that at one time or another someone among the Cubans must have known this elusive man.

* * *

Barter went to the Krome Detention Center to talk to the officers in charge of screening the immigrants and to go over Ramiro Ramos's records. "Very quiet, sweet, docile, and hardworking" were some of the remarks on his file, written in a neat, female hand. None of the officers really remembered him, even though all gave the standard reply that they remembered him vaguely. During the time he was there, they had processed thousands like him and there was really nothing special to remember him by.

While visiting Krome, Barter learned about the normal procedure for processing Cuban immigrants. First, an interview served to check the applications filled out by each one. During the interview, the officers would ask questions about several key issues—if they had a criminal record or had belonged to the Communist Party in Cuba, for example. Each application was checked against records kept in the computers. This step seldom brought up anything, except in some cases in which the applicants had travelled to, or stayed in, the U.S. previously. Other interviews were necessary only if something didn't check out properly. If the immigrants had relatives, or anybody willing to assume all economic responsibility, expressed by filing an affidavit of support on their behalf, the procedure to release them was very simple. Otherwise, jobs or some economic support for the newcomers had to be found before they were let out. Churches and charity organizations shouldered most of that responsibility.

Ramiro had stayed at the Krome Detention Center for almost three weeks because nobody claimed him and, at the time he entered, it had become difficult to find jobs for people in his situation. Barter composed a list of the immigrants who had stayed for over a week in the same section while Ramiro was there. From the list, he located six men who remembered him quite well. For all of them, Ramiro was a *guajiro*, a peasant, from the eastern provinces of Cuba. None had the slightest doubt about that. All were astonished to learn he was a high officer of the Cuban Intelligence Service.

* * *

Almost every day, King had long telephone conversations with Barter, usually at night, when the head of the Cuba desk was already at home and had little else to do. To support Barter's work, King was activating all the Florida organizations that usually collaborated with the CIA directly or indirectly on Cuban issues. King gave Barter full information on those organizations and their leaders, with advice on how to deal with each one in particular, as well as with the Cubans in general, "a difficult subject in which I have already acquired the equivalent of a Ph.D. from Harvard," King had once said to Barter, with a mixture of sarcasm and sorrow. Barter taped all his conversations with King and later went over them to make sure he didn't miss anything his boss ordered, suggested, recommended, or hinted.

Barter was determined to get results this time, to make full use of his capabilities, hampered until then by laziness, lack of interest in the jobs he had held, and this hellish inner need indulged since childhood to challenge all forms of authority through mockery. For a long time, he was haunted by the idea that he could have been a great actor if he hadn't been so inclined to read spy novels. Close to the dreaded watershed of his forties, he felt he had accomplished next to nothing in life, in spite of the fact that he had seemed to everybody so likely to succeed in whatever he chose to do. After two marriages, no children, and more than a decade in the CIA, he was still considered a rookie in a trade where others had made history by his age. Those were days of an ancient era, and times have changed, he used to say to cheer himself up. He had chosen a career that had dried up since the Soviet Union and its Socialist Empire had imploded and withered away. His philosophical conclusion was that he lived now in a world dominated by elderly people like King, marked by a confrontation with a rival that no longer existed. This line of thinking, he knew, was aimed at salvaging something of his self-esteem and making it possible to accept his evident half-failure in life.

During the daytime, Barter spent hours meeting with people recruited by King or by his own work among Cuban ex-military men. Soon, Barter realized that King's and most of the CIA's connections were with the "historic" sector of the Cuban community in Miami, the one that had come to Miami between 1959 and the middle of the sixties and had been actively involved since that time in the struggle to overthrow Castro and his communist regime. The first to arrive had been the ones deeply involved with the Batista government at the time of its downfall in 1959, followed soon after by rich and middle-class people fleeing from the radical economic and political changes introduced after 1959. But an enormous number of bitter and discontented people had remained stranded in Cuba, waiting for U.S. visas. The response of the Cuban government had been to let anyone with a boat in the U.S. come to pick up family members from Camariocas, a tiny coastal town near Varadero Beach, ninety miles east of Havana. This first boat fleet launched the final chapter in the changeover from capitalism to a militant communist government. The Cubans who landed in Miami up to that time were a fairly homogeneous group that formed the hard core of the exile community.

After more than a third of a century, the Cuban community had changed noticeably. The majority was now made up of younger people who had been brought to Florida as children or had been born in the U.S. to Cuban parents. In addition, a large mass of immigrants had arrived, mainly for economic reasons, in migratory waves and day-by-day trickles. The largest exodus took place in 1980, after the Peruvian embassy in Havana was taken over by a mob wanting to get out of Cuba. The incident triggered a new and enlarged edition of the Camariocas episode. This time, the Cuban government allowed free departure from Mariel, a port town twenty miles west of Havana, on boats arriving from the U.S. Many of the boats that had come to fetch relatives were actually filled up with common delinquents, as Castro responded with grim humor to Jimmy Carter's offer of "open arms for Cuban exiles" by emptying

Cuban jails. Finally, the last migratory wave, in that summer, 1994, was composed mainly of rafters, leaving Cuba not from a single place but from many points on the island, aboard whatever floatable material they could get hold of, fleeing from an economy that had almost totally collapsed after the fall of the socialist bloc.

Among the people who had come in the last twenty years were those who could help him most, Barter thought, men and women who had gone to school with Ramiro Ramos/Roberto, worked alongside him in the Cuban Ministry of the Interior, or played and gone to school with his kids, if he had any.

Barter posted enlarged copies of Ramiro/Roberto's photos taken at Krome all over his rented house. Often, he would stop before one of them, glancing at the man—in his early forties, maybe late thirties, five feet, ten inches tall, one hundred and seventy-five pounds—who was looking intensely into the lens of the camera, as the curious peasant he was impersonating would do. All his features were regular, average, as were his weight, his height, his complexion. Only his eyes, those clear brown eyes feigning amazement before the camera, betrayed him as someone different, unique.

When he coordinated the work with the FBI, Barter asked them to question the two boys and the girl who had been involved in the death of the mulatto and were rescued from aboard the lifeboat. He wanted to make a final check on the incident, still hoping that something new on the yachtsman would come up. The FBI sent an officer of Cuban descent named Gabriel who spoke fluent Spanish to question the youngsters. A day later, the officer met with Barter and gave him a copy of the tape he had recorded in case Barter was in a hurry to know the results of the interview, because he wouldn't have the report on it for three or four days.

"Did you find anything interesting?" Barter asked, trying to avoid spending several hours listening to the tapes if there was nothing of importance.

"I don't think it added anything substantially different from what you've got on the mulatto's death. In the beginning, they all tried to conceal it. I had to get rough with them before they started singing. I read them excerpts from the affidavits you wrote, then I accused them of lying and obstructing justice. They said they left Cuba from a town ten miles east of Havana, from the same pier those other guys did. Like them, they found rough weather as soon as they got a few miles off the coast. They were on a raft on the verge of drowning when they found the half-sunk yacht. After that, they told a story very much the same as the one you already unraveled."

"Anything else?"

Gabriel shrugged, trying to remember.

"Those kids really liked that yachtsman. There was no way they could avoid praising him. The girl almost hit me when I said the man was a cold-blooded murderer."

Barter tucked the tape into the glove compartment of his car and forgot about it until three days later, when the FBI officer came by to deliver the interview transcript personally. Barter was busy at that moment and promised to read it at once and to call him back. As soon as he had a chance, he glanced over the two-page report, noticing that the officer again remarked on the girl's attitude toward the yachtsman. Barter decided to listen to that part of the tape. He ran the recorder forward until he located the part in which the detective was pressing the kids by accusing the man they were defending. Barter slowed the tape down and listened carefully.

"Self-defense, my eye, this man is a cold-blooded murderer!" The voice of the FBI man was full of authority. Up to that point, the youngsters had been very coy and respectful in their answers.

Suddenly the voice of the girl came out louder, speaking very fast in Spanish. "You understand nothing! You haven't paid any attention to what we've told you. You weren't there when all of this happened, and you already have a set opinion on what this man did and who he is. Then I have the right to draw my own conclusion about you, mister. You are a complete idiot! Let me ask a question, since you care so much about this mulatto son of a bitch and the other beasts. What about us? We were going to drown. They kept kicking our fingers every time any of us put a hand on the boat to rest. There was no place we could get a hold on the yacht because the bow was sinking and the rear was lifted. The waves kept throwing us against the hull. How long could we resist? In what other way could he stop them from taking the boat away? He only had a little pistol this big. It was so small it looked like a toy. It didn't even make any noise when he shot it. He had to take them by surprise. Listen. We have thought about it and discussed the matter among ourselves a thousand times. He did the best thing he could do. If it was me who had the gun, there would be no fool making any inquiries here; those five hyenas would be nothing but shark's shit and there would be nobody to tell about it."

Barter decided to call Gabriel to thank him, but couldn't resist kidding him about the rebuke he had received from the girl.

"Oh, I love Miss TNT," the FBI officer admitted, laughing. "She's a true Cuban girl—so passionate, so full of life, so beautiful." He added sorrowfully, "If she weren't so young, I wouldn't mind marrying her, even knowing she'd be capable of killing me one day if she ever suspected I was with another woman."

Out of curiosity and a slight feeling that it might lead somewhere, Barter visited the youngsters in the house they had rented on Eighteenth Street East in Hialeah, introducing himself as a member of a religious charity organization that helped young Cubans arriving in the United States. He made them believe that, in order to aid them better, he had to know their background, education, and abilities. Also, it was important to know about their plans for the future and their dreams in life. Barter liked the three of them from the beginning and repeated the visit. Little by little, he was able to put the story of their lives together. Their mother had committed suicide four months before they left Cuba because she was very ill and knew she would die soon anyway, they told him. They hadn't seen their father for the last three years, and he hadn't been present at their mother's funeral. They had always had little contact with him and they had decided to come to the U.S. since they had no other relatives in Cuba.

They showed Barter photos and other family relics they had been able to bring, sealed in three packages they had taped to each other's backs. Barter noticed there was not a single photo of their father. They seemed uneasy and defensive every time the conversation touched that subject and tried to keep him out of everything. Their story seemed to be a very common one these days: single mother raising three kids, father out of the picture.

Barter didn't know why he kept poking around those kids. The only relation they seemed to have to the man on the yacht was casual. Since he had saved their lives, their admiration for him was understandable. Perhaps the explanation for his interest was a simple one: he liked to watch and talk to Claudia, and he didn't mind the age difference . . . At the same time his trained eye started noticing a few things that needed explanation. They had enough money to get by very well and none of them were working. He decided to make one last investigation into the matter before leaving them alone.

"Now, I have two questions for each of you. What are you doing now, and what would you like to do in the future?"

Antonio explained that he was trying to get a job that enabled him to continue with his studies in some field related to medicine. His ambition was to become a physician. His strategy was to first become an X-ray technician or something like that while working part-time in a hospital. At the same time, he would learn to speak English well and become acquainted with his future career in the U.S. After that, he expected to enter a school of medicine and become a doctor before the age of thirty. Barter thought to himself that the boy was dreaming, but he didn't have the heart to wake him up. He promised Antonio he would try to get him the job he wanted in one of the hospitals in Hialeah. Claudia was already attending high school. Felipe had purchased a whole set of costly painting equipment and materials and was busy creating a series of paintings with Miami backgrounds that Barter considered very good. Nevertheless, when Barter tried to help him with the commercial side, Felipe told him he wasn't in a hurry to sell any yet. He wanted to start his career in the U.S. with a personal exhibition in an art gallery when he had what he considered at least twenty outstanding paintings.

"How long will that take, Felipe?"

"I'm painting fast, two a week, but I like maybe one out of three. It depends. I don't think I'll be ready for another five or six months, maybe a year."

Yet, they were able to afford a six-hundred-dollar-a-month apartment, had bought plenty of good clothing, and were asking his advice on selecting a used car, not too old. Barter was going to ask who was financing all of that, but decided to find that out by himself.

Claudia had followed all his questioning and the answers with interest. She went with Barter to the front door to see him off. When he was about to leave, she said, as if reading his mind, "Mister, you may wonder where we get the money to live. Felipe failed to tell you he's getting one hundred dollars in advance for each painting he finishes from a gallery that keeps them on deposit."

"Oh, well, then he's already selling his work."

"I don't know. I don't know."

"You just said he's getting a hundred dollars for each picture he makes, and he said he's painting two per week."

"As an advance. Also, he's taking the lady owner of the gallery to bed two or three times a week. I think she's paying for that, too."

Barter looked into the clear brown eyes of the girl, who stared at him with a very serious face, as if the remark she had just made was the most natural thing in the world. There was something familiar about those eyes . . . Could they be Ramiro's eyes? He shook his head, concluding that he was going nuts. But he did ask her, "Claudia, whose eyes have you got, your father's or your mother's?"

"My mother's. Why?"

"You're a beautiful and strange creature, Claudia. You surprise me."

A piece of supplementary information Barter received from the FBI revealed that the youngsters had been released two days after their arrival in the U.S. because an affidavit of support had been provided on their behalf, backed up by a fifty-thousand-dollar account in their names in a Miami bank.

Who had deposited that money? Why hadn't the youngsters said anything to him about that source of support? After some thought, Barter decided to intercept the telephone line outside their house. A week later, he would retrieve the recordings and listen to all their calls to see what might have come up.

Barter retrieved the hidden recorder he had placed outside the house of Antonio, Felipe, and Claudia. A woman had called them every day, some days twice. She had long conversations with Claudia about the daily affairs of the youngsters. Using CIA services, he obtained the telephone number where the calls had originated. It belonged to Marjorie Turner, a widow residing in Manhattan. Barter told King his findings and they decided the best move was to conduct a full investigation on this woman through the FBI. Barter called Gabriel, who was now his official liaison with the FBI, and explained his findings without going into detail about how he'd obtained the information.

Gabriel took a deep breath and paused before he spoke. "I already did." There was another moment of silence before Gabriel added, "After I talked with those kids, I wanted to know more about them, and then I hit the jackpot. You'll be amazed."

VERY RAPIDLY, HIS days fell into a routine. He got up at six, and by six-thirty had his and Michael's breakfast ready, making sure that the boy was awake in time to eat and catch his school bus. It took him ten minutes to walk from the house to the university campus. He was one of the first to arrive at the library and worked there until noon each day on a systematic survey of the historical records of the Vermont settlers, trying to follow the tracks of their descendants up to the present day. He also had a keen interest in old and new maps of the area surrounding Burlington up to the border with Canada. The head librarian, Mrs. La Motte, was very helpful. She herself was a descendant of one of Vermont's oldest families and contributed to his research with a lot of first-hand information. She was a widow whose husband had been reported missing in a sailboat wreck off the coast of Maine five years before.

He carried out a good part of his quest using a library computer. Aside from the information from local sources, he had long sessions on the Internet connected to other university libraries and related centers in the northeastern states neighboring Canada, searching for similar information. He also used the Internet to keep in touch with Marcelo through several email accounts. Internet and email had become dream tools, mainly because they involved very little risk of detection.

He usually ate his lunch at the university cafeteria. After lunch, his leisure time started. He strolled back to his room to pick up his art supplies, then hurried to the areas surrounding Lake Champlain, where he spent the rest of the day painting and drawing. Michael soon began to join him after his classes ended, asking all sorts of questions that he would answer while he painted furiously. Sunset was quitting time. When they arrived home, dinner was waiting for both of them, a courtesy from Michael's mother, apparently in payment for the boy's early breakfast. He contributed with food he purchased twice a week.

He became curious about Michael's mother and the illness that kept her secluded in her room when he was around but did not prevent her from doing all the household chores. Once, the boy handed him a pack of photos taken when Janice was younger, some of them in a bathing suit at the beach. They showed an attractive woman with thick brown hair, a fair-sized bosom, and sexy lips. As time passed, Michael began praising his mother so often that he suspected the boy had already picked him as a potential stepfather.

Along with his routine activities, he opened a bank account and readily obtained several identification cards in John Wilkinson's name, one from Costco with his photo on it at a cost of thirty dollars, another from AAA. Nevertheless, he still considered it unsafe to use Wilkinson's name to make his next move from his hiding place. He was working as fast as possible to obtain other identities.

Janice was astonished at how much and how quickly Michael had changed since the arrival of the new tenant. In a short time, she told herself, this man had been able to gain more influence over Michael than she had ever had. Now the boy couldn't stop praising what John did, and what John said or thought about everything. It was like a miracle before her eyes, and she was startled and confused by it.

Really, she reasoned, it was in all the books she had read about child psychology. It only proved what she had known the whole time: Michael very much needed a constructive relationship with an adult male figure to make up for the father he had never had. She soothed her conscience by telling herself that she had always paid close attention to him, and had attained what she considered relative success. Until these last two years, Michael had been a totally normal boy. She had also made an attempt to give him a stepfather—although that had been a total catastrophe.

The stranger had come asking to rent the room two days after the last incident with Milton, and he had talked only with Michael. She had been in no shape or mood to speak with anyone, but they had needed the money, so she had accepted the renter, taking into account Michael's description of the man: ". . . almost as old as Grandpa and he said this place is very convenient for him. It's within walking distance of the university library, where he'll be doing research for *quite* some time." It also occurred to her that renting the room could provide an outside witness in case she needed it.

On several occasions, from behind a curtain in her room, she had watched the tenant as he went out in the morning, limping slightly from his right leg, heading for the university and coming back after lunchtime. The tenant usually went out again soon after, carrying his painting gear, this time walking toward downtown Burlington. After sunset he came back with Michael as a faithful companion. Once or twice, he had glanced back toward the house, as if sensing he was being watched. Her son had fooled her; in spite of the gray hair and the old-fashioned glasses, it was easy to see at that distance that the tenant wasn't a very old man. Actually, they had already met by telephone when he had called her from outside, asking for permission to use the house address for credit cards and to give the telephone number on an application he had to fill out— and his voice was also not that of an old man.

Michael had asked her to invite the tenant to lunch on Sunday.

"Don't make anything special," he said. "Just put on an extra portion of fried chicken." Knowing Michael as well as she did, she recognized in his insistence the inner urge to have a dinner like the ones he had seen in many of his friends' families, with a father-figure presiding at the table.

Since the last incident with Milton, she had stayed isolated in her room most of the time, avoiding questions about her black eye and bruises, keeping her misery to herself. Only after she had taken off her dark glasses and scrutinized her face closely in the mirror in broad daylight did she consent to the invitation. She was now full of curiosity to meet the man who had been living in her house for almost two weeks and who, in some matters, had managed to displace her with Michael. When he showed up at exactly the hour set for lunch, twelve-thirty, she felt awkward and tense—partly because it had been ages since she had invited anybody for lunch and partly because she realized she was overdressed. The tenant also seemed uncomfortable. Acting as if he wasn't sure what he was doing, he gave her a package with a bottle of French white wine. She smiled at him, feeling an empathy with the man.

She seated him facing Michael and herself to avoid having to decide who would head the table. She had also prepared herself for starting a conversation with the guest. Michael had told her the tenant had been seriously injured in a car accident not long ago.

After serving the appetizer, Janice asked the first question she had prepared. "Have you recovered from your accident?"

"Nothing's really wrong with my body, but I have memory lapses now and then. It's very annoying. Sometimes, in the middle of a conversation, I forget names or things that everybody ought to know very well. Doctors say it's only a matter of time before I recover completely."

"How are you doing with your research?" Janice continued with her prepared questions.

"I've found quite interesting information in the library regarding the first settlers of this region. I've really come to the right place."

The man kept staring at her like a schoolboy at a teacher, waiting for another question to be graded on. She felt strange being in command of the situation.

"Michael has told me that you paint very well."

The tenant made an evasive gesture of modesty.

"Do you have any children, Mr. Wilkinson?" she asked, getting into themes more interesting to her.

"A boy and a girl. They are already in college."

She wondered if the tenant was married but decided that matter was out of bounds, leaving her with no further questions. "If you'll excuse me, I'll serve the meal." She smiled at the guest again, leaving Michael to take over the chat.

She finished serving the food and the wine and rejoined them. The tenant had turned the conversation to sailing, tracing the sport from the time of the Phoenicians and Vikings to modern days. Michael became enthralled by the procedure for christening any ship regardless of size and stories of solitary sailors circumnavigating the world in sailboats not much bigger than the one resting in the backyard.

Michael continued to pester the tenant with questions in spite of Janice's efforts to restrain him. "Mr Wilkinson has to eat," she reminded him. But the guest had managed to eat everything she served him while answering all the boy's questions and telling some wonderful stories. Janice noticed that Mr. Wilkinson had excellent table manners, a broad education, and, most of all, was a born storyteller. His high spirits were catching, and Michael's fascination with his new friend was easily understood, she acknowledged with a sense of relief. Janice felt more relaxed than she had in a long time, and joined Michael in conversation with their guest.

GABRIEL GOT INTO the front seat of Barter's car. Barter had driven to the FBI man's house in Kendall, a Miami suburb. As soon as the car took off, Gabriel opened a thick file he had brought with him and began searching for select information to share. "Marjorie Turner, born in Brooklyn, 1942, of Cuban parents. Her maiden name was Margot Armas. She changed it to Marjorie when she married in 1962, at the time that both of her parents and a younger brother went back to Cuba."

Gabriel read on: "Carlos Manuel Armas, a.k.a. Ramiro Ramos, Marjorie's brother, was born in Brooklyn in 1950." Then he pulled a page from his folder and handed it to Barter.

Barter slowed down almost to a stop to glance at the photo of a group of kids at a junior high school in Brooklyn. Encircled was the face of a boy of about twelve with a stare he knew all too well.

Placing the folder on his lap, Gabriel began speaking again. "I went to New York to meet an old Cuban lady who had lived at 677 Lincoln Place, Brooklyn, in the same building as the Armas family, from the forties until 1962. The old lady knew the family well and loves to talk about those days. In a couple of sessions, I learned most of the gossip about the family. Margot changed her name to Marjorie just before she married 'because she never did like being called Margarita, a name that couldn't be pronounced well by her English-speaking friends and made everybody think of a Mexican drink.' Carlos Manuel's and Marjorie's father was a veteran of World War II, born in Cuba, exiled to the U.S. in 1940 for political reasons since the Cuban police were after him for conspiring to form a democratic government in Cuba. That happened during the first Batista regime.

"In 1943, Armas volunteered to go to war, fought in Europe, and was decorated four times. He belonged to a special group that was deployed several times behind enemy lines on very risky missions. He ended the war as a major and went back to work as a welder at the same dockyard where he had worked before the war. It was only logical that he became an anti-Batista militant in 1952, the year that Batista took over the Cuban government a second time with a military coup. In 1953, after Fidel Castro failed in an assault on an army garrison in Santiago de Cuba, he formed the 'Tweny-sixth of July Movement.' Many chapters of the movement were organized in the States, every place that had a Cuban population. Armas founded the Brooklyn chapter. As time went on, Batista's government became a bloody and corrupt dictatorship, and the war hero, Armas, became a strong supporter of Fidel Castro in his long struggle to overthrow the Batista regime. In 1961, the U.S. government sponsored the Bay of Pigs invasion of Cuba. Armas was deeply involved in demonstrations and active propaganda work in New York against U.S. government policy toward Cuba.

"The FBI decided to warn him and other supporters of the Cuban Revolution. They were summoned to Washington and told that if they persisted in their activities, they would be prosecuted. Armas felt threatened and decided to go back to Cuba. His wife and young son followed him a few months later, in 1962. The daughter, already a sophomore at the School of Arts at New York University, was engaged to Arthur A. Turner, an electronic-engineering student in his senior year. They were married in 1962 just before Marjorie's mother and brother left."

Barter felt furious by what he considered Gabriel's unfair play. "Why didn't you tell me anything before? How long have you been working on this?"

"Actually, I'm not authorized to tell you anything. This got out of my hands. The FBI is making a hell of an inquiry into this matter. I'll tell you why: After Marjorie's husband finished school, he helped perfect radar and sonar, working for Bell Engineering, and became rich with some patents of his own. When this whole thing came up, with Marjorie possibly being a sister to a Cuban spy, the FBI opened an investigation on the possible ties between Turner and Marjorie's father. The inquiry is aimed at trying to find out if Turner was ever recruited to pass vital information on U.S. weapons. Turner died of cancer in 1982. His personal life insurance and his company life insurance totaling nearly two million dollars were left to his widow. If they find anything, Marjorie may lose most of her money and properties, and could end up in jail."

"Where does this leave us now?" Barter asked.

"Wait, there's a lot more." Gabriel showed the thick file to Barter. "For many years, the FBI kept close tabs on old man Armas and his family while they were living in Cuba, to check any attempt he might make to carry on his activities in the U.S. through third parties. From his war record, it was easy to see that he was a very daring and resourceful man with a lot of experience in covert action acquired in Sicily, Spain, and France. After Armas reached Cuba, he apparently settled down on a small farm on the outskirts of Havana, where he and his family seemed to live happily ever after, growing vegetables and fruit trees. The last time this was checked by a qualified FBI officer was back in 1985, when Armas was supposed to have died. His wife had passed away in the early seventies. This officer met the son, Carlos Manuel, a respected medical doctor, who was living in the farmhouse filled with family photos and World War II trophies, even with some of the old furniture brought from their former home in Brooklyn. The FBI file on Armas was closed.

"When this new investigation started, we sent another officer, a Cuban descendant whose family are neighbors of the Armas, to check on this story in Cuba and find out why there seemed to be two Carlos Manuel Armas. It turned out that Carlos Manuel Armas, the M.D., really has his two parents alive in Santiago de Cuba, six hundred miles away from Havana. The FBI has been fooled all this time.

"To answer your question now, the FBI has created a task force to deal with this case. Catching this guy has become quite important. The FBI has asked the CIA for permission for you to work with us on this task force. Have you been told yet?"

MORE THAN THREE weeks had passed since he had arrived in Burlington, two months since he had left Cuba. He was ready to get out of the U.S., cross the Canadian border, and return home, but every day he postponed sending the message to Marcelo to let him know that he was prepared. Finally, he forced himself to do it. The answer from Marcelo came almost immediately. It was Friday morning, October 14, when he checked his email and received the message: Everything would be set for the next Tuesday, October 18. His old Swiss passport would be waiting for him at the DHL office in Montreal from Monday on. He would have a first-class seat on an Air France flight to Paris, and then back to Cuba.

He still had four more days to relax and enjoy his "vacation." He didn't go painting that afternoon. Instead, he gave the hull of Michael's boat a thorough examination. From what he had gathered, Michael didn't like the man his mother was with and that was the reason why the boy was reluctant to accept the boat. He had finally convinced the boy to accept the gift and give it a decent try on the lake. Carlos Manuel thought that was a good way to mend the relations between the boy and his mother's friend. It was also a good way to check on surveillance around the lake, knowledge that might be useful in the future.

* * *

Janice decided to go on the "maiden voyage" of the boat Milton Lafayette had given Michael. After the tenant had volunteered to teach him how to sail the boat, Michael had changed his mind about the gift, something that would never have happened, Janice was sure, if the tenant had not intervened so intelligently. It could very well be, she said to herself, that Michael had already abandoned his feud with Milton, a situation that constantly haunted her. But this change of mind, after he had committed himself, was unusual in Michael, who tended lately to be very stubborn, sticking to his decisions often beyond reason.

She had mixed feelings about the boat. She feared the dangers of the sport and dreaded the idea of Michael taking such risks. When Milton gave the sailboat to her son, presumably an apology for the last incident, she had a premonition that the gesture had a sinister purpose. Michael's presence had always irritated Milton in a vicious way, as an obstacle to his total possession of her. On a certain level, she was suspicious that the sailboat was intended more to promote an accident in the cold waters of the lake than for Michael's enjoyment, so she had felt relieved at Michael's initial refusal to accept the present. On the other hand, sailing was as common a sport as hunting for young men in Vermont, especially in the areas surrounding the lake.

The decision to go on the excursion was a battle she had lost with herself. She knew too well that she had to stop overprotecting Michael, but something in her heart prevailed over her reasoning. Michael was her most precious possession, and, as always happened, she could find excellent excuses for accompanying him.

On Saturday afternoon, the boat was going to be christened with a bottle of beer in what she considered a silly ceremony invented by the tenant for Michael's delight. Right after the christening, Michael was going to receive his first sailing lesson. This was something she had to watch rather closely. Besides observing how this new friendship worked—something she was extremely curious to witness—she had to see if the tenant really knew his way around boats. And despite her positive intuition, she was by no means sure how much she could trust this stranger.

The launching was a complete success. Some of the people on the pier of the boathouse gathered around and cheered when the bottle of beer was broken against the hull and the vessel, dubbed "Jan-Mitch," was safely placed into the water. After the initial lessons on safety and basic boat maneuverings, all was ready for sailing except the wind. They sat there, barely two hundred yards from shore, searching the horizon for the first gust of wind. The boat was drifting very slowly along the lakeshore, pulled by a weak current and splashed lightly by waves from the ferry and other passing vessels. The tenant filled the time with the story of what had happened during a long, windless spell on Columbus's first voyage of discovery. Janice watched Michael listening spellbound, and she longed for a stepfather like that for her poor boy.

A gentle breeze finally began to blow more steadily, as it should during a first sailing lesson for a thirteen-year-old boy and his mother who was suddenly interested in sailing lessons, too. The man sitting at the bow and handling the rudder transformed himself into a merciless ship captain, giving rough orders to his two sailors, cursing at each mistake according to the best marine tradition. When she and her son managed to bring the sail to life and the boat began moving, increasing in speed with every moment, Janice suddenly felt ten years younger. In a short time, the boathouse was a tiny blur at the edge of a big blue plate. Soon, everything else vanished for her but the sensation of the wind, the squirts of water jumping at her, and the nervous animal movements of the boat in response to any shifting of its living load or changes in direction of the sail. Janice felt the wind caressing every part of her body with a million fingers and wished it never had to end.

The afternoon dissolved far too soon into a glorious sunset as the boat made a great circle and headed back to port. The magic ended when the boat struck the dock a little too hard. John jumped ashore, rope in hand, to tie the vessel safely after its maiden voyage, and there, standing on the pier, was Milton Lafayette.

She felt terrified and unable to move for a moment, but managed to take two steps to meet Milton. When he saw her coming toward him, he turned away, wearing his typical rude smirk. It was at that moment that she knew she had to ask her tenant to go. The man who had jumped ashore was, by no means, the "crippled old" tenant she had described to Milton on the phone.

"Who is that guy?" the tenant asked her.

"I don't know," she lied, very disturbed by Milton's presence.

Janice rolled over in bed once again, wondering how and when to tell her tenant he had to go. The whole past week had been unreal, not comparable to any other experience in her life. She had managed to get a job as a saleswoman, making phone calls from her own home, and, to her surprise, she was earning more money now than she had at her old job. Since she hated getting up early in the morning, she let the tenant continue preparing breakfast. In return, when the "men of the house" arrived in the evening, she had a good home-cooked meal ready to serve. She and Michael loved the "family" dinner with the tenant who told such wonderful stories. After dinner, they spent a couple of hours lazily watching television before going to bed. The previous Thursday afternoon she had been in heaven with John and Michael around, cleaning up the basement while she cooked a large roast. During the sailing adventure on Saturday, in spite of how much she rejected it as a foolish thought, the idea of the tenant as a perfect stepfather for Michael had come creeping back again and again into her heart, now with a different, faster, almost painful beat. These days had been giving her a sense, for the first time, of what true family life could be.

She got out of bed, unable to fall asleep. She couldn't get Milton's smirk out of her mind. She had heard the tenant taking a shower shortly before and decided to pay him a visit to thank him for the boat ride and all the time he had devoted to Michael. Then she would ask him to leave the house, telling him the whole truth. Actually, it wouldn't be hard for him to find another place in the neighborhood. She put on a kimono and walked out of her room. When she stopped at the tenant's door, still hesitant about what to do, it opened. The man was standing barefoot, wearing shorts and a pullover.

"In a wooden house, you can hear every sound. I heard someone walking to my door and thought it must be Michael coming to pay me a visit. Did I startle you?"

"I'm sorry to intrude," she said, as he let her in. "I just wanted to thank you." She glanced around the neatly arranged room and noted that it lacked the messiness typical of most men living alone.

The tenant showed Janice to the only chair before retreating and seating himself on the bed at the other end of the room. The chair was in front of a small desk, the top of which was covered by a large map under the glow of a bright lamp.

"I see that you've been looking at where we went sailing." Janice bent over the map on the desk.

"Yes, I was measuring the distance from the boathouse to Appletree Point and back. We sailed about twelve miles."

"Is that all? I thought we'd travelled a hundred. The boat seemed to go so fast." They laughed.

"What do you want to thank me for, Mrs. Howard?" The tenant's tone of voice was candid.

"For today's ride and for everything you've done for Michael. And please call me Janice." Sensing that the tenant was not at ease with Michael's mother in his room, she folded her arms and stroked her biceps nervously. The man shrugged and remained silent, staring into her eyes as if trying to discover in them her real intention. Suddenly, she didn't know how to continue.

"Michael has told me you're a *real* painter."

The man smiled and shrugged, as if embarrassed.

"Could you show me something you've painted?" Janice felt justified in insisting. This was a field in which she could make a qualified judgement. She had paid part of her way through college by working as a saleswoman in the only art gallery in town.

The tenant pulled two canvases mounted on homemade frames from under the bed. He also brought a suitcase out and sat on it directly in front of her. "When I was a child, I loved to paint. In high school, I took some painting lessons, but since then I haven't had the time to practice. I've only been able to draw, now and then, sketches of landscapes and people I want to paint one day." He then uncovered the first painting, a view of Church Street with the church in the background and some of the road's big boulders in front.

"Oh, this is a magnificent view of the mall," Janice said, taking a closer look at the canvas.

The man handed her another canvas with a view of Lake Champlain from Burlington's Waterfront Park.

"Both are beautiful!" Janice was surprised at how good the paintings were. Her trained eye appreciated a great deal of talent behind each work.

"Do you really like them?" The tenant's smile reflected contentment.

"I love them. They're really good."

"You can have them. They're yours."

"You're giving them to me?" She felt incredulous. "Thanks very much. I appreciate it, but it would be improper for me to accept them . . . You should be able to sell them easily at the art gallery downtown."

Janice had been taken by surprise. If she had wanted to be close to him, there he was in front of her, his eyes at an angle where he could glimpse the color of her panties if she didn't watch the way she moved her legs. Then he had thrown her totally off balance by offering her such a gift.

"I really can't accept them."

For the first time, Janice took a good look at the man who was now sitting very close to her. She saw an honest face, manly gestures, and respect. Most probably, the man was straight, but totally immune to her sex appeal. Many men became aroused soon after meeting her. It was a curse she had apparently been born with, a figure and a way of being that made men think about dragging her to bed—a curse that, by now, had her on the verge of hating all men. Few of them cared to see beyond her body. During the whole boating excursion, the tenant hadn't leered at her once, even when she had bent down before him to pick up a rope and had unintentionally displayed a generous view of her cleavage. The entire time, he had given her the same polite and respectful treatment she was accustomed to getting from Michael's schoolmates who used to come to the house to study or play when he was in primary school.

She had always longed for a man blind to all her womanly attractions, capable of looking into her soul. Now, for the first time, she was feeling a strong sexual urge, one not suppressed by the fear that closeness to a man had inspired in her since childhood, ever since her stepfather had visited her room in the middle of the night. What was happening to her now? She tried to ignore the signals her body was giving her.

The shadow of Milton Lafayette abruptly came to her mind, ending the reverie. As long as the problem with Milton remained unsolved, it was stupid even to dream about another man. She decided to leave. "I would like you to have lunch with us tomorrow; I have something to tell you," she said, postponing the bad news. Maybe she would invent some excuse instead of telling him the whole truth.

"Thanks, I'd be delighted. Take the paintings with you and sell them if you can. Let's make it a fifty-fifty deal?"

"Thirty percent is the usual fee for selling a painting," she said, smiling at the tenant. She felt, for some inexplicable reason, that she could fall deeply in love with this man.

T HE MINISTER LISTENED for five minutes to what the representatives of the High Military Court and State Security had to add to the matter that had been brought to his attention with a memo. At the end of the proceeding, he turned to Marcelo and asked: "Do you have any objection to giving the information requested by the High Military Court?"

"No. But it should be very clear that we don't have to relinquish any information about the identity of this man and the work he has done in the past," Marcelo said.

"What about you?" The minister turned his head to General Pablo and General García.

General Pablo, head of the State Security Department, shook his head, indicating that he had nothing to say. García didn't speak, either.

"*Compañero Ministro,* all we have ever asked for is information pertaining to the hijacking of the yacht *Elvirita* and the whereabouts of the man who did it. All we ever received was misinformation, to put it in the mildest way I can," Colonel Francisco said, to make clear the lack of cooperation from the intelligence service.

"What is the current situation with this man, Marcelo?"

"We're getting ready to pull him out of hiding in the U.S. He should be here in a week to ten days. I'll send Colonel Francisco a complete report on this incident today."

"If I had had cooperation, I wouldn't have taken your time, *compañero Ministro*," Francisco responded.

Marcelo opened his mouth to reply, but the minister ordered him to wait with the palm of his hand.

"Okay, Marcelo, keep the High Military Court well informed about this man until he comes back."

The meeting was adjourned at this point, but the minister signaled to Pablo and Marcelo to stay.

After the others had left, the minister said, "It is of the utmost importance that this man not fall into the hands of the CIA. You two have to work together on that."

"Our man is near the Canadian border, ready and waiting to go to Montreal. There, he will pick up a package we're sending him with one of his old passports, some money, and a plane ticket to Paris. From there he will return to Cuba," Marcelo said.

"I'll send one of my best men to Montreal. He will make sure this officer gets back to Cuba," General Pablo replied.

The minister nodded, closed his notebook, and left the meeting room.

Marcelo and Pablo stayed behind to coordinate the operation.

"This is very simple, Marcelo," General Pablo began. "My man will pick up the DHL package. I'll give you the address where your man has to go and we'll take it from there." General Pablo got up and left the room.

24

O N THURSDAY, October 13, Gabriel and Barter went to New York, where the FBI task force had its base.

The senior FBI officer in charge updated Barter and Gabriel on the investigations under way. "The first thing we found was that Marjorie's maid was an illegal, so we sent her back to El Salvador. The new maid Marjorie has hired is working for the FBI, as is the building maintenance man. We now have complete access to Marjorie. In Hialeah, the FBI is also keeping close surveillance on Carlos Manuel's children.

"We went over Marjorie's bank account and credit card expenditures since her brother, nephews, and niece arrived in the U.S. Most telling was her trip to Orlando. Before leaving New York, she cashed a check for ten thousand dollars. We think she gave most of that money to her brother. She paid for motel rooms and many other purchases with credit cards, including the car she rented to go with her brother to Philadelphia. From the credit card records, it's easy to establish her trail and itinerary almost to the minute. She told her new maid about a multiple car crash in which she was involved while driving back. She remembers vividly everything that happened and what she did to avoid crashing. She said that a relative who was riding with her saved a man caught inside a van that had been thrown off the road. An inquiry made into the accident revealed that John Wilkinson, a salesman from Philadelphia, was driving the van. When questioned, he recognized the photo of Ramiro Ramos as the man who pulled him out of the car and later went back to fetch his kangaroo belt. The only thing he found missing from his belongings was his driver's license. In Philadelphia, Marjorie stayed in the Wyndham Plaza Hotel. A John Wilkinson was also registered there. We think Carlos Manuel has been using that identity since then.

"Brother and sister separated in Philadelphia. Chances are that he went to the West Coast en route to Mexico, which is fairly easy if you have money to grease your way across the border. Another interesting thing is that she, through her lawyer, has applied for a passport in her brother's name. She's been receiving email messages in plain language that must come from him, the last one with some coded information. She's getting ready to travel to San Diego tomorrow and has made reservations in a La Quinta motel in Chula Vista for a whole week. That would probably be the meeting place with her brother. I want you, Gabriel, to travel on an earlier plane to San Diego and be there at the motel ahead of her. You already have a room reserved next to hers. The local FBI has been instructed to give you all the backup you need. Also, they have been ordered to detain anybody who gets in touch with Marjorie on her way to the motel. That would be the most likely way he would approach her. Any questions?" the senior officer asked to end the meeting.

"I don't have a question but a comment," Barter said. "From what I've learned about this guy, he's very professional, and it's quite clear that he must be working on the assumption that, by now, we know all about his sister and his real identity. The San Diego meeting smells to me like a fake trail he wants us to follow while he does something else."

"We've thought of that, too, Mr. Barter," the senior FBI officer snapped back. "In spite of that, you mustn't forget that, in the first place, he asked his sister for help. If he had wanted to, he could have called on his pals in Cuban intelligence from the beginning. They have plenty of resources to take care of him here. Maybe he called his sister because it was the fastest way to get some money he needed when you discovered him in Sarasota, or maybe for sentimental reasons. Or, because it's a clever and quiet way to approach us. Possibly he's making this contact as an invitation for us to offer him a deal through his sister, instead of hunting him down on behalf of the CIA. Have you thought of that, Mr. Barter? Maybe his plan all along has been to stay here in the U.S., and he's using this as a probe to find out how much we know about him. I'm sure you thought of all that, Mr. Barter." The senior FBI officer spoke with polite animosity, making it clear that he resented Barter's comment.

"Yes, sir, you're right."

"Mr. Barter, do you want me to make a comment about your work?" the senior officer asked with open scorn.

"Please, go ahead," Barter replied, smiling in a humble manner, trying to iron out the wrinkle that he had caused.

"I think the way this case was opened was a gross mistake. It's clear that by putting this man on the ten-most-wanted list from the beginning, we sent him a real threat, not a bridge on which to cross over. After a little work, it happened that we had four aces in hand, the three children and a sister, and the CIA threw them away. Now he's dead set on leaving this country, where he's being hunted for an act of clear self-defense in international waters. Do you know one thing, Mr. Barter? I'm considering asking to have this man removed from the ten-most-wanted list."

As if thinking this last blow should be enough for the CIA guy, the FBI officer went back to business. "Gabriel, get moving to San Diego. This is the only lead we have now, and we have to follow every lead that comes up."

For the tenth time, King reread the message he had received that morning from P.G. As always, the information was brief and valuable: *"The intelligence officer who fled from Cuba on the yacht*

Elvirita *will pick up a package in Montreal on Monday or Tuesday. The parcel might be coming from London by DHL and should contain a passport, money, and a plane ticket to Paris.*" As soon as King had read the message he had called Barter urgently back to Langley. Barter was sitting before him, back from New York, and for the last half hour had been giving him news about the FBI task force.

King rose from his seat, yawning and stretching his arms while he paced the room. "The elephant's in the tent and there's nobody else but me to blame for it. Now that the FBI has a motive, resurrecting a ghost spy from the Cold War, they'll handle this matter whichever way they wish on behalf of national security."

King spoke as if thinking aloud. It was Friday, October 14, ten minutes past six in the afternoon. As on every other Friday, King had an appointment with his barber at seven that he hated to miss. For most of his life, he had worn a crew cut that had to be trimmed every two weeks. He had to make a decision and there was no point in sitting on it any longer. He wasn't authorized to use P.G.'s information at will, but time was of great importance in this case. He would reach Cabot over the weekend to get his full approval. In the meantime he had to set Barter in motion.

"Listen to this, Mr. Barter. We have received inside information that our quarry is going to pick up a parcel in Montreal on Monday or Tuesday. The parcel will probably come from London by way of DHL. I ought to have more information soon from our London office. The whole scheme is crystal clear. Roberto had expected that, by now, we were on his sister's tail, intercepting her mail, her calls, and checking on everybody there. He wants us to believe he's ready to cross the Mexican border. I'll bet he's done a wonderful job of leaving all sorts of fake evidence pointing to Mexico while he's already in Canada, waiting for his passport and money to fly back to Cuba."

King stopped his pacing and moved closer to Barter.

"He's trapped now. For the first time, we know what his next move will be, and where he is. You go to the hunting site and set everything up for the kill. It will be like shooting a sitting duck. And remember, not a word to Gabriel."

In spite of what he was saying, for the first time since the chase had started, King began to think that they were actually doing something useless, like trying to catch a fish with their bare hands.

ON SUNDAY MORNING, October 16, two men in a pickup truck opened the gate to the back-yard with a key and towed away the trailer with Michael's sailboat on it. When Janice stepped out of the kitchen to see what was going on, she found Milton supervising the operation from his car parked across the street. She heard the front door slam and saw Michael walking toward Milton's car.

"Your mother told me that you didn't want the boat, Michael," Milton Lafayette called as he drove away, waving his hand and smiling. "I just hadn't had the chance to pick it up till today."

Michael stormed into the house, ran upstairs, and locked himself in his room. At lunchtime, he refused to come down to eat. Janice and the tenant sat down at the table without saying a word to each other for a long while.

"Janice, last night you thanked me because I pay attention to Michael. Can you tell me now who that man is who waited for us at the pier and took the boat away today?"

Janice stopped eating. Slowly, her eyes filled with tears and her voice choked up. "He's Milton Lafayette, the assistant to the state attorney. He's the curse of my life."

Both fell into an extended silence.

"Where's Michael's father?"

"That's another sad story," Janice replied. Suddenly she felt she should tell him everything about her love life. "I was a sophomore at the university when I fell madly in love with a professor who had come from Colorado. He told me he was divorcing his wife. He was over fifty, but was as helpless as a child. I had to choose the clothes he wore. Soon, I was pregnant, and I refused to have an abortion. I wanted very much to have his child. I dropped out of school and came to live in Burlington. He sold his new car to make the down payment on this house. One day he came to me, crying like a baby, and told me he had to go back to Colorado to his family. That nearly killed me."

Janice stayed silent for a moment, staring at her hands. "As time passed and my son got older, I realized that I needed a father for him. Three years ago—the same story. Milton Lafayette told me he couldn't stand his wife anymore, that as soon as the elections were over, he would divorce." Janice's eyes swam with tears again.

The tenant had finished his meal. She had barely touched the piece of apple pie with vanilla ice cream in front of her.

Carlos Manuel wanted to tell her how much he liked her. How each day he had felt more and more drawn to her. He couldn't resist her candid soul, and he longed to embrace her strong and supple, yet gentle body. That blue gaze of her eyes . . .

Janice lifted her head and looked at him as if she could read his mind.

He put an end to his fantasies. He couldn't do anything for Janice and Michael except get them into deeper trouble. He was a fugitive on the run, a man whose future didn't belong to him. "I must leave the house. I'm sure my presence here has complicated things for you. I'll be out soon," he said finally.

Janice was going to say something, but decided to remain silent, playing with her spoon and the ice cream.

Michael heard the steps of the tenant returning to his room after lunch. He waited another five minutes, then went to visit him. As usual, the door opened without his having to knock, and the tenant stood before him, smiling.

"Come in, Michael. Tell me what's on your mind."

"John, do you know much about guns?"

"A little."

"In today's paper I saw lots of handguns for sale. I want to know which is the best buy." Michael handed him a section of the *Burlington Free Press*.

"It depends on what you want the gun for. If it's for short-range target practice, a small-caliber pistol will do. If you're planning on robbing a bank, then you should look for a sawed-off repeating shotgun, easy to conceal and with a lot of firepower at close range. If you want to take something at a thousand yards—a deer or an enemy—an old Mauser, caliber 30.06, from the First World War, with telescopic sight, could be appropriate. What do you want the weapon for? It also depends on the money you have."

The boy hesitated for a second, then said very convincingly, "We need a gun in case a burglar breaks into the house."

"What are you going to do to the burglar? Blow his head off or just scare him shitless?"

"Scare him off."

"Then you need a weapon that makes a lot of noise. Again, the best buy would be a shotgun. Twelve- or sixteen-gauge shotguns raise a lot of hell in the middle of the night. A two-shot shotgun would be all you need, and you could use it for duck hunting when burglars aren't robbing the house."

"Actually, I have in mind a pistol, something handy."

"Let me see what's for sale today."

The tenant browsed over the ads with the handgun sale offers already neatly circled in red. "Here's a .357 Magnum with a five-and-a-half-inch barrel. Holster and cartridge belts with ammo included, all for four hundred dollars. That's a good buy if the gun and the rest are new, as it says here. Let me tell you, any burglar will faint just seeing you geared-up with all this stuff, ready to shoot it out in good old-western style."

Michael's childish eyes glittered as he smiled, maybe imagining himself as a cowboy sharpshooter. Then his expression turned sad. "I don't have that much money."

"Well, a .357 is pretty heavy for you. Something smaller and lighter would be better. What about a .22-caliber pistol?"

"Can you kill a man with a pistol like that?" Michael asked after a moment of thought.

"Yes, if you hit him in the right place. Robert Kennedy was shot dead with one of those guns. There's a catch to it, Michael. You have only one shot to paralyze the burglar. If you are not a good marksman, and the robber is also armed, then he could blast you out of this world before he dies from the .22-caliber wounds. If you want to, though, you can become a marksman in six months of daily practice."

After saying that, the tenant got up, went to his mini-fridge, opened it, and fetched two cans of cola with one hand. With the other, he took a pair of clean glasses from a tray over the fridge and gave a can and a glass to Michael. He then continued his lecture. "Maybe you don't have all that time to learn how to shoot." He glanced over the ads. "There are some fine short-barrel revolvers, .32 and .38 caliber, at reasonable prices. Revolvers are more dependable than pistols. You know that, don't you?"

The tenant laid the newspaper ads aside, filled his glass, and started drinking, all the while looking attentively at Michael. "There's the question of buying this gun. You have to inspect the barrel carefully to see if the grooves are too worn out; the hammer is another vulnerable point. You risk spending your money and ending up with a worthless weapon." Then he added casually, "Also, I bet most people won't sell a gun to a twelve-year-old boy."

"Thirteen."

"Okay, to a thirteen-year-old man."

"All people want is the money, and they don't care who they sell to. A lot of guys in my junior high school have their own weapons."

The tenant shrugged, finished his drink, and went back to his seat on the bed. Michael stood up and came a step closer to him.

"I wonder if you'd be able to help me buy it."

"Do you mean buy it for you?"

"Just come along with me to inspect the barrel and stuff."

"Does your mother know about this purchase, Michael?"

"I have my own savings," the boy replied.

The tenant started pacing the room again, thinking about the boy's proposal. He stopped in front of a window and looked into the backyard, where the trailer with the boat had been parked. Then he continued to pace the room until he finally stopped in front of the boy. He placed a hand on the boy's shoulder. "Michael, this is a man-to-man conversation. I appreciate your confidence in me, but you want me to help you behind your mother's back with something that might have serious implications. I'm only willing to help you if you hide nothing from me and tell me what you really want this gun for."

After listening to Michael's explanation, common sense told him again to leave the place at once and let these two people follow their own lives as they had before he entered the house. It was self-sabotage to stand in the way of an assistant state attorney. There was nothing a fugitive like him could do but try to save his own hide. He had new identities that would enable him to simply walk out of the U.S. and enter Canada at whatever point of the border he chose. Marcelo had already arranged his rescue back to Cuba. In the coming two days, he had to cross the border, pick up his passport, and catch a plane to Paris and another back to Cuba. *Still, common sense and personal interest had never carried much weight in his life.*

The tenant knocked on Janice's door.

"I came to talk to you about Michael," he said in a whisper when she opened it. He closed the door behind him, but refused the chair she offered. "When I met him, I felt he was facing a very big problem and was near the breaking point. I've tried my best to help him have a broader outlook on life." He was speaking slowly, as if picking the right words to use. "Nevertheless, he's obsessed by something I can do nothing about." His voice conveyed regret.

Janice felt as if she had been struck on the head. Her mouth dried up and she had difficulty speaking. "What is it?" she asked.

"I know I risk Michael's friendship and trust. But you're his mother and his father, and he's only thirteen. He is set on killing the man you're with, and I'm sure there isn't anything anybody can do to stop him."

Suddenly, it was as if the whole world had collapsed on her. She sat there looking at the man across from her until his image became blurred. She wanted to cry, but she couldn't shed a tear.

"Believe me, Janice, I understand the anguish of having a child in trouble and not being able to help."

"Don't worry, John. I know a way out of this."

The sorrowful face of his late wife, as he imagined she had looked when she committed suicide, flashed in his mind.

THE NEXT MORNING, on Monday, October 17, Carlos Manuel went ahead with his plans. If everything worked out right, he would be in Montreal by noon. He could move around in the U.S. and Canada with the identification documents that he had procured, but to travel abroad, a valid passport was still indispensable. Even if, for any reason, he should need to remain longer in the U.S. or Canada, he had to rescue his old Swiss passport, full of visas from multiple foreign countries, already in Montreal.

He went to the university library as usual. Soon, he found the man he was looking for: Bernard Fletcher was emptying trash cans in the library hall. After a warm handshake, Carlos said, "Come on, Bernard, don't work so hard. Take a coffee break. Join me for a cup."

Fletcher smiled, pleased by the invitation. John Wilkinson was his hero, the only person, with the exception of his mother, who had ever really paid any attention to him. John was a swell fellow— a man with a very high education doing research at the university who didn't mind talking with him, a simple janitor who everybody else considered half-witted. Besides, he was a generous man who had paid him at least a couple of hundred dollars over the going price in the used-car market for his 1982 Toyota. They bought two cups of coffee from the vending machine. Fletcher added plenty of cream and sugar to his cup, while his friend took it black with no sugar.

"Car's ready. I tuned it up, changed the spark plugs."

"Remember to bill me for that."

"That's nothing. I had a set of new plugs lying around the house for a long time and never used them. Changing plugs is a fifteen-minute job," Fletcher said, blowing on his hot coffee. "When are you going to pick it up?"

"I'll do it in a little while."

"You know where it is. Remember what I told you—if you don't like the car after you give it a good test drive, I'll give you your money back."

"I'm sure there's nothing wrong with the car. I'll see you around, Bernard. I have to get back to the computer now." Carlos Manuel again shook the hand of the red-haired man who was about his age, height, and weight. Bernard smiled back.

Bernard Fletcher watched his friend depart and kept smiling as he went back to emptying trash cans from all the rooms into a big bin on a four-wheeled cart.

Carlos Manuel was ready to leave for Canada with a new set of identification documents in Fletcher's name. He had procured them by applying with the proper procedures for each one, stating that he had lost the originals: driver's license, social security card, and credit cards. Plus, he now owned the car that had been in Fletcher's name for five years. He had used the name John Wilkinson for too long now.

Before leaving, he went to the library to check the Internet for any messages from Marcelo. He entered his first email address and received a message with a very simple code that he deciphered as he read: "*Cancel Montreal operation. Wait for orders.*"

Marcelo had sent the message on Friday night. He took another sip from the cup of coffee he had brought with him, and pondered the implications of this change of plan. *This is a sign from the orishas; they want me to stay here,* he joked to himself, interpreting the change as a believer in Afro-Cuban religions might. His thoughts moved immediately to Janice and Michael, and he decided to stay in Vermont for another day instead of leaving for Canada. Maybe in the meantime he could find a way to rid Janice and Michael of this man who was harassing them.

Carlos Manuel went back to the computer. He typed in a name, Milton Lafayette, moved the cursor to "search," then hit "enter."

BARTER STARTED HIS discussion with the Canadian police on the wrong foot when he stated that the man they were after was on the FBI's ten-most-wanted list.

"That's not so," replied the first Canadian officer, showing him the latest FBI list from which Ramiro Ramos had been removed.

The second Canadian officer then asked for his identification, and went very carefully over all the documents Barter had brought in a dossier on the case, as if suspecting fraud. One hour later, he was told that the information provided was sufficient basis for arresting the fugitive if he came to pick up the package at the DHL office in Montreal. The package was due to arrive Sunday night, to be released to the person who presented the correct code name and number. The Canadians made it clear that they had no authority to detain any person who came to claim the parcel unless it was the same man whose photos were provided by the CIA officer.

Barter protested: "This guy we're after is a master of disguise. He could walk in there looking like an eighty-year-old, a good-looking woman, or an opera singer. His hair could be any color or style. He could also show up totally bald, or tattooed from head to toe, using false teeth, covered in makeup. The color of his eyes changes every time he changes his contact lenses. Just to make sure, you have to detain anybody—*anybody*—who comes to pick up that parcel."

"What if he sends someone else? Somebody who can identify himself as a respectable, law-abiding citizen. There would be no grounds for detention."

"We're 100 percent sure the man we're looking for will be the only one who will come to claim the package. We have absolutely reliable inside information."

"As good as your FBI list?"

Seeing in the Canadian's eyes that his word wasn't good enough, Barter decided to go a step further. "Our office in London managed to take a look at what's in the package. I have a photocopy. By the nature of the contents, we know for sure our man—and no one else—will be here to pick up the package."

"What's in the package?" both Canadian officers asked simultaneously.

"Look here—it's a Swiss passport issued seven years ago in the name of Manfred Riklin. With this passport, this criminal has travelled half the world. He even has a permanent visa from Canada."

The two officers looked at the photocopy of the passport and checked it against the photographs taken at Krome Detention Center.

"Doesn't look like the same man," one of the officers said.

"Not at all," the other agreed.

"Do you see what I mean? It's proof that he's a master of disguise," Barter said.

That settled the matter. Anybody who claimed the parcel would be detained.

The two Canadian police officers insisted on discussing with Barter the protocol to be followed during and after the operation. Setting the rules took quite a bit of haggling, but the Canadian police would not budge on their primary point: The CIA officer had to remain in his room until he was allowed to see and question the would-be prisoner. Barter had to remain caged in his hotel room all weekend waiting for the call.

On Monday morning, October 17, a man came to claim the package. He gave a full explanation of where it was coming from, the DHL parcel number, and the code name and number required, proving that he was the owner. The female clerk went into a back room and emerged a few minutes later carrying a small package carefully in her two hands, as if it might explode. The woman wrote something down on a slip. Then the man signed the receipt, put the package inside one of his overcoat pockets, and walked out of the office. He was followed by two other customers. As soon as he stepped out of the building, the two customers and another four men waiting outside forced him against a wall with his hands and legs spread-eagled while they identified themselves as the police.

When Barter reached the location where he would be allowed to question the detained man, he found the two Canadian officers with whom he had coordinated the operation. The Canadians were in a merry mood, obviously pleased at the successful outcome. The three of them entered a heavily guarded room where a husky black man stood in his underwear, looking confusedly at the men surrounding him.

"This is your man, Mr. Barter. As you told us, he really is a master of disguise. We've made him take three showers with plenty of soap and water, and there's no way to wash off his makeup."

AFTER PICKING UP Fletcher's car in the
library parking lot, Carlos drove to highway 89 on
his way to Montpelier, the state capital, where he
intended to make some inquiries about Milton
Lafayette.

From the information he had collected on the Internet, he knew
that Milton was a married man with two sons and a daughter. He
was born in 1955, graduated from Harvard Law School, and, since
then, had been slowly climbing up the political ladder of his state.
Mrs. Lafayette was a tall, slender, pretty woman, who belonged to
one of the most prestigious Vermont families and was very active in
politics herself. In fact, in some ways she was surpassing her husband's career. Their eldest child was a boy of ten, and the youngest
a daughter of three. The Lafayette family had an aura of dignity and
tradition about them, bestowed by Milton's famous ancestor, the
Marquis de Lafayette.

In the short time that Carlos Manuel spent in the tiny capital of
Montpelier, he found little additional information about Milton
Lafayette. The last hours before sunset, he took a look at Milton's
house and also his parent's house, where two of his sisters lived
with their father. Up to that moment, he had no clear plan about
what he could do to stop Milton from harassing Janice. He had no

information that he could use against him, and information was the key to any intelligent move. The other alternative was simply to walk up to him and shoot out one of his eyes, but—despite his recent action—that wasn't his style.

The first thing he noticed when he got back to the house was the recent tracks of a car pulling into the backyard. It was impossible to see the vehicle in the thick darkness surrounding the house, but the tracks were clear on the thin layer of snow that had fallen early in the evening. Janice's room was lit up. He tried to listen for any noise coming from inside the house, but the wind blowing against the naked maple trees around the house dampened whatever noise could be heard from inside. He went into the house as quietly as is possible in a wooden house. Once inside, he heard unmistakable sounds from Janice's bedroom, as well as sighs and a weak cry he knew were coming from a thirteen-year-old boy waiting outside the room with a .38-caliber Smith and Wesson revolver, ready to kill the man who was abusing his mother.

Carlos Manuel remembered his own words to Michael: "Don't do it. You'll spoil your life and your mother's life forever. You two have to find another way out, maybe leaving this state for a while . . . But if you can't do anything else and feel it's impossible to go on living like this, and you make a final decision, then you have to know how to do it. A .38-caliber revolver with new bullets is best. Don't try to break into the room. You might be overpowered or hurt your own mother with a stray bullet. Above all, be calm, and think out every detail ahead of time. Wait outside; he has to come out sometime. Take him by surprise; don't give him any chances and don't say anything to him. Just fire twice at close range at the center of his chest the very moment he appears in front of you, from an angle so that the bullet, if it goes through him, won't have a chance of hurting your mother behind him. And, son, be mentally prepared to spend seven or eight years in a reformatory school."

Since their first meeting, he had opened his heart to Michael, who longed so desperately for a father. Until that minute, he had concealed how much he liked Janice, as much in need of love as her child, both involved in a deep problem that threatened to end in their own destruction. Again, his mind and his heart split, pulling in opposite directions. He had to go back to Cuba, maybe "to a dungeon for the rest of your life," as his sister had told him. His duty was there, with the people who had trusted him and helped him to save his children; where his father's and his own dreams for a better society for all people lay half-buried, half-washed away, half-alive.

But could he ever sleep again if he turned his back now and fled?

"It's all right, I'll take it from here," Carlos Manuel whispered to Michael, who hadn't heard him coming upstairs. The boy was staring at the door as if hypnotized, listening to his mother struggling inside.

"Lend me the gun, Michael. Let's see what I can do. Go downstairs and turn on the lights, and stay there until I call you," Carlos Manuel said quietly, pointing at the weapon.

The boy surrendered the gun and left, switching on all the lights in the staircase and in the entrance area on the first floor.

Carlos Manuel placed an ear to the door, then knocked hard. The sounds inside stopped.

"Mrs. Howard, the water is cold. I can't take a shower with that cold water. You forgot to turn the gas heater on. I need you to turn it on right now."

The unusual request brought another spell of silence.

Carlos Manuel knocked on the door harder. "Mrs. Howard, I insist on the hot water. I paid my rent in full. I have the right to hot water in the shower."

"Go fuck off, jackass. Scram!" the coarse voice of a man shouted from inside the room.

"Hey, mister. I want to talk to my landlady. I don't want to talk to a fag who needs to beat up a woman to get an erection."

Silence again for a few seconds, then the door flew open. The gigantic body of Milton Lafayette stood half-naked in the doorway, about three feet from Carlos Manuel, who had now placed himself right at the top of the stairs, leaning on the banister. Janice came after Milton and tried to pull him inside, but Milton pushed her back easily.

"John, he's armed. He'll kill you!" Janice shouted, then started to cry in her helplessness.

"So you're the painter! Let me show you what I did with your canvases." Milton bent down and picked up scraps of the paintings, torn into hundreds of pieces, and threw them at Carlos Manuel.

Six-and-a-half feet tall and weighing 260 pounds, Lafayette had a large paunch that had grown in the last ten years from too much eating and too little physical exercise. But he had been well trained in boxing and wrestling during the years he attended Harvard Law School. Facing him, Carlos Manuel looked small and thin.

"You're just a pitiful, frustrated homosexual. Nothing wrong with gays, as long as they behave like homosexuals. The problem comes when they try to play like they're men."

Milton, in a surge of blind rage, charged Carlos Manuel like a bull going after the red cloth. Carlos Manuel stepped aside and kicked Milton's genitals with his left foot. The giant bent over in pain. Then, holding onto the banister, Carlos Manuel swung back and shoved Milton off his feet. The heavy body of the man plunged down the stairs. As he was falling, Milton tried to reach for the gun strapped to his back. Carlos Manuel jumped with his full weight on Milton's paunch. The giant cried out, feeling as if something inside his belly had exploded. His gun rolled to the bottom step of the stairs. Milton edged down, trying to reach the gun but, before he could, he was hit again by the full weight of his opponent, this time on his back and head. The whole house reverberated with the weight of two heavy bodies slamming onto the wooden floor. Milton remained motionless for a few seconds, then moved in an attempt to get up. Carlos Manuel was at his side and, as Milton managed to stand, he jabbed him again in the genitals with his knee. The giant fell to the floor and curled up with an expression of unbearable pain. His mind went blank.

When Milton Lafayette regained full consciousness, he found himself tied to the banister at the foot of the stairs with a short nylon cord. The cord was fastened to a fishing hook that was deeply embedded in his fully extended tongue. He had to use both hands to keep his body steady in a sitting position, to lessen the pain and avoid having his tongue ripped out. His eyes protruded, his body was shaking with fear; every involuntary movement added to his agony. Janice, leaning against a wall ten feet away, watched the scene with horror and fascination. Michael stood closer, not wanting to miss a word that the mysterious tenant—who had transformed himself into a completely different man—was saying to this once-mighty giant, now immobilized by a thin nylon cord.

"Look, fellow, I have nothing against you. I'm just doing a job. Somebody paid my company ten grand plus expenses in advance to have you cut into pieces and thrown into the lake. When I get back to L.A. with the job done, this person will pay another ten grand. I accepted this contract because I thought it was a regular job. I'd have asked for twice as much money if I'd known you were so big and heavy. Now, I have a logistical problem with you. Usually, when I kill a normal human being, I put the body in a plastic bag and carry it by myself to the trunk of a car and then to some isolated place. There, I chop it up into several parts with an electric saw, using the car's electricity. Then, I put the pieces into smaller plastic bags and spread them around in different places. Or, I just dispose of the whole body. It depends."

Carlos Manuel stood silent for a moment. He then shrugged and said, "I have no other choice but to cut you into pieces in here with this ax that I found in the backyard. Shit! That's a lot of hard work and a lot of complication."

When Milton Lafayette started to tremble uncontrollably,

Carlos Manuel gave the nylon cord a little slack. A strange sound, like a moan, started to emanate from Milton's throat. A bad odor invaded the room and his urine began to run on the floor.

Carlos Manuel backed off and shouted, "This is disgusting!"

"Please, Mr. Wilkinson, don't kill him. Please." Janice's voice was weak, as if she were about to faint.

AT FOUR O'CLOCK in the morning, Roy W. Andrews, head of the FBI division in Vermont, was awakened in his house by a phone call. Stanley Beacon, the legendary state attorney, wanted to talk with him immediately.

"Roy, somebody beat up Milton very badly. He's in the hospital now. A surgeon is taking a fishhook out of his tongue. I want you to step into this case."

"Yes, sir. Who did it?" Andrews asked, half-awake.

"Nobody knows yet. Milton hasn't said a word. I sent Shortie to take a look and he just called me back. He says that Milton is very scared, as scared as he has ever seen a human being. He believes this was done by a pro, someone who knew very well what he was doing. Who paid this guy? Why does someone want to scare Milton? That's what I need you to find out."

"I'll get on it."

"Is there anything I can do?" Beacon asked.

"You could have someone look into the affairs Milton has been handling to see if there's anything relevant there."

"I've already ordered everyone who works directly with Milton to write a report on anything that may have any possible, even remote, connection with this. First thing in the morning, you'll have all those reports by fax." Beacon paused. "There's another thing I want to talk to you about, Roy."

Andrews had to wait thirty seconds before the old man spoke again.

"As you know, Milton has been involved in the past in some bizarre situations . . . Some of them ugly, very ugly. You get me?"

"Yes, sir. I follow you."

"This time, he's not a university student or a private citizen. He's now a part of something much more important than he is. Do you follow me?"

"Sure, sir, I follow you."

"Okay, Andrews, whichever way this investigation goes, be on top of it. I don't want scandals, nothing that could be exploited as a political issue, if by any chance Milton is into that kind of trouble again. Do you read me?"

"Yes, Stanley. I read you loud and clear."

On Tuesday, October 18, at 10:35 in the morning, in one of the Burlington FBI offices on Pearl Street, a computer set to receive the reports from the state attorney's office by fax started beeping. On the screen, the photo of a man blinked for a few seconds. Below the photo were the names John Wilkinson/ Carlos Manuel Armas/ Ramiro Ramos.

On Tuesday, October 18, in the afternoon, Gabriel went to see Barter at his Miami home. He found him packing, getting ready to move out of the house he had rented.

"What's going on?" Gabriel asked after the usual greetings.

"As you see, there's nothing else for me to do around here. It's a shame this chase didn't last all winter. I was beginning to like the weather here. How was your trip to San Diego?"

"Came back yesterday. There was a letter from our man waiting for his sister at the motel. The FBI in San Diego managed to open and photocopy it. It had been mailed a week before from Mexico

City. It's a nice farewell letter, long and intimate, full of loving thoughts. The sister read it ten times and ended up weeping. That was all."

"Maybe that was the last we'll hear of that guy," Barter said, going back to his packing.

"I don't know if it's ended yet. I came to tell you about a piece of brand new information that might be interesting," Gabriel replied.

"What is it?" Barter asked, applying tape to a cardboard box filled with the open information he had collected during his quest—photos he had taken in Florida and Nicaragua, and assorted mementos he had gathered during his work in the last few weeks. He was going to send the box to his parents' house in Utah. There, it would be put into in an attic where he had collected many boxes like this one through the years.

"The name John Wilkinson has come up in an investigation in Burlington, Vermont."

Barter dropped what he was doing and sat down in a chair to listen to Gabriel, who was lying on the sofa. Burlington is very close to Montreal, Barter thought.

"The assistant to the state attorney, a man named Milton Lafayette, was badly beaten last night. He's still in a state of shock. A report from a man who works with Milton says that his boss had asked him recently to run an investigation on a John Wilkinson. The computer flashed the red light this morning . . . As you may know, any information that goes through an FBI computer is checked automatically against a list with the names of wanted people. It works like a virus detector."

"Have they detained that John Wilkinson?"

"No, he was last seen yesterday at the university library where he used to work every morning. An interesting coincidence is that he first appeared there a couple of days after Carlos Manuel separated from his sister."

The photos of a deer-hunting trip Carlos Manuel and his father had taken in Vermont came to Barter's mind. He had seen those photos when he visited the FBI task-force headquarters in New York, along with many other photos and documents Marjorie's maid had managed to copy.

"What are we waiting for?" Barter asked, rising.

"I have to stay," Gabriel replied, scratching his head, a gesture he often made. "I have to catch up on a lot of my regular work with the Cuban community in town. I'll call the FBI senior officer in Burlington and he'll give you all the backup you'll need. Please, keep me updated if you can. I'll join you in a couple of days, if necessary."

Gabriel shook Barter's hand and left.

"My guess is that he rented a room in some private home close to the university. Much cheaper and more difficult to locate."

"Mr. Barter, we keep no records of the people renting rooms in private homes. There must be over five hundred rooms rented just to university students near the campus. I must remind you that there is a 99 percent probability that this guy left town Monday night, right after this happened. Now, he could be anywhere in the nation."

Roy W. Andrews, chief FBI officer in Burlington, was reluctant to start the investigation Barter was proposing. He had told Barter that they had tracked down all the Wilkinsons in the state of Vermont and none of them were the John Wilkinson mentioned in the report. They had already taken all the necessary steps to detain the man who was doing research work in the university library as soon he was seen anywhere in Vermont again. Barter was getting Andrews's message: *They had more important things to do than chase this alleged Cuban spy on the run.*

"We have inside information that this guy was ready to catch a plane yesterday in Montreal and was supposed to pick up his passport and airline ticket at the DHL office."

"Why not catch him there?" Andrews interrupted, impatient.

"That's what we tried to do, but someone else went to pick up the parcel. We believe that the whole plan had to be changed at the last minute, and there's a good possibility he's still around."

The FBI detective found that his cup of coffee was already cold. He fetched a thermos full of steaming coffee to freshen his drink. After a sip, he said, "The only thing I can think to do is publish his photo in the *Burlington Free Press*. Mr. Barter, to be honest with you, this doesn't make any sense. Look, this incident happened late Monday night. Today is Wednesday—thirty-six hours have passed. He could be anywhere now. Best way to locate him is to put his photo on nationwide television. That's the way we solve a lot of our cases."

"Do you mind going with me to the hospital to see this man, Lafayette?"

"Milton belongs to one of the oldest families in Vermont. He's a direct descendant of Marie Joseph Paul Yves Gilbert du Mothier, Marquis de Lafayette, who fought alongside George Washington in the American Revolution, participated in the French Revolution, and, among other feats, created the modern French flag," Andrews said, as they walked into the hospital where Milton was recuperating.

Barter wondered if the information he was getting from Andrews was meant to overwhelm him with his thorough knowledge of American history, or to prepare him to meet a living historical monument.

The hospital room accommodating the assistant to the state attorney was heavily guarded. The big man lying inside could not speak on account of an injury to his tongue, but he had full use of both hands, Barter noted.

They tried to question Lafayette, but the man wouldn't cooperate. It was clear that he understood all that was asked, but simply would not answer anything, even the questions that only required him to nod his head. That was strange behavior for a state attorney's assistant who was supposed to fill the post that would be vacant when old Stanley Beacon, who had been elected state attorney for the last five terms, decided he'd had enough or passed away.

Going down in the elevator, Barter asked Andrews, "If this illustrious character is so shaken up he can't speak a word, write a note, or nod his head, where do we stand now? Who said Wilkinson was involved?"

"Take it easy. The man is waiting for us downstairs."

"Yes, Mr. Lafayette ordered me to investigate John Wilkinson, and told me he was supposed to be doing some research at the university library."

The man who had answered the question was looking up from his five-feet-three inches—elevator shoes included—at the two tall men standing with him in the middle of the waiting room of the hospital.

Barter thought that a better atmosphere could help the interview and invited the two men to dinner at a nearby restaurant Andrews had recommended.

"Shortie, start from the beginning and tell Mr. Barter what you found out," Andrews said as soon as they were seated.

"This Wilkinson actually consulted a lot of old maps and books on the geography of this area and on the first Vermont settlers. That was the thesis he was working on, I believe."

"What else?" Andrews asked, impatient.

"Nothing else. Mr. Lafayette just wanted to check on what Wilkinson was doing. He didn't tell me to go any further."

"Did you see this Mr. Wilkinson?" Barter asked.

"Of course, I took a good look at him while I was trying to find out what he was doing."

"We already showed Shortie photos of John Wilkinson/Ramiro Ramos. He thinks it's a different man," Andrews said.

"Let's try it again." Barter pulled an envelope from his coat pocket and placed on the table a set of pictures that he had composed on the computer based on the Ramiro Ramos shots taken at

Krome Detention Center. He had changed the hair to gray, brown, and red, reduced the sideburns, and removed the mustache. Some of the pictures were with diverse types of glasses.

"This could very well be the man." Shortie pointed to one of the altered photos. "He's using a different haircut, looks a whole lot different, but, yes, I think it's the same person."

Barter smiled at Andrews. "Why do you think your boss ordered the investigation?" Barter asked.

"Private affair." Shortie smirked, as if he knew something about his boss he shouldn't say.

"What private affair?" Barter pressed.

The pint-size investigator looked worried, as if he had to keep his mouth shut if he wanted to save his job.

"You could be in mortal danger if we don't catch this guy. I know him quite well. Look what he did to your boss. If he knows you've been spying on him and you're able to recognize him, there's no telling what he could do to you. I advise you not to withhold any information, regardless of its nature," Barter warned.

By his eagerness to answer from then on, it seemed clear that Shortie had only needed that small encouragement to tell everything he knew about his boss. "I'd done a lot of work for Mr. Lafayette of a private nature. He is obsessed with the idea that his wife might be seeing other men, so I had to spend a great deal of time following her. I believe he thinks some of his kids are not his. On the other hand, sometimes he himself would disappear for a whole night, or even a day or two, and my guess is that he was fooling around with another woman. In the past he had told me to investigate some men that might be connected with these affairs. *Cherchez la femme*, French detectives say."

"Was this man seeing Mrs. Lafayette?" Barter asked.

Shortie looked at Andrews's face and suddenly changed the tone of his voice. "No. Mr. Lafayette only told me to find out if this man Wilkinson was really doing research at the library. That was what I did. Besides, I hated that kind of work, because the state doesn't pay me for it. I always gave the reports on these assignments to Mr. Lafayette personally. Never filed them. When this happened, Mr. Beacon ordered me to check Mr. Lafayette's files to see if there was something in them that could explain the attack and why Milton doesn't want to say anything. You know, Mafia business, blackmailing, something like that. I included that bit of information on Wilkinson in my report because it was the only unusual thing I could find. "

"*Cherchez la femme,*" Barter repeated, as if talking to himself. "What sort of a man is this Milton Lafayette?"

"A regular son of a bitch just like every politician," Andrews said quickly, to kill the question. He looked at his wristwatch.

Shortie, who was eating voraciously, corrected him: "A king-size son of a bitch."

"Mr. Barter, I'll repeat what I said when you came up. If this guy Wilkinson, or whatever his name is, is the one who worked over Milton Lafayette, he must be enjoying the sun on a beach in Cuba by now, after going through all this cold weather we have here. What else do you want to do?"

Barter thought of Andrews's idea of publishing a photo in the local newspaper but dismissed it, thinking that was the best way to send his prey away if, by any fat chance, he was still around. "Tomorrow I'll fool around town for a while before I call it quits and fly back to Washington. I'll call you if I stumble onto something worth your while."

"When Milton gets better, I'll drill him to find out about his connection to this Wilkinson, and I'll file a report on that," Andrews assured Barter. Then, changing his tone, he added, "There's another thing I should tell you. We don't want this investigation to become involved in state politics. Let's try to keep it focused on this spy on the run. Do you know what I mean?"

Barter had already received the message. "Don't worry about it," he replied.

* * *

The next day, Barter took a taxi to the university library to question the employees. He went to see the head librarian, Marietta La Motte. He produced from his wallet a business card with a phony name, stating that he worked for an insurance company. He told her that he was locating John Wilkinson to give him his indemnity check for a car accident.

"The last time he came by was on Monday morning," Mrs. La Motte said. "He told me he was going to do some field trips to get better acquainted with the state. I'm sure he'll be back soon to finish his research."

"Just for curiosity's sake—what sort of research is he doing?" Barter asked.

"Mr. Wilkinson is studying a select group of Vermont settlers and the role those families have played in Vermont's development. He's a very hardworking and intelligent researcher. He has already made some fascinating findings."

"Do you know where he's staying in town? I really need to meet him as soon as possible."

"No, I don't."

"Did he make any friends here? Date any of the women working here?"

The head librarian said no with a slight movement of her head. It was easy to sense that she didn't like that kind of question.

"If I'd hung around all this time, I'd have asked you for a date," Barter said, trying to break the icy layer surrounding the woman.

The woman blushed and shook her head, turning back to her work.

The young woman who supervised the computers made a curious remark: "He never sat in the same place. Everyone who comes here always uses the same seat if it's available. Mr. Wilkinson always came early when this place was empty, and never sat in the same seat. That's the damnedest thing I've seen. Maybe he's superstitious about it."

"You've proved to be a keen observer. Do you know anyone else I could question about Mr. Wilkinson?"

"Try the janitor, Bernard Fletcher. I saw him talking to Mr. Wilkinson several times. The other day, Wilkinson invited him for a cup of coffee. You might be lucky and get some information out of Fletcher."

Barter talked with the rest of the people who worked in the reading rooms and at the computers, but collected no other piece of information that added anything to what he had already learned. As he was walking out of the library, he saw a janitor washing a window.

"Are you Bernard Fletcher?"

The janitor stopped what he was doing to carefully study the man speaking to him.

"What do you want with Bernard Fletcher?"

"I just want to ask if he knows a man I'm looking for, John Wilkinson."

Fletcher went on cleaning the window for a while, seeming to consider how to respond. "Do you have a card or something?" Fletcher said, and added, "I know who John Wilkinson is. I can give him your card when I see him again."

"Do you know where he lives?"

"Nope, I don't."

Barter gave the janitor his phony business card and left, suspecting that Fletcher hadn't said all he knew about Wilkinson. Judging by the way he had behaved, it seemed clear he had the typical New Englander's mistrust of strangers, and it would be no use trying to question him again.

Cherchez la femme. The phrase returned to Barter's mind several times. Ever since their meeting the day before, he had become sure that Shortie knew a lot more than he was willing to let on in the presence of the local FBI senior officer. Barter decided to rent a car and go to Montpelier to talk to him again. He found Shortie in a tiny room, at the back of one of the many government buildings in the state capital.

"Mr. Collins . . ."

"Call me Shortie—everybody else does."

"Okay, Shortie. Yesterday, I didn't tell you that I work with the CIA. We want to locate this man if he's still around, or we want to find out where he went. I'm convinced that, with your information and knowledge about your boss's habits, you're in a better position than anybody else to do this job. I'd like to hire you as a private investigator for a fee—let's say five hundred a day? There is, of course, the 100 grand reward offered for this man that will be yours if we find him."

The eyes of the investigator flashed, but he collected himself enough to lay out his conditions. "This has to be confidential. If I hit the jackpot, it doesn't matter, but if I have to keep on working here until retirement, then I might run into big trouble."

Barter waved his hands in the air in a reassuring gesture. "Nothing to worry about," he said firmly.

Shortie smiled. He reached for a key chained to his belt, swung his revolving chair 180 degrees to face a steel cabinet behind him, and opened a middle drawer. He went directly to a folder and took a look at a page inside.

"I keep notes on everything I do," Shortie said, with a wicked smile on his face. "Let me check on somebody who lives very close to the university library."

He wrote a name and address on a piece of paper, then got up from his chair and said, "I got it. Janice Howard, age thirty-three, single, one of thirteen children. 420 Buell Street, Burlington."

THIS MILTON IS a weird guy," Shortie said.

"Weird? In what sense?"

"When he was in his third year in law school, there were some nasty rumors about his having homosexual relations with his roommate, a weight-lifting champion. Old man Lafayette was very upset about that. But rumors, only rumors," Shortie added hastily, "not any hard proof."

"You think Milton doesn't say anything about what happened to him because it may backfire on him?"

"I believe he's not talking because he's scared shitless. I was the first to arrive at the hospital shortly after he got there. He had shit and piss all over his pants. He was still trembling, and his eyes were popping out of his head. The doctors had to pull a big fishhook out of his tongue. His balls were swollen to about five times their normal size. When you saw him yesterday, he was heavily sedated."

When the pair arrived at Janice's house it was locked, and nobody answered the doorbell. Shortie asked the neighbors if they knew Janice's whereabouts. None of them had seen the mother or son since Monday. Barter took a peek into the garage and saw a car inside. In the backyard, another car was standing beneath a canvas. Shortie decided that they must have left in a third car. "Maybe this

John Wilkinson rented a room in this house and was having an affair with Janice. Milton came home and found this guy with his girl and tried to shake him up. Or maybe it was the other way around—this guy came home and found Milton hitting his lady and got mad. There are rumors that Milton likes to beat his women. Those are my best guesses."

Barter had no other choice but to call on Andrews, who didn't hide his disgust when he saw Barter again, close to five o'clock in the afternoon. It was Friday, and he had planned to be home early for a change.

"I need access to your information on two people: Janice Howard and Bernard Fletcher. Next, I want a search warrant for Janice Howard and her son, Michael, who could be kidnapped by this spy we're after," Barter said.

Andrews made a signal to a young man, who invited Barter to follow him. Ten minutes later, Barter cried "Bingo!" as he collected a sheet out of the printer.

The sheet stated that in the last three weeks, Bernard Fletcher had asked for and obtained a certified copy of his birth certificate from the Department of Health, and a duplicate of his driver's license. He had opened and closed accounts in two banks, acquired a MasterCard and Visa, and applied for a U.S. passport by express service.

It didn't take much imagination, Barter thought, to figure out that all of this was done by Carlos Manuel, usurping Bernard Fletcher's identity. With the sheet of paper in his hand, Barter ran to Andrews's office to call the New York task force and activate a nationwide, last-minute chase.

As Barter finished explaining his findings to Andrews, the young computer specialist who had stood behind him waiting asked permission to interrupt.

"Bernard Fletcher signed for and picked up his passport Wednesday afternoon. He's booked to fly to Cancún, Mexico from the Burlington airport in half an hour. He must be boarding now."

Pandemonium broke loose in seconds. Andrews transformed himself into a demon, barking orders through different phones and to people summoned to his office by the touch of a button. Barter later told King that he had been fascinated by the way the elephant moved.

Barter and Andrews arrived at the airport when all the invisible forces unleashed had completed their jobs to perfection. The man using a passport in the name of Bernard Fletcher had been detained and brought by a whole platoon of FBI agents to a room converted into the headquarters of the flash operation. In the meantime, the American Airlines plane had been held back, all passengers de-boarded, and the plane searched from one end to the other.

Barter closed and opened his eyes several times when the man using Fletcher's passport, heavily handcuffed, was finally brought before him.

"Hello, Mr. Fletcher," Barter said. "Have you seen your friend Mr. Wilkinson yet?"

"I was supposed to see him soon and give him your card as I promised you." Fletcher was stunned, unable to understand why he had been brought in such a way to answer the questions of a car-insurance agent.

"When was the last time you saw him?" Andrews asked.

"Monday night. He came by my house with his wife and kid to say goodbye. They were driving all the way to Cancún. I'm supposed to meet them there today. He said he speaks Spanish and he'll introduce me to some nice ladies he knows there."

On the way back to town, neither Andrews nor Barter spoke a word. When Andrews stopped his car to let the CIA officer out in front of his hotel, Barter said, "Just tell me the best place to spend this weekend skiing. I hope I'll break a leg so I can take some time off."

BULLSHIT! Don't ask me to believe that you spent nearly a month in a concentration camp and walked out undetected, right under the nose of the CIA and the FBI. That will contradict all my experience over the last twenty years." Colonel Francisco raised his voice for the first time in six days of questioning and stood silent, staring at the man before him.

The man being questioned did not move a muscle. The colonel might have been talking to a wall. Then, Francisco pointed a thick finger at him and, like a father talking to a child who is clearly lying, tried to reason things out. "Listen. The CIA knew about your trip from the beginning. Right after you left Cuba, they started asking questions everywhere, looking for any sort of information about an important intelligence officer who had defected from Cuba. So, they had to figure that there was more than a fair chance that the man they were looking for was in one of their refugee camps. And they have the means to check everyone who gets in there."

Colonel Francisco put on a tired, honest face and changed to a friendlier tone of voice, pleading, "Why don't you help us think in a more professional way? Why don't you tell us the reasons why they let you go? Did they do it to follow you and get your possible contacts? Did they offer you any sort of deal? Did you accept a deal just to come back to Cuba?" Francisco stopped for a moment, waiting for a reply that didn't come.

"Don't be afraid to tell us the truth," Francisco continued, amiable and relaxed. "The hard fact is that you came back. *That places your loyalty beyond any question.* Whatever happened in the camp and while you were hiding in the U.S. can be explained, and we're ready to understand it, to get through with all of this quickly and let you go. None of us like to keep drilling you, a man who has devoted his entire life to serving our cause. What really happened there? Why do you keep yammering on about a completely unbelievable story that we simply can't accept?"

Carlos Manuel smiled faintly, thinking that he wasn't going to be caught in so simple a trap. If he indicated in any way that the CIA had let him out of Krome Detention Center, knowing his real identity, he would be admitting that he'd had some sort of understanding with the CIA. From there, it would be easy to imagine that his time in the camp and his wandering around the U.S. had been nothing more than a cover-up.

"I'm sure they never detected me. I had a plan to pass through their screening, and it worked perfectly."

"And how long had you had that plan worked out? A month? A week before you travelled to the U.S.?"

"Between the time the Coast Guard stopped chasing me and the U.S. ship picked me up, I had plenty of time to think it through."

"When exactly was it that you cooked up your brilliant and infallible plan—while escaping a gunboat taking potshots at you? While fighting off the band of pirates? Or while paddling behind the lifeboat?" Francisco asked the questions with open scorn and mockery.

Carlos Manuel kept his voice calm and even, delivering his answers to the State Security investigation team sitting at the back, bypassing Francisco as if he weren't present. "To begin with, I put myself in the place of the American officers in charge of checking the stories of thousands of immigrants arriving there. I decided I could use a story that couldn't be checked unless they made a thorough investigation here in Cuba. I knew they didn't have my fingerprints, or even photos that resembled me. Even if they had information on someone defecting from the Cuban Intelligence Service, only a few people knew my real identity, and those people would never reveal it."

As Carlos Manuel talked, Francisco started playing with his pen and looked out the window, giving clear signals that he wasn't listening.

"I pretended to be one of the eight construction workers from the eastern provinces staying in the building where I was living in Havana. I knew them very well. At night, after dinner, they always invited me to drink coffee, some of the coffee they brought from their provinces to sell here in Havana to make some extra money. Also, I watched baseball games with them on their old black-and-white TV set. I got along very well with a couple of them. We used to talk almost every night until it was time to go to bed. I asked them all sorts of questions about what was going on in their provinces under the country's new economic situation. They loved to chat about their families and friends, the little things they used to do there every day. I listened to the stories of each one, explaining why they had come to work in Havana. I used all that information in my cover story, including the way they talk, the way they walk . . ."

"We've already listened to all of that garbage," interrupted Francisco.

"I adopted the name and life story of Ramiro Ramos, a man about my age and my build but with much less hair. He was born on a farm close to the town of Velasco, Holguín Province. Ramiro was the third son of a farmer, owner of a small plot where they grew plantains, black beans, garlic, papaya, and manioc. Ramiro never got along too well with his father and elder brothers. Besides, they were too many men for the amount of work on the farm. As often occurs with younger brothers, Ramiro had to leave his parents' home to earn his living. He did all sorts of jobs. For several years he cut sugarcane at harvest time in a sugar mill not very far from his home. Later, he decided to see the world, so he went to work on the Isle of Youth, picking grapefruit. He travelled to the west as far as Pinar del Rio. Finally, he became a construction worker in Havana, a much easier job and better paid than any farmwork, he told me. Ramiro spent most of his time off looking for a woman who owned a house or an apartment who might accept him as a husband, the only way for him to be able to move to Havana and live a regular life here. That was the story I told them. At the same time, I always tried to remain as inconspicuous as possible—a blank face in the crowd."

Colonel Francisco looked at Carlos Manuel with an expression of infinite boredom, as if he were totally fed up with listening to the same fairy tale for the hundredth time.

"They just accepted your story like that!" The colonel snapped his fingers with a sarcastic laugh. He turned to the State Security officers behind him, and added, "Listen to this, boys, an intelligence officer who arrived in the U.S. on a stolen yacht, suddenly becomes a peasant from the eastern provinces, and they believed it, just like that." The colonel snapped his fingers again and laughed.

"I told you that the yacht sank before I reached Florida. I believe that you have forgotten some of the things I said. I had better repeat the story from the beginning . . ."

"I've heard enough."

"Excuse me, Colonel, you should listen to it again." The prisoner raised his voice a bit.

"I've had enough."

"If you keep twisting things around, I'll have to keep untwisting them for you." The prisoner raised his voice still louder.

Colonel Francisco walked abruptly out of the room, indicating his refusal to hear more.

The three officers of the State Security Police in charge of the investigation watched as the head prosecutor abandoned the room.

When the sound of his steps faded away down the hall, they started their own questions, all of them aimed at pinning down details on everything the prisoner had declared since he'd been jailed, trying to detect any flaws and contradictions, and at the same time, collecting information they could cross-check with their own sources.

"We want you to focus now on the FBI or CIA undercover agents among the camp inmates," said the head of the group, a stolid and very tall man named Mario.

The cell was kept dark at all times. It was impossible to tell day from night. As soon as Carlos Manuel arrived each day after questioning, he stripped off his clothes and did physical exercises until he became exhausted. The small cell was warm during the daytime and cool at night. It was late November and the weather had definitely changed after six months of high temperatures, torrential rains, and high humidity. Food was plain and scarce. He was losing weight despite the little physical effort he did outside of his daily routine. When he wasn't being questioned, he spent most of his time trying to sleep. Nothing really worried him, not even the worst possible outcome of the investigation. He felt almost in a state of grace, having regained his children's love.

As time passed, questioning became rougher. Often, he would be suddenly awakened after two or three hours of sleep and taken out for many hours of interrogation under bright lights, then brought back for another short dose of sleep, and brought back again to answer the same questions. The State Security team worked relentlessly to break his self-control, to induce in him a state of mental confusion and insecurity. But he knew the system and how to beat it.

The only way to escape from his cell and the interrogations was by recalling everything that had happened in the last months that had changed the course of his life so thoroughly. Those memories were like dreams, and he had the power to retrieve them, erasing from his mind the situation he was in. He could go back in time at will, remembering each detail of the days spent in Orlando with his kids and sister and the long ride with Margarita to Philadelphia. He never tired of bringing Janice's face and every part of her body back into his mind. Sometimes he could even feel the little kisses she gave him when she thought he was asleep. Michael's intent face when he asked him questions and listened to the answers came often to him. The excursion on Lake Champlain; the first lunch he had with Janice and Michael . . . Those were secret resources that he used to endure the stressful conditions under which he was living.

No visits were allowed, except for a woman who came every week to bring him clean clothes and take away his dirty laundry. The woman would also bring him a thermos full of an iced fruit milk-shake that he drank to the last drop during the ten-minute visit. Every week the woman brought a different flavor: mango, banana, pineapple, red *mamey, guanábana*, guava, tamarind, *anón* . . . He knew his friends had sent her, but he never asked her any questions. The woman, a mulatta with solid round breasts, big hips, and protruding buttocks, smiled all the time with a perfect set of white, strong teeth. She told him how good a cook she was, promising to cook him all sorts of delicious dishes once he was out of jail. By the way she moved her hips when she walked away, he thought there might be something besides the food in her promise. Carlos Manuel perceived Floro's hand behind those visits, maybe trying to give him a carnal motive to keep up his lonely fight.

THE STATE SECURITY investigation team was at last ready to submit its final report to the High Military Court. When they took over the case, they had been ordered to limit their inquiry to addressing only one question: *Is Carlos Manuel a traitor?* The rest of the charges were well documented and had been sufficiently cleared in a previous investigation by the police and another State Security investigation team. If the High Military Court charged him with treason, Carlos Manuel had to remain in prison until his trial, facing from eight to twenty years of imprisonment if found guilty. If he wasn't charged with treason, he could go free on bail until the trial, when he would be facing much less serious charges.

The inquiry had been thorough, going into minute detail on everything that had happened since Carlos Manuel arrived from Africa. The investigators felt they already knew as much as could be known about the man under scrutiny and his family. The hijacking of the yacht in the Almendares dockyard was also clear down to the last detail. Floro had insisted all the time that he remembered nothing, as always happened when he drank too much. Only he or Carlos Manuel could implicate the man who everyone suspected was behind the *Elvirita* hijacking—Colonel or General Marcelo, nobody knew his rank exactly. But neither of them ever mentioned

Marcelo or anything that could connect him with them. Carlos Manuel and Floro had been friends since the eighties in Africa. It was only logical that Carlos Manuel had called on Floro for help when he needed it. It was also logical that Floro would help him, and highly possible that Floro had drunk too much.

The team led by Lieutenant Colonel Mario carried out most of the inquiries and completed all of the paperwork involved in the case. Mario was a tall, thin, green-eyed man of about forty, who spoke softly and worked everything out in painstaking detail. The team went over the material again and again before reaching a conclusion to be presented to Colonel Francisco, head of the prosecution, and to a team of three of his peers, who would draw their own conclusion and present it directly to the head of the High Military Court. Finally, the court would present formal charges against the accused, a high-ranking officer himself.

Francisco was a veteran of this type of work. He had actively participated in the famous case of General Arnaldo Ochoa, a national hero who had been put on trial for helping drug dealers smuggle cocaine and marijuana into the United States back in 1986, and had been condemned to death. Colonel Francisco had participated in a great deal of the questioning on the present case. But he also seemed to reject the idea of reading the written material prepared by Mario's team. There was something about Mario that Francisco didn't like. He thought perhaps Mario, who might be a bit slow, wanted to snow him under a ton of paperwork that he considered superfluous to the case.

The other two men on the investigative team were in their thirties and, like Mario, both were graduates of Russian military schools. Francisco didn't like them, either. He viewed their thinking as too much like the boring twaddle of Russian military manuals.

There was a lot about Colonel Francisco that Mario didn't like, including, first and foremost, the narrow scope of his views. To Mario, Francisco was always more interested in expressing his own set ideas than receiving information vital to the case. Mario considered that a fatal flaw for a man in search of truth.

On the designated day, Francisco opened the hearing. "Well, men, I think you've worked hard enough on this case. By now, you ought to know if this man is or isn't a traitor. Tell us your conclusions."

The colonel opened his hands, looking at the three men who were sitting at one side of a long meeting table. On the other side were the other three prosecutors, one of whom was a colonel like Francisco.

"After going carefully over all the material we have gathered, we have not found any grounds for charging him with treason," Mario began.

Francisco was startled. This was not the answer he had expected. He felt anger rising in his chest, but managed to collect himself and ask, "On what grounds do you base that conclusion?"

"First, there is no evidence that Carlos Manuel Armas had any contacts with the enemy before or after he reached the U.S. There's plenty of proof that the CIA and the FBI searched all over the United States for him, and that he was able to escape. Second, he came back to Cuba, as he said he would, to face the charges for hijacking a yacht. If he were a traitor, he wouldn't have come back."

Francisco got up and raised his voice. "So, a high officer of the Ministry of the Interior steals a yacht and runs away to the United States, betraying his country, dishonoring his Service, and making fools of his comrades, and he isn't a traitor? What else would he have to do to be a traitor?"

Francisco looked at the blank faces of the men in front of him and was amazed they weren't able to see something so simple. He decided to go into a detailed analysis. "Let me cite an important element you've overlooked. He didn't do anything on the spur of the moment, just because by chance he found his children running away on a raft and wanted to save them from bad weather. No!

Everything was carefully planned. Listen to me, *compañeros,* I honestly believe you're missing the main points: When Carlos Manuel came home from Africa, he found himself in a very difficult situation." Francisco lifted his right hand in a fist and then stuck out a finger. "In the first place, his daughter had been in contact with her aunt in the U.S. His kids were already living very well on the money their aunt was sending them regularly. Many people in the neighborhood knew about that. They had lost public respect and they didn't care at all.

"At the beginning, they hid their counterrevolutionary opinions the best they could, but after their mother's death, Felipe and Claudia both became very outspoken. They had already decided to leave the country, using any means necessary." Another finger went out from the fist. "It was very evident that, from that moment on, Carlos Manuel Armas knew that in this situation he couldn't be trusted in the same way he had been until then. And"—Francisco took a dramatic pause—"he was dismissed from his Service." Francisco opened his hand and walked around the table before continuing.

"*Compañeros,* the accused had to come to a simple conclusion: It was impossible to mend his family life *in Cuba.* Those, you see, are very important facts you mustn't forget. All of these determined his final decision: *to leave with his kids and build a new life in the United States.*"

Francisco was a born actor. His gestures were vivid. The tone of his voice was strong and agreeable. He had a sense of drama and suspense. Mario began to think he'd been selling him short.

"Once he decided what to do, he carefully studied how to carry out his decision, and found the best way to leave the country with his children. Since he knew very well how we do our work, he moved to a room by himself as part of the plan he was inventing."

"What was the purpose of that?" Mario asked dryly.

"Like the great deceiver he is, *he wanted us to believe he had no part in his children's plans.* If they were living under the same roof, he couldn't claim he knew nothing about their plan to abandon the island. He also had to work under the assumption that he was under close surveillance by State Security or by his own Intelligence Service. It was obvious his Service wouldn't allow him to go off on his own to the United States. Do you realize how many operations had to be changed when he left? Can you imagine how much this man knows about the people who collaborate with us in those countries he worked in? His Service had to consider it very possible that his children might try to leave Cuba by raft like so many others, so it was only logical to keep an eye on the father." Colonel Francisco felt he was beginning to sway the young men.

"His plan worked perfectly: He made believe that his children's trip caught him by surprise, with a lot of witnesses to verify that. Then he played the role of a desperate father who wanted to save his only family from drowning. He went out to see two old friends and convinced them to facilitate his escape. Since he had thought everything out ahead of time, he knew exactly who to go to and what to say to them, and in less than five hours, he managed to leave Cuba in a yacht with no great difficulty. He even had a perfect alibi."

"Why did he come back?" Mario asked.

"There was an incident during the trip that changed his whole plan. He had to kill a man. If he had been alone, most likely he would have killed all five men who tried to take his lifeboat in order to leave no witnesses, but he couldn't do that in front of his children. They would have never understood a slaughter like that. So he had to leave four witnesses alive, knowing that sooner or later one of them could squeal. Up to that moment, he could have gone into the concentration camp in Florida and walked right out on an affidavit of support from his sister. Nobody knew him there. Later, he could have claimed his citizenship and lived with his children in a place not frequented by Cubans. Nobody would ever have detected him. Perhaps his plan never included turning himself in to the CIA, or betraying the country in that way. That much can be admitted."

This was a clever and subtle change in Francisco's arguments, Mario thought. During the whole time the prisoner was under questioning, Francisco had tried to incriminate Carlos Manuel as a possible CIA agent, and all his "persecution" in the U.S. as a cover-up. Now he had taken another tack.

"But, on account of that incident, he had to change his plans and consider the possibility of coming back to Cuba. He couldn't be sure what the Americans would do with him if he were captured and accused of murder. Most likely they would use that murder rap to blackmail him, and, if he didn't play along with them, he would go to the electric chair, or the gas chamber, or receive a lethal injection, or whatever the Americans are doing to execute prisoners nowadays. Then, he changed his plan; he played undercover in the camp to have control over the men from the raft. He's a master at undercover work. Like an actor who can play any character, he can impersonate anybody. When he got out of the camp, he discovered he had been exposed; his game was over. He decided to take the lesser risk, and he came back to Cuba."

Colonel Francisco started to walk about the room, thinking life had given him a hell of a job. He himself didn't believe anything he was saying. He had worked it all up to half-convince Mario and the rest. *But the core of the problem wasn't whether it was true or not.*

"Besides everything I have mentioned, the most important thing, above all other considerations, is that we have to recognize that the Revolution is at its lowest point since it came to power. If that man does not receive a strong punishment, it would be another demoralizing blow to the Ministry of the Interior, to the armed forces, and to the government as a whole."

Mario, in his colorless way of speaking, said, "Colonel, what you say could be an interpretation of the facts. We could put forward many other interpretations, just as plausible." Mario kept talking, raising his voice to throw his dart. "If Colonel Francisco had taken some time out to read the work we've done, it would be very clear to him that we couldn't find a trace of a lie in what the

prisoner has stated. We have no reason to think the facts are different from what he declared."

Francisco glared at him. "On the contrary, the most logical conclusion from the evidence that you've collected—all of which I
have read—is that he masterminded everything. He planned everything ahead of time. It was the only way he could get out of this
country. *And let me point out that quitting—going away—whatever
the reason, is a form of treason.*"

Again, Francisco could see that he had scored high.

"He had very good motives for betrayal. First, a sense of guilt,
because his children were leaving him. They blamed their own
father for their mother's suicide and the emptiness of their lives. He
felt that he owed them a lot. Second, he felt a sense of defeat and
isolation. He had been pulled out of the Service for which he had
worked for almost twenty-five years and where he had risen all the
way to the top. At the same time, he felt a sense of shame because
he had failed the Revolution as a father. How could he face his
comrades after his three children left? Third, revenge. Since the
Service didn't want him anymore, he didn't have to be loyal to the
Service. Fourth, he began to feel economic insecurity for the first
time, because of the lack of purchasing power of his salary. In conclusion, he had lost his faith in the Revolution, its leaders, and his
own country. That's why he stole a yacht and went to the United
States. Why do you say there is no reason whatsoever to think he's
a traitor?"

"Our conclusions point to a no," insisted Mario, this time louder
and clearer. "If he had been in contact with the CIA or the FBI,
they would have given him a good cover and we would never have
seen or known about him or his children again. He would be too
valuable to them to allow him to come back. If he had decided to
turn himself over to the CIA, the killing of that man wouldn't have
mattered at all. Also, if he had wanted to, he could have remained
undercover in the United States. He had prepared himself for that
all his life and had done that in many countries where living

undercover was much more difficult. *The indisputable fact is that he came back to face charges of his own free will. That's the absolute proof that he's not a traitor.* We can charge him with many things, but not treason."

Colonel Francisco cut in. "He could have come back for many reasons. He had no way of knowing what the CIA would do with him with that accusation hanging over his head. He was listed as one of the top-ten criminals in the U.S.! The game he was playing got out of hand, and he chose the safest alternative. That's my opinion. Maybe he came back out of loyalty to his two friends who were in trouble for helping him. Maybe he was just playing the hero again. Being in danger, accomplishing difficult and daring tasks, may be the only way for him to live. That's what he has done all his life. It's like a drug for him."

Francisco stopped, paced once around the long table, then continued quietly, "Why he came back is irrelevant. Again, I'm going to ask the same question. If a high-ranking officer abandons his Service, steals a yacht to flee—for whatever reason—to the United States, according to our laws and the regulations of the armed forces and the Ministry of the Interior, is he not a traitor?"

Mario sat silent, considering his answer.

"Technically, yes."

Floro reached Marcelo's house close to midnight. A light in a room on the second floor let him know that Marcelo was up. Marcelo came down when his aide told him Floro wanted to see him urgently.

"It looks like Carlos Manuel is doomed if you don't do something quickly," Floro said.

"I know." Marcelo nodded.

CARLOS MANUEL woke up suddenly and clapped his hands over his eyes against the light of the brightly illuminated cell. The door was wide open and his father stood on the threshold, looking young and smiling. The temperature was very low and he was trembling, covered only by a linen sheet.

"Why are you still here, son? Hurry up—we're going hunting. Let's catch those deer before other hunters do. You know the old saying, *'The early bird catches the worm.'* Come on, boy, don't be lazy. I know it's cold, I know it's freezing, but that's the way it is in this neck of the woods." His father invited him with his hands, his eyes glittering with joy.

His father took a step back to make room for him to come out the door, his figure turning whiter as he kept stepping back, his boots burying themselves in deep snow. The air was fresh and thin.

"What's that? Snow?" Carlos Manuel said it without having to utter a word.

"What did you expect? It's winter in Vermont, my boy."

Some guards came into the cell and, grabbing him by his arms, started to pull Carlos Manuel off the bed.

"*Está ardiendo,*" said one of the guards.

"*Está ardiendo,*" repeated another, after touching his forehead.

"*Está ardiendo,*" said a third guard, placing the back of his hand on his cheek.

"What are they saying, Father?"

His father was by his side. He appeared taller and the same age he had been when he had come to visit his school in Russia. His face was wrinkled and looked worried. He clasped one of his son's hands with his own big, strong hands. His father's hands were very cold.

"They say, literally, that you're on fire." His father laughed. "Why are you here? Who are those policemen? Why are they here?"

"This is a jail."

"What are you doing in a jail?"

"They accuse me of being a traitor."

"No son of mine can be a traitor, and you're my only son. Let's quit all of this nonsense. Let's get out of here. Let's go hunting in Vermont." This time, Carlos Manuel got out of bed and tried to follow his father into the snow. As he fell, his head struck the floor, and everything became dark again.

Carlos Manuel, with a high fever and in a state of delirium, was taken to the Pedro Kourí Hospital for Tropical Medicine on the outskirts of Havana. The diagnosis was a severe attack of a rare strain of malaria. Years ago, he had had a treatment that didn't work as well as it should have, and the disease was now coming back to him.

Slowly, he started to recover his health after a week in the hospital. Visitors were allowed. Floro went to see him almost every day, bringing newspapers and books. At the hospital, he was able to speak on the phone with his children and sister again.

After being held a month and a half for questioning by the Department of State Security of the Ministry of the Interior, followed by two weeks in the hospital, he was released on December

30, 1994, and told that he had been discharged from the Ministry of the Interior. He was now just a civilian, still subject to investigation. Some time in the future, he would have to face the charges against him.

He was given back his apartment and his old Lada. He knew that his case wasn't an easy one to judge, and the end result was impossible to guess. He was sure that, at best, he would have to spend a few years in prison. But it was good to be free again, even if not for long. In no hurry to look for another job, he planned to indulge himself in a long vacation until his trial was over—there was no point in worrying too much about anything. In the meantime, he would have to sell some furniture and clothes to get money on which to live.

One day he walked to the sea, just a block from his home, for a swim. He took along a diving mask to explore the sea bottom, something that had fascinated him ever since he had first come to live in Cuba and swam in the clear and warm tropical waters around the coral reefs, teeming with colorful life. Later, when he was at school in the Soviet Union, he had been trained to dive in much colder and darker waters, dangerous work with little pleasure in it.

On his first exploratory swim, he saw some edible fish around the reefs just a few yards from shore. He knew that several youngsters from the neighborhood went fishing almost every day, selling their catch to the neighbors. He soon began spearfishing to catch food for himself using a complete set of diving equipment, including an aqualung he had bought for his son, Antonio, four years earlier. Looking for more information on the subject, he approached a friend of his older son, a kid about Antonio's age named Roger, who lived on Eighteenth Street a couple of blocks from his apartment on Twentieth. Besides spearfishing to earn extra money, Roger filled air tanks with a small air compressor he had, and charged a dollar each to those who could afford it.

Roger was delighted to have his company and, in a short time, disclosed many secrets of the trade, giving him tips on the best fishing spots in the surrounding waters and on the dangers he would face. The hunting area extended from the mouth of the Almendares River to the Comodoro Hotel, along about two miles of coastline and less than a quarter of a mile into the sea.

"A few yards from shore, the bottom drops to about forty feet, sloping gently toward that area out there." He pointed to a place where the color of the water changed to a dark blue. "Shortly beyond it is the open sea. That's the *pretil*. The catch there is good, but you should never go there on your own because it's too deep and the current is too strong.

"A hundred yards from shore, at a depth of sixty feet, there's a sandbar about a hundred feet wide. Some lobster venture there at certain times of the year, but normally that zone is barren. Another hundred yards from the sandbar there's a set of small rock ridges, and in many places there are large concrete slabs and other debris from demolitions along the coast or rubbish from passing ships. In the crevices of the ridges and the debris there are always fish and lobster. Beyond the ridges, there's a place covered with seaweed and some big sponges, and the depth of the water there drops to seventy or eighty feet. This is a favorite spot for sea turtles. When you kill one, its belly is full of that weed, nothing but weed. Turtles are the cattle of the sea." Roger kept pointing to the locations of the places he was describing. He moved over to a higher spot to show another place farther out in the water. "Many big fish come prowling along the coast just at the *pretil*, always swimming against the current to collect the plankton and food in the waters that come from the land into the big stream. The current shifts direction. It comes closer to the coast and moves out into the sea according to the time of the year and the mood of the weather."

Roger stood looking out to sea as if wondering if there was any other advice that he should give Carlos Manuel. Suddenly, he remembered. "Take good note of what I'm going to say: You should never go alone into the few big caves in that territory. In the caves you'll find enormous *guasas*, some weighing a hundred pounds or more, as well as other powerful fish, hiding in the shadows. Don't ever spear a big fish unless you're absolutely sure of hitting it in the brain and killing it immediately. If you're not, and you just want to lose a spear, untie it from the nylon cord before you shoot; otherwise you could be tangled up with the cord, and the fish could drag you to the bottom of the ocean. A twenty-pound fish pulls much more than you can. A bigger one can play with you like a toy."

Carlos Manuel absorbed all the advice and put it into practice by spearfishing as often as he could. The physical exercise did wonders for him. He lost the extra pounds he had added in the hospital, going back to the weight he had been for the last fifteen years—170 pounds of smooth, solid muscle. He loved to stay in the water for hours, exploring the reefs, forgetting the outside world completely. Little by little, he went deeper and deeper. At first, he couldn't go past twenty feet. Two weeks later, he could reach sixty, and, with Roger around, ventured up to ninety. He swapped Roger a pair of Antonio's cowboy boots and a shirt for an extra air tank because he was afraid to go down so deep with only one.

One day, he found no more room in his refrigerator for another fish. He offered a six-pound red snapper to a neighbor, who fiercely insisted on paying for it. To avoid a quarrel, he accepted the money—five dollars—which was as much as he used to earn in a week. After that, he started giving his extra catch to Roger, who sold it and brought back the money. Later, he began to help Roger with the sales.

Floro was a daily visitor at dawn. He always refused the invitation to drink a beer, claiming he was through with alcohol. Then, as he stayed longer, he ended up drinking a couple of beers, since beer was "the only thing that really quenched his thirst," and a doctor had recommended it for a kidney problem he had.

By this time, most of the people in the neighborhood had learned about Carlos Manuel saving his kids on the high sea, going to the U.S. with them, and coming back. Cecilia and the boys had always said he was working as a radio and television technician, helping to set up networks in African countries. Now, some of the neighbors would approach him, asking if he had news from his children, or telling him how much they had liked Cecilia. He always cut his answers short, playing the same guy they used to know, closed in on himself, polite, shy, and a bit distracted, as if he were always thinking about something far away, maybe in distant Africa.

The mood in the neighborhood began to change. Rumors began to circulate that Carlos Manuel and Roger were illegally spearfishing and selling the catch to foreigners who frequented the Comodoro Hotel beach, right at the edge of their hunting waters. Someone said Roger had boasted they were "earning as much as eighty to a hundred dollars a month each, and even more during the tuna and sea bass seasons."

"Those guys are on their way to becoming rich," one neighbor complained. "That amount of money means about two thousand pesos a month, when the average monthly salary is two hundred. No wonder that fellow who looked so nice and quiet was put in jail for some time."

Carlos Manuel still had his defenders, though. "You have to subtract ninety percent of everything you hear from Roger," another neighbor insisted. "Probably they just sold a fish or two, and it's a matter of five or ten dollars," the neighbor continued, when a police officer came to check on the rumors. The neighbor, who was in charge of vigilance for the block committee, knew that Carlos Manuel and Roger really were fishing and selling some of their catch to foreigners. After thirty years of watching everything that went on in the block, elected by his fellow neighbors, his attitude had softened from the early days.

In the beginning, the Revolution had been fighting for survival and it was vital to keep an alert eye on the rich people who still lived on the block as well as on the few who had no visible job and thrived doing all sorts of shady business. As time went on, most of the counterrevolutionary activities died out, and the only thing to worry about were the burglars who increasingly raided the neighborhood to snatch whatever was left unguarded. Their main targets were the state-owned grocery stores, always easy to rob.

Now things were much different, to the point that most people were forced to break one law or another to survive. There were so many laws forbidding almost everything that the block-watcher had decided that he wasn't going to be a stool pigeon for the police to crush little people like himself. Rather, he used his position to cover up many things that were going on in the neighborhood. He himself was doing some work as a plumber and didn't have a license, meaning that he was paying no taxes. He hated to do that, but he couldn't afford to pay seventy pesos month after month for a plumber's license, while he earned, on average, less than a hundred for the plumbing work he did.

The block-watcher, whose name was Agustín, waited until Carlos Manuel came back from fishing, then pulled him aside and told him he had something very important to tell him. Carlos Manuel invited him for a cold beer in his apartment. Since he had become a good fisherman and a better fish salesman, his refrigerator was well stocked with beer that he bought for seventy-five cents a bottle in the dollar shops.

Agustín repeated three or four times what the policeman had asked and the clever way he had misinformed him. After the second beer, he became bellicose. "What do these guys want from you? Your whole family leaves you because you spent your life Godknows-where, aiding other countries, sent there by the Revolution. After all of that, what do you get? A good kick in the ass, and now they want you to starve to death. Fuck them! Good strong beer, this *Mayabe Negra!*"

"Want another one?" Carlos Manuel asked.

"Sure. Why not?"

YOU HAVE TO DO IT! You owe that to me!"
As soon as the words were out, King realized that he
had made a gross error by trying to give such an
order. He could not talk like that to Hernando
Pereda anymore. Pereda had come a very long way since the
Nicaraguan war.

"I don't owe you anything! You hear me? Nothing!" Pereda's
anger flashed in his eyes, turning them cold and merciless, a reaction King knew well.

"As a favor to an old friend," King said hastily, trying to mend
his mistake. He softened his facial expression into a smile, then
gave a short laugh.

Pereda, behind his big mahogany desk, stared at King, then
seemed to regain his good humor little by little. "T.S., you haven't
changed a bit after all these years. Always demanding everything,
as if the world were at your command." Pereda's sudden smile
seemed to King more like a sneer. "Okay. Why not give a hand to
an old friend? Sure, I'll help you. Let's drink to it. Come on. I
know you're not much of a drinker nowadays, but this is a special
occasion."

Pereda selected a bottle from a cabinet behind his desk, opened
it, and poured a colorless liquid into two glasses. "Let's drink

chamba, the sacred beverage of the *paleros*. That's what I drink when I make a promise."

"I want you to take me to a *palero* one of these days," King said, always intrigued by the tales he had heard about them.

Pereda didn't bother answering. He spilled a bit of his drink on the floor, behind a door, then drank his shot in one fast swallow.

King, who in the old days had imitated all these macho gestures, followed suit in spite of the nauseating odor of the stuff. The beverage hit his throat and stomach with the intensity of napalm. He repressed his impulse to throw up, feeling in desperate need of ice water and fresh air. He managed to stand like a statue in front of Pereda during the moment of truth, until the horrid sensations started to fade away, but two thick tears rolled uncontrollably down his cheeks. Pereda discreetly turned around and walked to the bathroom to laugh by himself.

"You haven't changed, either," King said when Pereda came back. *"The same son of a bitch as ever,"* he was tempted to add.

"I can't get myself involved in anything like that anymore. I'll get you a good man and he'll work directly with you. The less I know of what you two are doing, the better."

"It's a deal," King said with a false smile, as he got up to leave.

King had come to Miami claiming to be on a mission to exchange views with the leaders of the Cuban-American Foundation. He always used these visits to Florida to chat with some of the many Cubans who had worked with him in "Operation Mangoose" under the Kennedy administration when he was starting in the CIA, and, later, in Central America, carrying out low-intensity warfare against the Nicaraguan government when Reagan was president.

King had told Barter to meet him in Miami after a short vacation in Utah with his parents. During his visits to Florida, King stayed in one of the CIA's safe houses in Coral Gables. Barter met him there.

"I have a new task for you," King said, when the woman who served them coffee left the room. "As you know, the whole Cuban economy has been collapsing since the fall of the Berlin Wall. We should be prepared to give advice on how to deal with a Cuban government interested in changing their economic system without making major political changes. Of course, that would be in opposition to the policies every administration has carried out since Eisenhower. Most of the leadership of the Cuban exile community and a lot of our politicians only think of a change in Cuba in terms of a total surrender by the Cuban government. In the first place, they want to take back all the properties taken away in the sixties. And from that point on, they plan to enslave the whole country until doomsday to punish the Cuban people still living on the island for supporting a communist government for so many years. And that's not a realistic goal, even with a collapsed economy. Under those conditions, there simply will be no change, ever. It's like asking somebody to kill himself if he wants to be your friend. That's a stupid approach."

Barter seemed startled by King's words. King continued.

"The only way to bring about a substantial change in the political system in Cuba is if the U.S. opens strong economic and political relations, thus provoking a change in the economy for the better, as a first step. Once we have economic leverage in Cuba, changes in politics will follow slowly and painlessly. Cuba has now twice the population it had in 1959. Many of the changes made since then simply cannot be reversed overnight; it would lead to chaos and civil war. We have to play our role by advising our government in an intelligent way. To do that, we have to have a much better understanding of the Cuban economy and the implications of the changes undergone since 1959, especially the ones taking place now, after the collapse of the socialist bloc. Barter, you have a degree in economics, this work is right up your alley."

The new job sounded interesting and important to Barter.

"How should I go about it? There must be many people and organizations whose job it is to study and follow the Cuban economy."

"Yes, but they're focusing on enforcement of the embargo and how to harm the Cuban economy. Some think tanks are trying to measure the economic impact on both sides if the embargo is lifted. Nobody is working on the assumption that our policies have to be radically reverted on many crucial points before any major political change can be expected in Cuba.

"My idea is to hire, from among the émigrés that have arrived from Cuba in the last five years, a team of knowledgeable people in key economic branches. With a comprehensive work program, we should have a thorough understanding of this matter in a reasonable amount of time and be able to follow events in Cuba as they happen—in some cases even make them happen. Let's keep the house you rented in Miami Beach and use it as a headquarters for this group you have to put together."

In the days that followed, Barter had several work-breakfasts with King to discuss in-depth the plan he was to carry out. He became convinced that King was using these visits to sunny Florida to take things easy for a few days, far away from the gloomy winter at the CIA headquarters in Langley and the always-pressing work in the section. In spite of that, King's humor had changed in the last two days. He seemed absent, as if his mind were on another problem, even while discussing aspects of Barter's new task.

"How is your work here coming along?" Barter asked, to see if King wanted to speak his mind.

"It isn't easy to see Pereda or any of the other big bosses of the Cuban-American Foundation nowadays. They've taken over many of the chores the CIA performed in the old days regarding Cuba, and they feel mighty independent," King said, then added, "As time has passed, the Cuban exile has gained enormous wealth, representation in Congress, and incommensurable political power through alliances made with the most conservative personalities of both parties, Republican and Democrat. And, most of all, the *Cuban factor* in Florida."

"The Cuban factor?" Barter asked.

"Haven't you heard? Even though Cubans are a small minority

in the state of Florida, they vote in block for the candidate their
leaders select. While less than half of the Americans bother to vote
in a presidential election, over one hundred percent of the Cubans
get out and vote. The Cuban vote is supposed to tilt Florida's election one way or the other. Since Florida's votes for the nomination
of the president are decisive in most elections, that has given the
Cuban exile leaders unusual clout in our whole society."

"Is all that fact or legend?" Barter asked, playing dumb.

"I don't know really, but there must be some truth in it.
Nevertheless, the ultimate source of their political power is the bitter
and endless war with the communist Cuban government. If that political issue that keeps them united ever ends, the Cuban community
would split its vote according to the particular interest of each person,
as happens in the rest of the country. All that political power would
deflate to its proper proportion. The exile community dreads that."

Barter was well aware of what King was saying, but continued to
draw him out.

"Do you mean that the exile leaders are, in fact, against a policy
that could change the government in Cuba, because that would
mean the end of their power here?"

King looked at Barter without answering, thinking he had spo-
ken his mind too openly.

Barter and Martha arranged to spend the weekend together in
Miami; they hadn't seen each other, except for brief moments at
Langley, in almost two months. King was scheduled to travel back
to Washington Friday morning, and Martha would arrive in Miami
that afternoon, to avoid casual encounters with her boss. Barter and
Martha had decided from the beginning to keep their relationship
quiet, and were fairly sure they had been successful so far. Martha
arrived in Miami late Friday afternoon. After checking into her
hotel and changing clothes, she met Barter where he was playing
squash. When he finished the game, they went to his rented house
so he could take a shower and dress for dinner.

Martha decided to take a look at the house while she waited. She was walking toward one of the bedrooms when she heard a car stop in the driveway. After the split second that it took her to realize King was visiting the house, she emitted a hollow cry and took off running into the nearest bedroom. Barter didn't realize what was happening until he heard the doorbell and opened the front door to see King smiling before him.

"I had to change my flight back to Washington because I had some matters to clear with Pereda and one of his men. Since I have some time available before catching my plane, I decided to pay you a visit and see how you're installed here. Besides, I've thought of a couple of new things I want to tell . . ." The minute King entered the house, he smelled the perfume he knew so well. In fact, the fragrance permeated the place. King left what he was saying unfinished and took a look around, sniffing in all directions, his eyes opened wide like a bird of prey searching for a hidden victim.

"It's a nice place, indeed," said King, walking about the living room, the dining room, and the kitchen. "How many bedrooms?" he asked Barter, who was striding behind him barefoot.

"Three bedrooms . . . Mr. King, I'm glad you came by. I'd like to discuss a few . . . a few very important subjects with you before you leave. Can we sit down right here?"

King paid no attention to Barter and continued his scouting. "Maybe I can use one of these bedrooms myself in a future visit. Is that possible, Mr. Barter?" King moved toward the room where Martha was hiding, guided unerringly by her scent.

"Of course! You're most welcome here any time you wish to use the house . . ." Barter heard panic in his own voice as King reached the bedroom door. "Did you see that over there?" Barter said in a loud voice, pointing frantically to a slice of the beach that could be seen through one of the living room windows.

King glanced quickly toward the place Barter was indicating, then opened the door of the bedroom wide. "Yes, I saw that fat old lady naked with her big tits hanging down to her belly. Disgusting, isn't it?"

King walked into the bedroom and looked at a closet door. He then wrinkled his nose and turned around. "I have to go now," he said.

On his way to the airport, King asked himself why he was so angry. The whole affair between Martha and Barter should not really be a surprise to him. The woman had been behaving like a bitch in heat ever since she met Barter. Her transformation into a different female was the main theme of small talk in the section. Actually, the only thing he had to feel bad about was losing his old touch, failing to sense that Martha was madly in love. He hadn't seen her like that until now. He had been totally blind to something happening right in front of his very eyes. Was that why he was reacting this way?

He had to confess to himself that the real reason was the sense of loss of a personal possession. For many years, he had believed that his relationship with Martha was the classic platonic love of the secretary for her boss. Why had he felt so hurt, so cheated, when he was sure she was hiding inside a closet in Barter's house? He really should be glad to see Martha going out with someone. She was a good girl. She deserved some fun out of life, too. It was selfish of him to feel so mean about that relationship. In spite of how much King fought with himself, however, he felt a surge of anger every time he thought of Martha. Couldn't she see she had been used? Cold calculation instead of love had to have prevailed on Barter's side, a man much younger than she was. King tried to take a nap on the plane. He dozed off for a few moments, then woke up with a sense of discomfort. Suddenly he realized that his first negative reaction had been guided by his infallible instinct: *There was treason lurking in that relationship*. King felt another surge of blood to his head. He tried to react and think positively. "T.S., you have to be practical," he told himself. "*The time will come when the executioner has to swing the ax to chop off both their heads.*"

35

CARLOS MANUEL LOOKED at his wristwatch to check the day of the month, then looked at a calendar to see what day of the week it was. Since he had been released from prison, he had lost track of time. It was Friday, February 24, 1995. Two days before, Marcelo had called on the phone and told him he wanted to have a talk with him; he'd drop by his apartment on Saturday afternoon. He decided to receive his friend with rum and something to eat. He had plenty of lobster and fish to offer, but was unsure whether his friend liked them. Instead, he bought a ten-pound piece of pork from a vendor who sold regularly to some houses on the block. Fried pork and *chicharrones*—that, he was sure, Marcelo loved.

He paid the going price for pork, a dollar a pound. The black-market vendor, still with another load of meat to sell, had to hold off on leaving Carlos Manuel's apartment until a couple of policemen on the street walked away. While waiting, he showed Carlos Manuel how to cook *chicharrones*, since his new client had complained that they always turned out greasy and soggy when he cooked them. The vendor skinned off the piece of pork, leaving all the lard and some of the meat with the skin. He cut all of it into small squares about an inch thick, salted the pieces, and began cooking them. After most of the fat had come off, he added some water. The *chicharrones* came out crisp and dry this time. The key—the vendor told Carlos Manuel—was using the right amount of water and knowing the exact time to pour it in.

Marcelo came on foot, wearing an old pair of dungarees without a belt and a white T-shirt. Carlos Manuel decided that maybe Marcelo wanted to take a stroll. They met with a strong embrace, and Carlos Manuel felt again that it was the same pal he had always known, just a bit older.

On the terrace table were several glasses, forks, halves of key limes, and a bowl of ice. Other bowls held the *chicharrones* and pieces of fried pork. On a platter were four large lobster tails that had been boiled and roasted with butter and two types of fried fish. Beside all of that stood a bottle of seven-year-old *añejo* Havana Club rum.

They sat in aluminum rocking chairs with a view of the sea and started to eat *chicharrones* and drink the *añejo* straight, as old rum drinkers like to do.

"Pork, lobsters, and fish. There's no doubt that you're on your way to becoming a millionaire. I think I'll join your fishing enterprise one of these days," Marcelo joked, as he prepared a piece of fried pork with some drops of lime juice.

"You're welcome any time."

"Did you cook these *chicharrones*?"

"Of course."

"My wife never gets them right."

"It's an old family secret. One of these days, I'll tell you."

"In the meantime, I think I'll go after the lobster. I know you're trying to lure me with the fried pork because you know I'm still a country boy at heart."

When they finished eating, there was a long silence. Marcelo poured another shot of rum into his empty glass. Carlos Manuel sensed that the visit didn't portend good news. Marcelo's mind and time were always devoted to his work. He wasn't going to spend a whole afternoon telling his friend things he already knew or bringing back memories of the good old days. Nor did he often console people. He had no sense of melodrama, always shielding himself from that sort of situation. Marcelo had invariably been the person who used his time most effectively, going straight to the heart of what he wanted to say, in a clear, often simple way. Trying to guess the purpose of the meeting, Carlos Manuel told himself to prepare for what was coming.

"Listen, man," Marcelo began, "*I have a poison pill for you.*" He stopped the swaying of his rocking chair and looked into the eyes of his old friend. "Your case has become a political issue. Opinions are split. Some understand why you had to do what you did, and those people say your return to Cuba and your eviction from the Service closes the case, that it's insane to pick on you anymore. On the other hand, Colonel Francisco, backed by General García, is heading a crusade against you, and he's very convincing. He feels that, in a situation like this, if you don't receive harsh punishment, it's going to be demoralizing for the whole Ministry of the Interior and the armed forces. That's the core of his argument. He starts his plea by recognizing how good a soldier you've been all these years, and then points out that this worsens what you've done, just like in the Ochoa case."

Marcelo stopped. He played with his second shot of rum for a moment and continued. "The ones who think like Francisco and García say that the reasons for what you did, no matter how human and understandable, do not matter. You still have to pay; otherwise, it will create a precedent the Revolution can't afford at this moment. This country has been at war with the most powerful world power for more than a third of a century. Our only weapon—and our main defense—is our morale. You were a high-ranking officer on the frontline. You couldn't do what you did. We can't let you go practically unpunished; it could lead to chaos. There are many who will not rest until they get nothing less than your head."

Carlos Manuel froze a bit, thinking it wasn't at all like the old days when they had shared a room at the special school they attended near the Black Sea. Neither was it like Angola, close to the border with Namibia, where they waited for the South African army to strike. Nor like the wet days and humid nights in the northern hills of Nicaragua. It was Cuba of the nineties, a much more difficult place and time, and Marcelo wasn't in the same boat as he.

"Why was I let out of jail?"

"You might say someone won the first round, but not the battle."

Carlos Manuel remained silent for a while, looking out at the sea. There was a cool breeze coming from the east, charged with moisture and salt. The sun, a big red ball directly above the horizon, had begun to set, and he could look directly at it. There was almost no traffic on the streets below, and very few other noises.

Carlos Manuel spoke calmly, his eyes almost closed, watching the horizon. There was no hatred or sadness in his voice, just a great peace. "The other day that sea almost settled this dispute. I got tangled up in a cave at sixty feet while pursuing a big bass. I almost drowned."

"You shouldn't go deep-sea fishing alone," Marcelo said sharply, an order.

"When you're hunting a big one you get carried away. It's the call of the wild—something written in our genetic code since the time man lived off what he could hunt."

"That's no way for an old warrior to die."

"Old warriors get old . . . and tired."

"You still have battles to wage."

Again there was a long silence, filled only with the thoughts of the two men and the stillness of the sunset hour.

"If I die at the bottom of the sea, promise me, Marcelo, to publish the news in all the newspapers, so my enemies will be satisfied and my soul can rest in peace."

"I promise!" Marcelo said. He drank a bit of rum left in his glass, took a handful of *chicharrones*, and got up from his seat.

"Don't forget."

Marcelo slapped Carlos Manuel's shoulder. "*I never forget!* Call if you ever need me."

Marcelo's last words were as good as gold to Carlos Manuel. It meant that the High Command of the Intelligence Service had found no trace of treason in his behavior. It was like a taste of honey at the bitter end of his career.

THAT NIGHT Carlos Manuel went to Roger's house. He waited until Roger finished eating, then got up and walked away. Roger, puzzled by his friend's behavior, followed him. Carlos Manuel got inside Roger's souped-up Alfa Romeo and asked Roger to drive around town for a while. Soon, they were on Fifth Avenue.

"Step on the gas," Carlos Manuel said, looking backward.

The car jumped from forty to eighty miles an hour in a few seconds.

"Slow down and come back. There's a team of people following us, the man with the woman on a motorcycle, and the two men in the black car."

The next day Carlos Manuel didn't go fishing. He asked Agustín about the man and the woman on the motorcycle and was told that they were staying in the penthouse of the tallest building in the neighborhood. Carlos Manuel discovered that the place was being used to openly monitor his fishing activities with the aid of binoculars.

At about seven in the morning the following day, Roger came into Carlos Manuel's apartment, carrying two full air tanks for the day's fishing.

Carlos Manuel brought Roger his usual cup of coffee and asked him to sit down. "If for any reason the police or anybody else asks about me, tell them the truth. Never lie to cover up anything you may think I'm doing wrong."

"Why do you say that?" Roger asked.

"You know my situation. I just don't want you to get into trouble for hanging around this house or for helping me."

"I don't give a damn."

"I know you don't. That's not what I'm saying. I'll feel bad if you get into trouble. They just want information. Give it to them. If you don't, they'll think I'm hiding something. Just tell them the truth. It's better for you and for me that you become a reliable source of information for them. Otherwise, they'll begin asking a lot of other people, and they'll try to control me as much as possible. That will create a bad atmosphere in the neighborhood for me. Okay?"

"What about the fish we're selling?"

"Tell them. They just want to know what I'm doing out at sea. They already have enough on me to put me in jail for the rest of my life. What's another stripe on a tiger? Tell them that you're selling your catch also. They'll find out anyway, because you're being watched, too. If you tell them whatever you may be doing wrong, they'll trust you more. They'll feel they have everything under control. Everybody will be happy," Carlos Manuel insisted.

Roger remained silent, staring at the floor. "They have already come," he said.

"When?"

"A couple of days ago. I didn't want to tell you. I didn't want to worry you."

"He's after something," Colonel Francisco said, touching his nose. He scratched his left arm with the tip of the fingers of his right hand and his right arm with the tip of the fingers of his left hand. "I can feel it all over my body."

Colonel Francisco moved his seat closer to the people who were listening to him.

"Just to give you an example, all of a sudden this Roger, who has never in his life cooperated with authority of any kind, a typical rebel-without-a-cause kid of the new lost generation, starts giving all kinds of information on all the illegal activities he and this man carry out each day. How much they catch, how much they sell it for, to whom. What has caused this miracle?" Francisco opened his arms and kept silent a moment as if waiting for an answer from the men before him. Then he continued. "All of a sudden, again, Carlos Manuel changes his habits. He stops taking off at whatever hour of the day or night to wander about town, talking with everybody he meets. Now his alarm clock goes off at six sharp; in the next hour, he performs his morning chores—cleaning up the kitchen, making coffee, and doing his warm-up exercises—before going fishing at seven with his partner. Invariably, they get back at one o'clock, and for the next two hours they're busy preparing and eating their only big meal of the day. Roger goes to his house and this man goes on with his painting. He has taken up painting! He's even watching the Brazilian and Cuban soap operas on television. And after that, he has his horrible session of classical music before going to bed at eleven sharp."

Francisco looked at the men from the Security Police before him and studied their faces, where he always found a subtle hostility. It was clear that their sympathy was on the side of the fallen intelligence officer. Nevertheless, he charged on.

"It's very easy to see he's creating a behavioral pattern, a predictable routine. So predictable that you start getting confident. You . . ."

Two of the men listening to Francisco looked at each other. One of them raised his hand, and Francisco stopped.

"We don't agree with you. This whole change has a simple explanation. After a couple of days tagging him, we realized we didn't have the manpower and the means to cover everything he does. So the next time he went out, we became visible, giving him the message that we were watching him. As a courtesy, he has made things easy for us. Don't you worry. We know what we're doing."

Francisco stood a moment, staring at the two men with a disapproving look.

The second man spoke this time. "If you want to put it another way, we told him he had to quiet down because we had no resources to follow him. If he kept on, we would have had to restrain his movements in some other way. We can barely keep after the Alfa they have with that lunatic at the wheel. He also knows very well that to follow him in the water we have to have a couple of divers and a motorboat that we don't have. He wants to go on fishing and stay free, so he's got to keep quiet. That's all."

Francisco shrugged and left, very disappointed.

When Colonel Francisco entered the Ministry of the Interior in the early seventies, he was a young lawyer fresh out of law school. He had been recruited by the *Unión de Jóvenes Comunistas* to work for the armed forces. He soon realized that scaling the ladder of command was nearly impossible without a war record from the early guerrilla warfare in Cuba, or later in Latin America or in one of the African wars in which Cuba participated. He had no such background, and he always tried to be out of range every time people of his expertise were selected for missions in war-torn countries. To avoid being involved, he became an expert on Cuban and international penal law, and maneuvered to work on many of the committees that were drafting the laws for the new society in the making. He had even been selected to attend a two-year law course sponsored by the International Court of Justice in The Hague.

Since entering the army, he had made a brilliant discovery: *The best way to prosper in his trade was to always be at the very far left,* ever ready to criticize any deviation from the most orthodox line. He armored himself with a whole set of fundamental ideas that he expressed everywhere at all times, creating around himself the aura of a hard-liner—a self-appointed watchdog of the system in its purest essence, a bare-ass communist, as bare as they came. Besides, his peers considered him, in the words of one of them, "a very able man with a resilient butt, capable of sitting for long hours in front of books nobody else ever reads, participating on working committees with elderly law people who endlessly discuss the exact wording of a single paragraph." Any normal human being would die of boredom doing the kind of work with which Francisco thrived.

Then, Francisco discovered another way to climb the ladder of command. He became highly disciplined, fulfilling the orders of his superiors to the last detail. Nothing pleased the chiefs more than absolute obedience. He discovered that the exercise of power was the main drive in life for many people, especially in the armed forces and the higher government echelons. As time went on, he became a master at doing as he liked, but always under the safe umbrella of the orders he'd received. And to provoke the issuing of those orders was an art that he felt he had invented. Francisco had learned very well how to handle his many bosses.

This time it was different. He had decided to get even with Marcelo, a man he despised because Marcelo ignored him all the time. He knew Marcelo had called him an opportunist and an empty windbag. He was going to show this conceited bastard, who had been through all the wars ever invented by this country, that he could outsmart him.

37

W HEN CLAUDIA ARRIVED home from high school at six, she found her brothers unpacking a satellite dish and setting up a new DIRECTV system. To avoid his sister's scolding for his spending habits, Felipe quickly explained that this was another gift from his new employer. Claudia nodded, half-disapproving and at the same time, half-approving. Felipe had a Midas touch with women, she thought. He converted his bedroom adventures to gold. He was now being courted by a female photographer, well-connected in the advertising business and twice his age, who, according to her story, had "discovered" Felipe while developing some pictures taken at a party. She had hired him to model for some of her ads, paying him handsomely. To compete with the new rival, the gallery owner had raised Felipe's deposit per picture to two hundred dollars. He was now receiving more money than they could spend, his sister concluded. She had to invent a way to make him save all the extra cash.

Claudia went on with her chores while her brothers struggled to install the system, trying to locate with the antenna the signal of a satellite that was both on the equator and at the same longitude as Texas.

"How could it be on the equator and in line with Texas?" she asked. When nobody answered, she shrugged and went on with her tasks.

Antonio was taking measurements with the compass he had used during the voyage from Cuba, and following the instruction sheet, but he was still failing to pick up the signal. He went over the instructions several times before declaring, "This manual is wrong."

Felipe assented firmly with his head in such a way that Claudia wondered if he was, in fact, mocking Antonio. The brothers went to a nearby house where the same system was successfully installed and working. Claudia decided to go to a supermarket in the neighborhood to buy some soy sauce for the Chinese meal she was cooking. She left a note on the table for her brothers, stating where she was going and the time, 7:20.

At the store, two employees who were collecting shopping carts in the parking lot saw Claudia park her car and lock the driver's door. As she turned around to walk toward the market entrance, she suddenly seemed overcome by dizziness. An elderly couple passing by her on their way toward the store rushed to help before she fell to the pavement. Then Claudia started to tremble.

"Hey, you, help us here! This child is having a seizure," the old woman yelled to a man pulling up beside them in a green van.

The man jumped out to help and carried Claudia's inert body to his van just a few feet away. The old woman opened the back door on the driver's side of the van and helped arrange Claudia on the backseat. She then continued to direct the operation. Calling to her companion, she ordered, "Paul, lead the way to Jackson Memorial Hospital. Hurry up!" Then, she climbed into the van through the other back door, carefully placing Claudia's head and shoulders on her lap. The van left in a roar of squealing wheels, following a 1992 black Chrysler. The whole incident lasted just under one minute.

Antonio succeeded in locating the elusive satellite. "Just what I said. The instructions in the manual are wrong."

The two young men started cruising through the guide until several pornographic channels stopped them.

"How long has Claudia been gone?" Antonio asked after a while.

"Almost an hour," Felipe replied, looking at Claudia's note.

The brothers jumped up from their seats at the same time.

"Why did she have to go alone?" Antonio asked. "Let's go. No, I'll go. Felipe, you stay home in case she calls. Maybe she had trouble with the car. The carburetor isn't working well."

Antonio decided to run, using the jaunt as an exercise session. When he reached the store at 8:50, only a few cars were still parked in the lot. The store closed at nine, and the last customers were leaving. Their car was parked toward the end of the lot. He looked into it first to make sure Claudia wasn't there. Then, he hurried into the store, searching the whole place, including the ladies' room. The woman who was cleaning the place told him there was nobody there, but allowed him in to check for himself when he explained he was searching for his sister.

As Antonio was leaving the store, a man of about fifty spoke to him in Spanish with a Central or South American accent: "About an hour ago, a girl fainted in the parking lot and was taken to the hospital." The man called to a female employee who had witnessed the whole incident with him.

She explained in detail what had happened to the girl. "She was wearing this beret that fell on the ground." The woman reached into her pocket for the beret. "Take it. I didn't know what to do with it."

Antonio recognized Claudia's beret. He rushed to the telephone booth and called Felipe.

The brothers went directly to Jackson Memorial, the hospital closest to the market, where they located the people who had taken care of Claudia. Her name was on the hospital register. The doctor who examined her was an American, but a nurse, apparently a Cuban, spoke fluent Spanish.

"She was okay. I couldn't find anything wrong with her. The spell she suffered and the seizure could have many causes. I prescribed a complete medical checkup," the doctor said, then went off to see his other patients.

"Where did she go?" Antonio asked the few people gathered there, listening.

The nurse stepped in. "When the doctor finished his examination, she thanked him, me, and the old couple who brought her here. Then she went off with her boyfriend."

"Boyfriend?"

"While she was waiting for the doctor, she made a phone call. Shortly afterward, her boyfriend came to get her."

"How do you know it was her boyfriend?" Felipe asked.

"They kissed on the lips when they met. They held hands the whole time he was here . . . Wait a minute, I remember she asked me where she could find a phone to call her boyfriend."

The telephone rang twice before Carlos Manuel picked up the receiver. He glanced at the watch on his wrist; it was four o'clock in the morning. The caller was Antonio. His voice was distorted, as if he was in great distress. He kept repeating, *"Papá! Papá!"* just like when he was a small boy. Finally, he managed to say, "Claudia has disappeared!"

Then, both sons started to speak simultaneously from different phone extensions, trying to convey the same dreadful information. Finally, with Carlos Manuel's help, a coherent story began to emerge.

"Are you sure it was Claudia?"

"Yes, Daddy, her beret fell on the pavement. A woman who works in the supermarket gave it to me."

Finally, they gave an account of what had happened at the hospital, and the unbelievable story of an alleged boyfriend picking her up. Neither of the boys believed Claudia could do anything like that. Have a boyfriend, yes, but not without them knowing him.

Not walking out of the hospital and not coming back home. The last thing they had done before calling their father was to file a missing persons report at a police station.

"A fat, bored detective listened quietly to our story, assuring us that the police would search for Claudia. We think that nothing effective will be done, because this cop was sure that Claudia had eloped with her boyfriend. We don't blame the guy, that's what happens in most of the cases they get there," Antonio concluded.

"*Papá*, there's a chance that when she called home and nobody was here to answer, she called somebody she knew and she's now at a friend's house," Felipe said, trying to soften the news and to stay optimistic.

"Get some sleep and call me when you get up. Let me think this over," Carlos Manuel replied.

When he hung up after more than an hour of talking with his sons, he sat silent, thinking that his children were beginning to pay a very high price for pursuing their dreams, far away from their homeland.

I T WAS A FEW MINUTES past five in the morning on
Sunday, March 11. Carlos Manuel went to the kitchen to brew
some coffee and to think about Claudia's disappearance. A little
after seven, he tried to reach Marcelo at home. His wife told him
he was out of town, six hundred miles away in Santiago de Cuba,
and gave him the telephone number where he could be reached. He
caught Marcelo on his way out and told him he needed to see him.

"Your calling me here means it's something urgent, doesn't it?"

"Very urgent and very important for me. Claudia has been kidnapped."

"I'll cut short my visit here and get back as soon as I can. I'll
send someone to pick you up as soon as I reach my office. Okay?"

"I'll be waiting."

Carlos Manuel went over the recording he had made of the conversation with his sons. He always taped phone conversations and
reviewed them once or twice before erasing them. It was surprising
the amount of information that could be lost hearing something
only once.

The main thing that caught his attention was how fast everything had happened in the parking lot; "the whole incident lasted
about one minute," were Antonio's words, repeating what the eye-

witnesses had said. He started listing the factors involved for events to happen that fast. The first was the old couple close to Claudia when she had the dizzy spell, *so close that they could catch her as she fell*. The second factor was a man strong enough to easily lift and carry Claudia in his arms. The third was the van just a few feet away to take her to the hospital. The fourth was the old woman taking the lead and giving fast orders to everyone.

The most striking elements in the hospital were this boyfriend coming from nowhere and this strange Claudia, thanking everyone and uncharacteristically forgetting her brothers. She had no parents to run away from. She didn't need to hide a relationship like that from her brothers.

At mid-morning, when Antonio and Felipe called again, Carlos Manuel told them to take some of the most recent pictures of Claudia and show them to the doctor and the nurse and ask them if it was the same girl.

"Father, there's no doubt; she was wearing Claudia's clothes. I checked on that."

The boys weren't able to do what needed to be done, nor could the police do anything, at least for a while. He asked himself what he could do, sitting in his apartment, waiting for his sons' calls.

That afternoon at two, Carlos Manuel met with Marcelo in his office and told him the whole story. It was the first time Carlos Manual had been in this office. He found the place gloomy and disagreeable, especially the bad paintings hanging on the walls.

"What do you think?" Marcelo asked.

"Claudia is very mature for her age. It doesn't ring true that she just walked off with an unknown boyfriend."

"That's what I think, too." Marcelo paced around the room for a while, then stopped and said with enthusiasm, "Let's use one of the golden bullets that we keep for very special occasions. As you know, in this game, sometimes you've got to ask your enemy for a favor. It means that you contract a sacred debt that should be paid with another very special favor. Once I helped a man in a very high position within the FBI. He was most grateful, and promised to pay me back. It's time to collect."

Carlos Manuel continued to wait in his apartment for calls from Marcelo and his sons. That same afternoon, at six, Marcelo called in high spirits. "I located the FBI guy right after you left. I asked him to look into Claudia's disappearance. A moment ago, he called me back and said the FBI is now in charge of the investigation. Instead of a missing person, she is now a kidnapping case. Kidnapping has been in the FBI domain since Charles Lindbergh's son was abducted back in the thirties."

The FBI placed a permanent post in his children's house, checking on everyone who made a call to the house. By the end of the third day, no one had claimed responsibility for Claudia's kidnapping. The FBI had the boys view the corpses of two unidentified females about Claudia's age. One was found in the Everglades, near Ochopee, and the other in an empty house in Tallahassee. Both bodies were disfigured with injuries. It was a horrible experience for both boys, but neither corpse was their sister.

Claudia's photos were sent all over the United States. On March 15, four days after she disappeared, not one solid clue had turned up as to who could have done it. Carlos Manuel started to think that the early presence of the FBI on the case might have disrupted the plans of the kidnappers, and he couldn't tell whether that was good or bad. His two sons wanted him there very much. He had not told them yet that he wasn't allowed to leave Cuba since he was awaiting trial. It would only have made them more bitter, he thought, and prompted recriminations about his decision to return to Cuba despite all of their pleas. His boys' patience began to deteriorate from one call to the next and started to unravel badly at the end of the fourth day. On the fifth day, Felipe took the phone from his brother's hand and spoke in a harsh tone.

"What's stopping you, Dad? Why aren't you here with us? You're an American citizen; you don't need a visa to come here. You just have to take a plane to get here. We can barely make ourselves understood in English. Some people advise us one thing, others say the contrary. We don't have any experience with this sort of thing. We don't know what to do. Aunt Marjorie has been here with us since yesterday, but she isn't very much help. She cries all the time. We need you here! *Why don't you come help us before it's too late?*"

AT NOON ON MARCH 16, Marcelo's personal aide picked Carlos Manuel up and took him to a house in Reparto Flores. Marcelo was sitting in a rocking chair, taking a nap. He woke up as soon as Carlos Manuel entered the room. After the greetings, Marcelo kept silent for a moment, then spoke slowly.

"The FBI, after integrating all the information from the eye witnesses at the parking lot, has a detailed account on how Claudia was kidnapped. She was followed to the store by at least two vehicles. The old couple in a black Chrysler followed her car very closely, arriving at the parking lot at the same time she did. When Claudia turned around after locking her car, the old man started to walk toward her. The woman was behind Claudia, and as she passed by, she must have sprayed a chemical at her. Claudia immediately felt dizzy and started to fall. The old couple hurried to grab her, placing a cloth soaked in the same or another substance over her nose and mouth so she wouldn't utter a sound. Then, she seemed to develop a seizure, like a spell of epilepsy. It could have been produced by an overdose of the chemical applied to her or by another chemical product meant to produce that effect. Since the old couple seemed unable to control the girl, a strong man who had just arrived in a van was needed to carry Claudia. It all fits into the picture.

"The whole scene at Jackson Memorial Hospital was faked. They used Claudia's clothes and someone who physically resembled Claudia. It's only a ten-minute drive to the hospital from the parking lot. They needed a half hour because they had to take Claudia somewhere to remove her clothes. When the nurse saw Claudia's photos, she said emphatically that it was another person. The doctor wasn't sure. A Cuban-American patient waiting in line to make a phone call behind the alleged Claudia declared that she heard the girl speaking with a false accent. She said she was sure the girl was faking that she didn't know English. By the way she pronounced some words, it was easy to tell that she really knew English very well.

"The FBI is convinced, from this modus operandi, that the kidnapping was performed by highly professional personnel." Marcelo stopped for a moment to let Carlos Manuel grasp the significance of this turn in the investigation.

"There's more," Marcelo continued. "The FBI is on the trail of some people who had been checking on Claudia and the boys for at least two weeks before the abduction. The good-looking young guy who picked up the imposter Claudia at the hospital and a photographer had been around Claudia at several different places and times. They already have drawings of this guy's face."

Carlos Manuel, very agitated, interrupted. "This has to be a CIA job. This must be a scheme to get me there."

"Just to finish updating you," Marcelo added in a calm voice, "Colonel Francisco, who is following all this by listening to your telephone calls, is spreading it around that this was all prepared when you were there, a plot you masterminded to deceive us once more. He says this is the sort of thing in which you excel. The perfect escape hatch since things didn't turn out the way you'd planned. He's speeding the trial as much as he can, to charge you with treason and get you back into jail."

"Is that why I have a flock of people watching every step I take?"

"Yes, to keep you nailed down here until your trial."

"I want to know what you're going to do. If the CIA is using this method with me, it's doing it against the whole Service."

Marcelo stared sadly at Carlos Manuel. "To tell you the truth, I don't believe this is a regular CIA move. The CIA has to play by the unwritten laws of this game: Always respect the life of the enemy's officers, and the family is sacred. They know that if they start breaking those laws, it will backfire on them sooner or later. On the other hand, as you very well know, the CIA has many ways of doing things against us without showing their face or even getting their hands dirty. If they decided to get you by using your daughter as a hostage, they would cover it up with one of the anti-Cuba organizations they have in their pocket. Then the CIA can appear uninvolved and, even if the FBI discovers who the kidnappers are, they'll only find the people the CIA wants them to find." Marcelo shrugged, somewhat helplessly. "We're very limited in what we can do. I don't think this is a moment when the CIA would make a move like this just to get one of our men. Cuba is not that important now. We're not one of their main worries. A pain in the ass, yes, but not a worry anymore . . . This seems to me more like personal revenge."

"King?"

"Who else?"

Marcelo stood up to let Carlos Manuel know the meeting was over. As they walked to the entrance, Marcelo said, "There is one thing I'm going to do on my own. I'll see that the word spreads in Miami among the Cubans who serve the Big Master: *An eye for an eye and a tooth for a tooth.* I agree with you; this sort of shit cannot go unchallenged. Even if it's the last thing I do."

Carlos Manuel kept walking around his apartment, jumping toward the telephone each time it rang. This time it was Antonio's voice. "Dad, I'm calling you from a public phone. The telephone at home is being intercepted by the FBI."

"Always do that."

Antonio was calm. He sounded older, much older. "Dad, I've learned more about life in these few days than in all the years I've lived. It's a shame that we had to learn a few truths the hard way. This morning while I was at work, the man who got me this job in the hospital called me on the phone. You know the one I'm referring to, the one who came to our house several times when we first came here. Then he said that he was working for a Catholic organization to help young Cubans arriving in the States. He speaks Spanish with a Mexican accent."

"Yes, I remember who you're talking about," Carlos Manuel said.

"Today he sounded as if he were some sort of policeman with good information about what's happening with Claudia." Antonio hesitated before speaking again. "He told me that you should come as soon as possible, and secretly seek FBI protection; otherwise, we may not see Claudia alive again. He warned me not to tell anybody, except you, as if he were doing us a favor. I'm sure now that he came the first time looking for information about us, and, mainly, about you. Do you think this guy is involved in the kidnapping?"

"Listen carefully, Antonio. The whole purpose of the kidnapping is to force me to go there. This man will most likely come to see you or call you again to get the feedback after you delivered the message. *Tell him I need more time.* Do you hear me, Antonio? Try to gain time.

"There's another thing that's very important for you to know. I'm not free to leave Cuba. I'm in trouble for leaving the country without proper authorization, and I'm going to be put on trial very soon. And there's a good possibility that I'll have to spend some years in jail." He paused and drew a deep breath. "It seems my past keeps harming all of you. Please forgive me!"

Carlos Manuel called Marcelo at his office and told him the news he had received from his son. He concluded, "Somebody is putting full pressure on my boys to get me over there. It seems like King's style all right. Still, the message with the advice to look for FBI protection sounds strange . . . Do you have any news?"

Marcelo remained quiet for a while, trying to decide if it was right to tell this man, who was almost a brother to him, the outcome of their analysis. The facts were simple: If it was King's personal revenge, time was running out. To have the best chances of succeeding, a kidnapping has to last just a few days. The FBI's speedy entrance into the case must have complicated all the plans King had laid out. If nothing happened soon, the girl had to be released or killed. The psychologists who had studied King's profile believed there was a srong possibility the girl would have to die in order to satisfy King's need for revenge. Marcelo knew the analysts were seldom wrong. The only choice they now had was to send evidence to the FBI, alerting them that the kidnapping involved a personal vendetta by King. And that, it had been decided, wasn't a choice they could make, because Claudia might be killed to erase evidence.

"No, there's nothing new," Marcelo replied.

When he had hung up the phone, Marcelo paced his office, trying to think what else he could do for Claudia. Until that moment, even though he had to try to act and react as he would with any of his men, it was impossible not to take into consideration the close ties he had had with Carlos Manuel and his family. Now, he began to think of the demoralizing impact of Claudia's death on the whole world they lived in. *Maybe that was the political goal of the CIA behind this bizarre move from King—a blow aimed at dismantling the intelligence network Cuba has painstakingly woven in the U.S. over so many years . . .*

Actually, he told himself, he had no direct confirmation that King was really behind Claudia's abduction. He decided to play a card he still held. It was a long and complicated shot.

40

ARTURO MONTIEL woke up to the sound of a door slamming hard. It was close to two o'clock in the morning. He had decided to sleep fully dressed, sitting inside a closet with a shotgun on his lap and a dummy in his bed as a decoy. He had drilled holes in the wooden walls of the closet that enabled him not only to survey the hall toward the rear but also the entrance of the house, as well as the room in the front where Claudia was kept strapped to a bed most of the time, guarded by Inés, the old woman who had captured her. All the lights of the house, both inside and out, were kept on for better visibility. Peering quickly through the closet holes, Montiel saw the old curtains in the front window moving with the breeze and concluded that a gust of wind must have shut a door inside the house. When he had had enough manpower, he had maintained two guards outside during the night, letting him sleep in peace.

This was the tenth day of the kidnapping. The whole operation had bogged down, and now they were in this house near the edge of a marsh. Things hadn't turned out at all as planned.

The "project concept," as King liked to call the kidnapping plan, was brilliant. It was so good that Montiel had decided he might try it later on his own. "The beauty of the scheme relies on the fact that hundreds of young women elope with boyfriends daily. The police can't bother tracing every missing dame reported by her relatives. In 999 cases out of 1000, the girls return home, exhausted after a few days of sex-at-large," King had said at the beginning of his explanation.

Later, he had added, "To make the whole plot foolproof, if, by chance, the police stumble in, there will be a whole lot of pictures of the girl and the good-looking fellow she's supposed to have eloped with to prove they've known each other for some time and that she consented to abscond with him for fear of her brothers' reaction. Witnesses could be produced to confirm that if the moment came. Since there will be no ransom demand and no physical harm to the girl, it would be a matter of who the judge wants to believe, if the case ever went to court."

King had promised Montiel that the whole operation would last a week. *"Ten days is the limit for freeing the girl whether the plot succeeds or fails."* Montiel remembered King's words well and often: "The first five days, phase one, are to allow the father to come on his own to help find his child. If he doesn't, in phase two, he will be brought back by the proper means. As soon as the father makes it back, the daughter will be released."

The first hideout was perfect, located at the end of a five-mile-long pebble road in the backwoods of Alabama. The nearest town, Nanafalia, was about a forty-minute drive. The house was a stone's throw from the Tombigbee river, on a piece of property registered in the *groom's* name, to make the whole case smooth, even in the remote possibility of a flop.

To keep in contact, King had given Montiel a sealed cellular phone, hooked up to a laptop. When he heard the laptop beeping, he had to open it. On the screen, he received King's orders and any other information he needed. He could type his comments on the laptop while the communication was open, but he had no way to call King or anyone else on his own.

The operation had begun to crumble when the FBI got into the act the day following the kidnapping. Descriptions of four of the people directly involved were quickly disseminated throughout the country, one of them identified by name. Montiel had followed the news on the ambulance radio and on TV in their first hideout. On the fourth day, King had ordered Montiel to pay off the whole team except Inés. King had decided not to replace anybody, telling Montiel to keep the girl sedated most of the time to reduce the need for surveillance.

Before he disbanded his team, Montiel went to Tuscaloosa, the nearest city, to have a decent meal and to make an important call from a place that, if traced, would be far enough away from the hideout. He drove around town for a while, ending up at the University of Alabama campus. He had promised his stomach a big T-bone steak well-done, with plenty of hot sauce on it, some French fries, and a few ice-cold imported beers. In a hurry to make the call, though, he had had to settle for fast food at the Corner Drugstore on Tenth Street. While his order was being prepared, Montiel went to a telephone booth to make his call. He knew it was early for Alcazar, but it was the best time to catch him at home.

"Do you know who's speaking?"

"Your sweet, guttural voice is unmistakable."

"I need some advice."

"Before you shoot, let me warn you that *you know who from you know where* is passing the word that all the people implicated in *you know what* are going to pay according to the biblical rule '*an eye for an eye, a tooth for a tooth.*' The word is also going around that you're responsible."

"They wouldn't do that. That's never been their policy."

"This isn't a political matter. This is a personal vendetta. Better tell your family to stay out of sight."

Montiel remained silent for a moment.

"Do that for me, please. Look, man, I'm in a hell of a jam."

"You really are." Alcazar snickered.

"I've been left alone with an old woman to handle this whole shit. I smell something fishy. This guy might want to bump us all off. What should I do?"

"I don't know. I'd hate to be in your skin right now. The only thing I can do for you is talk to the boss as soon as I can. He might or he might not call this guy and tell him you're out of bounds. You know the boss."

"I can't call you again. Why don't you tell me what I should do and then tell the boss you gave me an order?" Montiel was feeling panicky.

"Look, man, you know very well the only order I can give you is to hang on. But to be honest with you, if I were you, I'd drop the load and see that she gets home in one piece. Then, I'd get the hell out of the country and come back when I'm ready for retirement. The FBI will be waiting for you then and they'll feed you and take care of you as long as you live. "

"Fuck you, man. Always joking! You should've been a circus clown."

"You're the one who's fucked already."

Once the rest of the team was gone, they had moved to another hideout in southern Georgia. Montiel kept only the ambulance, letting the other vehicles go, because the best way to move Claudia was heavily sedated, strapped to the ambulance stretcher and guarded by Inés, clad in a white nurse's uniform. They had several sets of license plates, and he changed to a new one on each trip. Travelling from one place to another in the ambulance was easy and fast. Montiel especially liked having the police open the way through heavy traffic, while he turned on the siren, lights flashing, and drove eighty miles an hour.

The new hideout, near the Okefenokee Swamp, was much worse than the first. It was an old, long-abandoned house, with a few pieces of dilapidated furniture scattered around. At least some-one had repaired the plumbing, replaced all the lights, and done some cleaning. The sheets were new. The telephone line to the house had been stripped off for several miles, as in the first hideout. As a consolation prize, they had nice neighbors: a flock of very talkative Canadian geese on a nearby pond.

Montiel knew he was the only one who could connect King to the whole operation, and he had detailed knowledge of how it had been planned and carried out. Sooner or later, the FBI would lay their hands on him. The only way he could escape spending the rest of his life in prison was by playing dumb, saying that he thought this was a regular CIA operation, like the ones he'd participated in many times in the past. Then he could make a deal with the prosecutor for squealing. He was sure that King knew that he was thinking this, too. Every detail of this last arrangement smelled of the work of a hit man who could be sent to terminate all of them, erasing King's tracks. As time passed, Montiel, and Inés even more so, began to fear the worst.

These thoughts often tempted Montiel to release the girl and go to some place in Venezuela or Colombia, getting lost there forever, as Alcazar had suggested. But he fought against those ideas, telling himself that he had been recommended by Pereda and he couldn't do a thing like that to him. He feared Pereda even more than he did King. Besides that, he would lose half of the money coming to him when the job ended. There was no use calling Pereda to tell him his worries; he would say nothing on the phone. Montiel could even guess Pereda's exact words: "Who's Montiel? I've never known anybody by that name in my life."

Montiel decided he could do nothing else but hang on.

41

MARTHA BROUGHT KING a brief message marked "URGENT" she had just received from Miami by fax. *FBI caught loverboy this morning here in Miami.* Signed P.

King stared at the note for a long time and then told Martha he wasn't feeling well and was going home. While driving to his house, King thought about the consequences of the news Hernando Pereda had sent him. *Loverboy* was the code name for the young man who had acted as Claudia's boyfriend. He was supposed to be in his hometown in Argentina now, very far away from the FBI. His foolproof project had received another blow, King thought. Now the stupid kid would point his finger at Montiel, and Montiel, if caught, at him. The whole "project" had reached a point of no return, and he had to make the final decisions. Once home, King served himself a good shot of whiskey and began pacing between his dining room and kitchen.

"Is it worth it?" he asked himself for the thousandth time. "Yes, it is worth it." His answer came back weaker every time. Why, if the need for revenge had been his salvation—physically and mentally— now, when it was at his fingertips, did he hesitate so much?

His first impulse had been to kill himself when he discovered the full extent of the damage inflicted on his body. How was it possible to keep living crippled? What was the use of struggling for the rest of a wretched life? Pity, pity, pity was the only thing he saw all around him—in his mother, his brother, the few friends allowed to see him, the whole flock of nurses and the two fucking doctors who must have handled situations like that a hundred times and who should have known better.

Of all people, his father, whom he despised most, was the one who provided the clue to his salvation. "Hello, boy. Yes, I know I shouldn't be calling somebody past forty 'boy,' a top officer of the CIA, wounded in combat. But to me you're still a boy. No matter if you went to all those schools to learn how to kill people single-handed and took part in some of the most disgraceful business your wretched institution has engaged in over the last few years."

"Jesus, Pop. It isn't noon yet and you're already drunk."

"That's pretty good, son. I thought you weren't even listening. You never listened; you're one of those people who don't have to listen to anything. You were born with a whole set of ideas about what's wrong, what's right, where's north and south, just like your mother . . . Now what?"

"What do you mean, Pop?"

"Where do you go from here?"

"Since when do you care?"

"Just curiosity, my son. Just to know what your set of values tells you to do in a situation like this. Your mother's best insult is calling me a philosopher, which in her code of ethics is the epitome of idiocy. Just out of philosophical curiosity, I want to know where the hell you go from here."

He didn't know how to answer his father. He really didn't know what to do. He was even, to his horror, beginning to enjoy all that pity directed toward him.

"Listen, boy. You have to live long enough to kill the mother-fucker who did this to you," his father said, with a strength and passion King had never seen before. "You got to stand up and get going on your only foot and run after that son of a bitch. Grab him by the balls, take out his heart, and show it to everybody. In a case like yours, there's nothing like revenge, my son. Come on, come on, it's time to start chasing that devil."

For the first time, he saw his father in a new light.

His mother resolved the matter in her own peculiar way, just as she had gotten rid of his father. She paid for his house in full and replenished his bank account. Then she visited him every Saturday for half an hour, always bringing a beautiful bouquet for everybody to admire.

"She never changed a diaper for any of her children." That piece of conversation had stuck in his mind ever since he overheard his nanny saying it to a maid when he was still so small he wasn't supposed to understand what they were talking about.

"Sonny, to get the rest of what's coming to you," his mother said, "you have to wait until you read my obituary in the papers." He wanted to yell at his mother that money wasn't what he needed from her. Money was the least of his worries, now that, on top of everything she had given him, he had the CIA insurance money paying dearly for every piece of his body that was gone. But she had taught him never to speak his mind.

"You'll outlive all of us, mother. You know that, don't you?"

As time passed, his father was the only one in his family who remained by his side. His mother, sister, and brother slowly moved away, but during the six months after the accident, his father stayed near him day and night, sober most of the time, teasing him in his spells of desperation or self-pity, reminding him of his revenge at all times. His father stayed until the seed began to grow in his heart and became a powerful tree on which he was able to climb out of the deep hole into which he had fallen.

So why all this hesitation now? There was only one way to bring *Roberto* under his foot in order to smash him like a cockroach. It had been clear from the beginning that he would have to act on his own. In an earlier epoch, carrying out an action like the one he had planned would have been easy. In those days, men of the caliber of Hernando Pereda would do anything they were told at the snap of a CIA finger. Now, they all had their own fat interests to look after, their own goals: mainly to keep milking Uncle Sam for the deeds they once did and for keeping their mouths shut. The man sent by Pereda this time, Arturo Montiel, was nevertheless experienced and efficient. But he was disposable, too, when the time came.

Why had the whole operation, so carefully laid out, started to fall apart from the very beginning? Why had the FBI stepped in with full strength just a few hours after Claudia was snatched? Was Montiel, somehow, passing information on to someone else? Maybe Hernando Pereda himself was playing foul with him. He had to find out who had warned the FBI. Could it be Barter? He had tried to keep him away from this affair, but Barter was smart and knew very well how to add two and two. Also, he had become very friendly with those kids; he probably had an eye on the little chick. He had ordered Barter to leave on a two-month tour of five Latin American countries to review their economic ties with Cuba, but Barter hadn't swallowed the pill, smelling something rotten in the sudden change, and had found a way to stay put. Martha, who knew the CIA inside out, had undoubtedly helped to arrange things so that he had to go into the hospital for a compulsory medical checkup.

King reviewed his plan again and could find no flaws—there had to be a stool pigeon. The whole thing should have worked perfectly and, within a week, he should have had *Roberto* at his feet. Coming back to help his sons find Claudia should have been his normal reaction. A nice false trail had been laid out for him to follow, leading directly to a mortal trap. Instead, a whole squad of FBI detectives specialized in kidnapping was swarming around the place the following day. If he had had any sense left, he would have quit then. Instead, he had let days pass, trying to allow time for the boys to put pressure on their father.

It was the eleventh day since Claudia's abduction. He had no choice now but to go on with phase two: Pull the bastard out of Cuba and bring him over to the U.S. And if that failed, move quickly on to phase three: Kill the fucking girl and clean up the rest of the mess.

AS ROGER OPENED the gate of the steel fence surrounding his house, his girlfriend appeared in one of the windows of the top floor, calling to him. "There's a man waiting for you in the garage. He wants you to fill two air tanks for him. I told him to leave the tanks and pick them up tomorrow, but he wants them filled now." She rubbed the index finger and thumb of her right hand together, meaning good money was to be earned.

A tall mulatto was playing with two of Roger's stray dogs. Roger had started to feed stray dogs two years earlier to pay back a promise he had made to *Babalú Ayé*, the powerful *orisha* who heals venereal and skin diseases, helps fallen people in life, and is always followed by a couple of black dogs. The man waiting in the garage had a pair of air tanks inside a heavy canvas sack. Roger noticed that the man wore an expensive pullover and tennis shoes.

"I charge a dollar for filling each tank from one day to the next. If it's more urgent, it's double the price."

The man reached for his wallet and pulled out a hundred-dollar bill. "Fill them up. You can keep the change if you do Carlos Manuel a little favor."

Roger glanced again at the mulatto, looked around, and

motioned the man to follow him to a place in the patio of the house where he was sure no one could eavesdrop. The man kept the bill in his hand and moved behind Roger, carrying the sack with the air tanks.

"What is it you want me to do?"

"I brought Carlos Manuel a tape from his daughter." The man reached into his pocket and gave Roger a sealed plastic envelope. "I also want you to give him this." The man pulled a package from inside his canvas bag. With a pocketknife, he opened it for Roger to see what was inside. It contained a box with an object about the size of a tennis ball, a booklet, a map printed on a plastic sheet, and a sealed envelope. "This is an electronic buoy. Inside the envelope, there are instructions. Those air tanks are for him, in case he needs them."

Roger started preparing to fill the air tanks while he considered the proposition the man was making. He pushed a button, and the compressor started to fill the first tank. Then Roger took the hundred-dollar bill from the mulatto's hand. "I'll give this to Carlos Manuel, too," he said.

"I need you to deliver the tape and the package to him right now. I have another hundred-dollar bill here for your trouble."

Roger put the tape and the buoy in his pockets and placed the map and the sealed envelope under his shirt. He walked a couple of blocks to a store where he bought a pack of cigarettes and surveyed the building where Carlos Manuel lived, finding nothing unusual. The tall mulatto followed him at a short distance, buying another pack of cigarettes for himself. Roger stopped at Carlos Manuel's apartment and stayed inside for a few minutes. When he came out, he joined the mulatto, who was watching him from under the shadow of a tree on Third Avenue. There, Roger showed the man that he had nothing in his pockets and beneath his shirt. The mulatto handed Roger the hundred-dollar bill he had promised, and walked away with long strides.

Papá,

I have so many important things to tell you now, but I've been told that I only have a minute, so I should try to choose the most important.

Papá, I know quite well what's at stake and the only thing I have to say is do what you have to do. Do what you think is best. If it's my fate that I have to die, I'll never again question your immense love for me and my brothers. My last thought will be a kiss for you. I love you and nothing will ever change that.

Please, forgive us for blaming you for Mama's death. We blamed you for not being there to help Mama and us with the situation we were in. We had never known a real need for anything and we demanded things she couldn't give us.

She felt responsible for the change in our attitudes and ideas. The times she tried to explain things to us, we outnumbered her. We were very critical of every argument she used, we mocked her ideas and . . . Oh, God, if life could be reversed, like in a film!

You were the greatest thing that happened in her life. She married a dream man and devoted her life to making a dream home for him, full of dream children. No woman ever worshipped a man so much. She tried so hard to spare you from the problems we began to face. When she lost a lot of weight and looked older, she didn't want you to see her like that. I often saw her staring in the mirror, crying. Everything was gone— her beauty, the model kids you were so proud of . . . She had nothing to live for; she couldn't bear the idea of facing you again.

Don't have any regrets. As time has gone by, we've been able to absolve ourselves because you have taught us that everyone has the right to live his own dream. And we believe that Mama, if there is something beyond death, will be happy to see us now. Love, forever.

A note inside the sealed envelope gave instructions to Carlos Manuel to be at the point in the sea marked on the map, about two miles north of the Comodoro Hotel, the next day at noon. When he reached the area, he was to activate the electronic buoy and let it float while holding the cord tied to his belt. He should wait ten feet under the water for a yacht that would pick him up and take him to the U.S. to join his daughter.

Carlos Manuel noted that it was March 22, the twelfth day since Claudia's disappearance. "All the cards are on the table," he said aloud.

COLONEL FRANCISCO knew he worked too much. He was up at six every day, took his Doberman out to pee, helped his wife prepare breakfast, spent some time on the computer checking his email, and by seven-thirty he was out, driving his wife to work and his daughter to the university. His day at the High Military Court never ended before six-thirty in the afternoon, and he seldom reached home before seven each night. Since the days when he was in The Hague, he had learned to take some time out to relax and to do some physical exercise. That time started as soon as he got home, with a shot of whiskey from his reserve, well hidden behind an old suitcase in the uppermost compartment of a closet, away from his wife's sight. Then, putting an on old pair of pants cut off as shorts and a T-shirt and sneakers, he would go off with the dog for a half-hour stroll. After the walk, and before taking a shower, he would drink another shot of whiskey. Dinner was usually at 8:30. Following dinner, he would go to the living room, where he listened to some pop music while reading the newspaper, or watched a Brazilian soap opera on television. At ten, he would do some chores he had brought home from work, and would read for about one hour before going to bed around twelve. He had noticed that he could sleep much better if he had a final shot of whiskey then.

That night, Floro called him on the phone right after he reached home.

"Colonel, I need to talk with you, privately, tonight. I'm calling from a place near your apartment."

A glint flashed in Francisco's eyes as he smiled. "You're welcome to come to my house," he said.

"I'd rather not. Several people who know me live in your building. I'd like to talk with nobody around. What I have to tell you is very important."

"I'll go out in a minute to walk my dog along Forty-first Street up to the Cira García Hospital and back. Meet me anywhere you wish."

Francisco readied himself for the walk while thinking about the possible meaning of Floro's call. He concluded that it was only the ripe fruit of the plan that he had steadily carried out to break Floro down. Floro must have gotten word that the case was ready for trial and had come to plead for mercy, or to drive a bargain. How much was Floro willing to pay to keep out of jail? Francisco had a price in mind and was not going to settle for less. This call deserved a celebration with an extra shot of whiskey.

"Colonel. You know me well. I've had a few little problems before—nothing serious. When I was younger, I liked to get into a good fight for nothing, that's true. But this problem is different. I feel both sides have squeezed me and that's unfair. I don't deserve that."

Floro stopped talking, turned his back to someone passing by on the sidewalk, then looked at Francisco, as if expecting some remarks that didn't come.

"I can admit to you—man to man—that I wasn't as drunk as I've said I was, okay, but I have the right to defend myself the best way I can. Isn't that right?"

Floro again waited in vain for a response from Francisco.

After a long silence, Floro charged again, knowing that this time he had to change the nature of his message. "What I came to tell you is that, after a lot of thought, I decided I'm not willing to pay for somebody else's mistake."

Francisco moved some muscles around his mouth, giving signs the he was going to speak, then said, "Floro, this is very simple. You helped hijack a yacht worth 43,250 U.S. dollars, breaking a whole string of laws in the process. You pleaded not guilty for those actions because your mind goes blank when you drink too much. It is up to the jury to decide if they believe you or not."

"There's a medical . . ."

"Yes. Doctors have stated that when you drink beyond a point you lose control of your actions. But it hasn't been proved that you had reached that point that night. So, it is for the jury to decide if you did or you didn't reach that point. If they believe you knew what you were doing, you'll be facing quite a long stretch in jail."

Floro seemed shaken by what he had heard, as if he had suddenly seen the hopelessness of his only defense.

Francisco began walking again, to the evident pleasure of his dog, who had waited patiently but with visible boredom. After a few steps, Francisco said, "Of course, it would have been a different situation altogether if you had been under orders. Then there would be no charges against you."

"Everybody knows who's behind all of this. Everybody knows I'm nobody's fool. If I hadn't been authorized, I'd have left on the yacht, too, and today I'd be driving a Cadillac all over Miami with a couple of chicks, one at each side."

"Would you say that in court?"

Floro looked at Francisco and made a gesture of despair. "Colonel, all I want is to have a man-to-man conversation with you to tell you exactly how everything happened. If you accuse me after that, you'll be doing a great injustice. You'll be crushing the little guy while the big fish goes on drinking beer. Is that the justice you stand for?"

This time Francisco was the one who remained silent, considering. Finally, he spoke. "I see your point, Floro. From the moral point of view, you're right." Francisco seemed to carefully weigh what he was about to say. "Okay, if you tell me everything, answering my questions to the best of your knowledge, then I'll see how I can keep you out of this . . . maybe by a medical affidavit. But, if you try to save yourself and cover up Marcelo at the same time, then there's no use wasting my time."

"I don't owe that son of a bitch anything. He let me rot in jail for twenty-one days. I lost ten pounds there. I thought I was going crazy, caged like a bird. He didn't move a finger for me. He could have gotten me out of jail by just snapping his fingers, and he didn't. I tried to reach him so many times before coming to talk to you. His secretary, who knows me very well, always says, 'Florito, Marcelo just left the office and won't be back for the whole day. Florito, Marcelo is with the minister now, where can he call you back? Florito, Marcelo tried to reach you all day yesterday, but you weren't anywhere to be found.'" Floro imitated her condescending tone.

Francisco repressed a smile and thought for a minute about what to do. Floro was acting sober, but judging from his breath, he had had a few drinks. He could change his mind very rapidly, so the best time to question him was right away. On the other hand, he had been away from his home longer than usual. His family would worry unnecessarily if he stayed much longer. Besides, he would have to tape the conversation to have an ultimate weapon against Marcelo.

"Wait for me fifteen minutes. I'm going to take the dog back, tell my family that I have something important to do, and bring my car over. Then we'll go to an isolated place where you can tell me everything with no witnesses. Okay?"

"Okay."

Ten minutes later, after activating the wire recorder, Francisco pulled up in his car and picked up Floro, who was still waiting in the same spot. He drove toward the sea, thinking about a good place to stop. He decided to go to the park on Twenty-sixth Street and Fifth Avenue. Under the shadows of the gigantic trees there were many dark places with very few people passing by at night. At the same time, the park was located in the heart of Miramar.

As soon as the car had stopped in a dark, secluded spot, another car with a young couple parked nearby.

"Those people are going to think we're a couple of fags," Floro said.

"Start talking and get this over quick," Francisco responded dryly.

At that moment, to Francisco's total surprise, Marcelo came out of the shadows behind them, and Floro drew out a pistol and pointed it straight at him.

"What the hell are you doing?" Francisco was startled, outraged, and scared.

"We need you." Marcelo spoke softly and calmly, as he always did.

"I'm not interested in helping you in any way. Please, let me go. This is highly irregular, but I won't make any report; I won't say anything. Just forget this nonsense."

"Francisco, we know with absolute certainty that you are passing information to the CIA."

"What have you been drinking, Marcelo?"

"A couple of days after the hijacking of the *Elvirita*, the high command of the CIA asked their station here in Havana for the identity of a high officer of the Intelligence Service who had defected. Only five people knew then that the hijacker was a high intelligence officer: Floro, who was in jail, the heads of the State Security and the Intelligence Service, me, and you, who happened to be at the meeting where I had to report the incident. Later, but only later, the minister also knew about it. The next leak was about the cache in Montreal. This time, I told only the head of State Security and you in the report the Minister ordered me to send. The head of State Security, as I thought, *instructed the man he sent to Montreal to intercept the cache at DHL as soon as it arrived to ensure that Carlos Manuel had to go to him.* That was a trap I set for the spy. If the head of State Security was tipping the CIA, it would have been stupid to have the CIA intercept his man when they were after someone else. Again, all the evidence points to you as the one who's been passing on information."

Colonel Francisco had regained his poise after listening to Marcelo. He smiled. "Okay, you're accusing me of being a spy for the CIA. Let's go right now to wherever you wish and make formal accusations against me. Take your brilliant arguments to court. If you succeed, you'll send me to jail for twenty years. Simple?"

"No, Francisco, we need you for something else."

"I don't have to take this from you two," Francisco said angrily, turning the ignition key in his car.

"Do you remember Mario Calabrese?" Marcelo asked Francisco, pulling the key out of the car at the same time.

"Yes, he was in my class in The Hague," Francisco said, trying to regain control over the situation.

"His name is Austin Cabot, and he's now CIA Deputy Director of Operations."

"You're making a great mistake," Francisco insisted. "What you are saying, including the possibility that some of the students at the school I attended in The Hague could be in the CIA, is not proof. It is just a lead. At the most, circumstantial evidence."

"Good lesson, professor. You're a brilliant lawyer. I always learn something from you," Marcelo said, and handed the key back to Francisco, who grabbed it. Marcelo kept ahold of the key, though, and with the palm of his other hand made a gesture to wait. "Just one last question, Colonel. Do the initials P.G. mean anything to you?"

Francisco shut his mouth and sank back in his seat. His face became very pale, and he gasped for air.

Marcelo pulled a laptop out of a bag in the darkness behind him. "Do you recognize this computer, my dear colonel? The biggest and sometimes most insurmountable problem for a spy, made simple and infallible. Just type whatever you want on the keyboard and a software program translates it into a coded message impossible to decipher. At the touch of a key, the message is sent directly to a satellite in a fraction of a second. That's the way to do real business, isn't it? It's a shame that you didn't notice that we'd switched your computer with another one very much like it, and we've been receiving all of your messages lately, in plain language."

Marcelo pulled the limp Francisco out of the car and shoved him into the backseat, where Floro was waiting to guard him. They then drove off in Francisco's Lada. Ten minutes later, they reached an isolated house in Reparto Flores, patrolled by several security men.

"Okay, just tell me what I have to do," Francisco said, knowing he had no choice but to play the new game.

"We have another task for P.G. You'll be overjoyed . . . I mean it."

VERY EARLY in the morning, Carlos Manuel prepared himself for fishing. When he was ready, he placed a letter in an envelope on the dining room table, along with the package he had received the day before, all addressed to Marcelo. When he wrote the date on the letter, he noted that it was the thirteenth day since Claudia's abduction.

"Bad omen," he said aloud.

Then he went to his bedroom to listen once more to the tape he had received. Claudia's poised voice once again filled the room . . .

Roger arrived shortly after Carlos Manuel finished listening to the tape. He was carrying an extra aqualung tank as they had agreed the night before. He served himself a cup of coffee and sat down close to Carlos Manuel, looking into his eyes. In the last week Carlos Manuel had gone fishing only twice because the weather hadn't been very good, and he hadn't been feeling well.

"You look like shit today, old man," Roger said.

"I feel like shit. I hardly slept last night."

"Take it easy today. Go back to bed and get all the sleep you need. Remember, you're your own boss."

"I need to catch a good fish for the wedding anniversary of two dear friends."

"I can get it for you. You better go see a doctor. Maybe it's a virus or something."

"I just need a dip in the cool water to wake me up, that's all. Maybe I'll follow your advice and come out early. Let's go. I'll come out as soon as I catch the fish I promised."

"I've told you I'll take care of that."

"Okay, I'll just swim around for a while, then I'll go see a doctor. If you don't catch anything, take a couple of four-pound red snappers from the freezer. It isn't the same as fresh fish, but it'll do. Call my friend, his name and phone number are written on that envelope on the table. He'll send someone to pick it all up. This letter and this package go with the fish. While you wait, have a couple of beers on me."

Roger glanced at the table and saw the box the mulatto had brought the day before and given to Carlos Manuel.

"Do you want that sent, too?"

"Make sure my friend gets that, too!"

Roger was going to say something, but changed his mind. As they walked together to the sea, neither said a word.

That day Roger went out to the *pretil*, where he was sure to catch good fish at that time of the year. He came out of the water about ten in the morning with a ten-pound *Dorado*, a delicacy even for a king's table. He decided to also throw in a five-pound red snapper that he had caught on his way to the *pretil* for Carlos Manuel's gift.

He opened his friend's apartment with a key hidden under a rock in the front garden of the building. As soon as he entered the apartment, he knew Carlos Manuel hadn't yet returned. His diving gear wasn't where he always put it when he returned from fishing. Roger followed his instructions and made the call. Some time afterward, a driver came to pick up the fish, the letter, and the package. Roger decided to wait for Carlos Manuel until noon. When noon came and went, he took his car and drove around the neighborhood, searching for his partner in all the places he might have been, even at the Comodoro Hotel. Then he went back to Carlos Manuel's apartment and made calls from there to the best clients they had, to ask if Carlos Manuel had called or if they had seen him. Roger didn't know what else to do. The phone rang, and it was Marcelo, who wanted to talk to Carlos Manuel. Roger told him what had happened, and Marcelo asked Roger to wait there for him.

Before leaving for Carlos Manuel's house, Marcelo again read the note inside the envelope the driver had brought: *"Considering the situation I am in, this is the only way I see out. I'm sure you remember what you promised me."*

Marcelo recalled Carlos Manuel's exact words when they had met at his apartment just before Claudia's kidnapping. They came readily to his mind: *"If I die at the bottom of the sea, promise me you'll publish the news in all the newspapers, so my enemies will be satisfied and my soul can rest in peace."* He had promised. And, as he was leaving, Carlos Manuel had insisted, *"Don't forget."*

The search for Carlos Manuel's body started in the afternoon, when it had become clear he had had an accident. Roger, three professional divers, and some of the fishermen from the neighborhood searched all the hunting waters from the mouth of the Almendares river to the Comodoro Hotel and beyond, even to places where they never fished. Late in the afternoon, Roger found Carlos Manuel's speargun floating at a depth of twenty feet. It was tied by a long nylon cord to a spear embedded in a big sea bass inside a small cave sixty feet below the surface, marking the spot where Carlos Manuel must have lost consciousness. Most of the flesh of the sea bass had been eaten away by other fish on the coral reef, indicating that the accident had occurred several hours earlier. At that time of the year, there was a strong current flowing northeast along the coast, and it was assumed it had pulled Carlos

Manuel's body into deep water off the island platform. The body wouldn't float to the surface because of the weighted belt he used to remain at fifty or sixty feet while diving.

As soon as Marcelo got back to his office, he took Claudia's tape, the electronic buoy, the map, and the letter Carlos Manuel had left him and went to see the old man at his house.

The next day, the Ministry of the Interior released an obituary to the newspapers reporting Carlos Manuel's death in a swimming accident. Technically, the Minister of the Interior had not yet confirmed his demotion and eviction from the Service at the time of his death, and the request was withdrawn.

45

BARTER RECEIVED THE news of Carlos Manuel's death and was unsure about how to proceed. *He had to do something to prevent King from harming Claudia, if he hadn't already.*

T.S. King had become a stranger to him. Barter had been abruptly pulled out of Miami, and the group to study the Cuban economy had never been formed. At the office, Barter had been "promoted" to attend to all the training courses going on in the "Company." King had also begun to snow him under paperwork that he now had to fill out, supervise, or sign. Barter wondered why King was doing all of this to him. They had become extremely close while they were after *Roberto*. Why had King changed so much? It had to be that he'd found out about his affair with Martha, in spite of the secrecy they'd maintained.

Three weeks earlier, he had received from King the sudden mission to travel to five Latin American countries to study their economic ties with Cuba in a trip that would last two months. There was no sense to that trip; all the information was already available and people in various government agencies were taking care of it. This mission could only mean that King was preparing to do something he didn't want Barter around to watch. He was scheduled to leave on March 10 for Sao Paulo, Brazil, and King himself was so eager to see him off that he was looking after his travel arrangements personally, making sure he would leave on time. On instinct, Barter delayed his trip until Monday, feigning an acute nephritic pain, something that he had suffered through once, ten years ago, the cause of which had never been determined, despite the many painful tests he had undergone. Martha called one of the CIA doctors, who came to see him at her apartment. The doctor gave him a shot of a strong pain reliever and prescribed a complete checkup at the hospital to determine the cause. He and Martha remained home all that day, mainly because the injection put him soundly to sleep for hours.

The following week he stayed at a hospital having a complete medical checkup. He couldn't stop thinking about what King could be plotting. The only explanation that returned repeatedly to his mind was that King was planning to do something to *Roberto*—King never used another name—possibly involving his children.

Barter had been calling Antonio regularly to check on how they were doing. He tried to tell himself that keeping tabs on them was part of his job, but he had to admit that he liked those kids, each with a different, charming personality. While at the hospital, he received a message through the CIA remote phone system that Antonio was trying to reach him. Barter did not want to reply from his cellphone. Once out of the hospital, he reached Antonio from a public phone. The news of Claudia's kidnapping hit him like a blow in the solar plexus. So, that was why King wanted him far away. He told the boy what he thought was best for his father to do.

What could he do? How was it possible to wage a fight against King, a man who wouldn't hesitate for a second to wipe him out? It was clear that King no longer needed him. He had to be very careful about anything he decided to do. King was a shrewd operator, a man he couldn't outmaneuver easily. He tried to reach King again and again to have a man-to-man talk with him, but he was always away on one of his visits to Florida, and, upon his return, he dodged Barter's messages.

Barter went back to his laptop and started to carefully read all the information he had stored on Timothy Sidney King. By the end, something was very clear. Even before he had entered the CIA, when he was a good-looking tough guy, the favorite of many dames, he had been the object of a couple of nasty accusations of brutality, although he had always been able to shake them off. Dispensing with the scientific jargon of the psychologists, it was clear to Barter that King was, in the end, a ruthless son of a bitch who would kill his mother if it served a purpose for him.

When King turned his black Mercedes Benz to enter his garage, its lights shone on the figure of a man jumping up and down to avoid freezing. He stepped on the brakes, grabbing his gun with his right hand. The car slid a bit on the snow and stopped right next to William Barter, who had leapt aside.

"What's the matter, Billy Boy?"

"I came to see you here because I don't want to miss you this time." Barter spoke with difficulty through rigid jaws because of his long exposure to the freezing weather.

"Come inside before you drop dead. I don't want your body obstructing my garage door in the morning." King's voice seemed merry.

Barter was in no mood for jokes, so he kept his mouth tightly shut. He could have waited in his car, but the layout of the house and garage made it possible for King to enter the garage connected directly to the house and lock himself in before Barter had a chance to intercept him. Since King had avoided seeing him or answering his calls for the last few days, there was no reason to believe he would change his mind unless he was forced to speak, Barter told himself.

The door of the garage opened at the flash of an electronic signal. Barter let the car enter, then followed it in swiftly. There was no telling what sort of intruder's trap might be waiting inside, Barter thought, as the door closed quickly behind him. He joined King as he stepped into his dining room from the garage. The room was warm and pleasant. The smell of recently broiled meat lingered in the air. Barter's mouth watered. God, he was hungry! King went directly to a bar in the dining room and collected a couple of glasses.

"I'm going to serve myself a big shot of whiskey. What are you having these days, Billy Boy?"

"Whatever you're drinking will be fine for me, too."

"This is a surprise. I thought you were searching for a kidney donor. How long have you been in the hospital taking tests to determine what's wrong with you, Bill? It must be something very serious."

Barter didn't answer the question. He wasn't there to let King provoke him with sarcastic remarks. "I have to speak to you about a very important matter, Mr. King."

"Important matter? In this cold weather, an empty stomach at this hour of the night is the most important matter I can think of. Have you eaten? Judging from the smell, there's a whole sirloin ready on the grill . . ."

"No, thanks, I'm all right. I came here to see you because I haven't had any luck reaching you on the phone these last few days. Something has come up that superseded what I wanted to talk to you about. *Roberto* is dead and is going to be buried tomorrow in Havana."

A sudden change flashed across King's face, but was quickly replaced with a feigned expression of good humor. "I appreciate your taking all this trouble to come here in this lousy weather to tell me that. As it happens, I was already informed."

"Why haven't you let Claudia go?"

The expression on King's face transformed into one Barter had never seen before.

"Who the hell do you think you are, coming to my house and talking to me like this?"

"I just asked a simple question. Why do you react like that? Why haven't you answered any of my calls?" Barter tried to talk normally, pretending to be surprised by King's reaction.

King took a long sip of his whiskey. He seemed to calm down, but the expression on his face had turned to a sneer of contempt. When he spoke again, his voice reminded Barter of a snake hissing.

"Why are you meddling in this affair? Do I have to spell it out for you? You're smart enough to know that I sent you off on a paid vacation to South America to keep you away, because you still don't have the stomach for something like this. That, of course, is the reason I haven't answered any of your calls. Your waiting at the door of my garage like a penguin isn't going to change my mind." King drank the rest of his whiskey and assumed an expression of regret. "I really thought you were smarter."

"I might be dumb, dumb enough to think that anybody who kidnaps a child, breaking every law in this country just for personal revenge, ought to be in jail, not heading an important section of the Central Intelligence Agency. Furthermore, even if I could ever lower my morals enough to accept this sort of thing, there's absolutely no reason why the innocent victim shouldn't be set free now that her father is dead."

King looked at Barter and chuckled. "*Roberto* dead? You're a perfect moron. How can you fall for such a farce? Anybody who really wants to kill himself takes a high-caliber pistol and blows his brains out. No, *Roberto* has to go deep-sea fishing, having his body conveniently washed away, turning up the next day so eaten up by fish that nobody can recognize him." King stared at Barter a moment, then added flatly, "Bullshit."

"Okay, let's suppose that *Roberto* is alive. You have no right to take his child; you're not above the law of this country. I'm warning you, let the girl go. I've taped this entire conversation. When I leave here, I'm going to turn this evidence over to the FBI."

"Sir Galahad, if you bring the FBI into this business, you're a dead duck within the company." King rose and came closer to Barter, with a smirk on his face and a menacing glint in his eyes.

Barter instinctively placed his hand on his pistol. "I'm leaving now," he said, moving toward the front door.

"If you believe anybody can find the faintest proof against me on that tape, you're really out of your mind. When you play that back, you'll find that you were the one who spoke all the shit that's on your mind. Billy Boy, I was mistaken about you. You don't really have what it takes." King followed Barter all the way to the main door, laughing and shouting at him. "Stupid fool! Is this the way you think you're going to get me out of my office so you can sit in my chair?"

King continued to advance as Barter retreated backwards, not daring to lose sight of his superior.

"I don't know what you're talking about. You're totally deranged."

"I've done my homework on you, Billy Boy. I know why and how you came to my section. And, since you're leaving, I'm going to tell you what I'm going to do next, challenging you to stop me." King passed a finger across his throat, clearly referring to Claudia. "See if you've recorded that." King slammed the door hard.

Barter didn't know what to do next. He hadn't been able to get a single clue as to where Claudia had been taken or who was keeping her. He knew that the FBI was after several suspects and that there was an arrest warrant for the person who had picked up the false Claudia at the hospital. The only thing he could do now was ask for an interview with Austin Cabot, telling him everything he knew about King, but that wouldn't stop this maniac from killing the girl. He cursed himself for having made things worse, much worse.

ON MARCH 24, at noon, Cuban radio and television announced that Carlos Manuel's body had been found. His burial, with all the honors due him, was set for the following morning. His body was brought to the funeral parlor at Calzada and K Streets late in the afternoon. Some of the personnel who found the body in fifty feet of water, twenty miles northeast of the location where he had been fishing, related details of their search. The corpse wasn't shown in the coffin, because most of the flesh and the eyes didn't exist anymore. At the Institute of Legal Medicine, Carlos Manuel was identified through his dental records. The twenty-three medals awarded to Carlos Manuel by Cuba and three other countries were placed on a board in front of the coffin. Marcelo and Mario stood the last guard of honor before the body was taken away in the hearse to the cemetery.

At the burial services on March 25, the head of the Intelligence Service delivered the eulogy. He praised the exemplary life of the deceased and concluded, "Son of a hero, a hero himself, whatever mistakes he made are insignificant compared to his proven loyalty during many difficult times, and to the great deeds he accomplished in a rather short life."

* * *

Austin Cabot summoned King to his office. King came promptly, seemingly in very good humor, stopping to chat a bit with Cabot's secretary. The second he entered Cabot's office, however, he knew trouble lay ahead.

"Look at this note P.G. sent." Cabot extended a sheet of paper. King took off his glasses and read:

> The Minister of the Interior has asked the High Military Court for advice on the legal actions that can be taken against Timothy Sidney King, based on hard proof in their possession, some of it directly from the FBI, about the kidnapping of the daughter of Carlos Manuel Armas in order to blackmail him and to force his desertion from Cuba, ultimately causing his death. The girl remains captive and it is feared for her life. Among the legal actions considered could be presentation of this case to a court in Maryland by an aunt of the girl, a U.S citizen.
>
> The evidence includes: The captain and a sailor of the yacht "Tycoon," anchored at the Marina Hemingway in Havana, confessed, shortly after being detained, that they had come to Cuba to force the defection of the above-mentioned Cuban citizen and smuggle him into the U.S. The captain is willing to publicly identify the man who hired him, Timothy Sidney King, head of the Cuba Section of the CIA. The Cuban intelligence officer turned other incriminating evidence over to his superior before losing his life in what was qualified for the public as a "swimming accident."
>
> The Minister stated that they have overwhelming proof that the head of the Cuba desk, with the evident support of the CIA Deputy Director of Operations, is behind the kidnapping carried out by Arturo Montiel. Montiel, they claim, is a well-known criminal who has done many such jobs for the CIA and on his own. They will present the proof when necessary.
> P.G.

King lifted his eyes from the communication and remained silent, staring at Cabot to see what his next move would be.

"Sidney, I warned you that you were on your own in this affair. You assured me that it was a fake kidnapping, easy to reverse if things didn't work out. This has turned out to be the stupidest thing I've ever seen in my life."

"They'll never be able to prove anything, I assure you. The Cubans are bluffing. I never talked with the captain of the Tycoon . . . except on the phone."

"Shit. You still don't see it, do you?"

King looked wide-eyed at Cabot, like a primary-school pupil caught shooting a spitball while the teacher was writing on the blackboard.

"The best way out of this shit-hole is your immediate resignation 'for reasons of health.' I expect it here on this desk in twenty minutes. I have a meeting with the general director, and I want to have that paper signed by you in my hands."

Cabot watched King gasping for air as if he had been hit with a left hook to the liver by a heavyweight champ.

"This doesn't sound like any of P.G.'s notes I've ever read. He never writes such detailed messages," King said desperately.

"Of course it's P.G. He's trying to warn us he's been caught. We burned the poor bastard, using the info he gave us about the cache your *Roberto* was going to pick up in Montreal, remember? It's clear this message comes directly from the Cuban Ministry of the Interior."

King brought the letter of resignation to Cabot's secretary and immediately went home to give Montiel instructions to disappear, taking the old witch Inés with him—broom and all—until things cooled off. He also had to change the instructions for the two men he had in a motel in Waycross, Georgia, waiting for his final order to make the hit. Instead, he would tell them to put the girl, unharmed, on the next Miami-bound bus. Their contract would be paid in full.

King sank into a chair to brood over everything that had happened, before cancelling the order to terminate Montiel, Inés, and the girl. He served himself a shot of rum to soothe his nerves. He was furious at himself for having given Cabot the motive he needed to throw him out of the CIA. For better or for worse, at every turn of his career, Austin Cabot had been there deciding which way he should go. With time, he had learned to hate the double-crossing bastard to whom nothing mattered but his own job. King also thought about the fact that the FBI was not going to rest until they grabbed Montiel. Having Montiel, they had him. That quest could take months, but eventually the FBI would get there.

What if he went ahead with his plan of wiping out everybody, anyway? He couldn't afford to have Montiel alive. King let his mind range over the possibilities. With Montiel, Inés, and Claudia dead, the FBI would have nothing in their hands—no witness to point a dirty finger at him—only a lot of accusations with no backbone to them. *Cabot and the company would have no choice but to stand behind him, no matter what.* He would not have to defend himself; Austin Cabot would do it wonderfully for him. He had nothing to lose and everything to gain by wiping out all his footprints now that he had been ousted from his job.

He decided to have another drink. This called for a toast to himself. This was a grand finale for his career. With Claudia's death, he would take revenge on *Roberto*, on Austin Cabot, and on the fucking CIA, all at the same time. He poured two shots of Bacardi in two different glasses. He took one in each hand, clashed them together, and drank first one, then the other.

THERE WAS ONLY one telephone Hernando
Pereda answered personally, and only a few people
knew the number. Not even his family knew of its
existence. It was only through that telephone that
Pereda felt free to speak. It was a very special, untraceable connection that he had managed to get when he built his house almost ten
years back. The telephone line was diverted from a commercial
center not very far from his house. The telephone bill was paid regularly by a small shop in the mall with no apparent connection to
him. He received fewer than a dozen calls a year through that telephone, although he often used it for outgoing calls when he wanted
to make sure nobody was listening. Pereda interrupted what he was
doing to pick up the receiver of his secret phone.

"Hello, Hernando."

"Who's speaking?" Pereda couldn't recognize the voice.

"This is a friend of *Roberto* from Cuba."

Hernando Pereda started to feel uncomfortable; something in
his stomach told him this wasn't going to be good news. If it was
what he feared, his secret telephone had been intercepted this
whole time, and he dreaded to even imagine who had been listening to his conversations.

"I know several Robertos," Pereda said, stalling.

The man to whom he was speaking laughed. "Same old Fernando. There's no way of sneaking up on you? I just want to ask you for a favor. One of your men, Arturo Montiel, kidnapped *Roberto's* daughter."

Pereda stayed silent.

The unknown voice continued. "Since you're Montiel's boss, please give Montiel the order to free the girl immediately and see that she gets home safely sometime tonight."

"I can't give any such order. Even if what you say is true, I don't know where Montiel is right now," Pereda snapped back.

At the other end of the line, the man laughed again. "Hernando, let me explain this to you more clearly. *Roberto* is dead. Some of his friends have decided to take action. If we don't do this now, tomorrow it could be someone else's kid. We just have to stop this shit at the start, once and forever, whatever the cost. Is that clear?"

"I honestly don't know where Montiel is, and I don't have a way to reach him."

The man at the other end laughed yet again, but when he spoke this time, his voice was commanding. "Pereda, we hold you responsible for this, as much as Montiel and as much as King. Don't try to squeeze your way out of it." The voice was increasingly menacing.

"That's mighty big talk," Pereda said, after a moment of hesitation. "Go and bark up some other tree. I don't have time for this bullshit."

Again the short laugh and the same even, self-assured voice. "We thought that since you have a lot to lose, being wealthy and having a large family, you would be wiser. But we were mistaken. Apparently, there's only one way to talk to Mr. Hernando Pereda. Just to give you a taste of what we mean, why don't you try to locate your son, Rodolfo?"

Hernando felt a rush of rage and fear. "Don't you dare touch any of my kids! I'll have every one of my men hunting down every fucking communist in this town."

"Don't panic. It isn't your style. Listen carefully. Pick up the phone and call King. You have just one hour to set Claudia free. *Make all the calls through this telephone. We're monitoring it.* If you want proof of what we're willing to do, we can have your son Rodolfo killed right now on his way to Fort Myers. Attached under his Volvo is one pound of TNT, and we have a car tailing him, ready to detonate the charge from the necessary distance. Don't waste your time trying to warn Rodolfo; somebody stole his cellphone. *Just do exactly as I tell you. And if you're still unconvinced, listen to the proof.*"

Pereda heard a big blast right outside his house, toward the parking lot. The windowpanes of the room trembled from the shock waves.

"Don't panic, Pereda. That was just a few ounces of TNT below your own car. We hold all the aces. Just play as I tell you."

MONTIEL, CAN'T YOU see what's staring you in the face?" Inés asked.

"Don't tell me again that we're trapped in here. Talking like that brings bad luck. Since the beginning, all your predictions, visions, and all that shit have brought us only bad luck. This whole thing got fucked up when you started making your *brujerías*."

"You know very well they're not witchcraft. *Caracoles* always tell the truth."

At that moment, the laptop started beeping. Montiel opened the computer and read the message on the screen: *"Two men are coming to take over the operation. Just leave everything to them. Take Inés with you. Try Brazil for a while until things cool off."*

Montiel typed on the screen, *"What do I use to get away? There's only the ambulance here."*

The answer came back immediately. *"Take it with you. It won't be needed anymore."*

Montiel knew this could only mean that Claudia was doomed, since the ambulance was the only way to take her from one place to another in broad daylight without risk. If she was going to be killed, so were he and Inés, as easy as adding two and two.

Montiel turned to Inés, who was searching for something to eat among the few cans of food left in a box. "Why don't you throw your *caracoles* and ask them what's going to happen today?"

Inés, surprised by the request, looked at Montiel, ready to mock him. Then she noticed he seemed worried, very worried. Obviously, the news on the computer wasn't good. She held her tongue, realizing that she was also in mortal danger.

"I'll ask the *obís*."

Inés went to the room she shared with Claudia and brought back four round pieces of coconut shell, each one about two inches in diameter, a candle, a box of matches, and a half-empty bottle of *aguardiente*. She placed everything on the kitchen floor and went to the sink for a glass of tap water, which she placed beside the coconut shells.

Inés took off her shoes and sat on the floor spread-eagled, the glass of water and the bottle of liquor at her right side, the shells and the candle before her at arms' reach. She lit the candle and fixed it to the linoleum that covered the floor. Before touching the shells again, she wet her fingers and flicked water to her left, to her right, and behind her. Then, she filled her mouth with *aguardiente* and spit it back out, spraying it all around her. She took another swallow and sprayed it toward the candle. The fine drops of the liquid caught fire, creating an impressive ball of flame. Montiel came closer and sat down on a chair to watch the divining session.

"*Anatunú ché oddá li fu aro mo bé aché.*" Inés's praying voice was low and monotonous. "*Aché mi mó aro mo bé amoi tutu, ana tutu tutu laroye.*"

Inés closed her left hand, and with her right touched the floor three times. Then, she continued in *Yorubá*, using exactly the same words that slaves coming from West Africa to work on Cuban sugarcane plantations had used when speaking to their *orishas* two centuries earlier:

> *Ilé mó kuo kuele mu untori ku,*
> *untori aro,*
> *untori eyé,*

untori ofó,
untori mó de li fu lóni.

Next, she took the shells and prayed to *Ellegguá,* the *orisha* who rules man's fate:

Obí ku aro obí eyó obí ofú, obí.
Ellegguá.

"*Akañá.*" Inés ended her prayer.

"*Akañá,*" repeated Montiel, who also knew these prayers.

Inés shook the shells with both hands and threw them on the floor. Three fell with the outer side up, while the last one fell with the outer side down.

"*Ocana Sode.*" Inés's voice seemed to break as she read the letter announcing all sorts of calamities. She rose and turned in a circle three times, pulling her ears, speaking obscure words in *Yorubá.* She poured the water left in the glass over the shells to cool them off and quickly made a last throw. This time all the shells fell with their outer sides down.

"*Eyekum.*" Inés stared at Montiel to see his reaction.

"What does that mean?"

"Death."

Claudia woke up. She realized that she wasn't strapped to the bed and didn't feel dazed as she usually did when Inés woke her once a day by throwing cold water on her face. The old woman was sitting on the floor, barefoot, looking intently at the array of *caracoles* between her legs. Claudia stared at the woman, trying to understand what was going on and why she was totally unbound and fully awake.

"Claudia," Inés said, without taking her eyes off the *caracoles,* "I have the most wonderful news for you. You're a daughter of *Shangó* and *Oshún.* You are the first one I've known in my whole life. You're blessed as a child of two of the most powerful *orishas:* the goddess of love and riches, and the powerful god of thunder. If I had known who your parents were, I would never have laid a hand on you."

The woman's words brought the image of her mother and father to Claudia's mind, and she was overcome by a strange feeling of awe before unknown forces that she suddenly felt very near.

Inés gathered her *caracoles* rapidly and stood up. "Get ready, quick! Some people are coming to kill all of us."

Claudia jumped out of bed and looked, bewildered, at the woman who a moment before had told her she had wonderful news for her.

"Put on the jeans, the long-sleeved shirt, and the tennis shoes. We have to hide in the woods."

Claudia hurriedly put on the clothes.

"Don't be afraid. *Oshún* will always protect you. With his index finger, *Shangó* will pierce the eye of anybody who tries to harm you."

A car with New Jersey plates drove up to the house at mid-afternoon. The driver blew the horn to announce the visit. All of a sudden, Montiel opened a front window and fired his .12 gauge repeating shotgun three times. The first blast burst the windshield. The second caught the driver in the head, blowing him out of the driver's seat, transforming his handsome face and body in a fraction of a second into a quivering mass of bloody meat. The man beside him received some buckshot in the head and neck from the first two blasts and a shower of minute particles of windshield that blinded him momentarily. He opened the door and fell onto the ground, bleeding from his wounds but still alive. He crawled under the car and, opening one eye, fired a couple of shots with his .357 Magnum at Montiel, hitting him in the belly through the wooden wall. Montiel fell back on the floor, feeling a ball of fire scald his stomach.

They heard the car horn, the slam of a window forced open, and the horribly loud explosions of gunshots from inside the closed-up house. They felt the wooden walls and floor tremble with the unexpected blasts. They heard the cry of the geese on the pond and the sound of their wings in their frenzy to fly away. The old woman opened the back door and started running toward the bushes near the swamp. Claudia followed her and was soon leading the way. They ran for a while, then hid amidst a thick cluster of shrubs, shrinking down against the roots, hearing only the beat of their own hearts and the sound of their respiration, smelling the grass and the wet, soft soil underneath them.

Montiel crawled to the main door, opened it, and kept crawling onto the veranda. He fired his last two shots at the man under the car, who was still aiming his gun at the window. The body of the man jumped a few inches from the ground twice, then lay quiet, bleeding from the many holes covering his body.

After the last gunshot, an enormous silence settled over the entire area. No sound was heard from any bird or any other animal in the swamp surrounding the place, and no wind blew the leaves and branches of the trees or played with the tin roof of the house.

After what seemed a very long time, the geese began to come back—one by one at first, then in small groups, until they were gathered all together and began to discuss the latest incidents among themselves. Claudia and Inés started to walk slowly in a great circle, wanting to approach the front of the house from afar to try to find out what terrible events had happened, before the night closed in on them. They approached a spot from where they could see two bodies lying motionless in pools of blood, one under the car and the other on the veranda. Moving cautiously forward, they reached the place where the slaughter had occurred. They smelled the pungent-sweet odor of the blood, and found a third man dead inside the car. Two vultures watched them from the top of the house.

When Claudia returned home, her brothers had everything packed. The three of them left Florida for an undisclosed destination.

49

KING STOPPED PACING in a circle around his chair. He glanced at the man behind the huge mahogany desk, clad in a dark brown suit that must have cost a small fortune. King felt as if he were appealing to a unique one-man court, where no jury, no lawyers, and no public were allowed. He had to be convincing in his last deposition because his life was at stake.

"After going over and over this whole thing, I can find only one explanation for why it failed—only one." King pointed a finger at the man behind the desk. *"Someone in your organization squealed. Told the FBI exactly what was happening."*

Pereda had avoided meeting with King for two whole weeks, blaming him for Montiel's death, and, above all, for putting his family in jeopardy. Only after Cabot asked him to listen to what King had to say had he consented to receive him. King had been talking for almost half an hour, trying to convince his longtime associate, while Pereda remained silent, looking at him with an incredulous expression on his face.

"The scheme was foolproof. I challenge anybody to find the slightest flaw in it. For a week to ten days the police wouldn't have moved a finger to find the missing girl. In most cases, they would do nothing, ever. And if they did anything, they would have found no grounds to prosecute anybody; thousands of young girls elope with boyfriends every day. And this operation was perfectly rigged to show that this was what had happened if, by accident, the police stumbled onto it." King kept reviewing the core arguments of his case before Pereda.

"There's no other explanation for the FBI jumping into the case almost immediately with all their resources. You have to face that hard fact, Hernando. Someone besides you, who knew what Montiel was doing, is also working for the FBI. I admit I should have cancelled the whole thing once the FBI got into it. I admit that I failed to recognize from the beginning that the FBI had to be working with full inside information and would thus progress very rapidly. My idea was that, since everything was so well planned, there was no real risk in carrying on for a few more days. Just to prove that, the FBI has the computer with the cellphone used to communicate with Montiel, with all the messages exchanged, but they can't decipher them. It would take a lifetime to break the codes.

"I also admit that I should have warned you that the girl was *Roberto's* daughter. He and Marcelo make a deadly combination, and I'm sure they're reunited again. When I failed to catch him in Havana, and knew of his disappearing act, I was sure he was going to pop up here with the full support of Cuban intelligence, whose men are swarming all over this city. I immediately sensed that the whole scenario had changed. Nevertheless, I told myself I should follow our agreement; you lent me only one man, Montiel, and you made it clear that you didn't want to be involved in the operation. 'The less I know, the better' were your words. I respected that the entire time.

"As for Montiel's death, I did exactly what you asked me to do in our last phone conversation. I already showed you the messages exchanged with him, in which I clearly stated that he should turn the girl over to these men I was sending and go away with Inés. But Montiel didn't obey my order and, instead, opened fire on the men I sent to relieve him. I also brought you the FBI report on the investigation, in which experts have concluded that Montiel shot at first sight."

King was sure that if he didn't straighten out this matter with Pereda, one of these days he was going to have a deadly surprise. Pereda never failed to collect what he thought was owed him. King had promised him in their last phone conversation to free Claudia immediately and let Montiel go away. Pereda had agreed to guarantee that Montiel would spend the rest of his life far away from the FBI's reach, working for a lumber company in the heart of the Amazon. King again paused, hoping to see even a slight favorable change in Pereda's face, but it remained immutable.

King was becoming desperate. He had reached the end of his speech and Pereda's expression looked as if it were carved in stone. "From the beginning, I had planned everything against any possible contingency, *except for a major information leak that can only have come from your side.*" King hammered again on this last argument to make Pereda indirectly responsible for what had happened, then sat down, to the evident relief of his only leg.

King didn't like Pereda's office; it was dark and emitted a mixture of damp, stale-smelling odors. He took a perfumed handkerchief from his jacket pocket and rubbed his face, as if drying sweat.

Pereda sat silent for a moment, looking at King—who was nervous, almost frantic—as if he had never seen him before. Then he spoke in the tone of a fair and severe Supreme Court judge. "You made your point on one matter. I'm going to look for that leak you mentioned, and as soon as I find the culprit, I'll take care of him. But that's not what I wanted to clear up with you."

Pereda pushed his chair back from the desk and stood up. The man was not tall, but had a powerful barrel-like chest and a strong neck. His skin was permanently tanned after many years of continuous sunburns. His big mustache was black and looked dyed. "The FBI has identified the two guys Montiel killed as common New York Mafia thugs, hit men by profession. They weren't there by accident. They didn't just miss the right road and end up in front of Montiel's hideout. *You hired them to kill Montiel and possibly Inés and the girl, too, to wipe out the only people who could point the finger at you.*" Pereda leaned forward. The cool and severe expression on his face had changed to one of hatred and anger. "Is that true or isn't it?"

Pereda came closer to King and regained his composure, but his voice held the anger. "Mr. King, do you believe that I'm going to swallow the story that you hired those New York killers to babysit this girl and escort her to a bus bound for Miami? What sort of fool do you think I am? Killing Montiel wasn't a part of the deal we made. You went ahead without my permission and without my knowledge. When we made our agreement, you assured me there was nothing to fear. That it was a fake kidnapping, and you could push the stop button the minute anything went wrong. But you pushed ahead until this was so fucked up it put my family in danger."

King looked at the man in the brown suit, astonished. Many years back, Pereda had been the swift, efficient operator who could carry out to perfection whatever order was given to him, in the blink of an eye. After they had lost contact for several years, Pereda had reemerged as a well-established businessman in Florida and in several Latin American countries, always pleased to meet King and enjoy a chat reminiscing about the good old times. Later, when King had begun to head the CIA's Cuba desk, Pereda had become one of the most important members of the exiled Cuban community, heavily involved in Florida's politics. Pereda ran a whole array of businesses in which he employed many men with experience in covert actions. It was not a secret that he kept these men organized as a militia, always ready to carry out all sorts of jobs.

Pereda returned to his chair behind the large desk and stayed silent for a moment, staring at the notes he had written. Then he lifted his head, looking again at the once-powerful head of the CIA's Cuba desk. "Is that all, Mr. King?" Pereda said, ending the meeting.

* * *

What was the verdict? King asked himself as he left Pereda's house, escorted by one of the guards. Worrying about it was useless; he would never know the answer until it was too late. Pereda, an extremely vindictive man, had called him at the last minute, in a panic, threatening his life if he didn't release *Roberto's* daughter at once. King had been so surprised that he thought Pereda had lost his marbles. He also had his own moment of panic, because he had no way of reversing her death sentence he had pronounced. Trying to warn Montiel on the computer only told him that everything was over and done with. Fortunately, under the circumstances, somehow it all turned out the best way possible for him: The girl was safe, as Pereda had begged, and Montiel rested in peace, leaving the FBI empty-handed forever. Why, now, was Pereda so upset? He had to figure out what and who were behind Pereda's anger toward him. The accusation of ordering Montiel's death was only an excuse—Pereda never cared that much for his hired hand. *Excuse for what?* King asked himself.

Once again, he sensed *Roberto* behind everything that was happening. Only a privileged evil mind, like *Roberto's*, could have managed—God knew how—to turn Pereda against him. It was very strange, he told himself, that "miraculous" things had begun to happen since the moment *Roberto* had "disappeared."

King couldn't help thinking that his *bête noire* was alive and in the country, and that all the evidence of his death, collected from different sources, had been placed there for his consumption only. If, by chance, his intuition was right, there was no time to lose; he had to find and destroy *Roberto* before *Roberto* destroyed him. Again, the Ariadna's thread leading to him was his children. He had to find where they had gone after they left Miami. *Roberto*, if alive, would be somewhere nearby.

50

WHEN ALEJANDRO Alcazar, better known as Alex, opened the door of Barbara Prieto's apartment in Boca Raton, he saw and smelled the blood staining the walls and floors. The sad looks on the faces of his two friends, who stood waiting for him with their guns drawn, told him that this was the end. He knelt on Barbara's carpet with the "Welcome" sign that he had always considered kitsch, and started reciting aloud the prayer his mother had taught him as a child.

> *Padre nuestro, que estás en los cielos,*
> *santificado sea el tu nombre,*
> *venga a nos a el tu reino,*
> *hágase tu voluntad,*
> *así en la tierra como en el cielo.*
> *Santa María, madre de Dios,*
> *ruega por nosotros ahora,*
> *y en la hora de nuestra muerte.*

The bullet hit him in the middle of the forehead. Alcazar collapsed backward, his hands still crossed over his chest.

The terminators, two men and a woman who had presumably

been Barbara's friend, had organized a surprise party for Alcazar and arrived with a huge birthday cake and several bottles of liquor. The plot, so common in gangster films, might have worked with better actors, but five minutes after they had entered, Barbara realized that something was seriously wrong. Becoming very nervous, she was detected trying to unhook the phone and set other warning signals for Alcazar. The farce had ended when the men pulled their guns, placed silencers on their muzzles, and fired upon Barbara.

ARRIVING IN MIAMI to carry out an investigation he was doing on his own, King learned about Alcazar's execution. He felt a great relief. Finally, Pereda had found a culprit for Montiel's death and his own troubles. Now that he no longer held an official position, King decided he was free to pay tribute to a longtime collaborator and brilliant man. He thought that Alcazar, who could have had a successful career in whatever he had wished to do, had met his fate at an early age by taking one of the world's most hazardous jobs. King was almost sure Alcazar had been killed because Pereda blamed him for passing information to the FBI. In a way, he felt responsible and sorry for Alcazar's death. But with Pereda, it was impossible to tell what had or had not been done and why, King told himself to soothe his conscience.

Many people attended the burial, but neither Pereda nor any of his men were there. It was clear to King that Alcazar's death was being used as a warning with a deadly message: *"Internal affairs of the clan must remain internal, regardless."*

After the burial, King went to the Hotel Fountainbleu, where he was staying. He ordered his lunch sent up to his suite and arranged for a waiter to serve at a small gathering he was having later in the afternoon. After lunch, King gave the waiter instructions about the other chores he wanted done, then dozed off for a while, watching television. He awoke to a call from the hotel lobby, announcing that his visitors were on their way up. A few minutes later, the waiter opened the door to a woman leading a team of four. The woman came forward with a big smile on her still-attractive face, preceded by a costly fragrance.

"Mr. Elvesham, I'm Mrs. Gutierrez. I'm delighted to meet you personally. This is my husband, Sergio Gutierrez."

A much older man standing beside the woman extended a cold and sweaty hand that gave King the impression he was shaking a dead fish. King wished he could go wash his hand immediately.

"Luis and Adrian will show you the paintings." The woman waved a hand toward the young men who were already setting up a private exhibition.

The waiter moved about with a tray, offering drinks to the guests.

"Enchanted to meet you, Mrs. Gutierrez. Glad to meet you, too, Mr. Gutierrez," King said, taking a daiquiri from the tray with his left hand, keeping his soiled hand in a pocket of his trousers.

In a few minutes, the fourteen paintings were on display. Most of them showed Miami landmarks and seascapes, and many of them struck King as excellent.

"I can assure you, Mr. Elvesham, this is the most talented young artist I've encountered in my twenty-five years in this business. Our gallery has made an exclusive contract with him. We're getting ready to handle his first show in this country, and we're preparing a strong promotion to assure its success. How did you learn about him?"

"One of my men likes to do volunteer charity work for his church, and he stumbled onto this painter and told me about him. He said this gallery has all the work he has done in Miami. I thought of helping the young artist by buying his paintings. I didn't know you had laid out such a major promotion plan for him," King said, conscious of Mrs. Gutierrez's perfume once more.

"Nevertheless, if you want to buy all the paintings, as you told me, we're ready to hear your proposition."

"How much do you want for the whole lot, Mrs. Gutierrez?"

"Taking into account your interest in helping the artist, we're willing to let you have them for one hundred."

"That's one hundred grand," Mr. Gutierrez intervened quickly.

"That's a lot of dough for the first work of an unknown painter," King said.

"That's what we've figured we can get for these paintings if our promotion is as strong as we hope to make it, Mr. Elvesham." Mrs. Gutierrez was smiling seductively at King, who looked ten years younger under a wig with abundant wavy brown hair.

"A great investment. Ten years from now they'll be worth five times that much," Mr. Gutierrez added.

King glanced again at the woman, already in her forties. She certainly had class, and a sexy body she knew how to move in an expensive dress, tailored in Paris, King surmised.

"I'm willing to buy the whole lot for seventy: five grand apiece."

Mrs. Gutierrez smiled. "Let's split the difference, and the paintings are yours."

"Seventy grand, that's my last bid."

"Well, taking into account that we won't have promotion expenses, we accept your proposition. They're yours. This calls for a toast." Mrs. Gutierrez locked an arm through King's and guided him to the suite's bar. Mr. Gutierrez followed, with a bottle of champagne in each hand.

"I want the paintings signed by the author before my eyes. I want to meet this lad."

"He's living out of town, but I meet him once a week to collect his paintings, Mr. Elvesham. Just tell me when and where you want to meet him."

"Another thing, Mrs. Gutierrez—I intend to sponsor the work of this lad. Please don't tell him anything about me in advance."

"As you wish, Mr. Elvesham."

"I'll give you a check for ten grand as a deposit. If you let me, I'll take that painting right over there to see how it looks in my house."

"As you wish, Mr. Elvesham."

52

ALICIA WAITED AT the restaurant entrance until the valet came to take her BMW model Z1, then she followed the car with her eyes until it was properly parked. She glanced at her wristwatch. It was almost two-thirty in the afternoon, and she was half an hour late. Madelyn and Ana would have already had their first drink and, as always when they had anything to drink, they would be laughing shrilly. Yes—Alicia could hear them as she walked through the crowded dining room of the elegant restaurant built on pontoons out into the ocean.

As she walked, she noticed a young man sitting by a window near her friends' table. He was very good-looking, although maybe too young for her taste, she thought, as she glanced at him scribbling something on a small board. He lifted his head, returning her gaze. During the few seconds their eyes met, she felt herself swept by one of those stares that undress you, and she turned her head quickly away. But it was pleasant to know she could still stir up interest in a man so handsome and young.

When Alicia joined her friends, she found them both excited about the lone customer, who had already been there, they said, when they arrived.

"That was quite a look he gave you when you came in! He's

paid no attention to either of us whatsoever. Isn't it true, Madelyn? Alicia, he's all yours!" Ana looked at Madelyn for confirmation, the two of them giggling like schoolgirls.

Alicia removed her bag from her shoulder, frowning. "Don't tell me your drinks have gone to your heads so much that you're flirting with a stranger at another table."

"No." Ana grinned mischievously. "We haven't flirted, but Madelyn has gone to the john twice already. He's a painter."

"Do you know him?" Alicia asked.

"While Madelyn was gone, I went over and asked him for a match. He said he didn't smoke and I told him I didn't, either. We smiled at each other, and I saw a sketch he was doing of a man on a boat outside. He seemed rather shy, so I . . ."

"That's why Ana's the best sales manager Sears Roebuck has in the whole country," Alicia said, not letting Ana finish her story. "She's a go-getter. She'll always be way ahead of us, Madelyn." Ana blushed. Alicia always scolded her for being so forward.

The three women had gone to high school and college together and had decided that they would not let jobs and family break up their friendship. They met once a week, every Friday afternoon, to have a couple of drinks, eat, and chat. Ana had married two years back, given birth to a boy, divorced, and recently come back to the club. Madelyn and Alicia had solemnly sworn not to marry before the age of thirty, still four and five years into the future. Alicia had picked the restaurant as their permanent meeting place because since childhood she had loved the smell of the ocean, the sound of the waves smacking against the pillars under the floor, the poised movement of passing boats visible through the windows, and, of course, the seafood.

The three young women ordered a round of drinks and began their ritual of choosing what to eat, before their conversation turned to the events in their lives during the past week. Two of the adjacent tables were occupied with English-speaking customers, so they switched to Spanish in order to talk more freely. Ana and

Madelyn often glanced over at the painter, who seemed completely absorbed in his work.

Before the food arrived, the painter rose from his seat and came over to their table with his drawing board in his hands. "Excuse my interruption," he said in Spanish, smiling at all of them. "I want to give you something that is yours," he added, looking directly into Alicia's eyes.

Alicia felt her heart beat faster and she suddenly felt out of breath. Why was she so affected by this stranger? He was very good-looking, but handsome men were a dime a dozen. Maybe it was his eyes. They seemed so kind, so alive. She reminded herself firmly of an iron rule instilled in her by her father in her childhood: Do not talk to strangers.

"You can't possibly have anything that belongs to me." Alicia let him know with the tone of her voice that the conversation was unwelcome.

"Ah, well, if you don't want it, I'll be delighted. It will be something precious for me to keep."

Ana and Madelyn were intrigued. They both wanted very much to invite the painter to sit down, but feared Alicia's reaction.

Ana then decided, for once, to defy Alicia. "Please, sit down. She's Alicia and she's Madelyn. This is Felipe, a painter."

"Thanks, I won't take much of your time. I'll be gone in a minute," Felipe replied.

"Whatever it is you have, you can keep it." Alicia avoided his eyes and peered disapprovingly at Ana instead.

"May I show it to Ana and Madelyn?" the stranger asked, looking again only at Alicia.

Alicia decided he had gone too far. She was not going to continue with this scene. "You can do as you please. I'm going to the john."

The newcomer seemed amused by Alicia's reaction. His eyes flashed with a glint of mischief. Alicia started to feel foolish and childish. Why had she stopped him so bluntly? He had been polite and seemed well-educated. Young men usually tried to meet girls with whatever excuse they could muster. She had better control her temper or she was going to spoil the afternoon. Since she had already announced it, she stood up to go to the ladies' room.

The stranger placed a sketch of a naked woman looking at herself in a mirror on the table. The woman bore a striking resemblance to Alicia, while the image in the mirror showed Alicia's face, but much older. She couldn't help looking at the picture, so surprised to recognize herself that she could not pull her eyes away from it. It was really her, even to the last detail! How had this man dared to paint her naked? But the portrait wasn't erotic or lascivious. Her face in front of the mirror reflected worry, while the mirror image was older and, at the same time, had a fascinatingly poised expression, as if the woman were satisfied and proud of the life she had lived.

After quite a long moment of staring, astounded, at every detail of the picture, Alicia became aware of the conversation going on around her. She sat down slowly to listen to what the painter was saying.

"It's just practice. A good chess player can remember the position of each piece on the board just by glancing at it. Some chess masters can play blindfolded as well as they play when they can see the board. All painters are trained to see and remember shapes, shades, colors . . . My passion is the study of people's faces and bodies. Once I see someone who attracts my attention, I try to decipher what's inside the image I've captured in my mind. Every wrinkle on a face has a reason; each smile and smirk has its meaning. Eyes are very telling, as are the way a person walks, their clothes . . . My task as a painter is to bring a new image to the surface that reveals the inner self of that person. Many painters can copy images, and a camera does it perfectly, but it seldom shows the soul inside."

"How do you see her? I mean, her inner self," Madelyn asked.

"In the sketch, I've tried to show her greatest fear—aging. Not really fear, that's not exact. What I sense in her is something more complex, maybe it's a self-imposed restraint on living the way she really and deeply would like, that gives the feeling that she's wasting her life. Then she worries about what she'll be like when she's older."

Alicia was very disturbed by the things he was saying about her. How could this guy, just from watching her for a few seconds, be so right about so many of her feelings? And how dare Madelyn ask a stranger such a question about her?

"How much do you want for the drawing?" Alicia asked bluntly.

"It isn't for sale." Felipe smiled. "It's a precious gift given to me. No?"

Alicia felt a surge of rage against her friends who dared dissect her with the stranger, and who now seemed amused by the bizarre situation she found herself in. She was also angry at herself for having acted childish and immature when the painter offered her the sketch. But her reaction was guided by habit. She reached into her purse and threw a hundred-dollar bill on the sketch.

"Is that enough for your work? Or how much do you want?"

The stranger changed his expression to one of sorrow. He retrieved the sketch from under the bill slowly, as if he didn't want it stained. He stood up and made a slight motion with his head to each of the girls, before turning to leave.

Alicia felt completely ashamed. She had done the worst thing she could possibly have done. Now it was clear to her that she had tried to humiliate him, although she hadn't consciously intended to. She couldn't let this man simply walk away with her picture. She sensed that the sketch bore a message that could change her whole life, if she could properly interpret it. She couldn't let him go away without knowing where to find him again. She wanted to ask him so many things, but not in front of her friends. Why had she been so vulnerable with this stranger? She was used to handling all sorts of situations like this.

She rose quickly, intercepting Felipe as he started to walk away. She caught his arm and held it softly, in a bold gesture that very much surprised her. She had never touched a stranger before in that way.

"I didn't mean to offend you." Something in Alicia's tone suggested that he was the one who should apologize to her.

Felipe was going to reply, but decided to keep walking.

Almost in a panic, Alicia took two quick steps forward, this time grasping his hand firmly. "Please, don't leave." She looked deeply into his eyes and then lowered her gaze submissively. She felt a strange, sweet feeling of surrender. "Okay, I lose. What is it you want?" This time her tone was warm and meek. She seemed close to tears.

The painter leaned forward and whispered in her ear, "I want you."

53

MARCELO CAME ALONE, driving his own Lada. The old man got into the car and told him to drive up to Calabazar to Octavio's house, where they were going to offer their condolences. Marcelo drove slowly, carefully avoiding the big potholes in the streets. In the past few years, most of the streets of Havana had begun to resemble a moonscape from lack of maintenance, especially in places away from the center of the city. Octavio lived in a small town long ago swallowed by the city's growth. Its name suggested that it must have once been a hamlet in the middle of a pumpkin field. But its deep, claylike soil had become the basis of a brick industry that flourished there for many years, until clay was replaced by cemented sand as the most popular building material.

Calabazar is very close to the Jose Martí International Airport. It begins at the southern end of the runway, where most of the planes land. The noise of planes constantly landing and taking off harasses the town day and night.

"He never got accustomed to the sound of the big planes arriving. As a child, he used to wake up at night crying, scared every time one of those big noisy aircrafts came in," Octavio said to his visitors, adding, "When he was old enough, he stayed away from home most of the time. He hated this place. Maybe I should have swapped the house for one in a better location." Octavio looked around the patio where his guests were sitting under the shadow of a big mango tree that spared the back of the house from the direct attack of the afternoon sun.

"This is where I was born, and my wife in the house next door. All our relatives live in this town, a stone's throw from here. I never really wanted to move away. I can work for hours in this patio, cleaning weeds, collecting coffee beans, pruning the trees, while my mind is somewhere else. From those plants back there we get all the coffee we drink year-round. Those two guava trees yield more fruit than we can eat. Remind me to give you some before you leave. These two trees produce hundreds of delicious avocados for six months out of the year. Have either of you tasted them? In a good mango year, this tree here can bear up to seven hundred mangoes. In that little piece of leveled land up front, I grow all sorts of vegetables during the winter and cucumbers and green beans in the summer. This old house with its high roof, on this little hill, is comfortable and fresh on the hottest summer days, always cool at night. The only problem is the noise from the planes. You have to get used to it."

Octavio sat down on a *taburete*, a strong wooden country chair with raw cattle hide covering the seat and the high back, designed to lean against walls and trees. "Maybe I was selfish, clinging to this place that he despised," he said in a low tone, as if talking to himself. Octavio remained silent for a while, his mind wandering to distant places. "He was overwhelmed with joy when we had to move to Europe. In every country we stayed, he learned the language in just a few months. He soaked up everything around us, as if his mind were a sponge always thirsty."

Octavio's wife opened the kitchen door, carrying a tray with three cups of coffee, two small ones with saucers for the visitors and a big one with no saucer for Octavio, who changed the subject of the conversation to again praise the quality of his mangoes.

When his wife left, Octavio continued. "He told me when he

called, 'I've lived a thousand years, Father.' This was the first time he had called me since he left us. I recognized his voice from his first word. I don't know why, but I was waiting for that call. All this week, I thought of him. And, by the way she kept to herself in her room, I knew she was also thinking about him. The day he called, I had decided to stay working at home. I felt nervous all morning, not knowing why, and I noticed that she wasn't well, either. His call was very brief. After he asked about me and his mother, he told me that he had called to tell us what we already suspected, that King had organized Claudia's kidnapping. Then he said that Pereda had ordered Arturo Montiel to work for King on that. He also told me that I could use that information. That was when he said he had already lived a thousand years. *'Papá, I feel as if I've lived a thousand years,'* were his exact words. I often wonder why he said that. Alex was such a special kid . . . and now he's dead."

On the way back from Octavio's house, the old man said softly, "General Pablo came to tell me that you withheld information on Colonel Francisco until the last moment, and that you had handled the case the way *you* wanted. If he'd had a say, he would have used Francisco to feed him the information we wanted to convey to the CIA's highest level. Francisco provided a unique opportunity to do that. You're the only one responsible for Francisco's defection. Of course, I played dumb, as if I didn't know about it."

Marcelo nodded. "I warned Pablo that there was some leakage. There were strong indications that Francisco could be the one tipping off the CIA. I told him I wanted his help to rescue Carlos Manuel and invited him to sit down and discuss it; then I was going to tell him about the trap with the passport in Canada. He wouldn't even listen to me. He just gave me an order to obey. He couldn't even see what was in front of his eyes. I can't do his job and mine at the same time. I'm sorry if he's too slow to live in the West. There are a thousand ways to convey information to the top CIA level. Francisco wasn't that important."

* * *

The old man was very sick. He didn't look as sick as he actually was because he had decided to spare his family worries, insofar as possible, about something that was inevitable. As a matter of habit, he stayed up very late reading all the information that Marcelo provided him each day. He put aside to discuss with Marcelo the matters that he thought his experience and advice could help solve. He had given up direct contact with the rest of the personnel when his health began to fail, letting Marcelo make most of the decisions. It was impossible to know what to do if he couldn't hear and weigh all valid opinions. Still, Marcelo always brought certain matters to him on which, because of their importance or his knowledge, he should have the final say.

This time, he wished he was in better health in order to help Marcelo. Because of the nature of the matters involved, he should have been consulted closely on a twenty-four-hour basis. Then he could have taken some matters to a higher level, or knocked on some doors that only opened for him. His health just hadn't permitted that. There was nothing wrong with his mind; it was this old, mistreated body that wanted to rest already. He had wanted to step down from his office some time ago, but the close relationships he had woven with so many people in key positions in so many countries over so many years were still a precious asset to Cuban Intelligence.

After carefully considering the whole situation, the old man decided what to do to maintain the delicate balance of power that allowed great independence for the Intelligence Section. "I believe that we have to improve relations with State Security. General Pablo and you dislike each other and will never coordinate work properly. He's too powerful to be ignored. He told me that he hadn't opened an investigation on Carlos Manuel's death because it would hurt the Section, and he respected me too much. And he doesn't want to know about what really happened to Francisco, either. He is not a fool, Marcelo."

Marcelo remained silent. He knew the old man hadn't yet finished.

"General Pablo wants you out of the department. In this case, it's better to yield than to fight back. The next thing they'll be inventing is that Carlos Manuel is alive and that we helped Francisco escape, or another fairy tale like that."

"I agree with you. I can't stand him and he hates my guts," Marcelo said, looking at his boss's poker face, always impossible to read.

"Carlos Manuel saved your life once, as I recall. What happened?"

Marcelo drove for a while without replying, then spoke softly, as if talking about something unimportant. "In a risky offshore operation in Africa, I got tangled in a mess of garbage at fifty feet. The rest of the volunteer divers got back except for me. They were exhausted, totally worn out. The captain of the rescue boat had orders to leave as soon as the operation ended—to wait for no one. Carlos Manuel stayed behind to look for the only man who didn't show up. He put his life at risk for someone he didn't even know. That was how we first met. Every time I hug my two sons, I remember him . . ."

The old man kept silent during a long stretch of bumpy road, then said, "The minister asked me for a man to reinforce the fight against drug trafficking. I hate to see you go, but under the circumstances, I think this is the best choice."

Marcelo nodded, accepting. He drove in silence for another short while, then said, "Once, a long time ago, I heard you say that when everything in the world disappears, the only things left would be family, love, and friendship."

"Did I say that?" The old man's face looked amused.

"Yes, you did."

"I must have been drunk."

I N SPITE OF the wet weather, the flowers that covered Alejandro Alcazar's grave had already withered.

It started to rain again. A graveyard employee working a few steps behind a man visiting the tomb decided to postpone the work he was doing for the next day. As he passed by, he heard the visitor speaking aloud to the person buried there.

"Remember, Alex, no matter what, your father always loved you."

The visitor placed an expensive-looking rose on the grave and quickly moved away, disappearing like a ghost among the tombstones and the rain.

55

H E INSISTS ROBERTO is alive and that he has proof. As long as he's after *Roberto*, he'll be chasing his children, and those bastards will be coming after my kids again, because they hold me responsible for whatever King does to *Roberto's* children. I can't keep my whole family caged up all the time. I've discussed this with King and he just tells me to join him in catching *Roberto*. He won't rest until he kills *Roberto*, no matter what. I've told him a thousand times *Roberto* is dead, but he won't listen. This is a stupid situation I got into because I thought he needed my help for an authorized CIA operation. I didn't know he was acting on his own personal vendetta."

"What can be done? You tell me." Cabot reversed the problem for Pereda, knowing that what he was telling was only half of the truth.

"King himself told me that Barter had threatened to kill him. He laughed and said Barter hasn't got the guts to do it. The Mafia people are saying their men were set up. The guy they were going to hit was supposed to meet them in a friendly mood, otherwise they would have done everything in a different way. In the first place, they'd have sent a squad and not just a couple of men . . . Some of Montiel's friends want King cooked alive. If that happened, the whole problem would be solved," Pereda said, looking out a window.

Cabot thought for a while before speaking again, also looking out the window. "Many people want King dead, but he's not easy to kill. King has powerful and influential friends, too. If he felt betrayed by the CIA, there's no telling what he'd do. On the other hand, the FBI has a lot against him. If he dies a sudden death, your men may be the first suspects. Remember, the FBI has all the details of the girl's kidnapping and Montiel's death. That might even reach you. Besides, his sudden death, whatever the cause, will bring the FBI prodding into CIA affairs again. They love to do that, and it has to be avoided at all costs."

"Do you want the whole truth?" Pereda's disagreement showed all over his face and body as he leaned forward belligerently. "King came to Miami to buy the paintings of one of *Roberto's* sons as a way of locating him. The next thing I know, my daughter, Alicia, after a very harsh argument with me, has left home and is living now in an unknown place with this painter. She seems to have fallen in love. She means a lot to me—she's the purest soul on earth. Now you're telling me I'm supposed to stand by, arms at my sides, while King is on the loose? I'm forced to move, with or without the CIA's blessing. I'm not going to let this stupid cripple hurt my child.

"Look, Cabot, I know very well that if King is killed, whatever way, the CIA will be deeply involved. So what? Since I came to this country I've belonged body and soul to the CIA, done exactly as I've been told. What I've done wasn't for the money I received, not because I liked the Americans one bit. I've done it because I hate communism. I had to take revenge for my father who worked hard all his life, saving every penny, never stealing anything from anybody, always giving a plate of food to the needy, until one day some people dressed in green fatigues took everything away from us. They took the land our family had worked for generations. They took the house where all of the Peredas were born since my great-grandfather came to America a century ago from Asturias in

Spain . . . the houses we had for rent and all of our other businesses.

"I swore to kill all of the people who murdered my papa, because he died the minute all his properties were taken away, even though he lived for another twenty years. In pursuit of that revenge, I've done everything that I've been told—becoming someone else. My mother said once that I'd lost my soul. I came to the U.S. almost a boy, now I'm fifty-one. As time passed, my world changed. I no longer care much for the lost family properties. I no longer care even if communism persists in Cuba until doomsday. My kids will never go to live in Cuba. They belong here. For them and the rest of the new generation, Cuba is a remote lost heaven that became hell and obsesses their parents. All I care about now is my family, my business, and my friends here. This problem I have now is affecting everything I care about. I can no longer be a pawn in your big chess game."

Austin Cabot did not answer. He went out of the house, feeling too hot inside, and leaned on the veranda overlooking the Chesapeake Bay. The temperature outside was chilly, but he liked it. It was painful for him to think about King's fate, remembering him as a tall, likeable young man with a crew cut, just out of college, where he had been an outstanding athlete. His first impression had been that King personified a paradigm of American youth. Later, he had seen a different King in Saigon, a violent man who could open fire on women and children and show no mercy or remorse. Then the macho man had turned into a crying, helpless creature in La Finca, Honduras, when he himself became a victim. And still later, he had made a remarkable comeback as a thoughtful man, full of profound ideas, totally devoted to his work.

Austin Cabot thought about the fact that he had been compelled all his life to make decisions that affected other people's lives. In most cases, though, they had been merely names or numbers on reports. When real people were involved, with whom he had shared his life at one time or another, things were totally different. Cabot's mind wandered again into another reminiscence, as he gazed toward the horizon.

The time he had spent in The Hague recruiting Francisco had been like a long vacation after a nasty divorce process when he came back from Vietnam. His chief, Curtis, had done well, sending him away from Langley for a while, giving him a taste of European culture and background that he had lacked. It had been a treat, going back to school days. This time he was a postgraduate student, but it had been just the same sweet, carefree university days, with plenty of sex and interesting people to meet—among them, Francisco.

The CIA had arranged for him to be Francisco's roommate, and they had liked each other from the beginning. He frequently invited the Cuban out to eat, because he noticed early on that Francisco ate sparingly in order to send most of his savings home. But Francisco loved food and was a big eater, always hungry. The Cuban was a born entertainer; no party was worth much without Francisco's organizing a conga when everybody was loaded. It was fascinating, the cunning ways in which Francisco, "the scholar who was always broke," used his gifts of big Havana cigars and his ability to cook Cuban meals to get what he wanted.

Reviewing dense reference books together, discussing Roman law, dating women of all nationalities, and visiting many places in Europe in Cabot's uncomfortable German VW, they had become close friends. One weekend, they had travelled together to a house by an orange grove near Catania in Sicily. The place had been prepared to lead Francisco to believe that this was Mario Calabrese's home. The Cuban got along well with his "papa" and his "mama" and a couple of "brothers." Then, it had been easy to recruit Francisco. He accepted almost immediately, as if he had already been expecting the proposal. He conditioned his acceptance upon two "sacred" principles: No one else could ever know his real identity, and he would only provide information that came his way. He was not going to seek out information for them, or do anything else that they needed done. This sacred agreement had been violated sparingly, always to clarify key issues.

Why and how had he been able to make the decision to burn him—openly using information that would most certainly uncover P.G.? When he did that, of course, he had also made the decision to pull Francisco out of Cuba and let him enjoy the fat savings account he had accumulated during his years of working for the CIA. But it had been too tempting to let time go by, checking on how alert the Cuban intelligence and counterservices were nowadays. He'd had still another chance to save Francisco when the CIA office in the Netherlands had sent him a message that someone had made inquiries about Mario Calabrese, the name he had used only while attending the course. It was evident that someone was poking into his past. In those days, recruiting Francisco had been his only job.

He knew Francisco had been caught the minute he saw a message from P.G. addressed to him stating that the Cubans knew about King's personal operation and had hard proof in their hands. No effort was made to hide the fact that they were using P.G., as if they were also telling him, "Hey, you! Look here, we've got your spy, P.G.—another ace in our hands."

And later, the open message to him, saying that P.G. was for sale, mentioning the price and the terms of delivery. He had accepted the deal. Francisco was safe and sound in the U.S., and now he had to find a way to fulfill his end of the bargain.

Cabot ended his reverie by turning back toward Hernando Pereda, who had followed him out of the house and was already half-frozen, awaiting his decision. "You're right. As long as King is after the phantom of a dead man, he'll try to get his revenge through those kids, one way or the other. That may put your family in jeopardy again, because—let's call them *Roberto's* friends—may want to use you to stop King again and again. But there is nothing we can do directly. Stop frowning. I said there's nothing we can do *directly*." Cabot turned once more toward the bay.

Pereda knew that Cabot would give him his decision looking someplace else, as usual, so he moved closer to him.

Cabot paused, then, after a long while, continued. "King has become a threat to the CIA and to your family, but the CIA cannot be involved in King's death, and you are the CIA, too. Just tell King you have accepted his terms. He has to get together two hundred and fifty grand, in used and unmarked twenty-dollar bills, in a handbag and have it handy in his home. *Roberto* will be delivered to him alive in the very near future." Hernando Pereda nodded, understanding very well the decision that had been made. The two men went inside the house to have the drink they both needed.

"Sometimes the most effective way to act is to sit tight and wait, and let life follow its own course," Cabot added.

A THANAS KYMINAS continued speaking without letting his scissors stop. "There is a lot to do around the house. My wife is always after me for something that has to be fixed. The other problem is the grandchildren. There is always a daughter or a son coming with their own children. They give a big hug to their mama, chat a little, and then ask her to take care of the kids while they go out to have some fun. I love our grandchildren one by one, but when they gang up together, they just kill their grandma. I've decided to retire to help her with the kids and to fix things around the house. Nowadays, nobody can afford a plumber or a carpenter—they earn more than the president."

The man in the barber's chair stopped reading the *Washington Post* and waited for a moment until the scissors rested before asking, "Are you seriously going to retire, Athanas?"

"Oh, yes. I was waiting for you to come by to tell you."

"This is high treason, Athanas! How dare you abandon your faithful clientele after so many years? You have no heart, no honor. If you were in Sumatra or in the Fiji Islands, you'd be dragged through the streets by a mob. Hung by the balls in Timbuktu." The client spoke loud enough for the barber at the next chair to hear.

"Mr. King, you'll have no choice but to let me cut your hair," the other barber said, keeping up the banter.

Athanas Kyminas was startled to realize that he felt loyalty toward his old clients. He looked at the other chair, imagining Mr. King sitting there, and he couldn't bear the sight. On the other hand, he had promised his wife, four children, and eight grandchildren that he would retire and be around the house all the time, like Grandma. He beamed as the solution came to him. "I'll go to your house every other Friday to give you a haircut."

"That's a deal, Athanas. I'm retired, too, and I'll play you a game of chess. If you win, I'll pay double. If you lose, the haircut is free."

"It's a deal, Mr. King."

When the haircut was finished, King crossed the street to the parking lot. He waved to one of the employees before boarding the elevator with some other customers. He got out at the third floor and walked to his car, a black Mercedes Benz 500 SE that he had owned for the last ten years and intended to keep for another ten. King drove out of the lot to his house, stopping at a Pizza Hut for a pie to eat at home with some white wine he had in his cellar. Four times a week, he had his dinner ready when he got home in the evening, but on Friday, Saturday, and Sunday he had to eat out or cook his own meals. He entered his garage and left the car, walking with the pizza in his hands to the dining room table. Just as he reached it, he heard the noise behind him. It sounded like someone tapping on the wall with a metal object to attract his attention. He placed the pizza on the table and made a movement as if removing his overcoat, actually reaching for his gun while turning around.

Standing in the open door of the dining room, a man was pointing at him with a small-caliber pistol in his right hand and a sawed-off shotgun in his left.

"Are you . . . ?" King said.

The man smiled faintly. King understood. There was no chance to draw and aim his own gun but he tried anyway, closing his eyes to meet his fate.

THREE AUTOMOBILES arrived at the house almost simultaneously, guided by a large oak tree towering above a neighborhood where all the houses and streets looked very much the same. The body of a former CIA officer had been found four days earlier by the police after the maid became concerned when her employer did not answer his telephone or doorbell.

Now, six days after King's death, the first to arrive and enter the house was the chief detective appointed by the FBI to the case. The three men who followed shortly afterward were very high-ranking FBI officers. The last to arrive were the CIA's Director of Operations, Austin Cabot, the new head of the Cuba section, William Barter, and the CIA's chief of legal affairs, Hiram Markovitz. As they met inside, other CIA personnel, together with FBI agents and city police, guarded the outside premises.

One of the top FBI officers began. "Thanks, Mr. Cabot, Mr. Barter, and Mr. Markovitz for coming here. Your presence should be helpful in completing our investigation. As our general director stated in the letter asking for this meeting, we've reached a point where we need top-level CIA cooperation."

The man who spoke surveyed the CIA men with a hawkish look that was enhanced by black-rimmed glasses and a large, birdlike beak. Seeing only blank faces in front of him, he continued. "If we all agree, I'll summarize our findings up to now. First, the killer entered the house—or rather, the attached garage—in Mr. King's Mercedes. That's a very important conclusion. This house is a fortress of reinforced doors, electronic alarms, and traps. To get inside, the police had to blast out one of the windows. So it seems impossible to break in, unlike an ordinary house. If Mr. King brought the killer in his car willingly, the whole investigation narrows down to King's closest circle." The FBI officer stopped, glancing at the faces before him but not noticing the slightest change. "So, the first question we want to ask you, gentlemen, is whether you know of a possible motive or motives for Mr. King's assassination, and probable suspects?"

"Do you want the answer now?"

"If possible, please, Mr. Cabot."

"We don't know who could have had any reason to murder Mr. King."

The CIA lawyer stepped in. "Let's put it this way: There could be endless reasons why Mr. King was murdered. He took a very active part in affairs that affected many interests and people. He was a very controversial man with a strong will. But the CIA, after careful consideration, concludes that since he lost his position and thus the power that goes with it, there is no situation that we know of that might explain Mr. King's murder or point to a possible killer."

The FBI man replied with the same even voice, selecting his words carefully. "Then, the next question is why King cashed in so many of his stocks and bonds and transferred the money to his home in recent months. Does the CIA know the reason?"

Mr. Barter nodded. "By chance, I might be able to answer that question. Since I was new on the job, I consulted with Mr. King on many matters. Once he told me he was going to invest most of his savings in a very profitable business in Central America. He had made many influential friends while stationed there. It appears to me that he was getting ready to take his money out of the country in cash, which isn't uncommon where Central American investments are concerned."

"Mr. Barter, Mr. Cabot, did you know that Mr. King had been carrying out an investigation, using the money from his accounts to pay the men he hired?" The FBI man's mouth snapped out the question like a steel trap.

"No, I didn't," Barter said.

Cabot nodded, indicating that he had known.

The FBI man put his glasses on a table and decided to take a shortcut. "Okay, gentlemen, this is the bottom line. We have enough evidence to prove that King had been paying a lot of money to several men working for him." The FBI officer stopped, waiting for comments, but the CIA personnel remained mute. *"Therefore, another possible motive exists: Someone didn't want Mr. King to continue his investigation.* If that's the case, I must ask the CIA to disclose the nature of this investigation, and the identity of the people who were working for Mr. King."

Barter appeared ready to answer the question, when Markowitz intervened. "You just said King was doing an investigation on his own, as a private citizen. He, of course, had the right to do that if he was so inclined. The CIA has nothing to do with it. The CIA knows nothing about it."

The FBI man smiled as if he had expected exactly that reply. "Mr. Markowitz, we know that King started his investigation while he was still head of the CIA's Cuba section. At that time, he was searching all over the U.S. for a Cuban girl who had been kidnapped and released some time ago, and her two brothers. We have a lot of information that points to King as the kidnapper of the girl. In the house where Arturo Montiel kept the girl, the FBI found very sophisticated communication equipment not available to anyone outside the CIA's top level."

The FBI agent stared at the CIA men as if trying to pierce their thoughts. After a few seconds of silence, he continued. "That brings us back to the motive. It wasn't a secret that Timothy S. King had been forced to retire. His announcement that he was writing his memoirs produced serious concern within the CIA, which had warned him regarding what he was and wasn't allowed to write about. But there was little that could be done until a manuscript was submitted to a publisher. The agency would then, of course, try to stop its publication in the United States if it revealed anything that shouldn't be published. But foreign publication was another matter. So, we have been looking for that unfinished manuscript in the house and there's no sign of it. The hard disk of King's computer has also disappeared. Any information regarding these points?"

The CIA people remained silent, but it was clear the FBI officer needed some sort of reply this time. Finally, Cabot shook his head.

The FBI officer kept talking. "After King was forced out of the CIA, he told confidants that Mr. Barter had set him up and caused his ouster, as part of a conspiracy with the Cuban Intelligence Service. He claimed it all involved a Cuban spy named Roberto, who supposedly drowned several months ago in Havana, but who King claimed was still alive and had engineered the plot to discredit him."

Austin Cabot held up his hand, stopping the FBI agent. "We're not going to answer any of those specific questions. I believe that you already know most of the answers. Let's stop this game, it's going to get us nowhere. I will give you our opinion about King's actions. As you know, a mine planted by a Cuban intelligence officer in Nicaragua injured him long ago. That mine destroyed his left leg, both of his testicles, and half of his penis. The incident changed his character and his life. The experienced field officer always hungry for action had to choose between retirement and a desk job. At the time of the accident, we feared he'd do something foolish if we forced his retirement. So we put him, together with other *dead wood*, to processing the enormous amount of information that comes in every day about Cuba. To our surprise, he adapted himself well to the new situation. He became a keen analyst, and as time went on, a true expert on Cuban affairs. There was nobody better to head the Cuba section."

Cabot was a remarkable man. Tall and massive, he could sit listening for hours without moving a muscle, as if he were just a mass of flesh with two widely opened eyes. But when he started to talk, his whole body became animated, his voice mellow, his diction perfect, all of which combined to produce a theatrical effect that always enthralled his audience. Now, in full command of the situation, he continued.

"For years, Mr. King devoted a lot of his personal and his section's efforts to following the tracks of this Cuban officer who had caused his tragic injuries. If Mr. King was right, this man was an amazing agent who seemed to appear in the most incredible places, always blocking our best efforts to detect him. If we were to believe Mr. King, this Cuban agent was behind every fiasco we've had in the last few years. Yet every time we tried to capture him, following Mr. King's advice, he disappeared like a ghost through a wall. A few months back, this Cuban officer was here in the U.S. for some time and then went back to Cuba. It was a most unusual incident. Apparently, he stole a yacht in Cuba and came to the States, where he stayed for three weeks in a Cuban internment camp right under our nose. Then he left the camp—still undetected—and stayed for another month and a half before returning to Cuba. Mr. Barter here investigated the whole affair for over a month. The incident was too much for Mr. King, and he became even more obsessed with this man.

"From that point on, there was no way to tell where reality ended and Mr. King's nightmares began. It started to affect his work. Then one day all the Cuban newspapers reported that this man with whom King was so obsessed had died in a swimming accident and was buried with all the honors due heroes of his caliber. We cross-checked the information with our own sources in Cuba and found he was indeed dead. The agency was certain it had seen the last of the Cuban spy we had known as *Roberto*. A month later, Mr. King came to my office, very upset, and told me *Roberto* was alive! Then he gave me some rather absurd details about *Roberto's resurrection*. That was too much for me, I must admit. We finally had to remove Mr. King from the CIA, prompted by his bizarre behavior during these last months. I must point out that we're here to help clear up King's death, not to review the CIA's work."

There was a heavy silence after Cabot finished speaking.

The FBI men looked at each other, and the officer who had been talking said in a sarcastic tone, "Then, the only reasonable motive we have left is theft. We have no other choice but to search for a very special burglar—a man well-versed in electronic alarms, safe-breaking, and personal computers, who can hit a dime at ten feet with a .22-caliber pistol."

"Since we're here, could someone tell us how Mr. King was killed by this unusual burglar?" Cabot asked.

The chief FBI investigator, who had followed the verbal wrestling of the top men from the two agencies with fascination, led the way into the dining room. He pointed to a door that opened to the adjacent garage, where a black Mercedes could be seen in the shadows. "The murderer gained access to the Mercedes while Mr. King was getting a haircut and the car was in a nearby indoor parking lot. Mr. King always had his hair cut every other Friday by the same barber. The killer only had to find a way to neutralize the car's electronic alarm, open the trunk of the car, and get inside, and he was guaranteed entrance to King's house, because the trunk can be opened from inside.

"Mr. King drove into his garage," he continued. "The doors closed automatically behind the car. He stepped out of the driver's seat and walked into the dining room toward that table. Then he must have heard or sensed someone behind him. He tried to pull his .357 Magnum out from his shoulder holster. Turning around was one of the most difficult movements for him on account of his old wounds. The intruder stood in the doorway, pistol in hand, apparently waiting for Mr. King to face him. Then, the killer fired one shot, a .22-caliber bullet, that went into Mr. King's brain through his left eye."

The FBI investigator smiled, lit a pipe that he had already loaded, and continued. "As to motive, theft is obvious. King had been cashing in a lot of his investments and bringing the money home. The killer could have learned somehow about that loot— around a quarter of a million—certainly enough of a motive in itself."

"Congratulations. We think you're on the right track," Cabot said, and began to leave, indicating that no more answers or explanations would be forthcoming from the CIA, and that they were satisfied with the conclusions at which the FBI had arrived.

Barter looked behind the dining room table and noticed for the first time a familiar painting on the wall.

58

BARTER REMAINED SILENT on the way to Cabot's house, reviewing in his head everything he wanted to ask his new boss. There was no special risk in talking in the backseat of Cabot's car, where all conversations were taped, as they would also be taped in Cabot's office, and even in his home. There was simply no way to talk to Austin Cabot without being recorded on film, tape, wire, or whatever new method might exist. Nevertheless, after a dinner home-cooked by Mrs. Cabot and a Cuban cigar Cabot had given him, it was a lot easier to begin the conversation.

"Before you ask, I'd like to show you a message I received the day after King had to abandon his post." Cabot handed Barter a sheet of paper with the message.

> *Dear Mr. Cabot:*
>
> *Although we have not met personally, we know of each other from the days you used to visit La Finca.*
>
> *As you must know, I have your dear friend P.G. securely locked up. As a courtesy to you, I am willing to send him immediately to the U.S. aboard the yacht Tycoon if you will have the courtesy to see that all charges against Roberto are dropped, and have the FBI stop their pursuit of him. As you*

know, Roberto is dead and it is in the best interests of both of us
that he remains so.

I believe that a small financial compensation for his family is
also deserved. A quarter of a million dollars seems an amount
within reason, taking into account the high cost of living in the
U.S. or Canada nowadays. I am sure you will find a way to
arrange this properly, too.
Sincerely yours,
M.

"Who sent this?" Barter asked, when he gave the message back
to Austin Cabot after reading it through twice.

"You know him. He was the other man in the photo Alex dug up
for you in Nicaragua."

"Is Carlos Manuel Armas really dead?" Barter asked after a
moment of thought.

"*Roberto?* Oh, yes, *Roberto* is dead."

Barter decided not to push for any more precision on the matter.
He sensed that Cabot was not going to answer many more questions, so he rushed to the core of the problem he faced as the head
of the Cuba desk.

"Why was King killed? Was it because of his opinions about
how to deal with Cuba? It seems that Cuban exile leaders and
many influential people here wanted him out of the way because
of his views on how to handle the Cuban situation." After a
moment of silence, Barter added, "His ideas seemed very reasonable to me. It's quite odd that the U.S. has renewed diplomatic
and economic relations with all the ex-communist and communist countries, including China and Vietnam, but not with Cuba.
Is the 'Cuban factor' in Florida's presidential elections the real
problem?"

"Dear friend, straight logic and reasoning have nothing to do
with politics." Cabot got up, inviting Barter to come out onto the
veranda, where he could take a look at the Chesapeake Bay and,

perhaps, escape his own recording system. It was springtime and the weather outside was perfect.

"To understand what really goes on in U.S.-Cuba relations, you have to go way back in time. History often has all the clues for understanding the present. We're facing a situation that has similarities with the situation that existed during most of the nineteenth century, when Cuba was a colony of Spain. In 1823, John Quincy Adams, then secretary of state, explained the policy that the U.S. had been following since its foundation. I believe I can still quote him:

'There are laws of political as well as physical gravitation. And if an apple, severed by the tempest from its native tree, cannot choose but fall on the ground, Cuba, forcibly disjoined from its own unnatural connection with Spain, and incapable of self-support, can gravitate only toward the North American Union, which by the same law of nature cannot cast her off from her bosom.'

"The Cubans fought and lost a ten-year war against Spain from 1868 to 1878, then started another war in 1895. For thirty years, the U.S. never recognized Cuban belligerence or, much less, helped them against Spain. To the contrary. In 1898, when both the Spanish and the Cubans were finally exhausted, the apple was, at last, ripe. The timely American intervention won us Cuba, Puerto Rico, and the Philippines.

"As to the present situation, the U.S. policy toward Cuba will only change when the apple is ripe again. It may not happen for another hundred years."

59

JANICE WAS CLEANING the stairs, a task she had always detested. Now she couldn't help doing it every day instead of once a week, as she used to. Starting from the top, each step she cleaned brought her a memory of those minutes that had changed her life.

Again, she felt the tremor of the house when Milton's body hit the floor. Again, she saw the great jump of the tenant hitting the paunch of the assistant state attorney with all of his weight, and heard Milton's mooing like a cow mortally wounded. She saw herself hypnotized, watching as the once-powerful animal who, little by little, had terrorized her into total submission, learned in his own flesh and soul the meaning of physical violence, the immense fear of losing one's precious life. Again, she witnessed the transformation of the tenant into a fierce cat playing with an enormous, clumsy rat.

She relived seeing Milton's excruciating terror when his master lifted the ax from the floor and touched his neck, aiming the sharp edge.

"Mr. Lafayette, you will have the rare opportunity of seeing your own headless body. It's a scientific fact that the head survives severing for a few seconds."

She watched, fascinated, the slow motion of the tenant swinging the ax back and could hear once more the words he shouted in a strange language—"*Cabrón, te voy a joder!*"—as he swung the ax forward, missing the neck by a quarter of an inch, hitting the nylon cord where he had really aimed. And the sight of Milton's body falling on his back as he fainted in complete panic into a pool of his own piss, shit, and sweat.

She remembered the tenant's words as he drew her to his side: "I have to leave now. One of these days, I'll be back."

Then she again felt his strong body against hers as she clung to him desperately. "I'll go with you wherever you go."

And his voice whispering in her ear, "You don't know who I am."

"My heart knows," she had assured him.

The shadow of a person blocked the dying sunlight coming from the front door. Impatient, she finished cleaning the step she was working on before looking up. She hated being interrupted when she was cleaning the stairs.

"Pardon me, madam. Do you have a room for rent?"

"Sorry, I don't rent rooms anymore," she answered shortly, without moving.

Then Janice turned around slowly, thinking that she was going crazy. There was no way she could keep this man out of her mind and out of her dreams. The gentle grip of his arm around her shoulders when they walked together visiting Niagara Falls while he waited for his passport to be delivered to him. The weight of his body and his hungry lips and tongue while they were making love again and again and again in the three glorious days they had spent together in Toronto . . . Now it was his voice haunting her.

When she looked down the stairs, she saw his silhouette in the doorway. She sank down slowly onto a step, feeling weak, empty, and devastated. When was all of this going to end? she asked herself.

"I don't need much of a room. Just about this big."

Against the dying sunlight, the shadow showed a space less than an inch between two fingers of his right hand.

"The tiny space inside your heart is all I need."

Also available from Akashic Books

COLD HAVANA GROUND
by Arnaldo Correa
320 pages, original hardcover edition, $22.95, ISBN: 1-888451-52-1

A riveting mystery based on actual events on the island-nation of Cuba involving three Afro-Cuban religions: Santería, Palo Monte, and the Abakuá Secret Society.

"Correa offers a tantalizing glimpse into the world of Afro-Cuban religion and folklore . . . With its detailed ethnographic background . . . this is apt to appeal to fans of such authors as Janwillem Van de Wetering and Eliot Pattison, whose mysteries contain strong spiritual elements."

—*Publishers Weekly*

BROOKLYN NOIR edited by Tim McLoughlin
350 pages, a trade paperback original, $15.95, ISBN: 1-888451-58-0
*Finalist stories for EDGAR AWARD, PUSHCART PRIZE

Twenty brand new crime stories from New York's punchiest borough. Contributors include: Pete Hamill, Arthur Nersesian, Maggie Estep, Nelson George, Neal Pollack, Sidney Offit, Ken Bruen, and others.

"*Brooklyn Noir* is such a stunningly perfect combination that you can't believe you haven't read an anthology like this before. But trust me—you haven't. Story after story is a revelation, filled with the requisite sense of place, but also the perfect twists that crime stories demand. The writing is flat-out superb, filled with lines that will sing in your head for a long time to come."
—Laura Lippman, winner of the Edgar, Agatha, and Shamus awards

THE COCAINE CHRONICLES
edited by Gary Phillips & Jervey Tervalon
269 pages, a trade paperback original, $14.95, ISBN: 1-888451-75-0

The best fiction anthology of cocaine-themed tales to blow through in years, featuring seventeen original stories by Susan Straight, Lee Child, Laura Lippman, Ken Bruen, Jerry Stahl, Nina Revoyr, and others.

"*The Cocaine Chronicles* is a pure, jangled hit of urban, gritty, and raw noir. Caution: These stories are addicting."
—Harlan Coben, award-winning author of *Just One Look*

SOUTHLAND by Nina Revoyr

348 pages, a trade paperback original, $15.95, ISBN: 1-888451-41-6
*Winner of a LAMBDA LITERARY AWARD & FERRO-GRUMLEY AWARD
*EDGAR AWARD finalist

"If Oprah still had her book club, this novel likely would be at the top of her list . . . With prose that is beautiful, precise, but never pretentious . . ."

—*Booklist*

"*Southland* merges elements of literature and social history with the propulsive drive of a mystery, while evoking Southern California as a character, a key player in the tale. Such aesthetics have motivated other Southland writers, most notably Walter Mosley."

—*Los Angeles Times*

ADIOS MUCHACHOS by Daniel Chavarría

245 pages, a trade paperback original, $13.95, ISBN: 1-888451-16-5
*Winner of the EDGAR AWARD

"Out of the mystery wrapped in an enigma that, over the last forty years, has been Cuba for the U.S., comes a Uruguayan voice so cheerful, a face so laughing, and a mind so deviously optimistic that we can only hope this is but the beginning of a flood of Latin America's indomitable novelists, playwrights, storytellers. Welcome, Daniel Chavarría."

—Donald Westlake, author of *Trust Me on This*

HAIRSTYLES OF THE DAMNED
by Joe Meno

290 pages, a trade paperback original, $13.95, ISBN: 1-888451-70-X
*PUNK PLANET BOOKS, a BARNES & NOBLE DISCOVER PROGRAM selection

"Joe Meno writes with the energy, honesty, and emotional impact of the best punk rock. From the opening sentence to the very last word, *Hairstyles of the Damned* held me in his grip."

—Jim DeRogatis, pop music critic, *Chicago Sun-Times*